I0613077

Xeno Gods and Demons
Space and Time

The Series

Written and Illustrated by   Kal Keller

Cal's Realm of Nightmares
Art by Kal Keller
COPYRIGHTS SERIAL #78/234,412
SCIENCE FICTION

ISBN NUMBER 978-0-6151-4151-0

Table of Contents
Sci-Fi Horror Adventure
Book One "The Xeno Project"
Thriller

SCIENCE FICTION

Cal's Realm of Nightmares PRESENTS
Book 1 of the Xeno Project SERIES

**SCI-FI HORROR/PROJECTIONS INTO THE
FUTURE/DRAMA/ADVENTURE**
Cal's Realm of Nightmares
BEE ROSES FEATHERS ENTERTAINMENT
41 Sutter Street SWT 1237
San Francisco, CA 94140

This story is based on actual facts and is a work of Dramatic Science Fiction. Any similarities to life situations in this story are purely coincidental and not intended to offend anyone. Dramatic recreations of what is in the future for the human species could be happening today. We are forecasting the future of the human species as we see it.

Book Two of the Xeno Series   Xeno Stars

Book 3
Xeno Gods and Demons

This is your page

CHAPTER ONE
"DOCTOR NICKLAUS KELLER"
January 1, 2010

Obscured windows blocked out the gloomy sunset with a misty haze hiding the horizon, as Doctor Keller was filling vials with his own medicine for Jarred. Soon it was time for another visit to the east coast, Jarred was one of Nicks trusted colleagues and once a best friend. Then Jarred went inwardly insane. Nicklaus cellar downstairs housed the best vintage wines along with a wall safe. Nicklaus was the man behind the Xeno Project and everybody knew it. Nick's experiments were successful and famous for his donations into the Genome Transcript map. Raindrops spattered loudly onto the windowsills as Nicklaus finished making the doses for Jarred.

Nick's father had recently passed away leaving his Estate to Nicklaus. Finances were good and the job was suited for Nicklaus, it was a troubling feeling knowing that his inventions and discoveries would one day be off limits to him. Nick was kicking back in his favorite chair and drinking a glass of wine, wines worth at least five-thousand dollars. Nick lifted his third glass of wine and took a long swallow. All that Nicklaus could feel was anger at the Xeno project and controlled by others. Nicklaus was far from feeling satisfied about his life.

In front of Nicklaus was a table with diagrams and charts. He was assimilating the Genome chart with his own Xeno chart discoveries. The similarities dumbfounded Nicklaus. He needed the resources of the Labs inside the Xeno Compound to finish his work. For this, he needed to steal his work back. Nicklaus needed files, many files. Laboratories to stock would have been nice. Certainly, 'somehow,' Nick knew that he would succeed in his assays.

Always staying active and full of fervor,

Nicklaus was not a bad looking man and what age he did have he wore it well. Nick sometimes spiked Lisa's drink and had his way with this student. She was infatuated with Doctor Nicklaus, they met at a Singles Bar in Seattle; it was love at first sight for the 19-year-old student. Every so often, Nicklaus took advantage of the girl.

Nick laid some more logs on the fire and then poured himself a bourbon and tonic. Liquor was the only thing that could relax him enough to research his findings. First, there was cyclosporine to explore into new areas of procedures. Nick had been putting his concoctions into Lisa's chocolate milk in the mornings during her sleepovers. Tonight was going to be one of those nights. Sitting on his black leather footstool Nick contemplated . . . . *"Cosmo's that contain most of the genes mapped to 11Q12-CD8. INT2, CBL2, ASSP13 YAC'S SOMATIC CELL HYBRIDS."* 'Doctor Keller was thinking out loud.' *" I HAVE FOUND THE LOST GENE INSIDE THE ASSP13 BY INSERTING MY HYBRID CLONE INTO ASSP13. 'Consequently,' PRODUCING AASA1313T2. "This Concept, my negative colleagues, will change the world one day."*

Nick heard the loud chimes of his antediluvian doorbell and knew that Lisa had arrived early. She surprised him like that sometimes. Secretly, Nick thought that Lisa wanted exploitation; some people want and like to exploit. After all, Nick was a realist. Nicklaus stood and walked to answer the door and he was in the right mood for anything. When Nicklaus opened the door it was pouring rain, outside the door Lisa was soaked.

"Well . . . can I come in and get out of this storm?" 'Little did Lisa know that the storm was just beginning for her?' Nick wanted to conduct an experiment and Lisa was his Subject. Nicklaus was being foolish; any good that existed in Nicklaus belonged to Lisa.

"I am sorry my dear, here ... Come on inside and stand next to the fireplace." Nicklaus led Lisa into his den and positioned Lisa by the stone-faced fireplace. Nicklaus offered Lisa a glass of something to drink. Lisa replied with an answer the doctor never expected to hear from her.

"Please Doc, would you bring me a tall glass of vodka on the rocks. I am in the mood to get crazy tonight. Would you mind if I borrowed one of your bathrobes and a towel to dry myself off?" Lisa was blushing while smiling at Nicklaus; Nicklaus was 15 years older then Lisa. At 35, Nick was the genius that hardly had to try and always got his way. He was slightly graying from the long hours and the stress that came with his work. Nick was in good shape and a slim man with a stringy beard. Nicklaus loved to smoke his pipe and loved smoking expensive cigars. Nick's left eye was going blind but nobody noticed.

Nick wished that they allowed smoking inside the Xeno Compound 'No Smoking.' Nick opened his bar and grabbed a bottle of vodka; during the process, he made himself another bourbon and tonic. In doing this he sidetracked and done a rare thing. Nick forgot to spike Lisa's vodka. Nicklaus was reaching for his pipe 'after laying the glasses on a crystal table.' For a little while it was time to forget about the Xeno Project

"Thanks Nicky, you are the perfect host." It seemed that Lisa had made her mind to seduce Nicklaus. Nick was astonished at the way his cute little shy girl was acting. They were always on a formal and respectful way toward one another. It was not something that the doctor was going to pass up. He knew exactly what he wanted.

It was the CYCLOSPORINE treatment. Along with the AASA1313 added to create the interaction of producing a fertile and sensually intoxicated individual. AASA1313 creates the liquid cyclosporine becoming living organisms.

Side effects included a tremendous appetite for reproduction and unable to think for themselves.

Procreative and loyal to the person responsible for this mutation, the subject is helpless to his demands. Control was what Nicklaus learned after this night of passionate and hungry lovemaking. Nicklaus decided that he would keep the house for his secret private get-a-way hideout. "Never sell it."

During the morning, Nicklaus washed Lisa's back in the shower and the two of them were making out. Nick is lucky to have a wonderful partner but at what cost? Nick instructed Lisa to live in the house until he returned. He did not know what that time would be. He assured Lisa that one day he would return. Lisa stared at Nick and asked . . .

"When are you leaving Sweetheart? I am going to miss you but I will be here waiting for you, count on that Nicky." Lisa seemed dismayed but did what Dr. Keller asked of her to do.

"There are two pigs and an Angus beef butchered and wrapped in the freezer next to the wine cellar. Fruits and vegetables ordered on the computer. They deliver and all my connecting web sites are in my folders in the Express files." 'Nicklaus was on top of things.'

"I have to go Honey and meet with John Sung. He has a liver infection and I inject my new restoration vaccine into him every three days. Please make yourself at home and I will see you later."

They exchanged one long passionate kiss and Nicklaus, out the door he went. Nicklaus was sure about Lisa Miller. 'Lisa was perfect for Nicklaus Keller.' There was Lisa to come back to if everything else failed. There was a vault in the wine cellar that safely held twenty-million dollars.

Lisa's kiss lingered on the lips of Doctor Keller as he sat inside the cockpit of his red sporty jaguar.

Lisa sat on a plush love seat using the remote control to turn on the big screen TV. She had 5000 channels to choose from using the new advanced electro magna Satellite dish. Kicking her feet up she hollered Yahoo! With the whole house all to herself, Lisa planned on redecorating and having social parties. Lisa was comfortable and content for the time being. Yet, deep inside her heart, there was Nicklaus and she dreaded the day that he was going leave and for who knows how long?

Lisa thought about the University and her studies. After a few moments, she dismissed the thought. She wanted to be sure that she be home when Nick got home. There was a fire burning inside of Lisa and it demanded satisfaction. 'Yes she thought.' I will love my Nicky forever. Nearby, there was another bar and Lisa poured herself a glass of champagne, 'In celebration of getting Nicky under her thumb.' There was no need for schooling because of Nick. Nick told her once that he was going to teach Lisa everything that there was to know about life. Lisa believed Nicklaus and enjoyed the secluded opulent easy life.

Perhaps Nicklaus was not going away for years. *'Lisa thought to herself.'* Perhaps Nick was teasing me. Lisa knew better and frowned. She did not want Nicklaus to leave. It seemed that Nick had perfected his love potion. With the work, Nicklaus had accomplished in the past putting a love potion together was child's play. Certainly, Nick knew that Lisa would wait forever and that she would barely leave the Estate. For now, Lisa was making plans for nobody. That is what Nicklaus made of Lisa, (His property).

Nick had gotten to work late and the experiments had begun without him. This made Nicklaus angry and worried. Obviously Nicklaus knew that the experiments were going to fail without his secret formulas. Other Researchers believed that they could copy Nicklaus but Nicklaus was smart. He never gave away all the data. He never compromised himself. They should have waited for Nick; they should not have tried to steal Nick's ideas.

Nobody seemed to notice him as Nick walked around inside the research facility and everybody was into his or her work unaware of his or her surroundings. Nicklaus entered his office and closed the shades. He then began searching for the site to build his own laboratories and a Research Facility. Nicklaus knew that once the Foundations had gotten hold of his formula's and data. They were going to erase him out, possibly make Nick disappear as Hoffa disappeared.

Staying late, doing his search after the others had left. Nick thought that he hit the jackpot when he saw the Lupus Estate on the large screen of his Foundation computer. He e-mailed the Broker and using his credit card put down one-million dollars on the Estate.

Now it was time to get back to his research and private doings. Doctor Keller was reading about Dr. Leonard Bailey. Almost twenty years past, a baboon heart was, transplanted into a newborn infant. They named this subject, Baby Fae. Nicklaus had made and is making breakthroughs with immunosuppressive drugs using his secret formula based with cyclosporinal.

First, Nicklaus examined his monkeys and his pigs for mutations. These creatures had been getting double doses of AASA1313T2 and they seemed normal. Two of the monkeys had human hearts and three of the pigs had ape livers. Nick believed that after a while when he bred the animals with normal ones. Their offspring would show amazing results.

Nicklaus was the only person with access to his office connected to his private research laboratory.

Who knew how long that was going to be authorized was anybody's guess. At least Nicklaus had Lisa to ease his mind. His house was eccentric, private and unlisted wherever nor anywhere. Many some nights Nicklaus stayed late while everyone else went home. He would perform surgery with Lisa as his assistant. It was time to regroup and get out of Dodge for Nicklaus.

Thinking it over carefully, Nicklaus decided not to bring Lisa into his Xeno future. One can easily think that Nick was in love with Lisa. In many ways, Nicklaus had it made. Yet Nicklaus always had to conjure up something evil or mutant. Some evenings' Nicklaus would have a Poker game and invite some of the Staff from the Xeno Complex. Lisa would be there periodically serving drinks and keeping busy with her chores. One fact that I can see is that the man is a genius and is as insane as a mad dog. Lisa was an innocent victim playing an ace in the hole for Dr. Nicklaus.

———————

Nicklaus finally gotten home from work at three in the morning and Lisa was sleeping on the couch with the TV on. Nicklaus quietly walked to his bedroom and went to his bed. Bed was ready and the corners were tucked. Lisa is a gem, which was the last thought that Nicklaus had before he fell fast asleep.

———————

Nicklaus was back at the Xeno Compound doing his regular job at his usual post. He was analyzing reports about the Xeno Project for the Board of Directors. When he glanced at the 'New Arrival' File, he saw something that set him aback. His endogenous retroviruses used for a bone marrow implant. HERV's and PERV's are 12 human and pig DNA combined to create a chemical reaction that causes mutations, (Unless, they injected his AASA1313 to combat rejection of the organ.) Nicklaus fabricated, lied and wrote in his report that the transplant would be successful, knowing that the patient was going to die without his AASA1313 injections.

Nick hid the file in his briefcase, there was the procedure diagramed in the file along with lab results from both the patients. Nick had been filling out false reports and stealing the new reports. It was no wonder that Doctor Nicklaus Keller was the most successful transplant surgeon in the facility. He had AASA1313 and results from experiments that were the true results.

For the rest of the day, Nicklaus turned in falsified reports to the Chairman of the Board. They were no good anymore because the true reports were hidden away. Nick was smiling and joyful. He worked with other researchers and professionals like himself all afternoon, 'Being happy about anything.' For the rest of the day, this man Nick was slyly calculating his next move.

"Dr. Keller, can you see what is happening in these Petri dishes? This is truly amazing Doctor. Please come and observe this." Dr. Hanson noticed a mucus slimy liquid-eating bacterium and deadly viruses inside of self-contained large Petri dishes. Dr. Hanson was a Resident of the Xeno Foundation.

"Dr. Hanson, please do not get excited. It is only liquid human cells mixed in with some of my formula. Remember Doctor, that the Xeno Project Board has not approved my formula. I would not say anything about this if I were you." 'Nicklaus had a stare in his eyes that spelled murder.' Dr. Hanson replied. *"Sure, don't worry about me saying anything. I have my own secrets to worry over."* This made Nicklaus think that the labs were a free for all. Nick wondered about Doctor Hanson being who he said that he was. More likely than not, he was a CIA Operative or a company snitch.

On his way home, Nicklaus decided to start packing

in the morning. Nicklaus planned to be late for work and while at work stealing, back what belonged to him in the first place. Nick had planned his big move carefully.

He had two assistants ready to join him. They were John Sung and Jarred. Jarred is a giant of a man while John is the small quiet type. They had not met yet, Nicklaus was sure the two would be fine together. Jarred was injected with the formula years ago. It was the old AASA13 instead of the AASA1313. John received the new serum.

These thoughts were in his head as he drove up his driveway as Lisa warmly greeted Nicklaus. *"Hello Darling, I hope that you had a nice day."* Smugly, Nick caught Lisa with a grin.

On this night, after some blood test's Nick learned that Lisa did not need more of his formula. It had stabilized and was reproducing fast enough to replace living AASA1313T2 cells that died. Nicklaus became ecstatic Nick was delighted.

"I had a wonderful day and there is a leg of lamb in the oven. It will be ready to eat in fifteen minutes. Honey, why don't ya go and wash up while I set the dinner table?"

Three bloodhounds ran out from the woods to greet their master, excitedly jumping all over Nick, waging their tails while licking him. *"Sure, I can do that."* They kissed and went their separate ways.

At dinner, Nick explained to Lisa that he was leaving in three days. She began crying and pleaded with Nick to stay. *"I must go, but I will be back in two or three years. Until then you will not hear from me. I hope that you will be all right here all by yourself?"* Lisa stopped crying and smiled at Nick. Then she promised. *"I will be here waiting for you and I have the dogs to keep me company. Do not worry about me. I will be here when you come home. I love you so much that I belong to only you"*

They had a nice evening drinking wine and telling stories. Nick was a good man at heart. With certain people, he was a pleasant fellow to know. Yet, he had totally gone mad years ago. His tastes were refined and his needs were great. Lisa was beautiful, a female full of charm and appeal. Intelligent and good to talk with, Lisa was going to be lonely for a long time if Nicklaus truly left her there alone for years. Tonight they danced and they played. They made love like lovers that had been apart forever.

Nicklaus slept well and was up early. He had an agenda and part of his agenda was improvising. Lisa was holding Nick as they stood by the car. ***"Honey, tonight I am fixing oysters and lobster tail for dinner, so you do not want to be late."***

Life could have been normal and the Doctor could have been sane. Then this story would end here. Delusions drove Nicklaus to madness, not his job that did it. Nicklaus Keller needed to play God.

This evening Nicklaus had to attend a lecture given by Stanley Brodmire. Nicklaus did not want to attend but it was required for him to be there. Nicklaus only has to catch the end of the lecture because he was an hour late.

Nicklaus walked into the Auditorium and had a seat waiting for him at front center stage. They were at the last Intermission of the Lecture and Nicklaus could barely wait until it was over.

There must have been twenty-thousand people attending, which impressed Nicklaus. People from all over the world appeared at the lecture and it was crowded. Doctor Nicklaus Keller hated to be in crowded places and this lecture annoyed him. Soon the lecture was about to begin so Nicklaus tried to get comfortable on his padded seat. In a minute or so, a speaker walked onto the stage. The audience applauded and gave a standing ovation.

Please let me introduce to you the Founder of the

Xeno Project . . . Mr. Stanley Brodmire the Third. Please give a warm welcome to the man that created this enormous Project. 'There was seven minutes of standing ovations.' Except for Doctor Nicklaus, he stayed seated.

Nicklaus was getting some nasty stares and a couple of boo's. Nicklaus did not care because Nicklaus was the person that had broken the genetic code. 'Not this thief!' His thoughts were selfish in nature and his endeavors were cruel. Nicklaus is a Dr. Frankenstein reborn, living in the new millennia. Technology has everything to make his dreams come true and so far, luck was on Nicklaus side. Everyone sat down as Dr. Brodmire entered the stage and stepped up to the podium.

"Hello everyone, I am glad that you could make it here tonight. First, let us talk about Eugenics. Let us ponder the fact that deformities and mutations occur in life. What causes this abnormally in living creatures one might ask?"

" I want you to know that we are trying to cure mutated living creatures. Our efforts are directed to help the human species evolve into perfect beings, overcoming environmental and heredity factors completely."

" This takes dedication by all of you to get the job done. It takes being a team, trusting each other with our lives. Certainly, we do it almost every day; we work together in disastrous environments. We are doing the dangerous work, taking all of the risks. I want to thank you from the bottom of my heart for your loyalty and hard work on the Xeno Project."

"Increasing number of genetic defects are being defined right here by you people. The Xeno Project is alive and well. Please stand up and honor us with a speech Doctor Nicklaus Keller . . ."

Nicklaus stood and the crowd cheered. They applauded Nicklaus for a couple of minutes and then took their seats.

Brodmire continued with his lecture. *"We are falling short keeping our Record Dept. in proper order. It should be easy to do; we have microdots now and Envision Computer complexes to hold this data. We need to take more care filling out the paperwork and processing data. Nanomites are the future, a threshold"*

Brodmire was eyeing over the rows of persons attending the Lecture. They had gotten more then they had bargained for. Nicklaus had to hold back a smile. It was worth the trip here after all.

Nicklaus stood and approached the podium standing beside Brodmire. Nicklaus stated flatly. *"There is much I need to say but I will not be humiliated again. I will say this much . . ."*

"Many Researchers are now calling for caution. Of course, they do not work on the Xeno Project and Mr. Brodmire does not sign their paychecks. If I told you that Defensive reactions depend on a multitude of additional biochemical and physiological factors then you would believe me. If I said that one of these is the presence of natural congenital anti bodies then you should know . . . they are a natural element vital to the immune system. Masked in mystery, not understood, I understand them and one day I will get the credit, me, where it belongs." 'Nick was enjoying himself, but his eyes ached and swelled, soon Nick was replacing his bad eye with a xeno replacement'

"You are out of line sir, will you please take your seat." Nicklaus sat and smiled. He knew that his days were numbered: at the Xeno Complex and that, he was leaving anyways. Nicklaus was wacky at times and everybody knew to ignore his outbursts. Yet if you listened, Nicklaus made a whole lot of sense.

Listening to the last fifteen minutes of the Lecture,

Nicklaus understood that Brodmire was a patsy. Brodmire was not knowledgeable of what was going on around him. He was a puppet for the Feds. Nick soon was on the road watching behind him for a tail. Nicklaus tried to put the lecture out of his thoughts.

Once Lisa seen Nick she knew that he was in a bad mood. He was looking a lot older then he was and Nick seemed nervous. Then Nicklaus said . . .

"I think that I am going to get fired sooner than I thought. Honey, will you fill the bath for me?" Nick was acting as if a bad event had happened but he did not care one way or the other. Nicklaus figured he had two days remaining at the Xeno Compound before they asked for his Resignation.

On this night, Nick was the boss. He had Lisa bathe him and do everything for him on this, hell-bent night. Indeed, Nick had a sex slave willing to die for him. It was time to leave the Project and begin his own program. There had to be a way that he could leave without turning in his resignation. He was rough with Lisa and hurt her in some ways; Lisa seemed to be enjoying the abuse. Nick had his formula and he was anxious to depart. It was sad that he had to leave Lisa behind. Nick knew that he was going to miss her.

Beating Lisa and making love to her heartlessly was Nicks way of saying *"I love you."* If there was, a thing of loving someone too much Lisa had it bad. AASA1313 was the ticket; it was Nick's way out, of being looked over the ranks again. I guess Brodmire angered Nick almost to the brink of jealousy. Hurt did not show but the pain lingered on and festered inside of Nicklaus. Nicklaus felt like pushing the doomsday button.

Nick could not sleep so after making love twice, he went into his den and began drinking. It was the Xeno Project and the lies behind it that drove him psychopathic.

You are supposed to get what you give but not at the Project, there unknowns decide everything. Nick wanted to destroy them and he thought that one day he would show those fools the unimaginable.

Lisa was glad to be near Nicklaus and it was because of her new immune system. There were the side effects of being complacent and passive. You become fun loving and mindless. These were the conclusions that Nicky had reached thus far in the study of his subject, 'Lisa.' Nick drank over half a bottle of bourbon before 4 A.M. and decided to leave in two days. Nicklaus went online and informed the Realtors that he was moving in. Nick finally fell asleep and woke up in the bedroom cuddled beside Lisa. Lisa was heavenly to touch Nick called her Buttercups.

Time passed quickly and Nick was working his fastest, mailing his files to the Lupus Estate. In another hour, Nick was finished with his downloading into the Lupus computers that were still there. Nick was going to have to sort it out later.

Nick told Lisa this morning that he was leaving and would be back in two years. Lisa replied, ***"Okay."***

Nick put on his suit and Lisa slipped on Nick's socks and shoes. She always has taken good care of the Doctors' feet. Lisa was his little foxy, puppy dog. Nicklaus knew that tonight was going to be the last relaxing night at the big house. The house made out of bricks and was sound as it was over a hundred years ago. If all went sour, Nicklaus would always have a place in his big house, with Lisa waiting for Nick to pamper. Bravo, thought Nicklaus

---

Lisa had her own visions of living alone. Knowing that it would be a lonely time with Nicky gone away, but glad that she would have it made while he was away for a couple of years, there was everything on the property to suit her needs and wants. Lisa knew more of what was happening to Nick then she led on. In many ways, she empathized with Nick and his appetite for power.

Lisa was truly in love with her Mentor; Lisa worshiped the ground, which he walked on. Great sadness calmed by the love Nick was showing her tonight as if it was the last time that Nick would ever see her. With a vow to remain at the Keller Estate until the day Nick returned Lisa had plenty to keep her occupied while Nick was away.

There were the dogs to protect Lisa and an Armory of Firearms that Lisa was well acquainted with. Her lover that night that gave Lisa the strength of five men that was a great asset for both of the lovebirds gave Xeno-hormone injections to Lisa. Lisa doubted that Nick could ever find another woman that loved him as much as she did, nor a woman as beautiful as she was.

Lisa was not in this relation for nothing, she planned to use Nick as much as Nick used her. Extremely smart and witty was reasons that Nick loved Lisa, he was glad that the best assistant that he ever had was also his soul mate.

If another woman did come along and seduced Nick then Lisa swore that person a horrible death. It raised the hair on her arms at the thought.

Lisa and Nicklaus hand in had, for each other and both knew in their hearts that in the very end they would be together.

The End
"Dr. Nicklaus Keller"

CHAPTER TWO
"XENO MADNESS"

If there is such a thing like hell. *"Can it be recreated on Earth?"* Possibly, you will find it in an old Victorian house and other real estate owned by Nicklaus Keller. My Xeno Project will take you a few steps further then hell and make you feel as if you were already there. It was not easy getting this story. That is why I decided to burglarize and confiscate medical journals, security video tapes and whatever else there was which would help me in writing this story. Be prepared to go to hell once you start turning the pages of this terror filled, thriller Mini-Novel. *"Oh, the pure horror of reality seems like fiction!"* I would like to be the first to welcome you to hell, and it will be my pleasure to hear you scream when you are reading "The Xeno Project" Remember that the road to hell is paved with good intentions, intentions like the Promise to Humankind with animal to human Xeno transplants. Indeed, the only promise that I can see is the promise of changing our genetic pool, creating a new species of who knows what.

You see, I want to frighten you and make you shiver in fear. This is my only goal in life, to reach those whom long to be terrified in the warmth and comfort of their own homes. This story is close to the truth and its horrors are real.

Nicklaus Keller was the chief scientist working on the Government Xeno Transplant experiments, at Top Secret Laboratories of the Xeno Tree Foundation Located on Broadway Avenue in Seattle, Washington.

'People wanted, they needed donor organs.' Unfortunately, people were dying because there were just not enough organs to go around. Every morning the Xeno Foundations lobbies filled with patients and their lawyers trying to secure a heart, liver, kidney, and it was always

a matter of life or death, money never a problem.

Doctor Keller had dedicated his life to developing an anti rejection drug to prevent the rejection of transplanted animal organs. Since the beginning, there had been new breakthroughs in medicine and science. Two examples of these breakthroughs are growing organs beneath the skin of lab rats and animal organs transplanted into human beings. After years of hard work and long hours in the lab, Nicklaus had discovered the formula that prevented organ rejection in humans and in animals along with other basic side effects.

For the simple fact that all inventions and innovations discovered and created at the Xeno Tree Foundation belonged to the Foundation, it was the primary reason that Doctor Keller had withheld his successful experiments and inventions from the Xeno Tree Foundation.

Lecturing on a limited amount of knowledge, it took Nicklaus little effort; he successfully transplanted a pig's heart into a human heart patient. It proved a complete success and extended the life of the heart patient ten years. Nicklaus had also successfully prolonged the life of a patient who suffered from a brain tumor, by a partial brain transplant from a baboon. Brain matter and tissue removed with the infected malignant tumor, which replaced by the Xeno transplant. Doctor Keller had not revealed all of his results of his two successful Xeno transplants and soon had fallen under suspicion that he was corrupting the Xeno Tree Foundation.

Nicklaus Keller was spending all his free time searching for the right house to buy. He had inherited fifty-two million dollars when his parents had died in a plane crash. That gave the good doctor plenty of finances to have his own research laboratories constructed. Now he found the perfect site, to apply his decision to resign from the Tree Foundation, and start construction on his new covert research project. Through a weird chain of events, Nicklaus Keller managed to buy the Van Lupus Estate and it seemed to fit his venue perfectly. With haste, Nicklaus closed the deal on the large Victorian mansion and the property with it. Nicklaus should have stopped searching for property after finding the Lupus Estate online at his home. Nick had the foresight to put a deposit on the Estate it was a good thing that he had done so before somebody else had.

Accidentally nabbed in the act, the Doctor concealing medical breakthroughs' in his formula research using Advanced DNA Technology, Nicklaus denied that he had the formula refined and that he was concealing his research from the Xeno Tree Foundation, *"XTF was a puppet corporation for the Department of Justice."* On January 5, 2000, a fire broke out in the laboratory which the good doctor was working in and when help arrived to extinguish the fire. Henry Boggs, he was the Project manager went through Nicklaus' opened briefcase and discovered manuscripts which proved Nicklaus Keller was concealing portentous information. That same morning, Nicklaus turned in his resignation to the Xeno Tree Foundation.

Nicklaus Keller was impressed with the huge Victorian mansion and the fifteen acres that came with it. Besides having fifty large rooms and eight bathrooms, along with three levels of full basements, it had everything that the Surgeon needed to create a Research Compound.

Perhaps the Van Lupus Victorian Mansion was on the market at a steal, only 2.5 million dollars. He paid the asking price for the Van Lupus Estate in cash and the next day he hired a Canadian General Contractor to begin construction of his underground basement Research

Laboratories. Estimated time of completion was set for three weeks, and that gave Nicklaus time to gather a research team together. Indeed, the Lupus Estate was perfect for the sensitive material involved with Doctor Keller's experiments. It had a locale Nick planned to use as a toxic dumpsite.

Nicklaus Keller's Grandfather was once a SS General in Hitler's Germany. Nicklaus' father arrived in the United States before America got involved in the war and sponsored through an Ivy League school where he earned a Master's Degree in Physics. Elmer Keller also sent his son to a private school and then on to Harvard University. Valhien Keller was able to rob and steal a great fortune and he entrusted his great wealth with Nicklaus Father. Who in turn left it to Nicklaus? Nicklaus never knew that his grandfather was a SS General and executed for his involvement in war crimes. I learned about him through intense investigations, which took me to Germany, Argentina and South America. Before long, Nicklaus had a Doctorate and Masters Degree displayed on his wall.

Doctor Nicklaus Keller is 6'1 and of a slim build. He was born on June 27, 1966 in Gary, Indiana at Saint Joseph's Children Hospital. His parents were in Gary, at the time in Indiana on a lecture tour at the local colleges and Universities on Nuclear Power, 'the safe energy of the future.' Doctor Keller is a good-looking man with thick sandy hair and a thick mustache when not sporting a beard. Nick walked with a limp, hardly noticeable; he wears gold-rimmed glasses during his working hours and drinks Whiskey on the rocks.

A dedicated and determined man Nicklaus passed up a social life for a life in the laboratories. Because of his long hours by himself and his oddness about his experiments, Nicklaus Keller was far from average and somewhat of a recluse.

There was some charity work that Nicklaus indulged himself with and he flew to Boston once a month to treat a mental patient suffering from dementia. Jarred Jefferson was an old acquaintance of his. Nicklaus was Jarred's Mentor. It was a tragic case and involved a total mental breakdown after unsuccessfully operating on his wife. A freak accident changed his life for the worse. A power outage during a bad electrical storm had caused the lights to go out and made Jarred do the most dreadful mistake in his life. Nicklaus truly felt sorry for the younger neurosurgeon and took the time to try to treat Jarred with AASA13.

Jarred attended school at Boston University and holds a doctorate in neurology. He made the mistake of operating on his stricken wife and when his fingers dropped the scalpel into her tumor, death invaded her brain. Jarred's world stopped to exist and he had gone insane.

Then he was committed into a sanatorium. Once you know Jarred, you might wish that you never had. One day Jarred escaped the sanitarium.

John Jung Sung was a student at Washington State University who volunteered his time at the laboratories of the Xeno Tree Foundation. In exchange for private tutoring by Dr. Nicklaus Keller, Sung was a foreign exchange student that wore out his welcome at the University with his host family. John tried to kill one of his Professors and expelled from school, soon his Visa revoked. Nick felt sad and took John in, offering John a job.

In his journal, I read an insert, which struck me as strange. It made me believe, that even in the beginning Nicklaus was losing his scruples. He had scribbled it on the back of a page in his personal journal.

"I want to think of my human subjects as heroes because they sacrificed today for your tomorrows. Let me tell you about my first operation. One of the first saviors

of the human race, and that is my honest opinion. What comes about, two hundred years from now is not my worry."

<u>*Nicklaus Keller's Journal dated February 13, 2010*</u>

Special interest groups and corrupt politicians want you to believe that Xeno transplants are safe and that the public is not in harms way. Faye Heim is the first one of my subjects to go under the knife and she is an unwilling subject. There are no other choices left, so I must force her to submit to my own will. Perhaps they are right, nothing bad will happen to the populace of our planet, and Faye will come out of this fine and dandy. "I doubt that's the case here" and I am going to prove my work to the world, for all to see it. You can believe whatever you like, but let's see if you change your mind once you have learned the successes of my Xeno experiments . . . .

Sung and I prepped my makeshift operating room as Jarred went to fetch my first subject from her holding cell, deep within the dungeons of the Lupus Manor.

<u>SECURITY CAMERA TAPES</u>

"Come on Faye, please lay down on the Gurney." 'Jarred Instructed at his test subject.'

"Go to hell you perverted bastard!" Snapped Faye venomously with hatred filled eyes.

Jarred eyed Faye from the top of her head to her toes and licked his lips. *"Now we can do this the easy way, or we can do this the hard way . . . The choice is yours, sweetheart."*

<u>JOURNAL</u>

Jarred is short on patience throwing his net over Faye's body. Then he grappled her to the Gurney and strapped Faye down. Faye was putting up her best fight but Jarred easily finished his assignment. You might be wondering how I know all of this. Well-let me let you in on my little secret . . .

Every inch of my estate is covered by concealed surveillance video camera's. That is why I know that he slipped his hand under her smock and felt what was there. Jarred is childlike in the curious manner that he gently stroked her privates in a completely benign manner. When Jarred tells you to do something, you had better do it. Jarred is a huge man now.

We must agree that there is no time to waste and a shortcut is necessary to get the results needed to prove my theories. For this reason I am not transplanting a liver, nor a heart my friends. I am transplanting sections of my test subject's brains.

Mia is one of my lab animals and she is the perfect match for Faye. Baboons' are extremely akin, closest to humans. This particular baboon is a smart animal and mellow. Faye is a fighter, most always hostile toward others. You see that they are a match for each other. What effect will it have on my human subject and what effect will it have on the baboon? We will soon find out. What sort of children will they bare, if they can have children at all?

Faye is cursing Jarred while trying to free herself from the straps binding her wrists and ankles to the hospital Gurney. Here comes and him Then Faye insisted to know what was happening to her but because of the nature of my experiment. I could not tell Faye, in fear of contaminating the results.

It is vital that I perform the operation on my subject while she is conscience. That is the only way that I know to assure a successful application of the transplanted temporal lobes between Mia and the human female. It brings me no pleasure to operate on a perfectly healthy human being, and if I could find any other way to prove my theory? I would do that instead of the Xeno Project.

I have also invented a surgical head apparatus

which makes this operation possible. Designed to exact specifications, to fit securely over any person's head, metal fasteners adjusted to keep the subjects' skull still while my miniature drill bits bore diminutive holes into the skull.

Once it is complete, then John Sung's acupuncture needles touch the exact pinpoints in the brain, which block the signals to different parts of the body. Thus, paralyzing my subject, unable to move a muscle, ready for surgery yet awake.

An electric pulse runs through the head apparatus, which gently massages the brain as the six holes drilled into the skull of my subject. Sung inserts and manipulates his needles until the subject feels nothing but is wide-awake and aware of the surgery. Once the head apparatus fitted, and then weighed down with one-hundred pounds, which attached to cables and hydraulically controlled. If more weight balances for a larger subject, then allow by adjusting the tension on the thin steel cables. With the electric pulse steady on the helm, surgery is easy on the patient.

Faye is the first, and at this point of my research, I will only transplant a small portion of the temporal lobes. It will be enough to show if new viruses will attack her body and if new human viruses attack the baboon body. Do you suppose that the baboon will retain human memory from Faye's past? I cannot help but speculate whether or not the temporal lobe tissue that I am transplanting into Faye's brain during this surgery will influence Faye. Faye is the first stepping-stone for a greater effort to find out the truth about Xeno transplants. Years will tell us what new species emerges from my creations, "New creatures, with endowed possibilities of science in the way of global progress."

Normally baboons are large, fierce, short-tailed mammals. Mia is out of the norm with her passiveness and docility. Mia is quite ugly with her dog like snout and long teeth. She has a large head equipped with cheek pouches that makes it hard to believe that she is so closely akin to the human species but internally she is almost exactly like us.

I will return to my studio and continue with this story after the transplant operation is finished. As I am adjusting the metal clasps and penciling in the area of the skull in which are made my first incisions. I gaze into Faye's eyes for a few moments and see the horror that she is experiencing. She is worrying for nothing because Faye is not in danger and she has no reason to fret about her future. There will be a detailed account of her progress in this journal.

We did it in precisely thirteen hours, and the operation seemed a total success. Jung Sung was a master at acupuncture, and did his job well. There were no complications, and both patients are in the recovery room. Sung was impressed with the head apparatus and congratulated me on my genius design. Jarred was hard at work washing away the blood and brain matter from the Gurney, and from the head apparatus. "I, Nicklaus Keller has done in thirteen hours what four surgeons working together could not have matched in a lifetime." I have performed a partial brain Xeno transplant.

Journal February 16, 2010

Three times a day I checked in on Faye and each time she was doing better then before. Most of my concentration and energy concentrated on Mia, because she was having a harder time adapting to human brain matter. 'Humans do adapt better than animals will during Xeno transplanting.'

We discussed renovations and improvements to our operating tables, devised a better and perfect way to perform surgery on our test subjects. There were several ideas we shared and constructed in the basement with materials we purchased at local area Specialty stores and Businesses.

It was time to celebrate our success because both subjects were doing fine and it's been more than seventy-two hours since the transplants. With great enthusiasm and with a little help from a couple bottles of aged bourbon whiskey that were kept in the liquor Cabinet. John and I were drawing up plans while discussing our next patient . . .

Liquor always seemed to calm the madness a bit but at times it could get out of hand. Everyone knew amongst the House that when Nick was drunk a person better hide or that person could become his next test subject. Success was great for everybody involved in the Xeno Project but not always for the people that sacrificed the most. For these unfortunate people life became a living hell. Liquor helped the lost and forgotten peoples.

Doctor Keller loved to get into details while speaking of his surgeries. Relishing the expressions on their subject's face as their victims watched in horror without being to save themselves.

Certainly, Doctor Keller loved to act out sadistic tendencies within the realm of his laboratory and at times, outside the lab. Many years ago Nick had murdered his best friend only to learn what it had felt like to be a murderer.

Now it was a time for celebration. Nick had finally reached his goal, now he had to finish his projects. John was going to become a problem; it was only a matter of time before it happened, Dr. Keller just did not know whose problem? *"Hand me another clean glass on the rocks so I can pour myself another Irish whiskey, would you please, John?"*

John was red-eyed and hungry for some new arrivals. He always did as Nick told him to do by. Nick was not a man to meddle with unless you had no trouble putting tour life on the line, if there was a head on the block.

Nick was sure to be the person swinging the axe. John had more fear of the mad doctor then he held respect for the man. Yet they were birds of a feather hanging out and celebrating their gruesome discoveries and inventions.

END OF CHAPTER TWO

"<u>Xeno Madness</u>"

CHAPTER THREE
"Jarred"
February 17, 2010
JOURNAL

Jarred likes visiting with the test subjects in their cells. He uses a bullwhip to keep the baboons in line and leather cat-o-tails on the humans in captivity. Because Jarred is still on the prowl for two more test subjects a male and a female. Jarred visited Emma to build his courage before his next kidnapping attempt. He is a natural at kidnapping. Jarred used a black limousine to get his human test subjects. That was for tomorrow; tonight he was going to play with Emma for a while.

Security camera films

Jarred made sure that both doctors were passed out cold from the liquor before he went to see Emma Harding. Then he opened her cell door and stepped inside. Emma ran into the corner and curled into a fetal position, terror stricken and traumatized because of her experiences with the sadistic brute that was her jailor. 'Jarred was Emma's Keeper.'

Jarred is equipped with extraordinarily large family jewels. He is a powerfully muscled insane maniac with a Master's Degree and a sandwich short of a bag lunch. He is loyal to Nicklaus for one reason. Nick keeps Jarred supplied with Morphine. When Jarred was not high he got powerful urges and they had to be ravished or he would hear the voices again. Those voices blamed Jarred for the death of his wife and for failing her in life. Jarred used his oversized organ like a weapon and he could hurt a female and make her bleed. If that is what he wanted to do and if a male got, 'on his wrong side' . . . Jarred was a sick man.

Jarred is perhaps needing some discipline, I believe that the AASA1313 created strange side effects.

Well, It was all the same to Jarred. Wearing his zippered black leather tights and grasping cat-o-tails in his right hand. Jarred walked over to where Emma was hiding and bent down slowly. Then Jarred reached with his left hand and grabbed Emma's ankles, yanking Emma out from beneath the bed. There was a thing or two that Jarred planned to teach Emma.

"Whoa now, you know that I always get my way in the end. Please do not make this any harder then it has to be unless you really want to suffer." (I could see in the video how the female captive was shaking like a leaf on a tree. She was whimpering and pleading with her eyes for her life. Jarred began to taunt her and tease her in ugly ways. Watching the event unfold on the video screen made me pity the poor woman. I was appalled at what I was watching.) It was all on film . . .

Jarred knew that Nick did not mind if the test subjects were abused as long as their brains were not damaged and there were no permanent disabilities as a result of perverted acts on the test subjects. I truly believe that by this stage of the experiments, all three of the residents of Doctor Keller's Victorian home were quite insane. They were living in a mad house but the experiments were works of a genius. They were doing what they believed was righteous, no matter how wrong and how sick their experiments certainly were.

Emma wished that her old man was there to see what was happening to her. He is the President of the "Steel Skull" motorcycle club. She knew that Gerry could easily beat the crap out of her tormentor and with one hand tied behind his back. Jarred's big hose did not intimidate Emma, hell . . . ; her Gerry's was even bigger. She was playing herself down and wanted to give off the impression that she was hapless to do anything, trying to save her life.

Without hesitation, Emma knelt before her Jailor and then she felt the sting of the cat-o-tails on her bare back. Emma hated that bastard with a passion and loathed to pleasure the half-wit. All she needed was a chance to escape, and then her survival instincts would come into play. Emma needed a break and luck seemed to be with her. In his haste, Jarred had neglected to shut the cell door behind him.

Selected as a test subject because of her size and build, Emma was a close match to the baboon chosen for the next transplant.

Emma's long auburn hair and stealth body went well with her olive skin. In her youth, before she had met Gerry. Emma won the Washington State Beauty Pageant. Her life changed and she toughened by joining in with the Steel Skull M.C. Some members had taught her to defend herself and put to their tests more then a few times. Finally she was going to give the bully pervert what he deserved and then some.

It was not going to be the first time that Emma fooled somebody by her size and was able to escape from rival bikers and molesters in her past.

Emma took Jarred in her trembling hands and started to massage him. She began crying because she knew that Jarred liked to listen to her cry when he raped her. In the weeks that she was in her cell, Emma neglected to trim her fingernails and instead sharpened them on the cement floor of her cell. 'Gerry used to always tell her that' *"If she wanted to control a man, just to grab a good hold of his balls and to squeeze them with all her might and then run like hell."*

With deliberate meditation and with the ferocity of a Bengal tiger, Emma dug her nails deeply into Jarred as she tightened her hold on he, and she squeezed with all the power, which she could muster. She got the results she had hoped for as Jarred howled in agony. When she rose to her feet Emma wringed Jarred's masculinity. He screamed as sharp stabs of pain shot to his brain. Gerry had taught her well as Emma led Jarred toward the cell door.

Emma planned to let go of him as she slammed the door on his face. Then it was just a matter of getting out of the building and finding help somewhere. There was something that Emma did not figure on and that was the baboons. They were frantic, yelling and beating on the sides of their cages with their arms. It sounded like the jungle gone crazy as Emma slammed the door in Jarred's face. Then Emma let go of his swollen scrotum with one last twist, Jarred's glands swelled and turned blue within minutes.

Emma was carrying out her desperate plan and it seemed that Emma had her chance to escape at last. She bolted the cell door and turned around to search for an exit out of the basement containment cells.

John Jung Sung heard the commotion because of where he was standing in the washroom. Noises traveled up the venting system of the house and so John heard Jarred yelling above the din of baboons.

Sung opened a panel on the wall and observed the surveillance video screen seeing the human test subject free in the holding area of the basement. John Sung laughed loudly and pushed the button, which released trained bloodhounds into the big house. He watched the screen closely to see how the female was going to react to five killer guard dogs.

There was no way that the test subject could escape from the house. It was a vain and a futile act to attempt.

John' laughing increased when the dogs entered the basement. (Viewing screens were found behind panels throughout the roomy mansion) and a high tech customized security system installed by Doctor Keller himself was the newest and most advanced in the world. It did not look so good for Emma. Today was June 19, 2010 and a full moon hovered over the mansion. If only Emma could make it outside to hide in the moonlight, but . . .

Emma had four Irish pit bulls at home. With a love of animals in her heart, Emma knew how to handle dogs, even mean ferocious dogs. It was too late for Emma to run when she saw the dogs coming at her. She stood her ground refusing to show any fear. All the bloodhounds stopped short of where Emma stood and then began to circle her. They growled and nipped at her but never broke her skin. She scanned the walls and saw an opening that lead to a flight of stairs. There was also an elevator to the left of the opening. Without considering what danger might befall her Emma darted for the elevator. All the bloodhounds converged on Emma, diving at her legs until she tripped and fell onto the hard floor. It almost reminded Emma of playing roughly with her own dogs but these dogs were beginning to get mean.

Rolling on the floor, she stopped at the foot of the cages that the baboons were contained. Then an idea hit her and she grinned as she opened the cages and the baboons released into the basement. It was a remarkable sight as the baboons attacked the bloodhounds with a coordinated assault. It was a bloody battle as both the dogs and the apes were biting each other and fighting to the death. Emma lay on the floor in a prone position just waiting for the right moment to sprint at the stairs and hopefully to freedom.

"That little sly bitch, she is a smart cookie. ' John. Said' *so you believe that you are smarter then us . . . Well we will just see about that!"* John Sung ran to the elevator grasping an assault rifle in his hands.

Emma ran up two flights of stairs faster then she ever ran in her life. When she reached the top landing, it was just in time to see the elevator door closing. She had missed Sung by less then a minute and she breathed a sigh of relief.

'Emma ran to one room and then to another.' All the windows were bulletproof glass with security steel bars on the outside walls. She tried the doors that would have gotten her out of the house but they found them locked then Emma started searching for anything, which doubled as a lethal weapon, she found it in a poker next to the fireplace. It was time for Emma to stop running and try to bash her way out the front door.

Narcosis induced visions were worsened by Emma's lack of sleep. Emma was having a tough time at it and her efforts to break the lock off the door were unavailing. With earnest, Emma decided to try and get out through the attic. She went to the far end of the house and used that stairwell to reach the attic entrance.

Meanwhile in the basement

Sung was lost for words when he saw that the crazed baboons had killed most of the dogs. He fired into two baboons that were tearing into the last bloodhound still fighting back.

In a flash, the other baboons ran into their cages locking themselves in. You can bet that they understood the power of an assault weapon. When John glanced around, he noticed that the female test subject was not in the basement, without making a sound and quickly enough to cut her off. John Sung ran up the stairs to intercept her before she got away.

When John stepped into the lobby of the mansion, he decided to fall back and just observed Emma for a while. He gave her credit that she had heart and made a private joke that the baboon would consume her. It was not her heart, that he was after, 'it was watching her writhe in pain.' John found her entertaining as he sipped on an extra dry martini. There was no way that Emma could see him standing behind the two-way mirror in a concealed security room above the lobby. There was no way out of the house.

Jarred was yelling for Sung to open his cell door so that he could help search for the test subject but Sung was not hearing him. Then he shouted and banged on the door of his cell. Sung was ignoring Jarred as he pleaded to be let out of his cell. It was good that Sung did not release the maniac because Jarred would have murdered the female test subject. Jarred needed time to cool off. Jarred's scrotum was the size of baseballs and were bleeding. Jarred was still crying over the pain in-between his legs.

Emma's hands were bleeding from the cuts she received swinging the steel poker. Then Emma tried climbing the ladder leading into the attic but slipped on her own blood. Emma never had a second chance to climb the ladder because Doctor Keller sneaked behind Emma and stuck a syringe into Emma's buttock. It was a good try and Emma caused a lot of havoc and damage in the basement. Bloodshot eyes spun in their sockets as Emma collapsed. Then the good doctor bandaged her hands and carried her back to her cell. There was a trail of dripping blood-tailing Emma as Dr. Keller carried back to her cell.

Nicklaus let Jarred out of the cell where Emma had left him. You fool . . . *"How could you allow her to escape!"* 'It is a good thing that Nick had awakened in time to subdue the test subject before she caused more harm.' Nick was tending to the wounds that inflicted by the female test subject on Jarred's privates. He was thinking about Emma and wondering if she was a bit too aggressive for a transplant. There was a risk to the experiment being contaminated by Emma's violence.

Jarred was keeping his mouth shut and for good reasons. That arrogant woman cost him a whole lot of grief and Emma had hurt Jarred. Every so often as Nicklaus was stitching together Jarred's privates, he scolded his clumsy attendant for allowing the female to escape from her cell. Sometimes Nicklaus thought of a clown when he observed Jarred.

After it was over, Jarred's composure changed. He was silent and now woeful most of the time. Jarred walked with a permanent limp and he detested women. That meant he began scrutinizing the captive men but he did not have time to Lully dolly around. Nick decided that he was going to spare Emma the transplant, but was going to keep her around for spare parts. That meant that Jarred had to find two females and one male to fill the Cells. It was never over, including when it was over, Jarred always found more victims.

Nick had gone maniacal. He was able to keep his raving and contempt for the human species trapped in his own mind. 'Beyond salvation and not wanting any,' Doctor Keller continued his macabre experiments without any regard for his test subjects, nor for God. There was no light at the end of his tunnel. He was lost in this horror. In the blackness of his wicked heart, there existed only hate.

June 21, 2010

Jarred picked up the lone rider at the limousine stop at the airport. Jarred used the customer's Gold Card to pay for the fare and left a better than an average tip. What the fare had not comprehended until it was too late. Was that he was going on a one-way trip and that he was in for the shock of his life? Jarred ogled over the young man in the expensive suit and licked his lips in anticipation of what was to come. He talked with the passenger for several minutes and learned that the man came from a wealthy family and was returning from a trip overseas. Now the yuppie was riding in a long black limousine. Not knowing that in reality, it was a Hearst.

Once Jarred reached the Keller estate, he quickly parked in the underground parking garage. Jarred turned the sleeping-gas on and watched as the sealed off rear seats of the limo filled with a misty gas. Then the passenger passed out and Jarred was positive the man was asleep. He brutally raped him on the hood of the car. Jarred decided that from then on out he was going to have sex with only unconscious test subjects. Jarred had his sick and demented fun on the man from the Sea TAC airport and then locked the victim into a holding cell. There was nothing better for Jarred than the Keller estate. He loved living there and planned to be more careful with his kidnapped subjects. For fear that, Nick would return him to the sanitarium.

A demon was in Jarred and that demon was on a one-way ticket to death. Jarred visited his subjects more but he was extra careful. *"Let me advice you that the more I read"* the more ghastly this all gets.

Nick was like a devil. Jarred hurt from Emma's clutch and vowed that one way or the other he was going to get even. Until then he was going to visit the tenants and stay on his best behavior. Jarred knew that Nick was all eyes. That demon had a name and it was AASA1313, Jarred was receiving daily injections of your drug and had made Jarred impotent. Jarred believed that Nick was not to be trusted and that one day Dr; Keller would kill him. Certainly, the serum was driving Jarred insane and it is just a mater of time before his nutshell cracked.

Jarred thought about his victims constantly and developed a nervous twitch. Jarred rarely had good thoughts about anything, he was obsessed with blaming the world with his beloved' death. Jarred had a way about him that made him appear stupid but Jarred was far from dumb about anything. His problem was that it was difficult for Jarred to stop once the inflicting of fear made him feel as a god would have. This power gave Jarred the ability to take out his grief, on somebody else's life for what happened to Jarred's wife.

The End of Chapter Three
"<u>Jarred</u>"

CHAPTER FOUR
"No Turning Back Now"
July 14, 2010

"*I have replaced the baboons that I shot and killed with two new ones.* 'Said John Sung.' *Plus I replaced the blood hounds with three Dobermans and three police trained German Sheppard's.*" 'There was a brief pause' "*Is there anything else that you want me to do?*"

"*No, I do not have anything else for you to do. You can go and do whatever you like, just do not forget to turn on the alarm systems on the estate. One never knows who might be lurking on the grounds.*" 'Then Nick added.' "*Ask Hauns ("The butler") how to do a test run on the alarm to make sure that it is operating properly.*"

Nicklaus was designating new chores to add onto the old ones for John. There were enough problems for Nicklaus to deal with besides Jarred neglecting his duties. Somewhere inside his darkened soul lay a conscience, Nicklaus was beginning to feel guilty about killing innocent people. Knowing the horror that occurred in his laboratory was ethically and morally wrong. Emma had reminded the mad doctor about morality and had awakened a part of him that died long ago. Damn that Jarred and his perverted antics, 'thought Nicklaus Keller.'

There was just too much work to do in the lab for the mad doctor to do alone. It was vital that he accelerate his experiments and start on the second transplants. It had been two weeks since the first transplants and John Sung could only do so much. Nicklaus listed in the paper advertising for a lab specialist and a computer data programmer. Within one week, he had received thirteen applicants for the job positions at "*Xeno L.L.C.*" Doctor Keller made appointments with each of the applicants and intended to thoroughly screen each one of them. More specifically, Nicklaus was searching for unmarried and unattached employees with the least family possible. It was elementary that Nicklaus could not do it all himself. He needed able assistants.

Nightmares awakened the mad doctor hourly as he tried to sleep. He was struggling to keep his composure together and drinking more alcohol. There had to be something that he could do to stop the nightmares so he tried smoking opium and it seemed to help him sleep. It was on his mind to quit his research and retire in Mexico. He did have a good mind to say the hell with it all, but it was too late to stop now.

There was no turning back now, and the mad doctor turned his back to his guilt, shutting away his conscience in that black hole, he called his heart.

Sung was as demented and more insane then his brethren at the house. What set them apart from each other were some distinct differences between their psychoses. John Sung was not a pervert or a sex fiend. He had given up love and sex for hatred. In many ways, he blamed humanity for the wrongs that happened to him. John blamed America for dividing Korea and for the murder of communist members in his family. He inflicted pain on others in an effort to ease his own mental anguish and suffering. Sung knew how to inflict pain and how to make it linger for days. John Sung was a living nightmare, 'being a bipolar manic depressive with homicidal tendencies.' Sung never had much to say so he managed to stay on the better side of Nicklaus.

July 20, 2010

"Are you going to rape me?" 'Emma cried when Sung entered her Cell.' John carried a briefcase in his right hand as he closed the door to the Cell with his left.

"No, I am not' but perhaps that would be better

for you then what I have planned. Lay on your stomach on the bed and place your hands on the headboard over your head. I am only giving you a check up, so do not worry because I have no intention on raping you."

"Do you always handcuff your patients when you give those examinations, Dr. Killdare?" Emma pronounced the words sarcastically.

"Just shut up and do what you're told, lady! Do not push your luck because you are expendable and the dogs are ravenously insatiable. In just a minute, you may make all the noise that you want to make. I promise that you will discover what hell is. Until then just keep your mouth closed."

John handcuffed Emma's ankles and her wrists to the four bedposts and then set his briefcase onto the mattress. When he opened his briefcase, his surgical stainless steel scalpels glittered in the light. There was also a velvet pouch, which contained acupuncture needles. John Sung hated Americans with a passion and he loved to impose pain on them. Sung decided to start with her feet because they were so dainty and delicate, they were quick and a risk to her captivity. 'He was making damn sure,' that Emma was not going to run away again. *"So you like to run, do you?"*

"I bet that you're not going to try that again. You have caused us a lot of problem's lady and now you're going to get what is coming to you." Sung was taking his time administrating the torture and he was loving every minute of it. John was speaking to Emma in a gentle and kind manner as he was neatly lining his needles in a row according to thickness and some were very thick.

"Do you know that there is grey brain matter in your spinal cord and that there are a thousand points on your body that causes agonizing pain when stimulated? We are going to converse with every one of these points,

yea, you and I are going to do some bonding honey. Ready or not here it comes, this little piggy went to the market, this little piggy cooked lunch, this little piggy grilled lunch, this little piggy baked breakfast and this last little piggy got stuck washing the dishes. " At that last word, Sung shoved the long needle under the toenail of Emma's right foot. It was going to be awhile before Emma ran anywhere again.

"Ouch, O. . . . ooooh. Ouch, 'oh my god it hurts, Yikes Ah . . . please stop hurting me, I will do whatever you ask just stop hurting me!" Emma started screaming bloody murderer long after Sung departed but there was more to help. With tears blurring Emma's sight and intense pain blinding Emma's eyes. Emma could not make out the face of her tormentor but she knew who he was just the same.

Oh, John was good and then was damn good. Taking each toe he shoved a needle into the tip and then pushing it in hard as it scrapped the bone. Oh it was pure agony, it was unbearable but Emma had no say about it. Her agony was at steady ebb when Emma started to whimper and moan in pain. John Sung was delighted in watching her suffering, and throughout the ordeal he did not spill one drop of blood, displaying his acupuncture skills.

Sung saw on his wristwatch that he had been torturing Emma for two hours. Time flies when you are having fun and Sung had not started in with the real pain yet. A grin appeared on his face as an afterthought hit John. Then he began stowing his tools and instruments into his customized briefcase and prepared to exit.

"Well Emma, it seems that I must leave you now, but do not worry because I will be back another time to finish our little talk." Emma replied half screaming and mostly raging as she cried.

"I hope that you rot in hell . . . Believe me, my old man will find you and send you there his self. You are a sicko, bucko . . ." Emma was going through hell and was beyond the realm of horrors. Perhaps a step above the normal thresholds of pain, Emma was fighting back any way she knew how and for the present time. She was safe for a while, although in severe pain she was able to wiggle her toes, hurting like hell to do it. As Emma watched the sadistic doctor walk away, she yelled at him to remove the handcuffs from her wrists and ankles. He ignored her and slammed Emma's cell door.

August 28, 2010

Doctor Keller and his sidekick were examining the transplant patients for infections and behavior patterns. John Sung was taking blood samples while Nicklaus was studying cells under a microscope. It seemed that they had been wrong and there were no side effects from the transplanted brain organ sections. Nicklaus was not convinced that new foreign antibodies and germs did not affect the test subjects in one way or another. Viruses mutating into genocidal magnitudes, even though the test subjects were not producing medical objective evidence showing new strains of diseases and physical mutations. Both Doctor and Intern believed mutated viruses infected their Subjects.

"Faye how are you feeling today, did the medicine you have been taking doing you any good calming your headaches?" Nicklaus was taking advantage of Faye's memory loss and had Faye convinced that she had been in a car accident. Faye asked about where she was and how she had gotten there. Nicklaus responded with an easy and comforting voice, 'expressing compassion for his patient.'

"You were brought here by a rescue helicopter and you are presently in my privately owned and operated hospital. My name is Doctor Nicklaus Keller and you are

under my strict intensive care unit's best people. You are recovering from a severe head injury and brain trauma. 'Believe me or not, you have been here for six weeks now.' Today is the first time that you are coherent, and can understand the seriousness of your condition. We are a long way from being out of danger with you. If your condition keeps improving, then the prognosis looks good. However, there can be some side effects from your surgery."

September 5, 2010

Peter Lewis is a wiz on the computer and he met all the demands of the job. Lewis was single and knew of no living relatives anywhere. At twenty-six years the young man had enough of the city and the rat race, surely excited about living on the Keller Estate. There were many good reasons to hire Peter; among the foremost were his manners and education. Peter was welcomed aboard and then sworn to secrecy by Nicklaus. *"Welcome aboard, please make yourself at home. Call me Nick."*

(The high ceilings with the hand-sculptured walls of the old house exhibited scores of demons and creatures never seen before by men. Ten feet tall, bay windows wonderfully garnished the house with more beauty to watch in the gardens below. Forbearance in the air brought on images of the olden days. Wooden oaken floors shone effulgently as the sun hit them from the south bay windows. Magnificent and adoring, the Keller Estate was mystical in every aspect of its being. In the parlor the walls were twenty-feet high and bore the name of the builder of the old Victorian house. Images of demonic play along with the name of the Cult Sect he belonged to, "Daimon Daevas Legions" neatly inscribed into the woodwork.

Children of today are children of the grave was the

maxim. **VAN LUPUS ESTATE** etched onto solid gold on a Coat of Arms anchored onto the wall beneath the cult's engraving, expertly plated in three-inch 20K gold shields.

Daimon was a powerful devil, which appeared before the Greeks over four-thousand years ago, Daevas was an unmercifully powerful devil who enslaved the Persians eight-thousand years past. Whatever they were into and for however long the Sect occupied the house. All were a mystery to the Real-Estate company from where Nicklaus had purchased the old Victorian mansion. Perhaps the Real-estate Agents stayed mum to sell the house.

Doctor Keller was having a tough time deciding on the last job position. That person had to be able to work long hours, get along with the mad doctor and go along with the program. It was between two people and it proved to be a hard choice to make.

Nicklaus did the unthinkable and hired both of the applicants on the condition that in three-month time. One or the other will die. Both of them agreed to the terms of the contract and Nicklaus wasted no time at putting them to work.

September 13, 2010

Everybody living in the house was atheist and like most scientists, they did not believe in the existence of gods and devils. That was going to change with new employees living and working there at the estate. Peter Lewis was a nerd and his young appearance and pimples made him look like a teenager. Peter wore black hard-rimmed glasses and a bow tie but he was a genius. He was an atheist who believed in UFO's and was into heavy metal music. Lewis was going to fit right in at the Keller estate but there was a question about the two new lab Assistants.

They were Joe Hansen and Becky Zenda, the first was a Reformed New Age Baptist, and Becky was Irish

Catholic. Both candidates for the job opening were over qualified and that made both ideal to work with the mad doctor. It was going to be a test with the loser fed to the dogs and the winner becoming a part of the Research Team. Becky was heavily freckled and she wore her red hair long. Zenda is from what I saw on the security videos, a sexpot, and a knockout stone fox who spoke with a deep feminine husky voice. Joe Hansen was reserved and quiet. He was not the kind of person to rock the boat. Joe went with the flow and attended church whenever he had the time. At six-feet four and two-hundred pounds, and Joe athletically gifted, bringing along with him to his new tennis rackets and his golf clubs. There was a tennis court and private Golf course adjoining the Lupus Estate. Dr. Keller bought a lifetime membership to the Country Club.

September 22, 2010

I was watching the security videos and noticed that there was friction building up between the two applicants vying for the same job. It seemed to me that it was the feisty red head was causing the trouble. She was born in Dublin, Ireland and raised in a radically political family. Becky Anne Zenda hated living in a war-torn Country and came to the United States to get away from it all. It was obvious on the video tapes that Becky did not like the way Joe treated and acted toward her.

Something else caught my eyes as I was watching the tapes. It was Nicklaus staring at Becky when she did not know he was and obviously, that Nicklaus was more than just fond of Becky. Becky Anne was sweet as cherry pie every time that the mad doctor was near her but when he was not, Becky was a cold-hearted bitch. Too many years in a war zone had taken its toll on Becky and she agreed on the same issues as the other doctors did. Becky was an advocate of Xeno transplants and she worked closely with Nick *(as she started calling him Nick* to the point of becoming Nick's top aide. Lisa went to the back of Nick's mind as a maybe.

Nicklaus was having a sincere talk with Becky in his study. He decided to bring her into the net and to learn if she was going to be troubled with Xeno experiments.

"I agree with your research doctor Keller and I whole-heartily will support it in any way you ask me. I have total faith in you to do the right thing morally and ethically. When you informed me of the test subjects, I did not believe you. Now that I have seen, and you have explained you're reasoning to me. Yes, I will stay by you to the end. It would be an honor if you take me on your Team and be my Mentor."

" Please understand that some of the projects that you might be assigned you might reconsider working here, could be life threatening to our human test subjects. Certainly, they will try to escape if you give them the opportunity. 'We must sacrifice a few to save the majority and that's if we are not too late.' Are you sure that this is what you really want to do with your life, my dear?" The mad doctor asked.

"Yes I am one-hundred percent sure but what about Joe. I know that he will not like your style of running an experiment." Becky was dead serious and she was searching Nicklaus' eyes for an answer. *"Well Nick, what about Joe?"* It seems that Nick corrupted Becky.

"Do not trouble yourself with that loser, I know what to do with the likes of Joe." Said the Boss with the convictions of a hanging Judge. *"I will give Joe a chance to adapt but that is all that he will get is one chance."* Becky seemed pleased.

"I have just one more question before I throw in with your Xeno Project, Doctor." 'Becky Added.'

"Anything Becky, what is it?" Asked Nicklaus, he was willing to do whatever needed to satisfy Becky.

Hauns, 'the Butler' was eavesdropping from behind the wall.

"How much money are you going to pay me for a salary?" This issue was a major concern to the future Xeno L.L.C. Lab technician/researcher. Becky was excited over the dangerous line of work and that she was getting into it over her head. Becky was an aberration with an IQ of 195, and she was bored. It was part of Becky's nature to live life on the edge while living an expensive lifestyle.

"Five-hundred thousand-dollars a year and you will be helping me convince the world to stop Xeno transplants forever. You can play a major role in the success of this research and there might be a Nobel Prize in it for us. There is no turning back now."

"I am convinced of your motives Doctor Keller and that they are in the benefit of science. Without doubt your main concern is to rescue the human race from over zealous Governments and their Sponsors. You can count on me sir, as I told you earlier . . . It is an honor to work under you, I look forward to showing you how important I will be in advancing your research."

After one month of working with the two prospects, 'using hands on assignments and responsibilities for his test subjects.' There was no doubt in my mind that it was going to be Joe getting axed from the team. It was obvious in the films that Nicklaus was avoiding all the restricted areas when he was tutoring and scoring Joe Hansen on his progress.

****

November 27, 2010

There was just one week left of the three-month probation period for Becky and Joe. Nicklaus was giving Joe one last hand's on examination. Moreover, it involved treating one of the test subjects' wounds. Emma's feet were infected and swelled because of Sung and his fat needles.

"Who is she? 'Joe Asked as he was attending to the patient's wounds.' *What monster inflicted these horrible puncture holes on her feet? Do you think that we should inform the police because it seems to me that there was foul play done here?"*

"She is a mental patient from the Sanitarian who has shoved knitting needles into her feet. She is a sad case indeed, said the mad doctor. *Her name is Jane Dole and I have taken over her treatment, she is my patient now. There is no need to contact the Authorities! I saw her inflict the wounds on herself. This is a classic case of self-abuse and I have her under control now. Do not call anybody or you can pack your bags and go home."*

"He is lying! My name is Emma Harding, he kidnapped me, and one of his goons tried to rape me. Please get me out of here or call the police. Do something . . . help me."

" Please help me." Emma was crying and pleading with innocent eyes staring at Joe. was Emma moved Joe by's pleading for her life.

"Now, now, do not start inventing stories again Jane" 'Nicklaus returned Emma's with stares of his own.'

"Remember the last time Jane? When you released the apes from their cages? I know that I remember it all to well. Joe, hold her down for me while I give her an injection and be careful that she does not bite you. 'What are you waiting for Joe?' Do it now!"

Joe was concerned about the wounds in the woman's feet because it was not self-inflicted and he was willing to stake his life on it.

Without using his head when he said it, Joe blurted out a suspicious question to his mentor. *"What is in the syringe Doctor Keller?"*

Emma saw her chance to try and sway the new doctor, trying to convince the intern that she was a victim and not a patient. *"Don't let him stick me; there is nothing wrong with my mind. He uses the Xeno transplant experiments on his unwilling test subjects because he has gone mad."*

"If you do not believe what I am telling, you then just ask the other prisoners in the cells next to mine. Please do not let them hurt me. See what they have done to me and please call the police."

"Are you going to help me Joe, you going to get the hell out of here? I told you that this woman is mentally ill, now will you please grab a hold of her so that I may give her a dose of her medicine?"

"Yes sir, sorry for the delay sir but she seems to be telling the truth.' Here, I am holding her still for you." Joe was holding the test subject down while Nicklaus shot her full of Demerol.

Emma Harding slowly wilted as the strength to resist left her and rushes of pleasure swarmed over her body as a smile invaded her face. She was high as a kite and content for a while. Emma drugged and for the time being everything was fine. This was the first time that she did not feel pain in her feet. Doctor Keller smiled quite warmly at Emma and put his hand on her hand in a comforting and caring manner. Then he stared at Joe and said . . .

"You see Joe, we know how to take care of our patients and Jane is all better now."

Emma had done her fair share of illegal drugs while with her brothers in the club. Demerol was one of Emma's favorite narcotics, so the dose, which Joe injected into her by the mad Doctor, did not hit her as hard as it would have a normal person. Quickly, the last remark by Doctor Keller set her off again.

"My name is Emma Harding, and everything isn't better now and not by a long shot it isn't. Joe, please call

the police now." Emma jerked her hand away from the doctors, spit at him, and screamed out. "Let me out of here! I want to go home." Emma was desperate.

Nicklaus stabbed her with another syringe and pumped ten units of Demerol into her vein. That was enough to put her out. Emma slumped over deeply into unconsciousness. In the mad doctor's eye's, Joe had failed his test and failed miserably. From this moment on Joe had become a security risk to the Project and the residents of the house. Nicklaus Keller frowned, because he knew what had to be completed, to save the Xeno project experiments.

November 29 2010

Doctor Keller had second thoughts about murdering anybody. That is when he had gotten a brainstorm and reasoned out a justification for another murder. He believed it to be other than murder, convinced that it could benefit the Project. Joe was going to become a test subject, said the mad doctor to his assistant who was helping to carry the intern to a holding Cell. For the first time in weeks, Nicklaus was feeling upbeat and optimistic about the Xeno Project.

"Face it Sung, there is no turning back now because we are almost at the threshold of success. You are free to do what you do, but do not put the Xeno Project at risk. Emma is yours, but make sure that she does not give us any more problems. Keep her alive for another couple of weeks and then kill her. Save her heart and lungs and her kidneys because I can sell them in the black market. I have no pity for that bitch Emma is nothing but trouble. I want to thank you for all your help to get the project to this point in time. One day you will be famous for your contributions into the Xeno Project experiments." Bravo!

PERSONAL JOURNAL
November 30, 2010

I am concerned about Joe and it seems to me that he is overdue for an operation. He has jeopardized everything that I have worked so hard to achieve. 'I wish that there was another way to deal with this problem,' but there is none. Joe has threatened everything by wanting to call the police and now he has volunteered to become one of my test subjects. Gladly, I welcomed Joe into the program. Joe received cash for his work. In my professional opinion, Joe did not do a good job during his probation period. Failing miserably in his tasks, I am sure that he be better as a test subject in the Xeno transplant experiments. Lisa will always be there if Becky wigs out on me . . .

"The end of Chapter Four"
"No Turning Back Now"

CHAPTER FIVE
"Monkey About"
"December 7, 2010"

John Jung Sung was living in a private world where he was a god. He hated Americans with a passion and had good reasons. Half of his family killed back in the fifties during the Korean War. When the war ended, the Americans rebuilt his village and gave the people their money with loads of opportunities. What they could never return to the young sixteen-year-old orphan was his family. Jung invited and then welcomed Joe into his private world. Sung easily, by administering acupuncture treatments on Joe's brain during the Xeno transplant, performed by Doctor Keller could be between a thousand people and he would stay within his own realm, "his private nightmares." Jung rolled the skin on the skull back over the forehead of the test Subject.

Mia was not herself and every day she evolved into something better, brighter then she was before her transplant. Cat-scans had revealed to the doctors that the new cells were bonding nicely with their foreign hosts. It was unexpected and hard for the researchers to believe but just the same, cat-scans never lied. Mia was special and she knew that she was . . . "Special." Mia was a baboon yet seemed to be evolving into a mutant human.

Faye was special too and she had visions, which had come to her in the realm of her nightmares. Since the surgery, Faye had been experiencing awful toothaches and her jaws hurt badly. Her nightmares, Faye was feasting on raw meat. She tore into the raw flesh with the ferociousness of a beast. Loving it and feasting like a starving wolf.

She had Mia's DNA and it was melding with her own. Indeed, Faye was telepathically special as was.

Mia

Dr. Keller was feeling disheartened by the lack of scientific proof to back up his claims that Xeno transplanting of animal skin and organs can cause new strains of viruses, which would destroy humankind. He monitored and recorded everything about his test subjects but he could not note any bad changes in the transplant recipients, neither physical mutations nor any new viruses. Just because he could not find mutations did not mean that they were not there. Nicklaus was sure of it and 'one way or another.' he was going to prove it.

Becky was proving herself a fine assistant and an excellent colleague in microphysics, a Genetic Techno prodigy. Nick and Becky were becoming more then just partners in the Xeno experiments and she was starting to be more then only a friend. Becky was falling deeply and madly in love with the middle-aged scientist. 'Feisty Becky preferred older men as her lovers. She loved a good mystery.

Becky was preparing a holding cell into a stage for the next experiment, which involved human behavior in baboons. Mia was the test subject and she was being mated with Joe who had received a similar operation as had Mia. It was going to be an effort by the researchers to prove that human procreation would cease, once Xeno transplants had become widespread.

December 20, 2010

Mia was not showing any significant progress as far as intelligence went. Her eyes had changed color to that of Faye's eyes. Bright blue eyes replaced the brown, almost black almond-shaped eyes. Something in those eyes spelled intellect and cunning, yet the female baboon refused to show improvements in her behavior.

Faye was regressing in her development but her health was good. One problem kept nagging at the mad doctor. it was the nasty gum disease, which had infested Faye's mouth. She was in agony for two weeks and last night her pain subsided. Emma was easy to dupe and extremely cooperative in a child like way. Doctor Keller laughed at her madly and at times insanely.

John Jung Sung gave to her a gift and said that it was from all the Staff. Faye loved the rag doll and treated her as if she would have her own child. There was a big change in Faye and it was not good but not so bad neither.

March 20, 2011

Three months flew by and the mad doctor and his Associates performed three more Xeno transplants. All three human test subjects had survived the operations and transplants but all three baboons had died. Emma was forced to complete an experiment that involved tissue transplants from all species of lab animals. Many events had taken place in Doctor Keller's basement of horrors during these six months and Becky was the rising star of the Project.

Times were tough for Emma and she was disgusted at the horrible things that they did to her. It never ended and when she looked at herself in the mirror. She cried from a broken heart considering killing herself. They had ripped her skin off her right arm and grafted onto it pigskin. Then a week later, they did the same to her left arm, except they used baboon skin instead of a pig. On her thighs there was patch skin grafts from god only knows what animals. Emma was living in a realm of despair and hopelessness. New anti rejection, drugs were making a hell out of her life. Only her drive for revenge kept Emma alive.

Paying special attention to the last two human test subjects Jarred left in the holding cells. They were Virgin meat, yet untouched by any of the experiments going on in the Xeno Project. They were untouched by the mad doctors but Jarred was having his way with them.

Joe was expendable so Nick utilized Joe for several experiments that were happening all at once on Joe. He was also the product of Xeno skin grafting and was in a state of shock all the time. It happened after the mad doctor skin grafted a baboon's skin from its penis onto the raw and tender organ between Joe's legs. It was an unbelievable event, which proved to be a complete success. Joe was Becky's pet project and she spared the right wing asshole no pain. If it were up to Nicklaus then Joe would have been dead days ago. Becky hated Protestants and loved to prolong torture on Joe.

Becky had her vile ways to get what she wanted and the mad doctor was a sucker to her allures and teasing. She hated Protestants with a passion and Joe was her way of getting even in her own private war. One could easily say that Becky is a pure Irish Catholic militant.

Becky and the doctor never showed affection toward one-another in open view of the others in the house. Yet when they managed to find the time to be alone, they were crawling all over each other like two long lost lovers would have done.

Nick is a good-looking man with a hefty fortune to kick back on and he was an equal to Becky's intellect. Becky was a hard person to get along with, 'from what I saw on the surveillance video tapes.' She had a whole different way about her when Nick was near and always seemed to get what she wanted out of him.

Peter Lewis worked eight hours a day and rarely socialized with the other people in the mansion. Lewis was friendly with one of the maid's that came once a week but that is all Peter and the maid was friends. Pete was great at keeping the books and taking care of all listings and Project activities in alphabetical order. He mailed out the bills and paid for others, with online banking. Lewis did not know anything about the nature of the experiments going on in 30 basement laboratories. After Peter finished his eight hours, Peter went into his room and did online Trading with his laptop computer. Peter was working out well for the mad doctor and Peter was making more money then he ever had in his life. What made Peter Lewis special was that he did not care what the experiments were about and he minded his own business.

April 10, 2011

Mia was in the Cell with the best view of the three human holding cells. She watched both Jarred and Jung Sung as they hurt their test subjects and Mia would mimic these rogue acts in her cage.

Hauns the Estate Butler or Keeper watched Mia from the peephole in the hidden passageway behind the cement walls. Hauns was the only person in the huge house who knew of the secret chambers and passageways behind the walls of the old Victorian mansion.

Every time Mia was moved from her cage. Mia studied the manner in which her cage opened. One night when there was nobody around in the holding area, Mia opened her cage and sneaked about the premises until morning. She moved about on the blind side of the security camera's searching for a way out of the huge house. Mia went unnoticed and one night she did find a way to get out of the house. Then she returned to her cage closing and locking the door.

Mia made sure that each time she left her cell that later she would return without being seen by neither the security cameras nor the people that lived in Nick's gloomy damp rooms of the mansion.

Toxic wastes and other byproducts produced from the Xeno experiments that needed to be dumped somewhere. Nicklaus bought and paid for in cash one-hundred acres of rainforest near Timber Lake in the North Puget Sound area. With the help of his trucking business partners in the outside world, Nicklaus planned to haul the waste to his property and dump on the low marshland, which was an area of almost forty acres. Even during long droughts, the marsh was under water. It was the perfect site to dump Xeno waste products. It was a beautiful land with an awesome sunset but Nicklaus Keller did not consider that. All that Nicklaus cared about was dumping his toxic waste somewhere that nobody would know about.

<u>April 18,1011</u>

I removed from the house evidence that there was some cannibalism present during the weeks and years of the Xeno Project. It must have been Gothic in the mansion before the mad doctor and his associates moved their operation to Timber Lake. There were Police Detectives nosing around searching for missing persons. I suspect that one of the occupants of the house was indulging in the dead of the night, most likely stealing children off the sidewalks of Seattle. I found the bones in the boiler room of the Victorian house and then learned that they were those of the children . . . I expected that a serial killer had lived at the Lupus Estate during Nick's rein.

Children never used as test subjects so what were they doing in the boiler room. All that I could think of was that they were murdered. I found teeth marks on some of their bones. What else could have happened to them? There were skulls whose insides were scraped clean. From the indications of the scratches, including the gouges on the interior of the skulls, I concluded that an animal had eaten their brains.

Becky and Nick were grafting animal tissue onto their two test subjects. Emma was doing better then Joe was, but they were both slowly dying. Samples of their D.N.A. showed changes and mutations as the skin drafts adapted to their new hosts. Becky helped Nick with his revolutionary transplanting chemical agents and together they made breakthroughs in preventing transplant rejections for just about any type of tissue. No matter what their species was. Proof was definite objective medical evidence, which proved beyond a doubt that Xeno transplants should be banned. Perhaps they should not have gone as far as they had with the human test subjects that it was too late now.

It seemed that the two heartthrobs were enjoying themselves so much that the grafts continued. Mia did not understand why the doctors were grafting healthy tissue unto healthy humans. She thought that perhaps it was because it was fun to do. Mia was seeing things for the first time and understood that she was smarter then before the transplants. Studying the way, the skin drafts were performed Mia memorized in everything she could. Mia was feeling more at home every day. She paid close attention to the two doctors because if she ever had to do it herself. Then she wanted to do it right.

———————————

John Jung Sung and Jarred were walking in the yard together. Troubling both of them by the presence of Becky and they were talking about ridding themselves of the bitch. 'Jarred began the conversation.'

"She is one two-faced backstabbing bitch and one day she is going to push me too hard. Then I'm going to cut her heart out and eat it for lunch."

" You know what?" stated Jung. "I bet that it has been you eating them children and yes I bet you would eat her heart,' but let me at her first for just an hour. Then she is all yours, Igor."

" Do not call me by that name again asshole. You know damn well that my name is, jarred! Now what

should we do about Miss smart-alecky pants Becky?" 'There stayed a mean stare in his eyes.' *"No, I don't eat people Sung; I thought that it was you doing it? I believe that the child murderer is Hauns the butler?"*

" Hell no, it was not I who murdered those poor children!" 'Jarred was angry' *If it was not you either then I don't have a clue?"*

'Jarred hated Becky and knew she needed to die.' *"When and how do you want to kill the bitch,"* asked Jarred repeatedly.

"An accident and then Nicklaus will not suspect us. I know how but not when ... We can throw her into one of the ape cages!" Sung was dreaming about watching Becky get torn apart by the largest West African baboon that was housed in one of the cages. Valentine earned his name because he was extremely sexually active. Both men agreed that would be the best way to kill Becky. They were anxious to get it done. It was going to be difficult to get her alone and away from Nicklaus. Yet they were determined to murder Becky and were going to try the first chance that they got.

Valentine was a test subject of two experiments in the Project. Valentine was the recipient of grafted penile skin and his testicles traded for human ones. Ever since the operations, he was in a bad mood and was hostile toward even his own brethren. That was the reason behind the frontal lobe section transplant operations. You can bet that Valentine was always angry and sore. One very unhappy and fertile test subject is what Valentine was.

———————————

Paul Jacobs was a peaceful and kind man who worked for the County Public Defenders Office in Mason County, Washington. How was he to know that the people waiting for him at the airport were kidnapers and murderers?

Paul was mellow and passive in his nature and one of those bleeding heart liberals. Valentine also shared his body with Valentine and Valentine with his. It was all in an effort to tame down the baboon ape so that he could be a stud for breeding. I can tell you that Valentine had not changed much but that is because he was faking it. In reality, his mind had awakened. Paul believed that he was dying.

April 20, 2011

Doctor Nicklaus Keller's sister and her fiancé made a surprise visit to see her brother. She tried calling but Nick's phone was out of order and had been out of order for several months. It was no great wonder that she was worried about her brother Nicklaus.

Hauns the butler had invited the pair into the house and had them wait in the parlor while he summoned his Master. Hauns was an old man who owed his life to Doctor Nicklaus Keller and was the most loyal person Nicklaus had. 'Whether he knew that or not, I cannot say for sure.' Hauns were gone for several minutes but returned with Nick at his side. Nicklaus tried to pretend that everything was normal and that he was fine. Elizabeth was not convinced that her brother was being sincere and insisted that Nick take some time away from his experiments. They hugged each other warmly and then talked about their youths. Nick admitted that he had forgotten that he had a half sister and then invited them to stay for the weekend. He insisted that was all the time he had to waste and then he had to go back to work again.

Nicklaus knew that he did a poor job convincing his sister that things were swell and everything was going great in his life. Nothing more he could do, except hope that everything went well during the weekend.

Watching the tapes left no doubt in my mind.

Nicklaus Keller was a mad scientist and he was extremely insane. I noticed that Nick was a lousy actor but that he was a clever man.

April 22, 2011

"I'm baaaack and was wondering, did you miss me Emma? I still owe you for running away from me . . . Remember?" Jarred was staring down at what used to be Emma and taunted the abused and badly mutilated woman with threats. *"My, what ugly skin you have and oh my God, what happened to your boobies? Shit woman, you are so ugly now I would not touch you with a ten-foot pole, Yucky! Have you been taking those ugly pills again or have Dr. Frankenstein and his bride been playing gods at your* **Expense?"**

Emma wished that she were dead. Pain was getting the best of Emma's determination to survive the horror and mutilations to her once shapely body. When Emma heard, those awful words come out of Jarred's mouth. Emma broke down and cried. Then she sobbed in despair. Emma started ripping at the ape like hair growing on her arms as blood was dripping seriously onto the hard cement floor of her cell. Then Emma stared at Jarred and shouted at him. *"Kill me! Why don't you just end it for me, right now . . . Look at me? 'I am of no use to you anymore, I am dying so why don't you' just get it over with and kill me now?"*

"I cannot believe that you still have some kind of smartass mouth *and that you still look good to me Baby. You want me don't you Emma? I bet that your love canal is as fresh as ever and if I cover you with a blanket then your monkey skin won't be exposed. Yes, I do not see any funny skin on you where I want to probe . . . Your mine Emma, ready or not here I come. Believe this Emma!"* Jarred exposed himself to the terrified test subject. It made Emma's lips bleed because they were dry and cracked from

63

lack of water.

Jarred raped Emma on this gloomy morning and he impregnated her without realizing that he had done so. Emma wept throughout the appalling ordeal and pleaded for mercy. Jarred felt that he had it coming and he had to boost up his self-esteem for the big job waiting for him.

Kidnapping Becky and throwing her in with Valentine. Jarred doubted that he would ever get another chance at Emma so he was glad that he got pleasured before she kicked off. Becky was next on his list.

April 24 2011

Emma was not dying anytime soon because when the mad doctor learned of her pregnancy. Nick had visions of new experiments with the fetus and a newborn baby to study, eventually dissecting it, if not, and then he would breed it with an ape. Nick envisioned the future of man and the coming generations of evolutionary changes.

Meanwhile, Nick's sister and her Fiancé were talking about their recluse brother and his poor memory. Hauns had led them to the south wing of the house and to their guest rooms. To the affianced lovers, Nicklaus was a different man then they remembered. Dark rings under Nick's eyes told a story of their own. Elizabeth asked Greg Ryder, (fiancé) to walk with her around the house and help her find what has been going on with her brother. Elizabeth complained that the house gave her the creeps and that the butler was acting strangely.

"I am not so sure that would be a good idea and besides that . . . It would be rude for us to be snooping around in places that are none of our business, but if you really want me to go with you then I'm ready when you are." Immediately, Replied Greg.

"But I just can't help it, Greg. I am curious to find out what is wrong with my brother. What can we possibly

find that Nicklaus does not want us to see?" Said Elizabeth and she were sincerely concerned about the changes in her older brother.

Greg opened his suitcase that was sitting on the dresser table. From it he removed a flashlight and his small caliber pistol. Elizabeth saw the pistol and protested . . . *"What in God's name is you doing with a pistol Greg?"*

"One can never know when a gun can come in handy. Anytime I go away on a long trip it goes with me. I think of my pistol as a tool and with all of those insane criminals that are 'out and about.' It very well can save your life and mine. I have a concealed weapon permit and it is up to date, do not worry Sweetheart. 'Greg went on to say.' *Once I went on a business trip to Chicago, I drove my Rolls Royce and I was car-jacked and half-beaten to death. Like I said, you never know?"*

"Oh very well, but be careful with that thing, will ya? Said Elizabeth, then added sarcastically. *"Next times tell me about these kind of thing's and what else is there that I do not know about you?* 'She wasn't done yet,' *Do you have a house in the suburbs with a wife and children and a mistress or two?"* Both of them cracked up laughing and then they exited their guest room and started their exploration through the doctor's oversized Victorian home.

October 31, 2011

Mia was hungry, restless on the night of Halloween as the full moon shone down on the Estate of Doctor Nicklaus Keller. In her cage Mia waited for the day to end and for the attendants to leave. Mia was planning to go on a scavenger hunt among the children that were dressed in costumes. Mia had trimmed down and she was taking on some human characteristics. She still weighed in at three hundred pounds but that was two hundred pounds less then when she lived in the jungles of Africa. Without a doubt, Mia's fur and hairs were thinning out and her skin was becoming softer. Inside of Mia burned a fire, with an urge to murder. She wanted fresh brain matter, so fresh that it was still breathing. Since the transplants, Mia refused to eat fruits and vegetables; she would only eat human flesh.

Mia was ugly and sported a dog like snout but she was going through changes. Human cells that had been multiplying in her temporal lobes were attacking and replacing her brain's original cells. She was smart enough to carry out the food with her, out of her cage so as not to alert the keepers that she was not eating. Because then they might have suspected her of escaping at night for hunting. Ugly as a bulldog but cunning as a fox, Mia was on the loose.

Mia entered the air-conditioning ducts to crawl her way out of the basement. She had to lose enough weight to fit into the ducts and ever since, she had lost the extra pounds. Mia has been escaping at least twice a week to feast on human veal. Tonight was going to be the easiest hunting that Mia could get in. Thousands of children were roaming the streets after curfew. It was easy picking' for the baboon, she started to work the bolt free that kept her cage closed. In less then five minutes' Mia was crawling into the air-conditioning ducts.

November 1, 2011

Emma was desperately trying to find a way to kill herself. She was disgusted with the living fetus inside her womb. She did not look nor feel like she was pregnant, but she knew damn well that she was. It was sickening for Emma to recall the way that Jarred had raped her but at least there was something good that had come out of it for her. Knowing that her old skin, was grafted back onto her body and her bruises healing was not enough. . .
'Emma wished that she were dead.'

Emma was having a hard time getting onto her feet

because of the bandages. Bandage gauze wrapped tightly around her legs to protect the skin grafts. She remembered the patches of reptile and goat tissue that use to be on her legs. It seemed that those tissues were tougher to remove and when the doctors replanted Emma's old tissue. She did not heal fast enough, and her body was rejecting her own skin tissue. It took her two hours, but Emma finally did rise to her feet. It was all in vain because she lost her balance and fell to the floor. She screamed at the top of her lungs more in anger then anything else. Emma prayed that once the bandages removed from below her waist, that her skin looked normal. Just the thought of the grotesque animal tissue patches on her legs made Emma Gag. She was anxious to see if the grafts took hold, they were itching like hell. 'That was a good sign, unless she was growing more hair.' In any case, she was fortunate to be among the living.

After a week passed, Emma's pain was more bearable, she began to think about escaping again. Wiggling and squirming in her bandages and ripping at the back with her hands securely taped together it was possible to get free. Emma could feel the bandages loosen and then she stopped her efforts to get free. It was much wiser to wait until the right moment when the door to her cell was ajar. There was just one worry she had to deal with and that was . . . because of the bad treatment and the swill, they fed the test subjects. Emma was as thin as a toothpick, but because of the mammary baboon derived hormone shots. Emma's breasts swelled like water balloons. She was a freak show in the dungeons of Doctor Kellers Laboratories..

How could pencil pushing geeks and nerds get away with such blatant crimes against nature? Emma's pain was worse then physical pain, Emma felt bestially and unnaturally violated. In the shape Emma was now making plans of escaping were pipe dreams, not reality. Emma's body was mutating and disfiguring again. She cursed the Doctor and Becky for their diabolical scheme to destroy our species.

Mia had gotten out of the basements and off the Estate in four minutes flat. 'It was easy as ABC.' Once she was in the streets, Mia stayed in the shadows as much as possible when she could, stealthily jump swiftly through the trees to the rooftops. Sure enough, Mia was on the loose again.

It was a clear night with a full moon in the sky. Without detection, Mia moved like the wind. There below her she spied the children with bags filled with trick or treat candies. Her stomach growled with hunger and the noise of it echoed through the thick foggy Seattle air.

Within the Puget Sound, the air is always thick with water particles and you could watch them float aimlessly about suspended in air. It was colder then the tropical ape liked, but as long as she kept moving, it was warm enough. With Mia's primitive instincts and her new found intellect. Mia kidnapped three children and carried them back to the Keller Estate. Then Mia sat outside the walls of the gates and devoured the children. Ravenously, Mia tore into the children ripping their flesh apart and lapping up the hot steaming blood. Because the night air was so thick, none of their screams carried through the fog. Thus, nobody heard the children cry out. Children's brains were the most delicious and Mia carefully scraped brain matter out of their skulls. Then Mia slurped the brain matter down her throat, as if athletes do raw eggs.

Three children were only appetizers for the hungry baboon. Mia traveled back to the city neighborhoods four more times before her hunger appeased. Fifteen dead and half-eaten children lay in a heap on the front lawn at the west gate of the Keller Estate. Some of the children had their skulls busted open like coconuts and their brains were missing.

    'After Mia was through eating, then checking to see if the coast were clear,' Mia ran past the dogs and into the estate utility shack. Once in the shack Mia removed the covers and filters on the vent, and climbed into the air ducts. If she had eaten another bite, Mia probably would not have fit into the ductwork. Her baby devoured the proteins eagerly and in its world inside Mia's womb. It grimaced as a new creation opened its eyes.

    It was two hours before the workday was to begin and that give Mia ample time to lick herself clean. When Mia finished locking herself into her cage, she saw Emma staring at her from the bean shoot of Emma's padded cell door. With a confident smile on her face, Mia realized that she could telepathically send pictures with Emma and in a vision showed Emma the dead children. Emma trembled for a few moments.

The End of Chapter Five

"Monkey About"

CHAPTER SIX
"Freak Lovers"
NOVEMBER 2, 2011

Alone and disillusioned, Faye was losing her battle with Xeno Experiments. She had developed a taste for human flesh. Faye could hear her rag doll talking to her and sometimes blink. There was nothing in the world that Faye had ever loved more then that rag doll. She held her baby close to her breasts and rocked her to sleep. Sensations of ants scurrying across Faye's skin felt half as bad as the pain in Faye's heart. There were no ants; they were only in Faye's mind.

Months passed and Dr. Nick had not let his sister leave. Now the pair was searching the place for the hundredth time. *"Come on we'll get something to eat and then we can lie down for a while. I hope that you're happy now because we have searched every room in the house and hadn't found a thing."* Greg was getting wary of climbing staircases and walking down endless hallways. *"We hadn't gone into the basements yet, nor have we been in the rooms that were occupied."* 'Complained Elizabeth' it was her character and Elizabeth always bossed Greg around. She tried too anyway and sometimes Greg allowed it to happen. Elizabeth was just five feet tall and ninety pounds but on her toes she packed quite a punch. There were a couple times when she walloped Greg and Greg tried to act as if it did not hurt. However, it hurt like hell.

"You know that we are not allowed to venture into the restricted areas, no way Jose. There must be a good reason that the signs say **Employees Only** *and* **Restricted Area**. *Moreover, the signs, which warn, of Hazardous Chemicals and the worst sign of them all,* Beware of the Dogs. *What do you say, Sweetheart, let's*

stop at the kitchen on the way back to our suites?"

"Okay Greg, let us go and ask Hauns if he can make us some sandwiches. I'm famished." 'Elizabeth Admitted.'

During the night, Greg and his beau heard strange noises coming from the air ducts. They had forgotten all about the strange sounds. 'That is, once they had eaten the Rubin sandwiches and downed three bottles of aged wine.' With the curtains wide open and the moonbeams shining onto their King size bed. Elizabeth and her man made passionate love until dawn.

November 4, 2011

Mia was pregnant and wondering if her baby would appear human. 'Joe had died during the night.' Becky had tested Mia because she suspected that the female baboon was getting a big belly. If she had known that Mia was bloated because she had gorged herself on Halloween costumed children. She would have had the ape put to sleep. Instead, she tested the baboon and discovered its pregnancy.

Hauns found the dead children just outside the south gate of the Keller Estate. He carried the children to the boiler room and hid them where they were unseen. He was more then glad to help his Master in any way possible. Doctor Keller had saved the Butlers life by doing a triple bypass and Hauns was indebted to the mad doctor.

This was not the first time that Hauns had broken the law for the sake of the Xeno experiments and Hauns was sure that it was not going to be the last. In my opinion, and I am a conservative. Hauns would have been better off to find another way to pay the bill for the triple bypass. Hauns knew that Dr. Keller was the answer to all his woes.

At this point of the Xeno experiments, the Project Staff should have foreseen what was happening in the old Victorian mansion. It was obviously possessed by an evil which was consuming everybody. Writings on the walls told of the next coming of the Anti Christ and his demons. Certainly If they had taken the time to study the drawings, paintings and writings on the walls inside the mansion. They would not have believed what they saw. I would have tried to prevent the contamination of the Project by the evil spirits on the Estate. It was Valentine with his newfound telekinetic thoughts, which caused evil to be created in the big house.

Hauns Bonhoff has been the Keeper of the mansion for fifty-two years and his father was before him, he knew from the beginning that the great evil one lived in the mansion. He also was aware of the Legions living in the basements and the wine cellars of the mansion. There were hidden passageways and crawlspaces, which only Hauns knew about. It was serendipitous for the Butler/Keeper that Doctor Keller had bought the mansion when he had, because of his triple bypass. Hauns had his near fatal heart attack as he was serving the doctor and his guest's tea. It was not in his destiny to die yet because Hauns had important duties to perform. Hauns was the Keeper and the

Years ago his Aorta used to belong to a pig until Nicklaus performed the transplant for Hauns. Old Hauns gained more time in his life to do evil acts against nature, hidden in the big house trying to find eternal life.

November 13, 2011

Walking the passageways Hauns was spying on the residents and the guests from peepholes and two-way mirrors. Sometimes he would take along Mia late in the night and very early in the mornings. Mia could talk fluently in English and every other language spoken in the world. Most often, the pair spoke to each other in a dialect from hell. It sounded as if they were speaking in wicked tongues as they walked through the secret recesses of the house.

Hauns and Mia were spying on the maids that worked during the night hours and on the Project Staffers. Lately, Hauns had been watching Greg, Elizabeth, and it brought back long lost urges. Urges which had lain sleeping for decades waiting for the day of the incarnation from Hell. When that day finally comes and Lucifer with his Legions released. At that time, Hauns will be one of the devil's generals and his youth returned to him with a promise of everlasting, never ending and eternal life. "Immortality with a soul blackened by evil and carnal lust ruling his days and nights, Ruling the nights until all the good on earth has been vanquished.

Hauns believed this with all of his heart, soul, and being. Knowing it was Nicklaus that would do it, with some help from Valentine. One day under the protection of the underground laboratories, the Xeno Project will thrive as the world above it dies.

Mia talked to Hauns and gave him this message from Hell. She informed the Keeper that Lucifer was furious that he has not found any of the women suitable for his embodiment. Now Elizabeth entered the house and he wanted her to parent his child. Mia suggested that she could murder Greg and eat the evidence.

Hauns ordered Mia to leave Greg alone for now and that he was going to sleep on it and let Mia know his decision tomorrow night. He knew that Valentine was destined to be the sire of the devil incarnate and that Elizabeth was destined to give birth to the greatest evil ever born. Hauns had to have some time to think things through so that nothing would go awry.

Lucifer could see through Valentine's eyes but could not take possession of his body. There was the act of conception, which Lucifer was going to use to transform himself into human form. His son, the anti Christ and his daughter, the greatest witch and whore that ever existed been conceived within the wombs of Emma and Mia. Lucifer thought that his plans perfect, but sometimes things do not turn out as planned.

Lucifer could hardly wait to taste the sweet nectar that only Elizabeth could produce. Lucifer felt 'right at home' on the Keller Estate. Valentine was a premeditating and a cold-blooded killer in his old habitat in Africa and he did not change his habits. He was not as smart as Mia was, but was evolving quickly and soon would pass his sister up on the tree of life. Lucifer was watching it all and he was thrilled to death at what he was seeing. Lucifer is high evil, genetically altered human with inhuman masteries are his forte.

One day at a young age, he escaped and has grown one year in only two months. Time passes quickly and Lucifer grows. Lucifer has special abilities, staying hidden cleverly. 'Disappointed that he was not in human form, Lucifer scowled.' For the present time, Lucifer had to be content with being dead and aware, less than a spirit.

November 14, 2011

Nick and Becky was pillow talking after having sex in their second floor penthouse apartment in his Victorian mansion. Sometimes they slept in the master bedrooms on the first floor. Then there were those times which they stayed in the bedroom next to their office in the second level basement. On this stormy night, the two of them stayed in luxury, hidden away from Nick's relatives.' Elizabeth was a royal pain in the ass to the co-conspirators. They were trying to figure out a solution to their problems while getting some quality time alone together.

"Nick, will you please tell your sister to stay out of the restricted areas. Why in the world is Elizabeth and her

Beau still here anyway? I thought that they were only staying for a couple days and they are still living here. Why?" Becky disliked Elizabeth for no special reason, except for the influence of evil in the house. It was going to be a rude awakening for everyone when they found out that Lucifer was in lust with Elizabeth. Shrouded in darkness Lucifer entered Elizabeth's nightmares and coaxed her into falling in love with him. Lucifer is a ball of energy created in Valentine's brain. Energy released into the house and roamed with a will of its own.

"Elizabeth wants to get me to go back with her and take a vacation for two weeks. I think that she suspects something and her boyfriend eggs Elizabeth on. Perhaps they should stay until the experiments are finished. She just knows too much and what can I do to stop her from going to the Authorities?" Asked Nick with deep consternation in his voice.

"Well perhaps we should kill them so that they do not ruin us and expose our Project to the public. You know damn well that we will go to prison and perhaps the death penalty! I love you Nicklaus Keller and this Xeno Project means as much to me as it does to you, perhaps even more. Your sister should have departed us long ago, it is her own fault for being such a nosy body." Rebutted Becky and she meant every word of what she said.

An evil presence influenced all the decisions that the mad doctor and his Mistress conjured up together and that evil was getting stronger. Nicklaus Keller started the Project with Nobel intentions in mind. First the evil in the mansion stirred and then it awakened. Valentine was creating monsters with telekinetic-powers. Lupus Estate was never haunted; it was just an old Victorian. The Xeno transplants and inter-breeders produced these unnatural acts.

Meanwhile, John and Jarred were plotting the

demise of Becky, unbeknownst of the decree sent from hell to sacrifice Elizabeth to the great baboon ape creature. If they did manage to get Becky into the cage, Valentine would kill them instead of Becky. They were taking a big chance just by thinking of it because Valentine could read minds. John Sung seemingly was making a big mistake by employing Jarred to help him with his diabolical plot to murder their Master's Mistress.

NOVEMBER 29, 2011

Emma was having the most peculiar dreams of her life and for the last couple of weeks it was becoming difficult for her to distinguish reality from illusion. She heard a voice in her head, which sounded as real as if the devil was standing beside Emma. Yet there was nobody there. In the air she could smell the turbid swamp and the decay of the dense foliage. With the wind behind her Emma ran and swung on vines through the jungles of Africa chasing her prey. Emma could taste the blood in her throat from the tribesman that she was devouring. Ripping and shredding the flesh as she bore into her prey with her oversized teeth. Emma strangely enjoyed her visions, relishing the taste of blood. Every time that Emma dreamed as she slept, it was repeatedly the same dream.

By far, the most drastic and remarkable of all the test subjects was Faye Hook. Her body features were changing into hideous and unnatural shapes. Unlike the baboon, which was her organ donor and very different from looking human, Faye was deformed and her eyes seemed to be glowing. Doctor Keller put her on video cam twenty-four hours a day studying her closely. Nicklaus had an idea of what was happening to Faye and with all the horrors; she had to endure for months. Doctor Keller noted in his journal that Faye was adapting well to the transplants and that Faye was melding into a new quintessence.

Pointed ears and a misshapen nose, were between

the warts, boils littering Faye's body. Her feet now cloven and she was growing a tail. Doctor Keller asked Faye if she felt any pain at all. Faye replied an ecstatic no. Faye was turning so ugly that she was hard to gaze upon. Faye felt good about herself; her animal instincts were becoming natural to the once beautiful Faye.

NOVEMBER 30, 2011

Jarred was the first person that entered the holding cell area and the stench sickened him. A few moments later Jarred collapsed onto the floor. It seemed that just about the entire test subjects had died of complications related to their organ and tissue transplants. There were only seven test subjects not affected by their transplants. They were Mia, Valentine and another baboon named Fury. Among the human test subjects were Emma, Faye, Magen Berks and Wayne Jordan. By the time Jarred awakened, almost everybody was in the holding area investigating the cause of his or her premature deaths. For some unknown reason the carcasses of the dead test subjects were rotting and emitting a lurid smell.

Valentine had gone apes on his neighbors and crushed their skulls. The Master of Evil, the Dean of Cruelty, and the Wizard of Mayhem, 'Lucifer' instigated this onslaught. It chose who would die and with delight glowing in his eyes, Valentine carried out his Sentences without remorse.

Elizabeth was having some wicked dreams of her own that were even stranger then Emma's nightmares. She was dreaming about a baboon and a Halloween-haunted house. Elizabeth was in love with a baboon and they were holding hands as they explored the haunted house at the carnival. It was an eerie state of mind where she was floating aimlessly with her baboon lover. Nothing mattered anymore that belonged to her old world and there was only one thing that mattered to Elizabeth in her dreams. It was the one who called himself Valentine.

"Elizabeth baby, wake up honey. Open your eyes and wake up, you're having a nightmare." It was light outside and well into the morning when Greg noticed that Elizabeth was having a bad dream. He was trying to snap her out of the deep trance she was experiencing but his efforts were ineffective. Greg could not awaken Elizabeth so he did the only other thing he could think of . . . Greg splashed water on Elizabeth's face, using water from the pitcher on her night table beside the bed.

Elizabeth finally woke out of her dream, sat up yawning. *"Oh I am wet, where did the water come from? Oh my, I had an orgasm."* Elizabeth seemed shocked about this revelation.

December 2, 2011

I was quite surprised and impressed with the mad doctor's security video cameras. Miniature, undetectable, and cleverly concealed with clarity beyond anything that I have seen in quality, tiny microphones picked up the slightest whispers and that made it impossible to contrive a plot against Nicklaus Keller without doing it on video tape. Soon recorded on a compact micro disc and stored in files. There was nowhere on the estate grounds where one could say, nor do anything without the insane mastermind being privy to it. What was even more impressive was the password needed to access the security camera tapes because each camera had a different password. Nicklaus Keller was the only person at the Xeno Project laboratories to possess all of the passwords for the security surveillance cameras.

Inside John's spacious and plush suite that had been assigned to him. John Sung was crying and talking to himself. He did not care that Nicklaus had most likely installed cameras in his quarters because he was on a down swing. Sung was having one of his episodes again and he knew to keep to himself when his mood was at a low ebb.

"I wish that I were dead! **'Said John Sung,'** *and I wish that I could take everybody in the world with me. I loathe, I abhor, I detest and I hate you! You think I'm mad and perhaps I am, but I'm clever enough to beat the likes of you. Beat you two within one inch of your worthless lives. Why, oh why me, and what have I done deserving this fate? What kind of monster am I to inflect endless hours of torture on innocent people? Be damned the people, be cursed, their loves and desires! They can all go to hell wearing bells around their necks for all I care!"* (John expressed his intense sexual desires with violence) John needed an outlet for his anger tearing away at his soul and a body, not his own to inflict his love on.

John tried to get past his crazy urges with hard work. It was about that maniacal time again and Jarred had as of yet not returned with any fresh test subjects. That left John idle and restless for another session with Emma. Only Emma was off limits to him and so were Faye and Mia. That left 'Magen Burks and Wayne Jordan. Magen was recuperating from heart and liver transplants and Wayne Jordan was recovering from a Pancreas transplant. John knew that of those two Jordan was the one most likely to survive one, two-hour sessions. There was no way around his dilemma, Sung slung his medical bag over his shoulders and exited his suite through the door nearest to the elevators. It was time for John to visit Wayne Jordan.

Thoughts and ideas were beginning to race in John's mind. He was breathing fast and heavily, his blood pressure was sky high. John was anxious to begin his evil deed and he was shaking like a leaf on a tree. After stepping into the elevator John tried to calm himself down, but all he did was get angry that he could not calm down. The more he attempted to calm down, the madder he had gotten. Another thing that John Jung Sung hated with a burning passion was the racing thought patterns in his head. Sung was thinking so fast that he was insane with madness by the time he entered Jordan's' holding cell.

December 3, 2011

Twelve hours is an awful long time to spend with John Sung if you are a test subject. Jordan had endured being skinned alive, skin tissue from five different species of lab animals replaced his own skin. The only sections on his torso that had not been mutilated were his reproductive organs. It was the point of the experiment to try to change the genetic make-up of human sperm. Time dragged for Wayne as the good surgeon skillfully but painfully cut the skin off Jordan's body while leaving his reproductive organs intact. Dr. Keller ignored the side effects and stayed indifferent to Jordan's pleas for mercy.

Wayne Jordan was a weightlifter and a professional body builder. Jordan was horrified at what was being done to his terrific body and cried profusely when he saw the rabbit, rat, pig, sheep, and monkey skin where his own skin once was. Wayne was retching foodstuffs all over his bed and onto the walls of his cell. No strength that Wayne could muster was enough to break the Velcro straps that were binding Wayne's limbs to the bed.

Sung used a thin haired brush to spread the thick honey like chemical compound over the grafted areas on Wayne's body. It was Doctor Keller's formula and it worked wonders for healing and adapting to new-transplanted cells. Wayne Jordan sighed with relief as the anesthetic in the compounds relinquished the agony and left behind a throbbing pain that Jordan could live with.

Faye was in the adjoining holding cell and she heard everything that was going on in Wayne's cell. With desperation while horror struck. Faye rocked her rag doll Ann to sleep and sung her a lullaby. Beaten and abused,

Faye was dreaming that she was somewhere else and not in the hell that she found herself in. Faye was lost in the realm of her nightmare and a bloody rag doll.

———————

Greg awoke from a disturbing dream and tried to get back to sleep but he just could not shake the vividness and clarity of the nightmare he had experienced. Careful not to stir Elizabeth awake, Greg rose out of his bed and silently tiptoed out of their bedroom of their large suite. There was no-good reason for Greg to be leaving the confines of their suite but something was drawing at him and beckoning the bedazzled young man to walk bare footed downstairs. It must have been some sort of retro-hypnosis, which had roused Greg from his sleep.

A diviner accomplishes remote Hypnosis through telepathic means. Who that Diviner is was a mystery but that person is also a Prophet, as a Sorcerer and a prophesier created by Lucifer in hell with molten lava. It was a powerful clairvoyant and born from evil where there are agendas that 'must be followed.' This person is the guard who protects the beast to receive the devil incarnate. Whoever is the source of the hypnotic messages and directives of this we can be certain . . .

'It is somebody who lives in the house that is committing the psychic acts to manipulate Greg into leaving his room.' What is going to befall on the unsuspecting guest of the Keller Estate is yet to be determined. At least Greg had his pistol but did not know of the coming encounter with hell.

Lucifer never imagined a reprieve from hell so soon. He expected to wait another thousand years before God Almighty would consider giving the denizens of Hell a break from their extreme fires and freezing graves. It seems that the human race beat God to the punch. Lucifer laughed a mighty laugh. Lucifer was delighted at the Xeno experiments and approved of the beastly human hybrids that were soon to be born into the world of living souls. These lost souls would belong to the Devil and they would fill the ranks of his Forces.

Humans made in the image of God therefore, humans can create life as God had and Valentine had, with the help of AASA1313. That also means that Nicklaus can create demons and incarnate the devil into a mortal soul. Lucifer had no intention on repenting. It was only interested in conquering Heaven and Earth and assassinating God. Many dreams of screaming societies and cultures the world over. Bestial virgins sacrificed to its name aroused the evil giant. In a few more months, the waiting was over for the wicked and merciless obscenity from Valentine. Lucifer's new Kingdom would reign. *"God made man in his own image therefore I am made the mutants in my image."* Screamed Lucifer and God heard the devil loud and clear.

Greg wandered aimlessly until he staggered into the Butler who was carrying a tray loaded with a tea set. It made a crashing noise as the tray dropped from the butler's hands. Hauns ignored the mess on the floor and grabbed hold of Greg and then Hauns threw Greg against the wall.

With a remote control switch, the concealed doors opened into the corridors and secret chambers within the Victorian mansion. Greg was not aimlessly wandering anymore as Hauns carried him into a large chamber dimly lit by flaming torches. Greg was able to reach into his back pocket and grab his pearl handled 32. Greg fired three shots at Valentine before big Hauns slapped the pistol away and it fallen onto the hallway carpet..

Valentine and Mia were standing there in the chamber watching Hauns applauding him for his efforts.

Hauns was lugging Greg into the Sacred Chamber as Hauns was cursing and swearing at God. Valentine and Mia hopped over to Greg and easily tossed him like a beach ball back and forth, blood was soaking Valentines shirt and then clotted as the wound healed. Madly laughing, the baboons locked Greg into an old dungeon filled with scared bones decorated with modern furnishings. It was the strangest thing that Greg had ever seen. Mia threw the pistol in with Greg.

December 6, 2011

Elizabeth was searching the house for Greg because when she had awakened Greg was gone. She searched two floors of the house before taking the elevator down to the third level basement laboratory. There, standing next to Becky was Valentine while Jarred was holding a large burlap bag in his hands. Paul Jacobs kept barely alive since the tragedy. Now he was doing much better with the intro-biotic stabilizer that Doctor Keller had implanted in his brain, along with the baboon bone-marrow transplants had nearly cured Paul. Paul was also a freak of the evolution tree of life. Paul Jacobs has been Xeno active with goats, pig ears, baboon and rats. It was no great wonder that when Elizabeth saw the mutant test subject, she shocked ***"Oh my God, what kind of monster are you?"*** 'Elizabeth Screamed!

'Elizabeth could not believe her eyes when she noticed Valentine standing next to Becky. It seemed that Becky had a good relationship with her test subjects and that she was fitting in well in the program. It was only by chance that Becky happened to be the one to capture the nosy busybody and troublesome Elizabeth.

It was love at first sight for both Valentine and for Elizabeth. Perhaps it was a freak thing perhaps they were spellbound? Paul was agape at the sight before him and Jarred was angry because Jarred had not gotten to stuff

Becky into the burlap bag. Becky filmed the pair as they copulated right there on the cold floor. It was obvious that the evil within the mansion was behind these freak lovers. Evil introduced by Dr. Nicklaus Keller and Valentine.

Beauty and beast engulfed in each other completely sharing juices and doing what lovers did. Putrid odors reeked from the juices mixing of beast and human. Becky was confused as to why it was happening but she did not care . . . or fight her urges.

Valentine was bruising Elizabeth and biting her shoulder as he entered her. Both of them were making satisfied sounds between groans of pleasure. *"Lucifer gleamed with pleasure and gloated over his children."* At last Lucifer was going to claim the crown made from corrupted souls and the blood of the innocent. It seemed that the more Valentine beat on Elizabeth and the harder he pushed . . . Elizabeth loved it even more.

Jarred was getting jealous of the big ape and his seductress. It was the catalyst, which motivated the deranged sidekick to go on the prowl again. There was no point in trying to murder Becky because she was important to the Xeno Project and a close friend of Valentine.

Freak Lovers in the Xeno Project were going to be commonplace, eventually in the basements of the mad brain surgeon/scientists all over the globe. Unless Doctor Keller and his company ceased the experiments and stopped the Xeno Project dead in its tracks, life as we know it would disappear from the face of the planet and be replaced with unimaginable creatures of Darkness. Watching these tapes can be disturbing, Nick was a madman to the fullest meaning of the word. Nick started it all by allowing Lucifer to escape into the house. Nick had no clue as to the evil he had created in his research laboratories.

I hope that this chapter will make you aware of

Xeno transplanting here in the home of the brave. Is it worth another ten years of your life to betray our species by mixing itself with animal D.N.A.? Today, Xeno surgeries are financed by Grants from the Federal Government. What are you willing to see, what do you want to know? This Novel is Fiction now but our future is within the realm of the Xeno Project.

Valentine is a fluke of Nature, a product of genetic engineering. Valentine has become a menace, a creature of evolution going back ten million years. What kind of two-legged human roamed the earth then? Were they half animals, all animals, part human, evolving into the human species? These creatures had big brains and thick skulls perhaps they had telepathic powers?

Doctor Nicklaus Keller created Valentine and brought pieces of ten million years of evolution into his labs. What is going to come from this freak accident of nature lays in the pages ahead . . .

Faye was paying less attention to her rag doll as she stared into space. Nothingness and absolute terror had made Faye nearly mindless. Nightmares were making Faye freaky and narcotic. She was expendable once the results of experiments performed on her were complete. Then it was the end of the line for Emma.

Faye cried over her plight as she stared at the rag doll. She knew all to well that the rag doll was the only one that understood her feelings and felt her pain.

The Keller Xeno Staff many of whose names are still unknown to me orchestrated freak lovers. There were raffles being drown to see what kind of creature would be born by these freak lovers.

It seems that most of humanity is corrupt to it's heart, never leaving things be, always having to change something good into something better. There always have been costs, a price to pay to make these changes.

Sometimes the results were not to be what you expected. Humanity has spent more time and money learning how to kill than curing sicknesses. At first it was the Pentagon and the Defense Department that funded the Xeno Project, now it has become widespread and funded by private citizens and the Defense Department, 'what does that tell you?

By inventing new ways to crossbreed test subjects creatures were being born that had to be incinerated because of their deformities. Those that were born healthy were kept on ice and the ones born of mixed species that were healthy were nurtured and trained for simple tasks in the labs.

All of these practices sickened me when I learned about them. Valentine with his telekinetic breeding techniques worried Dr. Keller. Dr. Keller, Becky and me was working well together accomplishing many impossible feats. I wish that the two of them would have died at the mercy of their test subjects or better yet, it would have been nice if the whole Lupus Estate had imploded. Sad as it may be, dreaming is a waste of time.

"Perhaps the perfect soldiers can be designed?" Certainly, humanity never stops trying to create the perfect Army. With each passing day these offspring and creations at the Lupus Estate multiplies in their numbers.

Mating Xeno Prodigies had become a game among the Scientists globally and some resulted in positive creations. Others were not so lucky now that human cells live indefinitely.

What wonders in physic abilities will develop if they do in these mixtures of creatures. Freak lovers were jokes among the rich and powerful. Everybody wanted to own one they were becoming novelties. You can bet your life that these new life forms will change our world in the future and not for the better. Wonders and miraculous medicines have fooled the great nations in the world into believing that animal to human transplants are the promise that they were made out to be, we will see and then it might be too late by then. Our fate sealed, our species doomed.

THE END OF CHAPTER SIX

"<u>FREAK LOVERS</u>"

CHAPTER SEVEN
"Confirmations"
December 20, 2011

There were some changes in the Xeno Project which were spearheaded by Valentine. It seemed that Valentine had evolved into a genius overnight. Valentine was a bully and a pushy beast. Every day his long baboon snout shrank some more, its teeth however grew long and strong. Elizabeth used a file to sharpen Valentine's teeth because she loved to pamper Valentine. Within the last two weeks, there had been three accidents in the laboratories. Then just this morning a maid was discovered in one of the rooms and her throat was slashed. Drastic means was taken by the mad doctor to keep things under his control. Yet there was a crazed ape-human loose on the Keller Estate. Soon changes needed to occur or the impossible would happen.

Becky was good for Nicklaus and devoutly loyal to him. Working together they recorded breakthroughs in Xeno surgery, developed new life saving and life giving 'and life is creating Micro-bio-formula's.' Confirmations of the successful formula's and chemical compounds were forthcoming. With reluctance and reservation, Nicklaus allowed Valentine to roam free throughout the estate and entrusted Valentine with a top security Clearance in the Xeno Project.

Nicklaus ignored protests from Becky. It was only natural for Becky to become indifferent to test subjects suffering in the name of science. Valentine was taking away responsibilities that Nicklaus had originally counted on Becky for. With Valentine, causing disagreements between the two of them, in what I saw and read in both of their personal journals, Nick and Becky seemed to be soul mates. Lisa hid within the recesses of Nick's mind.

There was an eerie almost dreadful sense about the Journals that I had read. It seemed that each entry grew more crazy and desperate. In the beginning of the Xeno Project the Staff was nearly insane and with each entry into their journals. These lovers of the peculiar grew more lunatic. Nick worked hard on getting the right people to work for him. It was a pandemonium of hate.

Jarred had snagged three more human test subjects while using a rented taxi. Airport security was searching for a black limo seen picking up a well-known attorney. It was easy to find a remote place to pick up riders without their being witnesses around to worry about. Jarred was becoming accustomed to kidnapping and murder. It is hard to believe that Jarred was once an upstanding and decent man. There was a time in Jarred's life when he was a compassionate and caring man and a loving husband. Before he became a serial killer Jarred was an upbeat outstanding physician.

Once Jarred picked up the three riders, 'Jarred almost jumped for joy.' They were three virgin nuns going to the monastery on the outskirts of the city, three Catholic prep school girls who had committed their lives to God. Jarred never even had to gas the nuns and they never put up a fight. All the girls did to defend themselves was pray. It allowed Jarred to fall back into the good graces of Doctor Keller and hopefully an increase in his morphine doses. Indeed, the girls were worth their weight in gold to the mad doctors.

NICKLAUS PERSONAL JOURNAL

John Sung was in one of his good mood swings today. It was great to have the old John back and I wonder what has been getting over him these last few weeks. I have given John one of the Sisters from the Convent. Fine tuning his acupuncture skills in an effort to cheer up his tortured soul will do him good. It seemed to have done John a lot of good and I am hopeful that his hard work and dedication to the Xeno Project will continue throughout the duration of the Xeno experiments. 'After which he too will become expendable.'

I pity the man and if Jarred was not so good at supplying test subjects. Then I would have used Jarred as one, in hopes of curing his mental illness. Jarred has brought back three healthy humans again to be used as test subjects in the Xeno Project. I am increasing Jarred's morphine dosage two grains. Jarred deserves the increase and it seems he had not slept for days. It is anybody's guess how much longer Jarred will maintain his composure before he cracks and falls to pieces. It is the Xeno Project which overrides all other priorities. Poor unfortunate Jarred is expendable to the Project's needs. Jarred is a sad case and my sympathy is with Jarred, but my devotion to the project will not stand down for naught.

Never in my wildest imagination did I dream that Xeno transplants would cause such extreme deformities. There is a godlike aura around the experiments and to understand that I have created life like a god makes me rush with power. I tell you now . . . This is pure madness, yet I am perfectly sane throughout this fiasco.

I was out to prove to the world that Xeno meant death. Now I am manipulating life into a smarter and instinctive race of living beings. Improving their telepathic abilities and at the same time creating some larger and more muscular species. Now I am trying to save what is left of humanity in these hybrids and I dare to say that Valentine is more than mortal, it seems that Valentines' immune system is beyond anything that I have ever known before. It has resisted three different lethal poisons, which I had injected into his main bloodstream. Last night I, injected twenty units of pure mercury into Valentines Aorta and it did not even make him sweat. I have done more then just prove Xeno is productive, now I ponder the world's fate. If I do not find a means to exterminate Valentine it would mean that I have created a master race of monsters that can live forever.

All that I ended proving was that evolution was going to erase the human species eventually and all that I am doing with Xeno is speeding up the process. There have been many test confirmations that have shown a new virus, similar to the AID's virus. There is ample proof that Xeno transplants created the original AID's virus somewhere in a Government laboratory somewhere in Nigeria.

SECURITY CAMERA RECORDINGS
December 24, 2011

Sandra Collins had made her confirmations to God and the Roman Catholic Church. So had her best friends, the three girls grew up as neighbors. Mary Bird, and Rene Wallace followed Sandra in everything that she did so they entered the Seminary along with their best friend. One for all and all for one, and that one was God.

In the dead of the night, John Jung Sung whisked Sandra away from her friends. Rene and Mary were on their knees praying while they held rosaries tightly in their fists. Outside of their cell, noises that were straight from hell vibrated their eardrums. Screaming along with hideous gurgling and cries of pain shrieked out of the din. Both girls listened for Sandra's voice in the cries and screams. Reverently praying for their Sister, both nuns pondered what had become of Sandra Collins. It was suddenly dead quiet in their God forsaken prison.

John Sung had Sister Sandra up in his suite at the north side of the house. Sung had nailed twenty penny nails through her hands into the wall of his private bathroom. Sandra was suspended from the wall with the tip of her toes barely touching the floor. John had not harmed Sandra otherwise. He was in one of his better moods. Nick was going to be furious when he observed this video. John Sung was not as he seemed, there is a dark side to the maniac. Nick was infected with a supernatural mental illness. John was chemically deviant, a product of true insanity.

Peter Lewis worked hard at trying to maintain his complexion. Three times a day, Peter applied medicine to his face and chest combating his acne. It had been getting worse since Peter moved into the house and Peter was beginning to wonder if it was an allergic reaction to something. Just as Peter was setting down the medicine for his face, he heard the screams coming from the bathroom in the adjoining suite. Lewis worked hard at ignoring the pleas for help because of the way he looked at it. It was none of his business.

He was interested in only his direct deposit. Peter made sure that he got paid every month. Peter had no complaints living in his own suite. Equipped with room service, whatever else he needed at his fingertips. Making sure to please the Doctor no matter what it took to do it.

"Why are you doing this to me?"

'Sandra asked, between sobs.' Sandra, weeping in despair while John was grinning like a cat that just ate the mouse.' ***"Why does a bear shit in the woods? It beats the hell out of me, what's it to you anyway?"*** 'Responded John, as John was majestically standing in front of Sandra with his hands on his hips and his bag of tricks on the bathroom counters, John was ready for some action.'

John Jung Sung planned to take his sweet time with Sandra. His plan was to start slow and work the pain into Sandra until it was more then Sandra could take. Then inducing some more agony on top of the sting with his acupuncture needles, Sung started pinching Sandra on the tender places of her body as he was slapping the bottom of Sandra's feet. Sandra did not cry to God and then continued praying aloud to her Savior. *"Slow and easy, that's how I'm going to do it."* Sister, sister, sister, Sandra . . .

While assessing his new joy toy Then John stepped back to admire his work. Black and blue spots about the size of quarters were scattered all over Sandra's body, that were not covered by Sandra's religious dress. Sandra was serendipitous that John was in one of his better moods and after a few hours of toying with Sandra, he yanked out her nails and chained her to his king-sized bed. Then feeling better about his self, John returned to his work in the laboratories.

Anguish and suffering filled the days and nights of the unfortunate test subjects. To the Residents of the Xeno Project it was just another day in hell. There are lifetimes of knowledge in just a syringe of Nicklaus Keller's formulas. It was too bad for some of the human test subjects if they did not see things under the same light. *"They only suffer because they choose to remain in the dark."* Was one of Nicklaus' favorite sayings?

With all of the hidden passageways and secret chambers within the Victorian, you could say that there was a house within a house, a society inside a society. Inner Circle Disciples of Lucifer lived inside of the walls of the Victorian and had been there for a hundred years. I learned of them just a few minutes ago through providence. Returning to the Victorian in search of more documents, (and whatever else I might find?) They were watching me . . . need I say more.

CHRISTMAS MORNING

Mary and Rene abandoned without any food in an isolated cell. There was a sink with running

water and a toilet with an open-faced shower. There was a stack of woolen blankets and two sets of clean surgical smocks for the captives to slip on. Mary suggested to Rene that there was bound to be a missing persons report and that the Police were searching hard for their whereabouts. Rene was nodding her head in agreement with Mary and then said some encouraging words of her own. She said . . .
"Yea, I bet that there is an S.W.A.T. Team just waiting to storm the joint, Merry Christmas." Then the two women laughed and hugged each other warmly.

Becky and Nicklaus were eavesdropping in on the Sisters' conversation. Then Becky opened the door to their cell and confronted the Sisters and it started raining on the nun's parade. *"Fat Chance for that ever happening and you can get that nonsense out of your head now. There is no salvation waiting for you here or anywhere else."* Becky was all business and intent on getting the test subjects prepped for their Xeno transplants. It was time to stop standing around and get on with the work at hand.

Valentine ordered that the two nuns used as surrogate mothers for his offspring. Nicklaus felt that the Xeno Project was spiraling out of his control and into the control of Valentine. Nicklaus and Becky had to do as they were told, but together they secretly conspired the end of Valentine and his 'Coup de' tat.' Becky wanted to give Valentine 'Coup de' grace,' but they were running out of poisons to try on the genius monstrosity. Becky continued to vent her frustrations out on the two Sisters while Nicklaus watched her from the doorway. She would beat them with a belt using the buckle inflicting welts. Valentine had angered her. *"Now you hear this loud and clear, Sisters. You better get your asses into the showers and then get into these hospital smocks. If you know what is best for you, then do not make me repeat myself again."*

Mary and Rene stared at their captors through sad eyes as they froze in their tracks. They were wearing their thick black religious long wool dresses with cotton white trim. Dresses embroidered in gold and over their white woolen breastplates were conformation crosses.

Becky grew impatient and called out for Jarred and John Jung Sung who were waiting in the Holding area of the confinement cages. When they entered the cell the two Sisters were still standing in place with horror-struck expressions on their faces. As soon as the two captives seen the surgical knives in the hands of the two assistants their frightened stares had become terror-stricken.

"Merry Christmas" Said Jarred . . . *"And have a happy new year."* Added John Sung.

John and Jarred had become allies against Nicklaus and Becky. 'They were back stabbing fiendish villains.' Valentine allowed them to get away with more and he promised kingdoms among other treasures for their reverence. Nicklaus knew of the plot against him but refused to let them know that he knew.

Valentine was preparing Mia for a transplant. Her babies (twins) implanted into the wombs of Rene and Mary. Valentine's hands had become fingered and slender because of the Xeno transplants. His skull was getting larger and his face was getting smaller. Valentine's baboon snout had receded and his eyes became blue. At the rate Valentine was evolving, he was sure that before long he would be able to perform the transplants.

Mary and Rene did not resist their molesters as the demented assistants of the Xeno experiments cut their clothes away from their bodies. John was methodical in his movements of the knife, but not Jarred. Jarred was running his fingers along Mary's private areas on her body as Jarred cut into the black wool dress. It was sad to watch the two women praying while awful things happened to them.

Jarred nor John hurt the virgins and they were gentle but stern with the Sisters. Rene and Mary continued praying aloud while John and Jarred used long-handled brushes to bathe them. After they dried off with towels, the two helpers dressed the nuns in hospital smocks. There was not one word of protest from the two Sisters during the course of this awful event. Nor had the Sisters resisted in any way.

Lucifer was breeding demons using Valentine procreating the Virgin girls of the Church. Once Lucifer's sperm had conceived in Mia, a low animal of hell, not even Lucifer had anticipated twins so he was overjoyed to be bringing a pair of anti Christ into the world of the living. Lucifer was himself being reborn in Elizabeth, possibly cloned. All of this information and much more can be found on the walls in the Victorian house. It has taken hundreds of hours to decipher the ancient Latin writings. Too much, work for one person. With Valentine having his way, it was a sick situation. What if one of the twins was born to be Christ, Valentine never thought of that.

God made man and woman, and God rules the souls of humanity. Man and woman created creatures and monstrous deformities, hybrid mutants, beasts of human invention. New souls not bound to God, but welcomed by Lucifer and his denizens of demons and imps. Lucifer laid claim to the hybrid souls of the Xeno Project. 'Lucifer, a creation that was once only a thought in Valentines mind had become real.'

Nicklaus and Becky were now the Adam and Eve of hell and they used their laboratories to create life that has never existed in time.

So it came to be that both nuns were involved in the destruction of humanity, or its salvation. It was lucky for

the Sisters that Jarred had not raped the nuns and John
never gotten to practice acupuncture on their nerves. If all
went well for the doctor, six months from now the Anti
human would be born en masse.

---

*"Please sir, don't hurt me, what have I ever done
to you to deserve this kind of treatment?"* Sandra was
pleading with John to release her or, at least return her to
her friends. It was too bad that John Jung Sung was in a
bad mood today. He had heeded to Sandra's pleas thus far
in his game of pain. Every night he allowed Sandra to eat
and sleep well and John had mended her hands so they
were healing. It was solely a platonic relationship and it
seemed they were becoming friends. That is the reason why
Sandra kept pleading for her life it had worked before. This
time, not even God would save Sandra from John Jung
Sung.

  Valentine possessed a keen sense of hearing and he
glanced upward when he heard Sandra's cries. At first
Valentine considered investigating, Sandra's screams and
then he thought better of it. It was best for the devils'
servant to allow Jung to have his fun. There was a place in
hell waiting for the heartless and peculiar soul belonging to
John Jung Sung. There were times that Valentine could
hear Lucifer scream in agony and distress. Then there were
those times he heard Lucifer laughing and grunting. Indeed,
Valentine could hear many sounds, which mortal humans
could not. He could hear Lucifer inside of Elisabeth womb.

  It was good policy to encourage evil anywhere it
festered and John Sung was about as evil as it came. Many
times in the past Valentine had said that John was, a man
after his very own heart and Valentine was correct with his
assumptions. Lucifer watched the people in the house from
his perch and Lucifer was all knowing. Lucifer was all
seeing and approved of the evil he endorsed. 'Lucifer knew

that God Almighty was watching too.'

With his body constantly going through conformations and deformations because of the Xeno transplants and because Valentine's diet was lacking human protein, Valentine commanded Jarred to collect a dozen humans each week for his consumption. It was in the hopes of stopping his gums from bleeding and helping his body adapt to his altered genetic makeup.

Elizabeth detached herself from the horror trying not to look directly at her fiancé head on the end of the bedpost. Valentine had taken the time and sewn her lovers' eyes open, which gave the decaying head an insufferable face.

Gray matter was oozing from the spinal cord hanging freely reminding Elizabeth of a kite tail. Entranced by a voodoo spell Greg's head was there to remind Elizabeth of the past. The consequences of Lucifer' wrath Valentine did not want her to forget. All about her large master bedroom was hand-carved dolls and bowls filled with blood. Candles were abundant and silver platters containing powders and jewels were neatly set in rows on oaken pentagon tables. Painted black walls were surrounded by 6'x 4' feet mirrors. Valentine forced Elizabeth to eat human flesh for his baby's sake. Well treated Elizabeth was, and provided with wines from the cellars. Along with fresh fruits to make her conformation into hell a easier. With each passing day, Elizabeth adapted more to her new life, drinking more wine to shut out the horror. **December 30, 2011**
Evening 7:00

Mike's World History students boarded the Charter bus in a single file and began sitting in their assigned seats. A field trip made December 30, the best day of the school year. Every year the sophomore class went on a fieldtrip by bus to the State Capital Building to meet with Congressmen and Congresswomen. Professor Mike Halpin and his wife Beatty had been teaching at Washington University for twelve years and this was their thirteenth field trip together. After everyone was accounted for and their baggage was neatly stowed away, it started raining as the bus rolled onto the highway.

_____ 4:00 A.M._____

Jarred asked Jung Sung if he would help him with the kidnapping of his next test subjects because they needed people to feed Valentine and his mate.

"What do you have on your mind, Jarred?" Asked John and his demeanor were dead serious.

Jarred answered, *"well, I made all the necessary arrangements and have everything we need to pull off the best job of my life."*

"What might that be?" Questioned John Sung.

"I have bribed the Olympic Tour Bus Lines dispatcher and have the keys to the bus in my pocket. We need to pick up sixty passengers from the Washington Campus Commons area and haul them around for three days." Do not worry about exposure because the dispatcher never asked for my name. 'I bribed him with fifty-thousand dollars.' Corroborated Jarred.

"Of course you do not expect me to drive around a bunch of yuppies for three days? We can drive the bus to that dump site on the property the boss bought and bind the passengers. Then we can separate the people to be used as test subjects, from the plump and obese ones for Valentines food pantries." Suggested John Jung Sung.

"That is why I have asked you to help me my friend, because you're so smart. I would never have thought of that. Yet you did." John cut Jarred off before he started his rambling again. *"If you want my help, do not call me your friend and you better do exactly as you are*

told by me."

"All right John, you're the man. But how are we going to get the people over here?" Jarred seemed puzzled.

"Easy, 'said John Sung,*' we are going to employ the Company helicopters as they are needed. There is Confinement chambers built into underground bunkers. Those will become our primary housing for incoming test subjects and what not. Until that time we will do what we must."*

_____7:00PM_____

All chartered buses there are a driver and a relief driver. Usually the relief driver sits behind the bus driver, but on the bus to Olympia, the relief driver sat in the back seat of the bus for a better view of the passengers. Jarred was driving the bus as he picked up the microphone to speak through the loudspeakers on the tour bus.

"Ladies and Gentlemen, may I please have your attention for the next minute or so. Hi everybody, my name is Jarred and I am your bus driver. I regret to inform you that the highway is detoured for the next twenty miles so relax if you notice the change in our route to Olympia, Washington. Thank you, please remember that there is no smoking on the bus."

"Please stay in your seats unless you need to use the bathroom, the bathroom is in the rear of the bus. Thank you for your patience and we will be in Olympia in no time at all."

Jarred took highway 99 to highway 101 and in twenty minutes they were pulling off the freeway into Shelton, Washington. There was no way in hell that Jarred was driving to Olympia, no sir. Jarred was driving the bus nonstop to Timber Lake. It was a black night without a moon and it was raining. There were hardly any cars on the highways and the air was thick with moisture particles floating in the wind. They were supposed to be spending the night at Kings Inn's on Capital street in Olympia, Washington. It seemed that they were going to miss out on their reservations unless they turned the bus around and headed south again.

Before long, the bus was cruising down Trails End Road and then rolling down the long and winding dirt road to the dumpsite. They passed a contractor's job trailer and noticed construction-taking place on the mad doctor's Estate. John had been there before and knew about the hidden entrance leading into the complex. Deep beneath the dense foliage of the rain forest, low laying fog was enveloping the land, which was now a major part of the Xeno Project. Loaded with a banana clip with thirty rounds John Sung had the two professors held hostage in the back of the bus and was sporting an assault rifle,. It seemed that the professors and their students had reached the end of the line.

It was a sad scene in the tour bus on this late evening and thus far the students on the bus had not resisted their captors. One student on the bus had a pistol in her purse. Liddy's father was a Bounty Hunter and gave it to her on her eighteenth birthday, just in case one of the fugitives he had put in prison hunted after his daughter.

Liddy had protested at first but then agreed to carry the nine-millimeter semiautomatic in her purse.

Sitting calmly and collected in the seat behind the bus driver. Liddy contemplated her next move. With cool deliberation, Liddy scanned the scene happening inside the tour bus. She was a fighter; along with karate classes, Liddy was underestimated.

John Jung Sung handcuffed the professors to the back seats and turned his attentions on the passengers getting out of their seats. John discharged one round from his assault rifle and the bullet punched a hole through the roof of the bus. Then Jung leveled his rifle on the students standing in the aisle.

"Get back into your seats before you die where you are standing! Everybody sits and shuts up . . . and I do not want to hear another peep out of you."

It took Jarred ten minutes to do a Y-turn and back the bus into the pole building. Behind him slunk down in her seat was Liddy and she had her hand stuck inside of her black leather purse. She was using the rear view mirrors over the drivers' head to keep an eye on the man with the rifle behind her. Liddy's dad had taken his daughter to several war games in which paint balls provided for ammunition. Liddy was reviewing everything that her father taught her during the games. There was the obvious of Liddy unarmed; it was all over for Liddy. Liddy decided that as soon as the bus stopped then she would make good her escape.

Jarred stopped the tour bus and shut the engine off. Then he felt two bullets rip into his back, he did not hear the shots fired at him by Liddy. In that instant Jarred slumped over the steering wheel and passed out, counting his lucky stars that he was still among the living as he slept.

Liddy jumped from her seat and darted for the exit as she swung the bus doors open. In a New York moment, Liddy was out of the bus and running into the blackness of the rain forest. It was raining buckets and the ground was slushy and slippery. It did not matter to Liddy because she was running as fast as she could to get away from the mysterious terrorists.

In a matter of less then a minute Liddy was lost in the dense rainforest. It seemed that the deeper she got into the forest the more lost Liddy was. Repeatedly, Liddy tripped over crawling vines and fell flat on her face but she never stopped running. After running in a large circle for a couple of hours, Liddy collapsed on the ground. With her clothes torn away and with scratches and abrasions covering Liddy's body, Liddy convinced herself that she had ran far enough away from the kidnappers.

Then Liddy tried to get some rest and to find her bearings. Little did Liddy know that a pole building was only fifty feet from her position?

John Jung Sung used his cellular phone to contact the privately owned Security Police. It was a good thing for John and Jarred that Doctor Nicklaus hired twenty unemployed South African Mercenaries for security on the Xeno Compound. Within minutes, a team of security people was hustling the passengers out of the bus and into the underground lookdown area. John called Nicklaus on his private phone and informed him of Jarred getting gunshot. **January 13th 2012**

Jarred was laid up ever since the despondent bus rider had shot him. Nicklaus had operated on Jarred and saved his life with a heart and lung transplant. When she had shot Jarred through the driver seat, Liddy had hit Jarred's heart and right lung. With his body, taking to the new organs so well and his immanent recovery secured. Jarred thought of evil designs and malice toward the woman who shot him, Jarred slept and he dreamed when, he dreamed of the woman on the bus with the red hair holding a black leather bag.

Liddy was hiding in a storage bin filled with smoked salmon and honeyed ham. A stroke of luck allowed Liddy to sneak into the undetected storage building. There was one big problem that Liddy could not overcome and that was . . .

Liddy was locked in and there was no way out of the windowless pole building. There was no top soil, Liddy stood on solid cement.

Elizabeth was not herself anymore. Intense and realistic nightmares haunted her nights, and visions with hallucinations during the day. Elizabeth became a neurotic mess withdrawing into a world, within the thresholds of hell. There was only one thing that Elizabeth could do and that was adapting, acclimatizing, and conforming to a different way of life. 'A life stupefacient with horror and overwhelmed by despair,' was all that Elizabeth had left and that was better then being dead, almost . . .

    It was Hell and the writing and carvings on the walls of the old Victorian confirmed my conclusions. I have taken photographs and documented all the illustrations and other evidences of torture, mayhem and mass graves filled with nameless victims of the Xeno Project.

    Exhausted of the intensive collecting and documenting that needed completion, here at the old Victorian house, it was crucial that I bring into my work two of my associates, Val Hoffman, and Casey Kelly.

    (My name is Steve Kuzma and I am the new owner of the Lupus Estate. I am a Historian and bought the house in the hopes of uncovering ancient Indian relics and skeletons. To my amazement, I have found something that is unreal and hard to believe. Yet, as you view the evidence before you now, it is all real.) Many rooms in the house and buildings on the estate needed to inventory. Come with me in these pages to learn as I do what evil lies inside the Lupus Estate. Dare I say that I might, be caught up in this Mo Jo, the proof is in the pudding and that is what my grandma use to say all the time? There must be something to all of this evidence uncovered here at the Lupus Estate property. If there is then I will find it. When our excavations and searching are completed, then I will contact the Authorities.

JANUARY 27, 2012

NICKLAUS KELLER PRIVATE JOURNAL

There is no sense in fighting the demonized ape and all that I can do is conform or die. I am the father, of the Xeno Project and everything that has come out of it. There is only helplessness here and discontent. That is the reason behind my murder plot against Valentine and this time it should prove to be a success. Valentine believes our spirits to be broken and he thinks of me as a conformist. This is to my advantage and Valentine will suffer immeasurably when I am through with the beast. Let him think me not a threat to his power and then he will burn to death by my hands. I have confirmed that Xeno transplants cause deformations and new viruses. Now I will complete the experiments once Valentine is dead and I have regained control of the Xeno Project.

'Poor, Poor, Elizabeth.' How I wish that she had never come here, but now that Elizabeth is here. I must try to rescue and cure my half sister. I hear my beloved calling me to bed and Becky always knows what I need. Elizabeth made her own bed and now she can sleep in it.

The End of Chapter Seven

"Confirmations"

CHAPTER EIGHT
"THE BEQUEATHED CHILD"
April 4, 2012

Nicklaus used his ultrasound apparatus in his laboratory to learn more about the twins. It seemed that one of the twins was pure evil and the other twin did not seem out of the norm. Mary's baby boy was deformed and growing a tail. Rene carried the female in her womb and from the ultrasound it was a perfect baby. Nicklaus and Becky had a difficult time with getting a clear picture on Mary's baby. There was a red incandescent glow which obscuring the growing fetus. Both researchers were amazed at the rate both fetuses were maturing. It had taken half the time for the fetuses to grow compared to normal growth of a human fetus. Nicklaus performed the ultrasound several times before he finally believed that a tail did exist on the twin that Mary was nurturing within the safety of her womb.

I have not found any video tapes from the security nor the surveillance cameras for the date's February 2011 to April 2012. There were pages missing in the journals for these same dates. We will take off with the rest of what we gathered in the following pages of this horrific story. Some of these depictions are graphic and ugly to remember.

Liddy was in trouble and her plight in the Keller Industries Compound was stuck at a dead end. After unsuccessfully trying for weeks to find a way out of the compound, it seemed that all of Liddy's escape routes were dead ends. There were security patrols constantly patrolling the compound grounds and insects that caused huge welts on her body. Twice, Liddy had near misses with scorpions and rattlesnakes. Not far from her hideout lived a brown bear. What made it even tougher was the constant rainfall. It was beginning to look doubtful to Liddy that she was ever going

to get home. Liddy opted to play it safe and so she stayed well hidden.

Becky hated the touch of Valentine b there was naught she could do to prevent it. If Nicklaus had known that Becky had performed orally on Valentine, he would have lost his composure. Valentine abused Becky while Nicklaus was at his Timber Lake compound and 'Becky never told a soul about what was happening to her.' Becky smiled and thought to herself. Tonight is the night that ass wipe fries. Becky volunteered to set the blaze but Nicklaus insisted on setting the detonators on timers inside two fifty-gallon drums of $CO2+GENO\ 13A13=OXN'2+NTR\ +HNO3>TN13T$.

After unsuccessfully trying to set Valentine aflame with arranged accidents that failed, Valentine did not suspect a plot against him. Nicklaus decided to go a step further and explode the laboratory where Valentine spent most of his time. Becky knew of the plot and made sure to be away from the self-contained fire walled laboratory at precisely midnight. Valentine was always praying to Lucifer at midnight while he made his human sacrifice. Nicklaus was sure that the chemical fire that he rigged in Lab Level 3 would, completely incinerate the demonic baboon.

Nicklaus concocted a formula which burned hot enough to incinerate the baboon, but without detonating properties that would destroy the basement laboratories and the house. All the laboratories sealed tight from each other and fires could not spread to the other parts of the house. It resembled napalm and the formula named $13A13=OXN'2\ >HNO3$ in short, was more then perfect for the job of murder. Becky sent Jarred into Seattle to pick up supplies and then Becky directed John Jung Sung to fetch three male test subjects from the Xeno Compound in

Timber Lake for Valentine.

It was necessary to move two test subjects out of the Lab but Valentine refused to allow subjects moved. Becky figured that if it meant killing Valentine then the test subjects were expendable. After making sure that Valentine was alone, except for the sacrificial virgin in waiting locked inside of a 5'x5' cage. Becky went on to visit with Elizabeth and to make sure that Elizabeth stayed out of the laboratory. Life was cheap at the Lupus Estate.

Becky was getting ecstatic about her aim to murder Valentine. By the time, she entered Elizabeth's bedroom her face was flushed bright red. On the wall over the bed the clock showed 11:49 P.M. and Becky's heart skipped a beat. Then Becky vomited from the stench in the bedroom onto the floor. Feeling faint while trying to catch her breath, Becky regained her composure enough to turn her attention back to Elizabeth. Elizabeth's vision cleared and then her hatred for Valentine returned.

Elizabeth was depressed and openly disheartened. When Elizabeth saw Becky entering her suite, she did not bother greeting her. Nicklaus's stepsister was dirty and her clothes were torn. Becky was not thinking about the rigged laboratory because Valentine could read minds and she concentrated on Elizabeth. *"Please let me help you clean up and get some clean clothes on?"* 'Becky advised her as she began to lead Elizabeth to the shower.' Words had not seemed to help Elizabeth's despair, nor did Elizabeth try to prevent Becky from helping her.

Becky turned on the water in the shower and helped Elizabeth into the shower stall. Then both women heard the explosion in the basement that shook the house on its foundations. Becky exclaimed joyously . . . *"Thank God that monster is finally dead! You are free now, Elizabeth, Valentine is dead!"*

"No, he can't be dead, it does not die. All that you

have done is anger Valentine and bring down his wrath on everybody." Cried Elizabeth in disbelief and inflamed at what Becky had told her.

April 4, 2012
<u>11:55 pm</u>

Valentine inspected the young nude female and admired her body. Then he fought the desire to rape the female because of his fear of Lucifer. There was no way Valentine was going to risk inflicting neither a blemish nor a scar on a virgin sacrifice to the devil. After taking one last look at her, then licking his lips, Valentine lifted the terrified woman onto the altar. Then he strapped her onto a fixed inverted crucifix. Taking a step backward, Valentine admired his handiwork.

Below the sacrificial virgin's head, there was a golden bowl to catch the blood as the demonic dagger eased up into her cervix severing an ovary? With the twisted long slender blade pushing its way into the woman, it can take hours before death set in. Skilled Priests of black magic had performed this ritual sacrifice where it had taken days for the virgin to die within hells fires. Valentine was not as skilled but any less the wicked. Beneath the unfortunate young woman's head blood dropped in large droplets into a golden bowel. Valentine ate the virgin's bloody ovaries in spite of his fears of Lucifer. Lucifer angered and became incensed. Blood dripped from his eyes like tears.

On the last stroke of midnight, Valentine was dead on the midnight hour. A burst of flames engulfed the virgin sacrifice and in that same instant, her ashes trickled into the golden bowl of blood thus filling it. At twenty seconds past midnight the two barrels of $13A13=OXN'2$ exploded in a controlled blast within the fireproof walls of Lab Level 3.

Brilliantly caught on camera as the flames consumed everything in the laboratory, except for the evil sacrificial altar. For some unknown reason the flames did not touch the altar and the golden bowl filled with virgin blood and ashes. I did observe on the video recordings and the horrible way that the young woman was murdered. It was in the realm of a morbid shine of complete horror. I will briefly describe this event . . .

Certainly, it is hard to fathom that the virgin sacrifice was not dead but I can clearly see her crying and pleading for mercy. Meanwhile Valentine is laughing like a lunatic and dancing around the altar with the down turned crucifix. Then in a moment of frenzy the detonators set off the 13A13=OxN'2 and the camera filmed Valentine as he ran about the laboratory flinging his arms as he was completely engulfed in flames. I watched the great baboon grow so hot as to begin dissolving. I applauded Nicklaus for a job well done. Who the virgin sacrifice was is a mystery to me. There are no signs of her left in Level 3 and the only proof that she existed is on the surveillance tapes.

Two test subjects died instantly in the explosion. Valentine burned into a pillar of salt and that was the last of his realm of terror. Nicklaus carried on with the experiments and before long, deformed and mutant babies were born into the Xeno Project. At this point in my research of the haunted Lupus Estate, I am disgusted.

There is evidence that the Xeno Compound in Timber Lake has expanded to an adjoining property and that Nicklaus is running for a City Councilperson inside Seattle government. If that is true, then I wonder if I should go to the Authorities with this evidence in my possession.

With all the hideous crimes that had taken place on the Lupus Estate, 'Who would believe me?' "Could I be implicated in these crimes?" Not if I can prevent it by being thorough with my investigation. There is one thing that I do worry about sometimes like discovered by Doctor Nicklaus Keller. I am an affluent entrepreneur; I have instilled my own security people on the Lupus Estate. If the Xeno Project people find out about my investigations then my Security Force will provide for our safety net. My associates and I uncover more evidence of foul play, and each time it gets more gruesome.

Val Hoffman and Casey Kelly have been doing bang up jobs and I thank my lucky stars that they are working with me. Val's Specialty is deciphering the writings and the engravings on the walls of the mansion and has a Masters' Degree in languages. Casey's great talent is being an Authority on Cults and an Authority in microbiology. They like to think of me as their teacher but sometimes I wonder who is teaching whom?

Val told me the story of the bequeathed child as it chronicled on the walls of the old Victorian house. Evidently, Lucifer promised to send his son to live among the peoples of the Earth to rule them as their Prince. Then it told of Lucifer being born from a mortal and taking his rightful place on the throne.

There were drawings and illustrations of half beasts and half human beings serving their Master. "Lucifer" It also told of an Angel conceived by an ape and born from a human female. She was a twin of the anti Christ and the opposite of evil. 'Both children, one a boy and the other a girl were predicted.' I do not hold much weight with the prophecy, which read off the walls by Val, but I believed that the people involved in the Xeno project did. They still do believe in the prophecy and the Anti Christ. Val is Jewish and says that the pictures and writings on the walls are nothing more than nonsense. He claims that there are no such things as hell and the devil.

APRIL 20, 2012

On this sunny Spring morning an event took place that brought to mind epic legends of the Greeks and Egyptians, of half beasts and humans with super human strength. Horus, in the form of a falcon . . . Anubis, in the form of a dog and he was god of the dead . . . Pan who had goats hair, hoofs, horns, and tail but had the head of a human. Hauns and Mia were in the corridors inside the walls of the old Victorian house discussing the baby girl born to Rene. Perhaps they had taken on more then they could handle. Many events made this day a day of wonders.

"She could be the Christ child; we must kill the little misfit of goodness before it destroys us. Our Master Lucifer is blind to her brightness. God has poisoned the great horned one's eyes. We need to make sure that little Jessica has an accident." Hauns was trying to persuade Mia to murder the godchild on one of her rampages. Mia howled with laughter and said . . .

"You mean like the accident that Valentine had? 'Mia was smirking as she continued.'
"If it was an accident?"

Faye was becoming a blob of flesh because of the genetic cell mutations occurring in her body. With multi colored skin tissue were infections and a new strain of some flesh-eating bacteria. Faye was able to think rationally and comprehend what was happening around her. Clutching onto her rag doll with what was left of her hands and gently rocking the rag doll to sleep. Faye was beyond saving. At 112 this point in time from what I saw in the video tapes of Faye. She would have been better off if she were dead.

Paul Jacobs confined to a cell because he had attempted to rape Becky. It was lucky for Becky that she was able to dose Paul with an injection before he ripped all of her clothes off. Jacobs was growing uglier by the day and smarter. With a ravished hunger for procreation directly attributed to Nick's formulas.

Nicklaus had made it a rule to keep all the test subjects locked down at all times. All the apes and baboons were kept shackled, hands and feet. Nick was not about to make the same mistakes again and planned to tighten his control over the people involved inside the Xeno Project.

Emma tried to kill the fetus inside her womb several times. Now she is always strapped to the bed and hand fed. Constantly complaining and making threats against her captors angered Becky and soon severed Emma's vocal cords so now Emma is speechless. Enduring rapes committed by Jarred and subjected to breeding monsters no longer frightened Emma. It enraged Emma to a point of madness and Emma swore revenge. Surreal in Emma's realm of horrors, the baby's heartbeat caused insomnia.

With bustling activity around the daily transplants and surgeries, Nicklaus was feeling good about the Xeno Project again. Faye went into labor and had a miscarriage, or so everybody believed. Then, just before Becky performed the biopsy, she found it to be alive. Becky placed the living tissue into a glass containment incubator and bitten on the finger by the abnormality. By the days end, Becky's pinky finger needed amputation. It was just part of an average day inside the Xeno Project.

Nighttime brought on a completely different type of activity as the residents returned to their Quarters. John concentrated his efforts on making Sandra Cry in despair. John intended to make every minute pure hell for her. "Relishing every twitch in paranoia and every jerk of terror" Sung loved it as Sandra yelped like a dog as he practiced acupuncture on Sandra's pressure points at different areas of her body. 'Sandra prayed.' Sandra's nerves was shot and sometimes when John was not in the room, Sandra experienced spasms and convulsions.

Hauns decided that in the morning he was going to inform Doctor Keller of the evil he had brought forth from the bowels of hell. Hauns had been regressing in age as the bequeathed one was forming into a human being. Mia was becoming more human and Lucifer spoke to Mia of his plans. Lucifer had selected Mia to be the assassin and his first mark was Rene and her baby Jessica. Hauns was to protect Samuel from harms way. In many aspects, Lucifer was being reborn.

Both twins were born at the same moment but from different mothers. Rene named her beautiful baby girl Jessica and Mary named her boy Samuel. Soon the new born infants were set beside each other.

Samuel tried to choke his twin sister to death. Rene broke them apart while Mary laughed. Samuel was an ugly baby with horns on his head, which were two inches in length. Rene called the horns the mark of the devil.

After observing the boy, we learned that Samuel could retract his horns and his tail. Both babies were born with full sets of teeth and bright deep blue eyes that exhibited intelligence.

April 21, 2012

Hauns knocked on the mad doctor's doors and waited to get inside. Without a doubt, Hauns seemed twenty years younger on the video tapes then he was the day before. After waiting for several minutes at the mad doctor's doors, Hauns decided to tell Nicklaus on another day. It was the anti Christ who needed Hauns' protection and from this time and on. Hauns always stayed next to Samuel, also when nobody knew that Hauns was watching. One can bet that he was in one way or another. 'There were the denizens inside the chambers and passageways throughout the house to do his bidding.' They were lost and homeless people until Hauns recruited them from the streets. Now they had a home but their souls were lost to Lucifer. When they heard the news of the anti Christ being born, hundreds within the passageways celebrated this event by staging an orgy in Samuel's honor.

John woke up on the wrong side of the bed, again. He went straight to Sandra and then kicked her in her stomach. Then he began manically ranting and raving at the defenseless and terrified Sandra. *"Nothing is going right for me, and I hate, I hate, I hate your guts! Who gave life to these bastard children American Whore? Capitalist, merciless animals shoot out from between your legs to create children that murder innocent people! Let me show you what your children have done to my mother and my father, sister, and my brothers."*

John Jung Sung kicked Sandra in her chest three times and then he urinated on Sandra's head. John experienced in the worst attacks of manic depression in weeks and Sandra was there for him to ease his pain. Nick knew about Sandra and John. It was a good way to keep John level headed. Some people go bowling. Others walk their dog through the Park. John vented his stress by torturing other people. John hated Americans and held indignation for the deaths of his family in Korea, the tumor in his brain that created these false memories.

Rene tried to talk and pray with Mary but Mary changed into a different woman. Mary said that there is no righteous God and that only Lucifer is righteous in his ways. Because of the friction between the two mothers and that Samuel was always trying to suffocate Jessica. Soon Nicklaus had them put into separate rooms.

Rene believed in God with all her heart, soul and mind . . . 'Was God going to rescue Rene from her fate?' She seemed to believe it to be so.

Nicklaus was working out the final details for the next organ transplant. This operation was going to be the most advanced in the history of medicine and science. It was going to be at the price of two test subjects, a human and a baboon. 'If the brain transplants were successful, then Nicklaus was going to do experiments on mind control.' There was the problem of expanding the baboon's skull in the correct places to fit a human brain. Templar was the baboon test subject and Mike Halpin was the other test subject. Mike's wife locked down inside the Keller Compound somewhere.

Lucifer did not know if God would prevent his birth into the human populations of the Earth but he knew that God could not stop his son to be born into their world. That is because man made it possible for his son, "the Anti Christ" To be born. Beginning with the invitation through the Xeno Project, it would have happened in another century but Nicklaus made it possible for Samuel to be born. From the darkness of Elizabeth's womb Lucifer was no longer roaming about in spirit form and he almost felt like he was in the world of the living. That is because Lucifer was the fetus and the father who created the Anti Christ. Thanks to AASA1313X and Valentine.

"I hope that Elizabeth makes it through this imbroglio. Elizabeth is your sister and you should try to help her." Becky Said to Nicklaus compassionately. *"You are absolutely right my dear. However, what is there that I can do for her when her pregnancy is such a difficult one? IfI induce labor then Elizabeth will surely die so all we can do is to wait it out and see if the baby will be stillborn."*

APRIL 30, 2012

Mia had been waiting for her chance to get away and murder the God sent girl child. Lucifer was appalled at the thought that God used Mia to deliver the Christ, the daughter of God. It was going to be a pleasure for Lucifer to take part in the death of Christianity during the second coming of Christ. That would be the ultimate high for the master of evil, the foul fiend, our common enemy, the devil. Mia could not outfox Doctor Keller and new and better locks used to keep Mia in her cage. Inspiring her thoughts with human thought patterns of religion Mia hungered for human flesh.

Mike could think clearly and his wits were about him. Mike Halpin abhorred the body he possessed and was disgusted with his bad luck.

Once Samuel learned how to control his Muscles as he matured, Samuel became attractive and quite adorable but his heart was corrupt in its core. God had given free will to all his people. That meant he was going to stay out of Samuels life. Victory to the bequeathed devil child meant victory for Lucifer who was still clinging for life. None of this is in the Bible. An ape has a different idea of the devil. Once the notion of heaven and hell entered Valentine's thoughts, he created his own devil with telekinesis-channeled energy. His name is Lucifer, the evil one. Valentine, Lucifer's best Disciple was dead.

The End of Chapter Eight
"The Bequeathed Child"

CHAPTER NINE
"OMENS AND SIGNS"

Templar uttered as he was cradling his head, agonizing over being human. *"Well Doc, the easiest way to explain this is to compare the pain to Alka-Seltzer in my brain, hot wetness that I cannot see and bleeding inside of my skull. I'm not so sure that I would not rather be back inside my own body."*

Nicklaus was hopeful that his brain transplants had been a total success. Templar was healing and the bleeding had stopped in his brain. The melding principles of Nicklaus's formula caused the sensations in Templar's skull to create a crisis and mild panic within Templar's mind. Nicklaus talked Templar into believing that it was nothing and that eventually the side effects of the transplant would subside.

Then Nicklaus prescribed painkillers and mood elevators in the hopes of calming Templar and in effect gaining an easily controllable test subject. Templar asked Nicklaus not to lock him into a cell, demanding equal treatment in a mannered and mild way of speaking.

"Doctor Nicklaus, now that I am a human being shouldn't I be treated as one? Your conditions are deplorable and I know that I deserve better then what I am getting." Templar was importunate and pushy this time, most likely side effects of the drugs.'

"Sorry my friend, you must endure many more tests before I can allow you to roam about free. Now please stop you're fussing and I promise that one day you will be living a normal life. After all, you have a lot to thank me for and without me you will surely die."

"Well if you put it that way Doctor, Frick you!" Templar started walking toward the elevator and intercepted by Jarred. Who escorted Templar to his cell and

locked the rebellious test subject down.

Templar lay on his bed and before long and with a welcomed call by Templar. Hundreds of rats snuggled against the brain transplant test subject and comforted the half baboon and half-human ignominy. Hiding inside the walls and breeding in droves, rats driven by evil became the legions of helpers for the devil. With the painkillers, taking effect Templar was feeling much better as he nestled lovingly with his rats.

May 20, 2012

Heavy fog engulfed the Puget Sound area to the point of zero visibility over the last week. Highway fatalities were the worst's ever and the forecast for the future was more fog and rain. Sea-Tac airport had suspended all flights into and out of the airport today along with all of the Ferries on Puget Sound halted until further notice.

This morning at 6:45 A.M., an Amoco oil tanker rammed a Navy Destroyer and caused more than seven hundred thousand-gallons of crude oil to dump into Seattle's waters. As of last hour, the tanker was sinking and evacuation procedures were in effect taking place. Black tar and crude oil were washing ashore on the beaches of Puget Sound. Sea gulls among other sea creatures were dying in mass bevies.

In the dark and desolate streets of Seattle, a murderer searched for another victim. She went from yard to yard and sleeked through the alleys as a predator would in the jungles of Africa. Power outages caused the city to shut down and an evening curfew for seven o'clock was enforced.

Seattle has been rioting protesting the new mandatory D.N.A. laws and W.T.O concerns in the Northwest. Police enforced curfew and received needed 'hands on experience.' Changes in Law Enforcement were forthcoming.

Sergeant Colby and his partner Officer Rick Monty were walking their beats on First streets and Jackson in downtown Seattle when they stumbled upon two dead bodies lying on the sidewalk. After investigating the corpses, they determined that an animal had killed them. There were chunks of flesh bitten out of their bodies and their throats ripped out. Officer Monty contacted the zoo and learned of no wild animals on the loose. Both officers were baffled at the crime scene and began a thorough search of the immediate vicinity.

It was pitch black and wet in the heavy fog as the two police officers searched for witnesses. They heard noises but when they attempted to find their source, they came up with only blanks. It had taken two hours for backup and an ambulance to arrive to the murder scene, then the two police officers continued to walk their beat. By midnight when their shifts ended, the Police Officers had found eleven more bodies.

May 21, 2012

Mia sprang into Peter's quarters and burped loudly. A stench reeked forth from her mouth of the victims recently murdered. She planned to kill the Christ child but felt compelled to do otherwise. With bloodshot eyes and feeling down spirited. Mia left the Lupus Estate and moved through the fog unseen by anyone.

Hauns glared at Mia and demanded, *"Mia, when are you going to murder the Christ child?"*

Mia bowed her head in shame and defended herself the best way she knew how. *"That damn book keeper is always hanging around Jessica. He owns a large caliber pistol with a long barrel. There is no way to get near her, Rene has befriended the bookkeeper."*

Peter Lewis was falling in love with Sister Rene and her beautiful baby girl. With her curly locks of blond hair and soft olive skin Jessica was indeed special. It was a breeze, 'as Peter put it,' to baby-sit while working on the computer. There never were any women in Peter's life. Peter had never been in bed with a woman so Peter was extremely shy. Jessica was the perfect excuse to get close to Rene and even though Rene was a nun. Bizarre circumstances that Rene was part of the Xeno experiments that made her vulnerable. As far as Peter saw it, Rene was single with a baby and all alone. Until Peter came into Rene's life all that she knew was despair. Each new day the two of them got more involved into each other's lives.

Every time that Peter heard the cries coming from the suite next to his own, Peter wanted to find out who was screaming. Peter asked John Jung Sung what the noises were emitting from his residence and was told by him that she was a mental patient under personal care, his. John was polite and sympathetic in every way for the concerns exhibited by his neighbor. Later that same night the screams grew shriller and Peter banged on his wall yelling, 'Shut up!'

June 12, 2012

The mayor of Seattle and Governor Powell declared a state of emergency. Mobs had formed and were hunting the serial killer in the dense fog. Looting and riots had closed down all the businesses in Seattle and panic set in among its residents. In its darkest hours, pandemonium ruled the city. Anarchy ruled in many pats of Pierce County

All of the babies were born in these last few days and there were thirteen all told. Monstrosities of nature, horrid mutants breathed and lived in seclusion. Nicklaus designated them as numbers except for Samuel and Jessica.

All the babies were demons, pure evil in their natures. 313, 413, 513, 613, 713, 813, 913, 1013, 1113, 1213, 1313 were the designated numbers assigned to the mutant children of the Xeno Project.

On a foggy day a 7.5 Earthquake hit San Francisco, California. Thousands of people died in the five minutes the earth rocked and cracked wide open. San Francisco was devastated by the earthquake and countries worldwide hurried to help in this emergency. It seemed that one disaster after another was bombarding the west coast of the United States of America. Damages were the most horrific in the Sunset District and east of Van Ness Ave.

Mary was scrawling in blood on the wall of her room a passage into the bible and she was covered in her baby's excrements and urine because of a ritual performed earlier. An imp possessed Mary and it had control over Mary's free will. On the wall, a prophecy written in her own blood boldly proclaimed . . . ,

"The people of God who are destined for prison will be arrested and taken away; those destined for death will be killed. But do not be dismayed, for here is your opportunity for endurance and confidence."

JUNE 13, 2012

Becky was getting worried because Mary had been acting peculiar and was showing signs of several mental disorders all at once. She found Mary dead on the gray carpet in her room. Samuel was at Mary's breasts suckling and gnawing them to bits. Mary slit her own wrist and died while breast-feeding Samuel. It seemed that Mary did not have the endurance or the confidence in her God to keep on living. Becky had good reasons to worry but it was too late. Mary was dead as a doornail. Samuel was giving Becky the evil eye.

There were no reasons for Becky to read the writing on the wall but she noted it smeared in blood. Lifting the baby out of a pool of blood and then wiping the floor baby clean. Becky noticed that Samuel must have gained fifty pounds and it was amazing to her. With blood everywhere from the baby splashing and playing in it, Samuel forced his mother's death.

Hauns cleaned up the mess in the blood-littered bedroom and smiled as he did so because the mushroom tea, which he served Mary, caused the delusions she had experienced. Hauns was looking younger every day and nobody had noticed because of his disguises. Samuel orphaned so Hauns took over caring for the Anti Christ. Nicklaus allowed it to happen because he trusted Hauns. His fellows of making more messes knew Hauns then he cleaned up, if you get my drift. Yet Nick thought the world of Hauns.

Seattle was getting the nickname, "Fogattle" because of the unyielding heavy fog, which had invaded the city weeks ago. It seemed that the world was falling apart and that increased global warming was imminently going to kill our planet. ('I have not drawn any conclusions as of yet, but the more my colleagues and I dig facts out of the Lupus Estate. The more convinced I am that there are unnatural events going on here.')

JUNE 27, 2012

Sandra refused to give in to the devil and held fast with her God. There was no feeling in her legs and yet Sandra refused to give in to the psychopath who was still abusing her. In her heart, Sandra believed that God would rescue her as long as she was patient. She petitioned the Lord with prayer. If death did present itself and Sandra was to die then Sandra was confident that her soul would go to

heaven. Sandra prayed for death. Either way, the Lord God was going to be Sandra's savior. Sandra's defiance riled John Jung Sung with her refusal to renounce her God. John wanted, needed Sandra to call him god.

Smoke was mixing in with the fog and Seattle hospitals were over capacity. Electricity had been going on and off making for some extremely irate customers. Both ships had caught fire and were sinking slowly into the Sound. It was odd that the smoke from the chemical ship fires had not entered the Lupus Estate but instead had swirled around the property and the old house. Strange noises and sounds echoed within the confines of the heavy fog among the whispers of the dead and the soon to be murdered. Mia was out and hunting in the blackness of the heavy fog. On this ill-fated night, Mia was searching for new bodies to mangle and fresh souls to steal. Perhaps Lucifer would be easy on Mia if she kidnapped enough souls that would soothe his appetite for the baby Jessica. Smoke in the fog gave wooziness to humans but toxic smoke made it that much easier to stalk her victims. Mia was the serial killer in the fog roaming the streets of Seattle for easy meat. She was out of commission for a while, now Mia was back.

It was getting harder for Mia to find her prey because everybody was scared of the serial killer. With the night running into the morning Mia had not had gotten one kill. All the streets deserted including the police who also stayed out of the fog.

There had to be better pickings further up Hill Street thought Mia. Therefore, the direction Mia traveled and she was not disappointed. Running along the hedges and keeping her head low to the ground Mia moved like the wind through the neighborhood but much swifter. Up the hill, was a green two-story house with balconies overlooking a nicely kept back yard? Mia knew it to be a keg party with about twenty or so high school kids drinking and smoking dope. The partygoers were yelling and raising hell not caring about the Law crashing their party. Loud music made it easy for Mia to work her way near to the house. Once Mia was there then she waited in the nicely trimmed bushes within the darkest part of the yard for stragglers. Mia had found her prey and waited for a chance to get her fill of human meat. Mia had a craving that was powerful; it was a hungry rumbling in her gut for human meat.

In a few minutes, the first of many murders were to begin. Lucifer led Mia to find new victims. Lucifer was bored living in the womb.

Newspapers were reporting of worldwide earthquakes and floods, which were killing thousands of people. Never before was there such havoc on the planet in humankind's memory. Scientists were suggesting another ice age. Meanwhile, in his late night hours of working in the laboratory Doctor Keller and his mistress discovered another technique of dissecting D.N.A. Nicklaus was not about to report his findings to the media. Well hidden All of the experiments of Doctor Keller, secretly performed under covert conditions and.

Rene had moved into Peter's suite with her baby and nobody stopped them. Peter had been magnificently manipulating the records and other books of the Xeno Project. Nicklaus, greatly impressed by Peter's accomplishments and Peter's ability to hide the costs of the Xeno Project in other Keller owned companies. Peter's loyalty always repaid with favors and Rene, and baby was a small price to pay for Peter's loyalty and expertise. It was extremely fortunate for Rene to be safely under Peter's wing. Dr. Keller never had to apply his mind control drugs on Peter.

Summers were usually hot or at least warm in the Puget Sound area. Apparitions and other phenomenon were commonplace in the Puget Sound and five dead whales washed ashore on a Bremerton shoreline. *"What did this all mean and what can be done to stop it? All the evidence seemed to point at the Lupus Estate. Could it be that Mother Nature has revolted into its own form of vigilantly justice? Against humankind and their Xeno transplanting and with Xeno grafting ventures into the unknown. It was going to be a long hard summer in Puget Sound and the forecasts for the rest of the world were downcast. Researchers had manipulated the DNA of fish."*

Jarred and John Sung were proficient at recruiting test subjects, often offering free cigarettes and liquor to snare them into the Xeno Project. If there were no recruits willing to go with them on their own free will then the gruesome twosome had other more sadistic means to get their way with them. Laboratory incinerators were running twenty-four hours a day incinerating corpses. Jarred worked like a lunatic and loved every second of it. Ever since the gunshot wound, Jarred treated the test subjects harshly. John Jung Sung hated working with Jarred and wished that Valentine were still alive . . .

At just about midnight the fog lifted in the Puget Sound area and an intense electrical thunderstorm rolled over the skies. Unbelievably, our Lord's wonderful sun shone in Puget Sound before the black clouds obscured the sunlight.

Mia waited in the bushes until one guests after another entered the darkness to relieve themselves. There were two pairs of lovers were brutally murdered as they made love on the grassy knoll near the edge of some neatly trimmed hedges. After her hunger was satisfied, Mia ran all the way back to the Lupus Estate and slept like a baby until morning.

July Fourth, 2012

For nearly a week, the rain was pouring in torrents onto the Puget Sound area. Lightning had claimed more than two dozen lives and house fires were raging out of control. Fireworks banned for this holiday season and turmoil was the norm in Seattle. Deer were running into cars and birds were attacking people in some parts of the Puget Sound area and the world over.

Nicklaus entered Peter's suite and offered a deal, which was impossible to say no to. Of course, if Peter did refuse this offer then it was the end of Peter.

"Good evening Peter, do you mind if we have a chat?" Nicklaus Asked as he walked over to the kitchen table to sit at the table.

"Welcome into my humble abode and by all means make yourself comfortable. What can I do for you, sir?" Peter seemed nervous and he was trying not to show it, but obvious as Peter was ..., Nicklaus noticed it and grinned.

"What I have come to ask you, 'said Doctor Keller.' Were if you wanted Rene and Jessica for yourself, then you may have Rene, as long as you continue to serve the Xeno Project. Then no harm will come to you and yours. However if you want to leave here, then that is not permitted. Rene is mine to do as I please with as is her baby." 'Nick thought silently for a moment.' *"You can keep both of them but do not leave the grounds of the Estate. Now what do you say, Peter?"*

"What do you mean sir that I can have the woman and the girl?" Peter was confused and in his bewilderment envisioned what he had just heard come out of his boss' mouth. Could Peter have really heard Nicklaus speak about Rene and her baby as if they were his property? Peter knew that things were strange and that he was in it over his head.

"This is a Top Secrete Project where lives are expendable if the causes are justified. Even you are expendable son and you belong to the Xeno Project, as do the test subjects. I cannot compromise the security of this facility, even if it means disposing of you! Now, please, I do not care what you do with them, just never allow them

to leave the house or the Estate grounds."

"Thank you sir, I truly appreciate your concerns about security and you have my word that you can trust me. Thank you for giving me Rene and Jessica. Don't worry because I will take good care of them and they will never leave the Estate." 'You can count on me boss.'

"You are welcome, Peter. Keep up the good work and there is a bonus for you in it." Advised Nicklaus to Peter and then Peter relaxed over a job well done. Or so he believed . . .

"Believe me Peter that by the time these experiments are over the world will know what we have done. We will be Kings and rule the world through our advancements in our genetic pool." 'Nicklaus was speaking as he departed the room.'

Today was a disastrous day for Dallas Texas. Three tornadoes with tremendous power hit North Dallas and devastated the North side destroying everything in their paths. These tornadoes were larger and faster than anything ever seen by man throughout history. They left destruction in their paths that went unequaled in our history.

Dallas was in turmoil and more than a million persons killed or are missing. These tornadoes were thirty or more miles wide and the destruction was long past due. Most of the Mexican Gulf coasts devastated by tornadoes in the last two years and Galveston were lost last year to the intense storms that struck chaos there in the dead of the night.

Global warming has not subsided and the world was using more fuels then ever while industry and Chemical plants were spewing toxins into our atmosphere faster then ever before in time. Globally, Xeno Age Industries were the worse polluters and was the reason for the yellow tint in the Earth's atmosphere.

All over the world, storms were accelerating into stronger winds, larger hail, heavier rains, and in other parts of the world, intense and long-lasting droughts.

Most hard hit by the droughts were Canada, Germany, and northeastern United States. Africa was getting drenched with rainfall, as were other previously dry areas of the World. All coastal regions of the world were shrinking, and once there were wetlands were under water or dried by the powerful sun to a crisp.

Predictions by scientists and Researchers were dispirited at their best with forecast of a Polar meltdown. North Pole Observers reported that in less than five years the glaciers would have all but melted.

I consider these actions and events to be omens of things to come. Terrorist sympathizers and Countries were reconstructing Bagdad. At a phenomenal rate and death was no stranger as combatants between different religious Factions hindered the construction of New Bagdad. "Of course most of the monies for this project were provided by the United States.

THE END OF CHAPTER NINE

"Omens and Signs"

CHAPTER TEN
"The Earthly Incarnation of Lucifer"

It was going to take more than fearlessness to beat the devil. Lucifer was born into the Xeno Project and he was bound to be Earthly Incarnated now that the Xeno Project had advanced into its final stages.

Samuel had been born as was the girl Christ. Lucifer had a foot in the door of life and the clock was ticking. Elizabeth was on her way through the door and that avenue was now open for the shrewd and crafty Lucifer. There was the option of becoming an animal form and that did not suit the demented father of crime to humankind. Having his son born on the earth was inadequate for Lucifer because he wanted desperately to be there too, in the flesh.

Lucifer envisioned himself teaching Samuel the ways of the wicked. With his son by his side, Lucifer plotted to slay God. Lucifer reminded Mia that the girl Christ child was still breathing the air and its goodness beat life from her heart. Brainstorming and scheming, Lucifer was astonished by the twins. Certain that at last and forever, determined to get his way, Lucifer would initiate in one form or another Earthly Incarnation. With Samuel at his right hand to execute Lucifer's decrees on God's peoples, Elizabeth was only a vessel for the devil.

Collecting all of his evil allies and focusing his energies at Nicklaus Keller. Lucifer devised and revised his scheme to assure his Earthly Incarnation.

July 13, 2012

It smelled like death and the screams of the dying went unheeded by those committing their felonious acts against the doomed test subjects of failed experiments. There were those who covered with new types of bacteria that cultured into moss on human skin tissue. Then there were the hopelessly insane, they had no control over their bowel movements. The most serious threats to humans were the highly infectious virulent test subjects that were internally bleeding to death.

Each separate case documented, logged in the vast record's department on the first floor of the mansion. Nicklaus had employed slave labors who lived in circus tents on the Estate property. From what I can see on the security tapes in my possession, there were also cages stacked atop one another, which housed some of the slave laborers. There were hundreds of thousands of pages along with miles of video tapes in my warehouse. Descriptive bloody carnage that went on under Dr. Nicklaus Keller's fold, in time I will expose it all to the Public.

'I began having some realistic and graphic nightmares of my own during my investigation of the Lupus Estate.' Lucifer hated living in the womb and wanted to be among the walking, born as soon as possible. He was able to see everything happening in the house and its laboratories but Lucifer was unable to do anything about it. There was a sense of desperation and frailty for the Master of death and the father of liars. Elizabeth was complacent.

Thoughts of escape entered the soon to be incarnate and if he tried it. Then that was going to be Lucifer's downfall in his scheme of things to come. With every part of his soul Lucifer hated women and he hated children more then life itself. It was deploring and mortifying for the 'King of evil, the master of decay, the stealer of souls,' to be living inside of Elizabeth's womb, nothing short of a miracle was going to prevent the devil from staying in a place worse then hell, "the womb." Yet, escape meant death to Lucifer so he refrained from becoming still born. There was no escape except for one, death and death led straight back to Hell.

Elizabeth, surrounded by demons that were born in the labs saw that they were growing at a phenomenal rate. Covered with warts and boils the baby demons stood watch along with Paul Jacobs and Templar. Hauns let them out of their cells and led them to Elizabeth's room, instructing them to protect Elizabeth and the baby Lucifer with their lives. Paul and Templar were holding shotguns determined to stay free of their chains.

Of all the demons, two stood apart from the rest. 1213 and 1313 were demons endowed with special powers that included creating illusions. They also possessed glands that at a whim the demons provided invisible cloaks that operated at ten second intervals. All the demons were horribly ugly and vulgar in their characters. 'With ravenous appetites to be satisfied,' Hauns bought a semi-trailer filled with fifty-pound bags of dog food to feed the bottomless guts of theses demons.

Nicklaus was furious at what was before him and he moved at Paul to push him out of the way. Templar came up behind Nicklaus and Becky screamed out a warning but it was too late. Templar belted Nicklaus on the back of his head with the butt of his shotgun. It was light's out for the mad doctor as Paul caught Nicklaus before he hit the ground. 'Nicklaus had a personal problem with anger management.'

Becky went to help Nicklaus and with Paul's help carried Nicklaus to the first aid station to be treated for his wounds. Everything was out of Nick's hands again but it was not going to get as bad as it was during Valentine's Rein. Not for a while anyway, or until Lucifer's incarnation, 'when all of Hell will have broken free on Earth.' In order to complete his diabolical schemes and to reach his goals, Lucifer needed Doctor Keller and his expertise. Nick was not expendable and it cost the devil.

July 20, 2012

"It was snowing this morning. ' Jarred Said.' *Boy, can you believe it?"*

"I agree with you, replied John Sung. *It's hard to believe that we are in the middle of summer."*

Both men were walking toward the tent to retrieve two more humans for Doctor Nicklaus. They were carrying flashlights and cattle prods to help the task go easier. Jarred loved to use the cattle prod and he used it as often as possible.

Colors reaching shades of purple, orange, and red streaked across the hazed horizon. It was obvious that the signs were there of the coming of the end of time as we know it. Nuclear weapons were on alert status in world power nations as tensions grew over the worldwide disasters. Jarred nor John gave a rats ass about what was happening outside the walls of the Lupus Estate. Either one of the two sadistic degenerates would have welcomed death but death was not an option.

Jarred and John dragged one and then another person out of the tent. Then they dragged them back to the house. Jarred was poking his test subject in her ribs as he pushed the women forward toward the entrance to the basement laboratories. She had bitten her mouth when Jarred shocked her with the cattle prod. Bleeding profusely from her mouth, she was leaving a trail of blood in the fresh snow. Surrealists to the bone, Jarred and John continued to do the bidding of Doctor Keller and his mistress, Becky. Above, 'the skies were gone and blackness engulfed the forest.'

Nicklaus and Becky were doing some experiments in an effort to affect mind control on all test subjects. With their latest succession of experiments and with the results from ongoing experiments . . .

Nicklaus was close to perfecting the drug and

finally injected the new version of FK506-012 into the veins of the two test subjects, which John and Jarred had brought to his tables. It was essential for Nicklaus to find a way to control the Xeno experiments and thoughts of Paul and Templar pointing shotguns at him sent chills up his spine.

     If the body did not reject Nicklaus' formula, then the perfect mind control drug worked. Now all Nicklaus had to do was to watch the test subjects. If they did not die of its side affects, then, and only then was there proof in the formula of its usefulness to the lunatic.

     Nicklaus and Becky had developed the perfect anti rejection drug and they were playing god. Becky came up with the idea to add her drug into the properties of Nicks. Nick has been able to combine and mix the properties of Cyclophosphamide, Cyclosporine, Antilyhocyte Antiglobin, and Rifampicin to use on his transplants. They worked well enough but needed to perfection because of skin diseases and the patient's ability to hold down food. Becky secretly thought that about dosing the good doctor, she was a control freak and habitual in her needs in controlling everybody.

     Becky tried Erythromycin, a drug used to treat Legionnaires disease and Tinidazole to treat the eating disorders. She combined the two working on bonding their molecules. Then six months ago, she succeeded. Now with a drug that Nick named cycloslyhocyte, he performs the transplants. Then when completed, Becky gives two booster shots of Rifampicin. Soon Becky injects Erythrozole, her newly discovered concoction into the patient's liver.

July 30, 2012

Becky was disappointed with FK506-012, as was Nicklaus. Test subjects B-52 and B-53 were suffering extreme side effects. First, their faces were swelling, thus making test subjects resemble chipmunks and then there were other side effects more agonizing for the test subjects. Hunger infected the two test subjects to the point where they were always starving, no matter how much food they consumed. Of course, they had gained more than sixty pounds since the injections. Round shouldered and slightly hunched while their legs and arms were skinny.

Elevated blood pressure and stomach problems complicated matters more. Becky injected the test subjects with heavy doses of Steroids to try and counter the side effects of the formula. Then there were many psychological side effects, which also complicated things, mood swings and sleeplessness. It seemed that both test subjects were proving to be failures.

In other ways, Nicklaus' formula was very successful. All the test subjects did as they Nick instructed no matter how extreme the command was to them. Nicklaus wanted to create an army of these creatures, like Valentine, Paul, and all the other monsters in his den of horrors. As soon as the formula perfected, Nicklaus could control what was left of the world. If only, there were not so many side effects? Becky was working treating the side effects and was making good progress.

It had been a long day for John Jung Sung and he was dead tired. John had been treating Sandra better and had been kinder to her for the last week or so. With Sandra's spirits up and her body nearly mended. John thought it due time to work Sandra into a consumed frenzy of horror once again. This time John was more prepared and had carefully considered every form of torture. Then he figured a way to maximize the pain he was inflicting on the stubborn Holy Roller.

As it was, John began speaking to the kidnapped

nun. In a tired and worn out voice John started playing with Sandra's mind.

"Yes I am, John, God will reward you for showing me mercy. John, I have been diligently praying for you to see God's light, and dare I say that God has answered my prayers." Sandra was watching John closely from her seat on the bed. Sandra security chained to the bedposts by her ankles and prayed for the released by her captor. When John stood before her and was staring at Sandra it gave Sandra the sweats. It was too much silence for Sandra to bear so Sandra began speaking again.

"Please John, open these shackles and set me free, I forgive you and God forgives you too."

"Please, Please, Please let me go, in the name of Jesus Christ, release me."

"Just like that you want me to let you go so that you can go to the Police. You poor poor, lost child, do you know what I am going to do to you, Sweetheart?" 'John's eyes got cold and his skin paled as he listened in disbelief at what he was hearing.' *"Now you listen to me, sister, not even God is going to pull your ass out of the frying pan this time."* Sandra prayed that God would reward her for her faith in Him. That John burns in hell for his crimes against nature. Sandra felt dread but a thought occurred to her. She might be in Heaven soon!

Sandra started praying aloud and raised her voice for God to hear her pleas better. Lucifer began crying in pain and started to kick inside of Elizabeth's womb. It seemed 'that the louder Sandra prayed the harder Lucifer kicked.' Lucifer began cursing John Jung Sung for allowing the prayers to go on. Lucifer was helpless to stop Sandra from calling out to God. Lucifer was twisting in mom's womb while kicking outward flailing in agony for silence.

Meanwhile next door, Peter and his new family

held their ears shut with their hands as they tried to block out Sandra's screams. Peter could tell that the victim was praying and that she needed help. Rene realized that the woman next door was Sandra and then asked Peter to help her friend. All the noise had wakened Jessica from her sleep so Peter was thinking about going over there. Then he remembered the threats from John and Peter changed his mind to investigate the woman crying loudly next door. Peter pleaded with Rene to ignore the woman next door because it was probably not her friend praying.

Down the hallway from Peter's suite, Paul and Templar were running up the stairs to deal with the nun who was praying loudly. They knew that Lucifer was cursing the prayers because they could hear him plainly enough. Through the thin tissues separating him from the walking and the living, Lucifer's voice vented curse words from Elizabeth's womb. Paul and Templar aimed to stop the loud prayer finally, when they kicked in John's door crashing into John's living room.

Sandra got a good look at the two men who crashed into the room. Then before she gave up her ghost, Sandra watched chunks of flesh tear away from her body as the shotguns opened up on her. God was merciful in his glory because Sandra might have seen herself get killed but she never felt a thing when it occurred. Paul and Templar were the last things that Sandra saw before she died and I bet that if there is a heaven. Sandra screamed of fright all the way there.

August 13, 2012

Seattle was picking up the pieces of what use to be a prosperous and thriving city. All around, Nations were getting their second wind. Cleanup crews were trying to make the streets safer. Broken glass and banged up cars were common place. Tow trucks and garbage trucks were running on twenty-four hour schedules.

It seemed that the world had settled down and the time had arrived for the healing to begin. Then there were those that believed that this was calm before the storm, and that the worst was yet to come.

Every day, every hour and by the minute evil festered thicker and hotter in the realms of the Xeno Project. As long as Lucifer was alive and as he grew older, sinister and premeditated motives propelled Lucifer and his denizens of carnage unto the Lupus. Now renamed the Keller Estate to infect the goodness there and then to spread like a cancer, time was running out for life on Earth as we have come to know it with each new transplant.

Time might have been running out for us but it did not seem to bother the people of the Xeno Project. Activity was buzzing in the laboratories and people were dying on call. It was hell living on the Keller Estate and a bit more.

Seattle newspapers boldly declared a war on the flesh-eating serial killer. It stated that a Special Police Task Force organized by the mayor to hunt down the savage serial killer, or killers. Whichever number need apply? Mia was not worried about the News Report.

It was an unusually hot August day in Puget Sound and it was getting hotter by the minute. Scattered bits of bone and human flesh reeked on the grounds of the mad doctor's Estate property. It was so hot that taillight covers on cars were melting and people's pets were dying from heat exhaustion locked inside the cars.

Jarred learned that he had the HIV virus. Indeed, Jarred caught several venereal diseases in his sexual carnage's with the test subjects. Panic set in for a   minute and then Jarred calmed down. Without a second thought over his problem, Jarred ran to Nicklaus for help. Doctor Keller was more then happy to help Jarred and scheduled an operation for the infected pervert. Nicklaus had perfected Xerographic bone marrow transplants using a baboon as the bone marrow donor. Doctor Keller had developed a procedure of transplanting human sections of the pituitary gland to manufacture antibodies that kill all viruses. 'Creating virtually a flawless immune system,' Jarred was going to be the first to have this futuristic surgery.

Doctor Keller was giving Jarred more then what Jarred had bargained for. Nicklaus was injecting Jarred with FK506-013. It was the new version of his mind control drug and he believed to have worked all the bugs out of it. Jarred was the first to get the injection thanking the mad doctor for the injection. Side effects were good, improving the immune system.

Nicklaus had more pressing problems pending and to worry about than Jarred. Was there a chance of a conspiracy going on against Nicklaus by the mutant's guarding Samuel? *"Of course there was not, but Nicklaus believed there was."* Paranoia was consuming Nicklaus and his nightmares were getting worse. Doctor Keller was optimistic about FK506-013 and if it proved successful he intended to use it liberally.

Elizabeth's belly was extremely large and she was bedridden because of it. Lucifer was constantly punishing Elizabeth with vicious kicks. Bloody discharges lapped up by the demons guarding Elizabeth. As soon as Lucifer's nails were long enough, he planned to tear and rip his way to freedom. It was going to be his first mortal sin, murdering his mother. Then he was going to eat his mother before taking on God.

Elizabeth was always crying and whimpering because of the baby in her womb. Evil Samuel was four feet tall already and his intentions were as devious as his born Samuel wanted to be there when his father was born so that he could smother Lucifer with a pillow before he grew strong. Samuel was not about to share his Kingdom with Lucifer. It was not in the Anti Christ's character, besides, evil begets evil. Samuel was maturing threefold compared to a normal human child, as was Jessica. Elizabeth suffered through it all.

Peter Lewis knew that Doctor Nicklaus Keller and Becky were not going to let him leave the Xeno Project, not alive anyway. Discreetly, Peter skimmed the Project budget and covertly transferred monies into his own private investments such as gold and Microsoft stocks along with a large amount of Blue chip stocks.

Recently in the last two months, Peter had ten-million dollars stashed away in hidden assets. Peter also stocked up on ammunition for his assault rifles and the pistols he bought two weeks ago. Peter liked life and was not about to let anybody piss on his parade. Not even Nicklaus or his mistress, the bitch Becky.

Rene was extremely grateful to Peter and was growing more then just fond of the awkward and pimpled bookworm. She noted that Peter was not the normal nerd type; there was more to Peter's character then meets the eyes. Besides being so daring, he had a lot of good common sense. Even with blemishes on his face and wearing braces, Peter was not a bad looking man. It was all Rene had to protect her, 'her nerd survivalist.'

Like Rene, Peter felt a powerful longing to protect the beautiful little blond girl Jessica. Jessica was talking and walking and she was quite a young lady. Whenever a person would be near Jessica a sense of wellbeing,' and they would be embraced by hope. She gave off an aura of peace and goodness. Peter and Rene were convinced that Jessica was a special child.

Lucifer did not suspect either Samuel or Jessica to be a threat to him. As vain and egotistic Lucifer was, believing himself to be made supreme Lucifer subject to the powers of other forces unknown to his own. Because of carelessness and overconfidence, Lucifer was going to get the shock of his short life.

"Unless he was born when the others were unaware of it happening, only then did he have a chance to live."

Samuel moved into the attic of the old Victorian house well furnished with antique furniture. There he lived in the old house alone, but not forgetful of the deed he planned to tackle. Without a doubt the anti Christ was determined to murder his father, Lucifer. Surely it was more important then murdering the Christ girl child. Living in the attic was doing Samuel good and it gave him time to think things through carefully.

Mia was getting restless again, but the last time that Mia went into the city. Mia almost caught by the Police Dragnet searching for her. Mia's profile described as a large and fierce predator by the news on the Television Networks and they were relentlessly searching for Mia. That fact made it impractical for Mia to venture beyond the gates of her Master's Estate.

Today the freaks and devil worshipers emerged from their hiding places behind the walls of the house and joined Lucifer's small band of Disciples. Nicklaus could not believe his eyes but was helpless to do anything about the half brain dead living zombies. Then an idea struck Nicklaus and before long some became Nicklaus' best test subjects.

AUGUST 24, 2012

I found Val Hoffman this morning in his room and he was stone cold dead. It seems that he had tripped over his footlocker when the light bulb burnt out in his room. Val hit his head on the corner of a handsomely carved Ivory table. When the Police arrived at the old house and examined the body. They had come to the same conclusions as I had and deemed it an accident. I try not to think too much about the accident and there is an emptiness left forever in my heart for my good friend and colleague, Val Hoffman. He was working 12 hours a day and always there when I needed him. I am going to miss his jokes and all dearly missed hearty laughter, Val.

Casey Kinney took Val's death hard and cried for the whole daylong. I offered to drive her home but she insisted on staying on with me. We miss our dear friend immensely yet the work here at the Lupus Estate must continue.

———————

Jenny was waiting for the bus when a limo pulled up to the curb and motioned her to get in the car. Jenny worked for the Sheriffs Department in the Corrections Division and would have driven to work but her car would not start. Without any hesitation, Jenny stepped into the long black limousine. When Jenny's car did not start in the past it was usual for Jenny to be picked up by her brother in his limousine. Only this time it was not her brother Frank driving the limo, it was John Sung. Jenny pulled her service revolver from her purse and pointed it at the glass toward the driver . . . *"Stop the car and let me out before I blow a hole through your head buster."* Jenny was furious and had good reason to be so.

John started laughing like a maniac, and told her. *"You cannot shoot me through bullet proof glass, Missy. I have been seeing you at that bus stop every so often and realized that sometimes you was picked up by a black limo. Now here you are and here I am. Just relax and enjoy the ride Missy and do not try anything funny or I will release gas into your sealed compartment. I have to replace Sandra and you are that lucky girl."*
"Who is Sandra?" Jenny asked.

———————

It was the strangest bunch of people living in the

house, which could have ever been. Half of them seemed to have come out of nowhere and the rest belonged to the Xeno Project. Nicklaus kept pulling people out of the satanic worshiper's cults to use as test subjects. Odd as it were, the brain stunned groupies never objected.

Elizabeth was in a terrible predicament and she knew it. Inside of her Lucifer promised to rip Elizabeth apart and then shred her into pulp. Elizabeth was living in more then the realm of her nightmare, and she was playing the staring role as the breeder. If only Greg were still alive and if only they had left before all this happened. In her heart Elizabeth knew that Lucifer would keep his promise and murder her when he is born.

All the demon babies had grown so quickly that their bodies were going through puberty and they were having an orgy. With each passing day, Lucifer was that much closer to being born and the evil in the house intensified to a point of no return. Elizabeth tried not to watch them, but she could not help but hear them loud and clear. It all made her so horror-stricken that Elizabeth was numb all over her body. Inside of Elizabeth, Lucifer wished that he were free of her forever.

The devil's Earthly incarnation occurred this day. Lucifer did as he promised and ripped poor Elizabeth apart as a ferocious lion would have done it. Elizabeth's eyes did not express horror or fear they did express relief.

Lucifer looked like a little man fully mature in body and mind. Samuel was there too and he was fuming. *"You promised that I was going to be God here on Earth, what are you doing here father?"* Asked Samuel, Samuel was inventing a prophecy.

"How do you dare talk like that to your father, is you stupid, son?" Lucifer was giving his son the evil eye and frowning at him. Lucifer was covered head to foot with Elizabeth's blood. Suddenly Samuel started walking toward

Lucifer and the latter stepped back. **"I am as you are father; I am a liar and a traitor. Remember that you had taught me all your wisdom in hell, now you die!"**

"You are not in the prophecy's father but I am. If you think that I am going to let you steal my glory then you are mad!" *"There are a couple things that you need to understand Lucifer. One is that you are a mortal now so you do not have all of your dark powers and the other is that you can die because mortals die, sir. I was born before you were so I am bigger and stronger then you are Lucifer. My intentions concerning you are clear . . . I am going to murder you!"*

Lucifer yelled for his demons to overtake Samuel but not one of them moved an inch. Panic set in and Samuel saw it within Lucifer's eyes. It seemed that his demons were two-faced backstabbers. It was part of their destinies to follow the anti Christ, which was Samuel. With desperate eyes and quick feet, Lucifer made a dash for the exit. Samuel cut him off at the pass. With broad grins covering their faces and laughter spitting forth from their mouths they were mocking Lucifer and taunting the Anti Christ, the demons did not raise a finger to rescue their master. Revenge is a bitch.

It was a sad night in Hell when Samuel wrapped his fingers around Lucifer's throat and then squeezed with all his might until Lucifer was choking to his death. There were only two ways to kill the devil and they were, God Almighty striking Lucifer dead or the anti-Christ committing the dreadful deed his self during birth.

Once and for all time Lucifer was dead and the anti Christ ruled the days and the nights which filled with evil. Lucifer burned in the fires of hell as a servant to those that Lucifer had tortured in the past. This grade did not last.

When Lucifer was dead, Samuel devoured Lucifer's remains. When Samuel swallowed the last chunk of

Lucifer, "Samuel stood up and howled like a wolf." For billions of years Lucifer ruled the darkness and he tortured souls of the dead. At last, he was born into the world to torture and maim living souls in their flesh, only for Lucifer's mortal body killed soon after his birth by his own treacherous son. Samuel licked the blood off the floor and had Lucifer's bones made into clubs, knife handles and trinkets. Samuel fashioned Lucifer's skull into a candleholder and then had it dipped in gold. Samuel kept the candleholder on the nightstand beside his bed.

Samuel was worse then his father ever was but you would never know it by just looking at him. Quite a handsome boy with opal green eyes and long locks of curly hair, Samuel was polite in his mannerisms as he was a child prodigy Out with the old and in with the new was Samuels favorite saying and his tail would wag . . .

After devouring Satan, little Samuel was not so little anymore. Samuel compared in size to a fourteen-year-old teenager yet Samuel was less then a year old.

Jarred's condition had improved with Nick's daily injections of FK506-013, soon Jarred was transformed into a mindless slave. Just as Doctor Keller had hoped would happen it did happen to Jarred. Nicklaus did not want to use the injections on the others in the house now because since Lucifer was murdered, everything was back to normal again. *"What was normal to Nicklaus and Becky?"* Jarred was not hurting people anymore nor was he sexually active. Terrible Jarred was sterile. FK506-013 side effects were impotency and mindlessness. None of the test subjects missed Jarred and in fact, the atmosphere was better with Jarred almost out of the picture. Positive aspects were there too. Jarred no longer had the AID's virus anywhere in his body and his immune system was better then human.

Nick and Becky actually liked Samuel and

thought of the burgeoning boy as a mascot of the Xeno Project. Several intelligence tests revealed that Samuel had an IQ of over two-hundred and fifty. Other important factors swayed Nicklaus into accepting Samuel. Along with his followers into the fold of the Xeno Project there was a new dawn rising in the schemes of the evil one, "the slayer of the devil" 'Samuel, the anti Christ.' Nick was going for the Nobel Prize but he had no idea that he was only a puppet a puppet that changed the world. Both of the lovers were extremely fond of the boy and perhaps there was a way out of this mess after all. Samuel was their answer. Samuel put the odds on the side of Doctor Keller.

Unbeknownst to Nicklaus, he had established hell on earth to welcome the anti Christ. It was not his intention to do so. Nick still believed the test subjects to be the results of his experiments and surgeries. Nothing could convince Nicklaus that there were such things as demons and devils . . . and the anti Christ. There never was a time in Nicklaus life where he believed in there being a heaven. Never had Nicklaus believed in hell, he was living in it. Nicklaus was enjoying the ride. Nicklaus brought the idea of heaven and hell into the world with his Xeno transplants. Nick made it real through telekinetic consciousness with the creation of Valentine

Peter was watching the KIRO News on CBS out of Seattle when a segment showed the Lupus Estate on a News clip. Authorities were searching for the serial killer and all leads led to the general vicinity of the Keller Mansion. Police have not been able to reach the owners of the property and a butler named Hauns refused to allow the Authorities to search the residence and property of Doctor Nicklaus Keller. KIRO News stated that the police were trying to obtain a search warrant.

Nick and Becky were celebrating at noon by making mad and passionate love. They consumed two bottles of vintage wine. Comfortable in a cramped attic that seemed to serve their needs well enough Becky turned out to be a lusting tiger in bed. More often than not Becky clawed Nick's backside until he bled from his wounds during sex.

It was unfortunate for Nick that Lisa was watching the News on the big screen. Lisa felt pangs of jealousy and deep hatred toward Becky Zenda. Soon after the News broadcast, Lisa broke down in tears and vowed that one day she would find Becky and choke Becky to death with her own hands.

Peter became dismayed at the prospect of a Police Investigation into the Xeno Project. Then he saw Nicklaus and Becky on the News talking to reporters. He claimed the Estate quarantined because of the nature of his experiments. Becky went on to add that Privacy Acts protected the Xeno Project and that an inspection of the Estate would contaminate it, because it contained a sterile environment. Beside a team of lawyers that took over the interview represented Nick and Becky. Peter relaxed when he realized that the good Doctor had everything under control. There was no reason for Peter to fret. It was obvious that there was still plenty of time before the police busted the house. Glad that there was time to plan their escape. Peter comforted Rene and convinced her that there was nothing to worry.

Lucifer blew his only chance of Earthly incarnation and was bound to rule in the fires of Hell for eternity. That was more agony and suffering which not even God Almighty had cast upon Lucifer, but that Samuel. Lucifer's first born son had. Samuel removed all hope of Lucifer ever being mortal and condemned his true father to the fires of hell. The entire legacy was left for the anti Christ to carry out. Samuel was the millennium's Devil. There were millions of new ways to torment the people of the Earth and Samuel knew every one of them.

What was Samuel anyways? "Could it be possible that he was the anti Christ," Doctor Nicklaus did not believe so, do you? Was Samuel just another result of some Xeno Project experiment or was he more than that? I believe that he might have been just that, but I am not a religious man.

I cannot help but ponder about Lucifer; it is ignorant that he truly believed that his first-born son, his only son would betray him. Could it be possible that the devil possessed the ability to love?

No, that is out of the question because the devil is incapable to love. Obviously, the King of Liars bested by his own creation. Samuel was not a brave devil; he is very different from being loyal to anything or anybody. Yes, the devil got his due but was it enough to keep the master of corruption out of the picture? If there is a devil then I would say the Samuel is going to see that his father ruled hell and eventually Lucifer would reappear again in the future. I am but a Science Professor not an authority on religion, but what is obviously a fact is hard to ignore. Only time will tell us what will happen to Samuel and whether or not Lucifer will return among the living.

Are Lucifer and Valentine dead forever and not a threat to our world? There are so many unanswered questions and doubts about their fates, which I cannot phantom Samuel beating God without his father Lucifer at his side, perhaps Lucifer knew this and for this reason, this reason only, allowed Samuel to be born?

This Researcher believes that we have not heard the last of Lucifer or Valentine but it is only a guess. More inventories must to be studied before I can draw on any conclusions but for now, I have a story to finish. This story will change the world for the better, as long as people listen to these stories and fight the changes coming into our futures while we can fight.

Samuel feasted in the blood of the innocent and laughed loudly enough that he echoed for miles. All the servants shuttered during the scream as evil from the screams tried to creep under their skins. Samuel loved to splash blood around, swim in blood and play with it.

A desolate new Age has risen over the horizon; the question is this, are we ready for it?

THE END OF CHAPTER TEN

"The Earthly Incarnation of Lucifer"

CHAPTER ELEVEN
"THE LAMB OF GOD"
NOVEMBER 13, 2012

*"**Jessica** is a Lamb of God and I will do whatever I must to protect her, and you Rene. God spoke to me in a dream and explained everything to me."* Peter was whispering to Rene so that nobody could hear what he or she was speaking. 'Considering that they were in the confines of their suite.' Peter knew that the ceilings had eyes and that the walls had ears. Peter must have been getting delusional. With all the horror he was learning about Peter felt guilty playing a role in the Xeno Project. At the very least, he had to save Rene and her child.

As it was, the only decent people of the house were either dead or about to go under the knife. Almost all of those were doomed. Peter and his newfound family still had a chance. However, a small chance it was it was better than nothing was. 'I noticed that when people constantly live in horror then they become dulled to its effects on the mind.' Peter was no exception to this rule of thumb.

Rene was the perfect mother and housekeeper. It was just a part of Rene's nature, which made Peter fall hopelessly, and completely in love with her. Jessica fit in just right with the two lovers. Peter used to be a virgin before he met Rene and now Peter was a new man. There was a sense of responsibility and belonging in Peter's life that was once missing. Rene brought out that certain and special goodness in Peter. It seemed obvious to Peter that Rene was his soul mate and Rene believed the same about Peter. It was great to have someone around to help stack, separate, data process and file invoices. Who better then Rene, the woman that Peter adored.

It was getting toward evening and the noises started in the suite next to Peters again. Ever since the nun was shot to death by Paul and Templar it had stayed quiet. Recently screams began to vibrate through Peter's adjoining walls. Peter was in the shower when Rene decided to venture into the hallway and knock on John Jung Sung's door. There was blood at the bottom of the gray security door, which made Rene rethink her curiosity. Quickly, Rene turned around and ran home with her heart beating a hundred beats per minute.

All night Rene wondered about the screams and the blood under John's door. It was all quiet now but that did not mean anything in the Keller house. Rene decided that from that time and on, she was going to mind her own business. No matter what she thought was happening outside of their suite.

Peter and his soon to be Bride tried like hell to live a normal life but it was almost next to impossible in the Keller house to do. 'Diligently and with the cunning of a jewel thief,' Peter devised a plan that was going to free him from the Xeno Project.

There was not going to be an easy way out of the Xeno Project, if there was a way out? Things were in Nicklaus control again and he was a stickler with staff security then ever. Soon after Emma's escape attempt, Nicklaus had replaced all of the windows and exits with electro-hydra sliding insulated steel doors. There were only four people with the authorization codes to open the exits and they were Nicklaus, Becky, John Jung Sung, and Hauns the butler. In order for Peter to execute his escape plans, he had to procure one of those security cards. Even at the risk of losing his life, it was going to be the toughest task of all. Peter planned to give it his best shot.

Whenever she said anything at all, Jessica would speak in parables. Peter Lewis loved the way Jessica was so innocent almost like Shirley Temple in the old black and white movies. Jessica promised that when the time was right and the signs were there. Then she would help Peter open the doors of the house to make their escape good. Without batting an eye, Jessica claimed to be able to make the guards fall asleep at night at their posts. Peter thought it was cute what the girl said but he did not put much sand behind her words.

****

It was getting overcrowded in the holding cells and Jenny was put into the same cell that Emma was living in. When Jenny saw Emma for the first time it made Jenny heave. It was Peters' complaining that made Doctor Keller force John to hand Jenny over to the Xeno project.

John had broken Jenny's nose with a punch to the face. Jenny was lucky that was all that happened to her, it could have been much worse by the stories told by Emma. Emma used her own blood to write her stories on the walls of Nick's secluded dungeon.

Every part of the old Victorian house in one way or another possessed evil. For the brief moments that Lucifer was a mortal being, denizens of imps and devils along with Legions of demons invaded the house and stayed around for Samuel. They were invisible to the eyes but not to the nostrils. Evil entities are ice cold and when touching one of them. It feels like pins and needles all over your body. *"I know it to be true because I have felt and smelled them myself as had Casey Kinney, my assistant."*

Casey Kinney is a true humanitarian with a gentle touch in everything she does. I loved the idea of a picnic or a horseback ride around the Estate paths. When she asked me to go with he I seen that Miss Kinney was good at what she did and liked to keep our work area's neat and tidy. She always has something funny to say and seemed happy and joyful most always. I know that she is covering the fact that our friend is dead. We miss Val and his great sense of humor. Perhaps Casey missed Val a bit more.

There is one wing of the house that produced sweet rosebud odors, with a warm and peaceful feeling associated wit the smell. It was the suite of rooms that Peter, Rene and Jessica lived while they were in the house the emitted the odors. Last night, Val was in my nightmares blaming me for his death. Should I continue with this investigation or should I quit before it drives me insane. There are some truly nasty happenings and accidental narrow escapes. Walls have collapsed from rot. We have fallen through parts of the floors from heavy infestations of carpenter ants and termites. My intentions were to fix the house and make it livable again but I am having second thoughts.

Contaminations in the laboratories and spilled chemicals are making me sick. Yet I am compelled to relentlessly search for the truth about the Xeno Project. If for no other reason but in dedication to my good friend and trusted colleague, Val Hoffman I must continue this work.

HIDDEN SURVEILLANCE CAMERA'S
NOVEMBER 24, 2012

Doctor Keller walked with Becky over to where Jenny and Emma were donors to give Jenny an injection of FK506-013B. Jenny was doing well apart from the experiments of the Xeno Project and protected from abusive handling by the workers and demons of the house. Neither doctors believed that the results from Jarred's injections of FK506-013 showed more harm done to the patient than good. Becky made some modifications to Nicklaus formula and hoped that the improvements countered the more severe side effects of the original chemical compounds. Jenny was about to discover the disadvantages of FK506-013B and the advantages of being dosed with the mad doctors' altered anti rejection drugs.

Nicklaus walked into the cell first and then Becky followed him in. An Eerie stillness came over everyone as

Becky held the bottle and Nicklaus was drawing the formula into the syringe. In a minute, they were ready to inject Jenny with FK506-013B. It was then that Jenny began moving evasively around her bed. Her ankles chained Jenny to the concrete wall but her hands were free to resist the doctors. Becky felt slapped across her face as Jenny refused to allow the strangers to poke her with needles. Becky lost her self-composure and started plummeting Jenny with her fists. Becky knew where to hit a woman and make it hurt and was taking it just a mite too far with Jenny. Stillness returned to the cell when Nicklaus finally hit Jenny's vein. Jenny fainted when FK506-013B reached her brain and she lay on her back atop the bed silent as a lamb.

"Well, do you think it killed her Becky?" Nicklaus asked with doubt lurking in his eyes.

"No, she just passed out from shock. I am sure that she will recover. Just glance at the screen monitors, her pulse is seventy-two beats a minute and her blood pressure is normal. We should probably have her moved into a room by herself and keep a twenty-four-hour watch on Jenny's reactions to the revised FK506-013B." Becky was holding an ice pack on her face where Jenny had smacked her. Becky was sure of her work and was confident that Jenny was going to prove it.

Emma stayed mum and hid beneath her woolen blanket. With Emma's eyes closed tightly, she prayed that the doctors would not hurt her again. Actually, Nick and Becky barely noticed Emma hiding under the blankets. Emma was old news to the Xeno Project. They were only keeping Emma alive until the final bacterial tests were completed. After that, Becky scheduled Emma for the incinerator on Lab Level 2.

November 25, 2012

Samuel is a headstrong youngster with more then

enough confidence to move mountains. There was no need for Samuel to worry about Jessica because she was a girl. To Samuel girls were inferior to boys and if God wanted to have the second coming of Christ be a girl. Then the Anti Christ was glad that God was making it so easy to overcome goodness by letting a girl fight evil. "Jessica was a Prophet" It was in the course of his schemes to fool God and his lamb of peace into believing that Samuel was reborn in God. Samuel must have read every book in Nicklaus library and hit on every web site on the Internet. Every day, Samuel grew as if a month passed by and before long he grew into a young man. Nicklaus and Becky were excited about the twins and their fast growth rates and above genius intelligence. Neither of them suspected Samuel to be the Anti Christ. Most scientists do not believe in God. Samuel loved to say . . . "That the 11th Commandant was, thou shall not get caught."

Jessica was a happy child with enormous patience. Peter and Rene were astounded at Jessica's healing abilities with just a touch from her hand. It was miraculous to behold such innocence and frailty combined with the acumen of a thousand wise men. Today, was the first time that Jessica was expressing gloom, nobody could figure why?

It was early in the afternoon when the Authorities showed to search the Lupus Estate and Hauns allowed the Policemen into the house. Samuel appeared at the top of the stairs and stared down at them from the railed landing. It seemed to freeze everybody in place. Doctor Nicklaus entered the group of Policemen and Houseguests in the Reception hall, soon the room turned dead quiet.

Samuel had put a charm on the Policemen so that they would not find incriminating evidence against the Xeno Project. After an hour of searching, the Estate and drinking some of Hauns' tea made with one of his favorite herbs. Then saying they were sorry for intruding, the Police abandoned their search for incriminating evidence in the beastly serial killings. By the end of two weeks all the Policemen that were at the old house died horribly in freak accidents unrelated to the visit on the Lupus Estate. Was it possible that Samuel truly had put a hex on these unfortunate police officers?

Mia was restless again and her nightmares were of the girl Holy Child damning Mia into hell. It was a horrible dream filled with Centurion angels prodding Mia with spears thus making Mia fall into the pit that led to Hell. There had to be a way to stop the dreams, Mia knew of one way that could work. The Godchild that taunted Mia and she had to kill the girl child before it drove Mia maniacal. Jessica was after all Mia's offspring.

Mia left her cage and followed the air ducts all the way to Peters Suite on the second floor of the old Victorian house. Then she watched them from the slits in the cover of the vent, patiently waiting for them to go to bed for the night. Mia planned to get it over with quickly and she was sick and tired of failure. It was going to be Jessica or Mia. One of them was going to die tonight.

It was pure hell and then some. Jenny was in a league with the devil that was madder then a disturbed nest of rattlesnakes. Lucifer was back in hell again and the flames were higher and hotter then ever. Now there was a soul, which Lucifer wanted more then even God's and he wanted it in a bad way. Samuel had betrayed the one who gave him life and Lucifer swore retaliation. Jealousy was turning Lucifer green as his skin bubbled from the heat. A candle burning in his gold-plated skull boiled Lucifer's brain in Hell. Lucifer could barely wait to introduce his only born son to Hell for all the grief Samuel had caused him. Lucifer had been plotting a desperate plan.

****

Peter thought he had heard something in the ducts but shrugged it off. Then a couple of hours later when he and Rene lay in their bed he heard it again. There were rats in the walls of the house so after making love with Rene, Peter ignored the noises in the vents. Both of them fell fast asleep. Mia silently watched overhead Jessica's bed from her perch in the vent high on the wall. Mia made sure that she stayed quiet as she waited long enough to make sure they were asleep.

With the stealth of a cat and the determination of a murderer, Mia climbed down off her perch in the duct vent and landed on Jessica's bed. Jessica knew all along that Mia was watching her and that Mia intended to kill her. Jessica reached up and touched Mia on her hand as Mia sat beside Jessica on the bed.

There was a light that shone in Jessica's eyes which emitted warmth and love. With wide eyes Mia stared into Jessica's eyes and then started crying. Jessica blessed Mia with God's forgiveness as she held the half beast and half human being in a hug. From that night and on Mia stuck like glue next to Jessica. Watching her every move, Mia had become a bodyguard.

When Samuel learned of what had taken place between Jessica and Mia, he was furious and frightened at once. Samuel did not want a confrontation with God, not yet anyway. Not until he had control of the world, a time when his people would fight God by abandoning their religions. Samuel could feel Jessica radiate love and tranquility. It gave Samuel no other option but to move away from the Lupus Estate to the Keller Compound in Timber Lake. It was a wise move.

The girl Godchild terrified Samuel of being 'touched' decided to ask Nicklaus to dispose of Jessica, Doctor Keller disapproved and opposed Samuel's decision.

Nicklaus did not go along with Samuel because Peter was blackmailing Nicklaus. Samuel replied with allegations of a conspiracy but Nicklaus ignored the spoiled test subject bratty prodigy.

It was just too hard for Samuel to believe that a servant of the girl child would extort protection through blackmail. Nicklaus explained that Peter was not a follower of God, nor any other religion. Peter was an atheist but was madly in love with a nun. This made more sense to Samuel after Nicklaus detailed it for him. Quite indirectly, Jessica was making Samuel's life hell.

DECEMBER 1, 2012

Jenny was under the influence of FK506-013B and Lucifer's evil eye. In a moment of weakness Jenny had pleaded with God for help, no help arrived. Jenny turned to the devil for help. Promising to trade her soul for a chance to avenge the wrongs done to her person and for another chance at life, Lucifer heard Jenny's pleas and went to rescue Jenny. That was when Nicklaus and Becky dosed Jenny with FK506-013B and ever since than, Jenny was being treated better and free to roam about the labs during the day. Searching for Samuel so that her bargain with Lucifer could be sealed, Samuel was Jenny's target, she had promised to assassinate Samuel. Samuel was not in the old Victorian any longer with his demons, his followers had moved out to the Keller Compound at Timber Lake. Jenny felt impelled to do the biddings of Lucifer and Nicklaus. Lucifer made the mistake of directing Nicklaus to inject Jenny with FK506-013B and the formula was stronger then

Lucifer. In the end, Jenny did as Nicklaus told her to do. Nicklaus celebrated privately with Becky about the success of FK506B, the ultimate mind control drug.

Private Journal Nicklaus Keller December 2, 2012

"It is Paramount, in the best interests of all

human beings, for us to go through with all the Xeno Project experiments. I will not feel remorse, or guilt for the lives, beast and human life. That will be sacrificed to the Xeno experiments. " 'Nick was deranged in his manner of thought.' *"Because for every life lost, one-thousand is saved. It seems that the nature of my work has turned my heart to stone. What is compassion, I forget? The Xeno Project is clearly foremost to do to enable us to save our species in one form or another. "* Nick turned off his tape recorder and began to write into his Ledger.

My love for Becky is equal to my devotion to the Xeno Project. If I ever have to choose between the two, it would drive me mad but of course, the Xeno Project would be preeminent in my choice. I have been keeping an eye on Lisa, I have people watching her from a distance. Becky is a cool cat but Lisa is a Goddess.

I have deemed that an army be recruited to combat the forces of the Government and the selected wealthy. It will be an army without firearms and bombs; they will spread the news of FK506-013B to the masses in food and drink. I will sell it in the Projects and in the ghettoes through my army of saviors. No my friends, I am not crazy. As a matter of record, one of my test subjects has proven my formula. She has the strength of two men and an immune system equal to none other. Yet her mind is like wet clay ready to mold into whatever I choose. An army of test subjects ready to die for the Xeno Project, it will go down in history. That I, Nicklaus Keller with my army of gods has saved human life on Earth!

In my experiments, I have been able to develop a hybrid steroid that multiplies my strength and endurance tenfold. One hour to the minute, I injected Becky and myself with dosed strength steroid. So far there have been no effects from the injections, but I am hopeful, I ponder if Charles Darwin seen in his visions of what was to come in man's evolution. All that I can hope for is that the Xeno Project 116 continues undisturbed at my compound in Timber Lake. Darwin created the Xeno experiment on our world and we put it in laboratories.

December 4, 2012
Conversation in Peter's living room

"Horror, and death. That is the only thing that I can count on seeing here. I believe and am begging you to get us outta here Pete. How much longer before one of us gets hurt and what about Jessica?" 'We should get out of here before it's too late.' Rene was tired and somehow knew that Mary and Sandra were dead. In fear of retribution coming from sinister ghosts, today was the first time Rene ever complained about her living conditions? Nightmares about unanswered doors and pools of blood consumed her restless nights and before long, Rene had reached her breaking point.

"I can't get a hold of a security card Honey or we would have been gone weeks ago. Just relax because I think I figured out another way to escape from this house of demons."

Peter did not want to let Rene in on the details yet. For the present, the helicopter utilized to affect their escape, only Peter knew about this.

Certainly, I could feel destiny in the air at the old Lupus Estate. Strangers were coming from afar to meet with Samuel, only Samuel was across the Puget Sound in Timber Lake. There was no forwarding address for Samuel, 'only Nicklaus knew where Samuel was hiding.' Samuel had become Nicklaus' pet project. Not all of the demons born to the Project's test subjects had gone to the compound in Timber Lake and the ones that stayed behind were the fiercest of the thirteen. They were constantly playing tricks on the members of the house, tempting Jessica with lewd acts before quickly disappearing into what seemed like thin air. Bafflement that gave the house a feeling of distrust was a mix of chaos. All the demons being a new species of human, part animals, there was good reason for the disheartened to worry.

John kidnapped another two dozen people today and this time he had to go all the way to Olympia to find them. You can bet that John kept one of them for himself and that she was not going to be the last. He showed up at the local Catholic Church and offered free rides home as an act of charity. It was lucky for John Sung that a whole Bible class offered to ride the bus as long as John stayed for the Bible study. John listened to the Word but did not hear any of it. 'During the service John was saved.' John vowed to give his soul to Jesus but that was not possible because he was an atheist under the control of Nicklaus. After the Bible Study over, John gave the Bible study class a ride to the compound where they dropped into the darkness.

Inside the laboratories, Nicklaus and Becky were running experiments and preparing for another brain transplant. Sean Scott was a twelve-year-old boy who had run away from home only to find him in the Lupus house. Nicklaus was transplanting Jarred's brain into the boys' skull. Becky suggested that Jarred's intelligence and the boy's innocence would make for a winning combination. 'So they believed.' there nothing that the duo could not do, with speed and accuracy, Nicklaus and Becky were breaking performance records in completing their experiments. Blood and guts, and pieces of livers and other body parts strewn about as never before because of these atrocities. Ideas and notions were becoming clear that clouded before and the laboratories were bustling with gadgets and chemical reactions.

DECEMBER 5, 2012

Jessica wakened Peter and Rene in the twilight and told them to get ready; she said that it was time to leave. Peter did not know why he believed the child but it seemed to be the right thing to do. Mia was hopping around and getting excited, then the four of them walked down the stairs where they stopped and stared at the steel security door.

"Now what," Asked Peter?

Jessica lifted her arms toward the heavens and declared, *"Behold"*

Now I saw it happen with my own two eyes on the security tapes in my office. Somehow, the doors slid open and the four of them walked off the Estate property. John Jung Sung and the others stood in suspension, oblivious of what was happening. It was nothing short of a miracle and I have yet to find how they accomplished this feat.

These are the last records that I have found on Peter and Rene with the Lamb of God. However, within the basements of the old Victorian mansion we did find a wall with a prediction about the future. I am sure that there are tapes that we have not found, somewhere. I have not documented all the tapes that we have found to now yet, perhaps, this story never ends.

****

NEW YEARS EVE
THE BREAK OF DAWN

Liddy was impressed with the beautiful red streaks of sunlight slowly coloring the horizon crimson. It almost seemed to the eyes that the Earth was bleeding into the sky as Liddy moved through the rainforest like a cat on the prowl. It had been difficult to find a means for Liddy to get out of the storehouse that she was hiding. It had been a grueling and nerve-shattering stay inside the locked building and several times Liddy had to hold her breath when people were removing supplies. Liddy was taking long deep breaths as she ran deeper and deeper into the thick rainforest, the giant cedar trees and the thick foliage began blocking out the red sky as she ran.

MORE TAPES

Moving trucks were backing up the driveway to get a better angle at loading the crates, boxes and other things from the old Victorian mansion. Nicklaus Keller had arranged a week before Christmas and had been packing since that time.

It was a two-hour drive to Timber Lake because Nicklaus dared not try taking hazardous chemicals on the Seattle Ferries. There were ten semi trailer trucks waiting to be loaded and their drivers were anxious to get on the road.

All the test subjects been moved in the weeks before the moving trucks arrived and so had most of the laboratory Staff. During their rush to vacate the premises, five large crates were loaded with boxes that were filled with video tapes and journals that were mistakenly left behind. In the last days of the Xeno Project Headquarters at the Lupus Estate, Nicklaus and Becky were the last ones to leave.

Soon thereafter, I took possession of the Keller property once known as the Lupus Estate. Many files was written in scripts. More files filled with data needs to be deciphered. I believe that the scrawling and crude drawings done by insane people make some kind of sense. Xeno Project existed and these types of transplants are happening every day in places all over the world. I am glad that they are not happening here at the Lupus Estate anymore. Yet I wonder if we are truly safe from the past?

"What if you had to decide if it was death or a Xeno transplant?" Would it be so easy to refuse monkey bone marrow? Then on top of that, would you stop making love to your wife? 'What if, let's say what if?' She becomes pregnant and has a baby. Considering that five years ago you had three Xeno bone marrow transplants from a baboon, do you suppose that child might have altered bone marrow D.N.A.? One hundred years down the road brings many possibilities with Xeno transplants going on now. 'Through chance and through years,' people will begin to get infected with Xeno deformities and new diseases caused by mutated viruses and bacteria's. I would rather die then receive a Xeno transplant. Dr. Keller had one eye taken from one of his dogs placed into his own socket a while ago. Perhaps that will be his downfall. Not me, I would never give in to any sort of Xeno transplant, drug, or therapy! At the rate the Xeno Foundation is advancing in Kansas and overseas, in a couple of years a new species will be born and begin the Xeno Age?

Continuing my quest, searching for clues on this huge estate, I find old Indian bones. Do you suppose that the Estate once was a sacred Native American burial ground? If it was then there is time enough to make this fact public. I still have much to learn about this site. Although I know in the end I will regret not making it Public once, the findings had become conclusive.

Paintings on the walls captivated me. Emitting from some of these exquisite paintings was the aroma of death. There are the paintings in the foyer of Nicklaus and Becky's walls. Together, and in separate portraits, one of them walking down the red carpet through a hallway leading to the laboratories. Nicklaus and Becky haunting the mansion create framed photographs' of some of the creatures.

I have hired four new Assistants to help me go

over this Estate. I have found passageways that revealed treasures, diamonds, gold, platinum, and charred bones. I do not like to traverse the passageways alone; there must be a team so that everything gets uncovered. I am also letting a Journalist come along for the ride. 'I must say that the treasures are tormenting me to retire.' Please don't take me seriously. I have affluence of my own. At times, a feeling hits me of eerie natures. This is the reason why I am getting more people on the job. I need some company. I wonder if they too will hear the noises at night, the whisperings and such. I believe that there is an explanation for everything but not always an answer.

Timber Lake is a beautiful place in the mountains with many Trailer Courts and cabins scattered about. A few "Well to do Families" live in this beautiful lush rain Forrest. It is a place with a bad reputation of mobsters and gangs and a perfect place for the Xeno Bunch to hide out. After I am finished investigating the Lupus Estate, I am going to infiltrate the new Xeno headquarters.

Who knows what will be in the future, especially if a person does not what to see the truth. I expect to find dedicated fast movement for advances for medicine. A cure for Aids and cancer is around the corner with Xeno Brain Stem research.

If Xeno Research stops with breakthroughs in medicine and stays in the realm of saving lives, then perhaps it would not be such a bad thing. We all know that our species cannot help but create dangers for ourselves that were never there before. Many scenarios will occur that do not exist in our imaginations now. One can only wonder if the future will embrace the beginning of The Xeno Age, or if the world will smother the Xeno Project and cast it away into the void. I believe that if we embrace this new technology then it will bite us on the ass.

Perhaps the future is now. Congress has voted to

allow a law that will change everything we know about sports. Something called the Xeno Games Act and the Government Grants needed to build the Xeno Arenas. Yesterday this was all in the Headlines of the Washington Post and I had taken the time to read about it. There was also an article in the Post about Researchers creating fast developing life. Babies maturing twice as fast than normal infants and babies born with horns. We are treading deeply into the unknown but I can take a good guess about what I do know and what we uncover daily.

Everything destroyed that belongs to the Xeno Project before it goes idle wild. After seeing what I have on the tapes and all the other evidence, which we collected. I want to be there when Nick and Becky destroyed. 'I know this much. It won't be easy to bring the Doctors down because they are creatures of terror.' Studying these facts as I watch the yellow mist rise from the sea I know that humankind has taken things too far and that only God can save us now . . . If there is a God.

NEW YEARS DAY, 2013

If we make it off the Lupus Estate grounds alive then we have our work cut out for us and I am patiently waiting for my new colleagues to get here. If I were to believe in such a thing as a devil, I wonder if I am possessed. *"Just kidding, in this line of work you have to keep a good sense of humor or all you do is dwell on the horror of it all."*

Certainly, there is proof that Jessica is a product of God. 'I am speaking not religiously but as I see it.' No doubt about the fact that Jessica is not Jesus because Jesus is a man so this leads me to believe that she is some sort of helper, perhaps an Angel or a Prophet if not a Saint?

The End of Chapter Eleven

"The Lamb of God"

Chapter Twelve
"Nicklaus and Lisa"

Lisa was taking good care of the house and befriended Nick's vicious dogs. She was lonely and depressed but mostly lonely. There were many things for Lisa to do in and around the house. Lisa loved to play ballads on the baby grand piano that was a part of the old house. Always keeping the garden's lush and she kept the house immaculate. Lisa learned how to play the guitar and sing. All of her songs were love songs about Nicklaus.

Glass Flowers adored the walls in the hallways. Hallways that led into the gardens and the back yard exits. While watching the big screen TV, it showed Nicklaus with Becky. Lisa went into a rage for days. She beat on the dogs and one of them had bitten her on the leg. It was good that the gardens had a calming effect on Lisa and she had bonded with the dogs. She trained the dogs to leave her gardens alone and enjoyed a telepathic bond with them.

Lisa swore and promised that if she ever got close to Becky then she would rip out her hair and gouge her eye's out. It seemed that the AASA1313 marked a mean streak in Lisa. It had changed Lisa into a more sensual and passionate woman, more adoring than before. Other side effects were bouts of crying. She was crying in her loneliness for Nicklaus. Her leg had healed quickly from the dog bite and she seemed to have a newfound awareness. Becky decided that when Nicklaus came home. She would ask to see Becky.

Mostly, Lisa kept busy riding in the pastures on the beautiful stallions Nicklaus kept on hand. There were four horses and a stable's caretaker. He was an old man with nothing to say. Lisa saw him often in the yard trimming bushes and mowing the lawns. Rever James was handy with the horses and seemed to have the energy of an 18-

year-old. All the studs were extremely fond of Lisa and seemed to have a protective aura about them. Lisa loved the seclusion.

Lisa was up late tonight, thinking about Nicklaus. She was thinking about going to the Lupus Estate. Lisa did not know about Timber Lake. In her hands were letters from Nicklaus written about his undying love for Lisa. Yet there was the woman that seemed to be closer to Nick than Lisa liked. Lisa was thinking hard about Becky.

Stroking her long blond hair with a brush, Lisa was planning to braid her hair again. She was more beautiful than she was when Nicklaus was there. Staying in perfect shape, long and lean, Lisa could have gotten a modeling job anywhere.

After braiding her hair, Lisa lie down and fell asleep. She started dreaming about Nicklaus holding her as she slept. Morning came quickly and when she awakened, Nick was laying on the bed beside her. Nicklaus was stroking her braids with his long slender fingers. Nicklaus had left Becky in Timber Lake to run the Project. Afraid that things were getting out of his control, Nick trusted Becky to assert herself in the Project and gain control over its subjects.

Nick hired fifty Security people who were good at their jobs. All of them armed to the teeth. They were to protect Becky from the mutated Xeno transplant Subjects while watching over Samuel. Nick was ready to learn about Lisa and the effects that AASA1313 had on her. Nick planned to concoct mind control serums for Security Staff

---

Nick knew that he had made it out just in time to avoid detection and prosecution. It was a bad dream for Nicklaus and he was glad to be free of it.

Becky had a video phone and meant to keep in

contact with Nicklaus. It was a shame that Nick had his phone turned off. Becky had her job cut out for her and she protested when Nicklaus decided to leave. It went to deaf ears as Nicklaus packed three suitcases and had his private limo driver take him home.

"My Darling Nicklaus, oh how I missed you." 'Nicklaus knew that Lisa was going to appear beautiful but the sight before he was stunning.' *"Please tell me that you are never going to leave me here alone again."* Nicklaus kissed Lisa on her lips and replied, *"Never."* Lisa held her man tightly and rubbed her body against his.

"I am hungrier then a bear in the woods. What is you fixing us for breakfast and you look like a million-dollars, Sweetheart. I see that you have been keeping busy." Nicklaus was wearing his bathrobe and naught else. Lisa began exploring territory that a day before belonged to Becky. Making a big deal out of breakfast, Nicklaus asked Lisa if she wanted to go for a swim in the pool with him. Lisa was more then willing; she undressed first and gave Nicklaus a broad smile.

Nicklaus removed his bathrobe and Lisa became concerned about her man. Nicklaus had a bad bruise on his back and a deep stitched cut on his thigh that was and infected. *"Please allow me to treat your wounds first, oh my, whatever happened to you?"* Nicklaus explained the wounds by telling Lisa that a mental patient had attacked him. He told her that it was an isolated incident. On this night they decided that after Lisa treated his wounds, they would go into the hot tub instead of the pool.

They had leg of lamb for dinner and watched noncommercial TV until ten. Then they took a stroll through the gardens and talked about everything but the Xeno project. Lisa asked Nick about Becky and Nick tried to explain it off as a platonic relationship. Lisa had made a strawberry short cake for dessert and the two of them retired for the night. Nick did not fool Lisa for a moment.

In the morning, they played tennis and then rode Arabians to a beautiful pasture. Once there, they ate lunch. It was the best place to be for Doctor Nicklaus Keller, way out in the middle of nowhere. Lisa and Nick seemed to be made for each other but Lisa never believed Nick's story about Becky. On their ride home down the narrow trails, Lisa asked Nick if she could see Becky. Nicklaus said that he and Becky were not working together anymore and that he did not expect to see her anytime soon . . .

"If I see that bitch I am going to kick her ass for holding your hand on TV." Nick was surprised at what he had heard and stayed calm. Then he replied . . . *"Be my guest."*

Nicklaus changed the subject and started speaking more of Lisa.

"Tell me Lisa, how have you been feeling since I've been away?"

"Oh . . . "Better than I have ever felt, and I feel strong as an ox." Lisa showed Nick by lifting an anvil.

"What else would you like to know, Honey?" Nick thought for a second or two and replied. *"Will you have my baby?"*

"Yes Nicky Baby, I would love to be with child. We will raise the baby together here by ourselves. We do not even need a doctor because you are a doctor." Nicklaus laughed and gave Lisa a passionate hug. They stayed near the fireplace on the deck for the remainder of the evening.

They fell asleep Enjoying rum and colas, until ending up in each other's arms outside on the deck on the love seat,. On the red cedar deck overlooking the mountains, they slept without conscious.

Indeed, Nicklaus seemed to have it made in the shade. He knew how to join animal and human genetic pools into a mutated sequence. I asked a Baptist Pastor what he thought was going to happen out of all of this, and he said this to me.

He said that the human body rejects animal DNA and the only thing that keeps the animal organs from rejection from the human body are the continuance of anti rejection drugs and commenting that God would never allow this scenario to happen.

I explained that it was more complicated because bacteria and viruses have DNA.

What if taking these anti rejection drugs causes compliance by the host for so long that chromosomes mutate. This Author believes that if she has children, the body will have adapted enough to make a difference in her chromosomes. Thus, the baby would be the beginning of a new human species. That was many years ago and is now history. I have made it happen, *'thought Nick'*

Becky was having a tough time controlling Samuel. It was something that she had over his head that kept the brat in line. Machine guns and extreme security with the promise that one day, be allowed to leave his cage calmed the beast. Samuel was constantly arguing with somebody and was a nag. He wanted women put into his cell but Becky would not allow it.

Becky had all the mutants and all of the Test Subjects locked in individual cells. She banned procreation in the Xeno experiments, then she had Jarred put to sleep. *"She had Jarred incinerated."*

Becky was not at fault that the experiments in the labs canceled. After leaving dozens of messages and calling Nicklaus on the phone every day, there was nothing else to do but what she had done. It was obvious to

Becky that Nicklaus had his phone turned off. Becky was doing a great job with the help of the Staff and on call Security Force. Becky had to collect her thoughts and get her composure back before the Xeno experiments got out of hand.

John Sung had vanished without a clue of his whereabouts. Becky was glad that the sadistic creep was gone. She detested John and wanted him gone. Becky planned to kill John after Jarred and that is when Sung disappeared.

Becky never loved Nicklaus and figured that he bailed and was in hiding. From the start, Becky had her self-interests as her only intention. She hoped that Nicklaus would not return and postulated that he most likely would never return. Becky had a new Bookkeeper and along with the Staff, they allied with Becky. You did not have to be a genius to know that Nicklaus was going to be angry when he returned. Boldly, Becky intended on taking over the Xeno Project in a hostile take-over. 'If Nicklaus returned to the Xeno Project Hell would break loose but Becky planned a surprise for Nicky?'

An exquisite dawn filled with jubilant colors adored the sky as the two lovers walked to the swimming pool. Nicklaus has a glass dome covering his heated pool and a working bar. A mysterious woman ran the bar and oddly, she was mute. Nicklaus called her Ann Gonzales. Before long, the sun had broken free of the horizon and filled the morning with brightness. Splashing water drenched Nick when Lisa jumped into the pool. There was soft music playing as Nick followed Lisa into the water. They played as they swam around the pool. Laughter filled the dome with echoes' as the two love birds spoke about the future and the baby. While in the water, Lisa seduced Nick and the fertility pills she had taken did their job. Lisa was laden with Nick's child.

Each day the two of them lived life to its fullest. Picnics, horseback riding, swimming in the pool and their private spring-fed ponds. They danced at night in front of the fireplace and enjoyed every moment when they were together.

Next to the gate, entering the Estate is a giant willow tree. Beneath the tree are the graves of Nick's ancestors. Every so often, Nicklaus went there to pay his respects. All of his life Nicklaus consumed by his hatred for society. Quietly at night when Nick visited the tree he would rant and rave, cursing them for allowing himself to be born. Nicklaus knew that he was the beginning, of the end. That hope was diminishing more each day for the human species. Nicklaus did not care because he figured he would be long dead by then.

On this night, Nick was considering returning to the Timber Lake Compound, but in the end. He decided to wait until his child was born. Until then, he had Lisa. Nick did not know what comes after that.

Lisa was enjoying herself more then she ever had. She had more passionate hours with Nicky than ever before. 'Little did she know?' Nick was ingesting a potion that he made from a form of methacholine mixed in with another one of his formulas. It kept him potent for hours on end. Nick manufactured the drug in the old days and sold it to Entertainment sharks to distribute among corrupt and unscrupulous Businessmen. It was all the same to Lisa because Nicklaus is the best lover that she ever had. Lisa was not going to give Nicky up, she meant to keep him happy at home having fun and content with her. "No matter what!"

When morning came so did the rain. Lisa allowed the dogs to go in the house while Nick stoked the fire. Then they wished the sun to return but it was a futile request in

Washington State.

Bacon and eggs were good for breakfast and hot cakes with cherry syrup made it delicious. They enjoyed rainy days as much as sunny days. It was on this rainy day that Nick learned about the Boa Constrictor that Lisa had bought as a pet. It seemed to get along well with the dogs and quietly curled up on a chair by the kitchen table.

Time flew by and before she knew it, Lisa was six months and counting. It was going to be a welcome addition for the two Heartbeats. Besides that, Nick knew that the next time that he left home, Lisa kept occupied with the baby. There was seven months to pass before Nick left Lisa again. Nick planned to make the best of this time and always kept his video phone turned off the whole while. Because of his dog eye Nick was watching ghosts as they flew past him but knew that they were only illusions. Lisa stayed happy and cheerful knowing that she had her man back. Nick wished that he had gotten contact lenses instead of a dog eye. One day Nick intended to develop a serum, which would allow him to have color vision in the bad eye. It was quite madding for the good surgeon but he was a well-disciplined man. If Nick had any doubts ever . .
. He would get busy and with time, the doubts would vanish. Nick was focused on his goals and manically willing to achieve them at any cost. Nick believed that time was on his side.

"Nicklaus and Lisa"

ADDENDUM

"For the scripture saith, whosoever believeth on Him shall not be ashamed." It was the first time that Jessica had spoken a verse from the Bible. Peter was amazed because he did not have a Bible on the premises.

The four of them were hiding out in a cabin near Cougar lake outlying Shelton, Washington. Peter had bought a property there on the beach with a beautiful cedar home. Mia was mellow and ate regular human food now. Rene felt remorse. Rene was sad but seemingly glad that they had escaped from the clutches of Doctor Keller.

Jessica was a quiet girl with big blue eyes that seemed to stare into your soul. Since the time that she was born to the present she had grown, Jessica looked like a girl of 14. With long locks of light brown hair and olive skin Jessica nearly appeared to be Egyptian. Jessica is a beautiful girl. She spends most of her time by the lake or walking the trails with Peter's hound dogs. Peter had ordered the dogs from a web site. Peter used his computers for just about all his needs. He was learning that without any training in computers Jessica was a natural with computers. Jessica programmed Peter's computer week.

Today the foursome was going on a boat ride on Peters large 60 foot fishing boat. Jessica wanted to go on her first boat ride after she noticed that it was delivered.

Peter loved sports because before he had met Rene, he spent much of his time alone. Now Peter was never alone and he felt as if he was on the top of the world. Since he had been with Rene sports had left his life.

Jessica spoke after breakfast and amazed them all with what she said. *"Even as Abraham believed God, and it was accounted to him for righteousness."* Jessica smiled sweetly and then continued.

"Know ye therefore that they which are of faith, the same are the children of Abraham."

I learned of these events by hiring private investigators to monitor the four fugitives. I am several steps ahead of the Police because now I own the Lupus Estate. I should report my findings to the Authorities but my research has only begun. I kept getting reports on Peter daily via short wave radio. Certainly, the Police do not know about Peter and many of the others that escaped the Sting Operation to locate the serial killer. I hope that you will become an advocate to stop Xeno Projects all over the world. I learned that evil and good can come out of Xeno transplants. I do not think that it is worth taking the risk. This is my opinion, but then I was raised with values.

My Investigators are watching those that are watching Peter. 'There was a fiasco and now there is peace.'

Seattle Interstate Investigation Agency cost me a bundle but they are worth every penny. I have asked my uncle, Harris Kuzma, for help and he was more then willing. Harry handed me a check and told me to write in the amount.

These Investigators are better then good and most are Police officers running their own business. They own sophisticated listening devises and classified lenses on their cameras. Certainly, astounded by what I am learning.

All of the openings for employment quickly filled and my teams of Experts at this very moment are excavating and exploring the Lupus Estate. Casey Kinney is doing well organizing and running the teams. She is a bit jittery at times but Casey never loses her composure. Amy Morgan who is a great asset in my work has replaced Val. We miss Val; he had great character and a keen sense of humor.

I have built a six-hundred foot Vault and filled it with priceless jewels and gold.

Soon I will receive another Report about this mystical child called Jessica. Mia seems to have taken on human characteristics and follows Jessica from a distance if he is not on hand. Peter keeps Mia out of the house so Mia sleeps outside below the window to Jessica's bedroom.

Jessica once told Peter that there was time remaining to save his soul. Peter explained to Jessica that he was an atheist. That everything made sense in one way or another and that for every reason there is a cause, every action causes a reaction and that he was a Realist. Jessica replied, *"Call in the name of the Lord and you will be saved. There will come a time that in this way you will never die."*

I will continue to tell this story as I learn the facts. What to believe is for to you to decide. It is difficult for me to draw conclusions on the unnatural and the clandestine events that occurred on this Estate.

Peter plotted the course for his boat and tested the new radar. This was no ordinary boat. It was an eighty-foot-fishing yacht. Its previous owner was Mark Sands, on Board Member of a large oil company. Peter bought it for a steal, he paid a fifth of what it was worth considering that the manufacturer was Hull Craft Corporation.

Peter loved the large bed adjoining the Galley and the surround sound stereo system. There were shelves stacked with mini CD movies for the fifty-inch big screen television. Rifle racks and pistol cases were full of loaded weapons and Calvary Sabers adored the cabin bedrooms. There was not much room to walk around but the arrangements suited the new family fine. Peter loved the water.

At eighty feet long and twenty-two feet wide it had room for two turbo-charged Cummings powerhouse engines. There were three extra cabins in a hallway to the left of the Galley and two bathrooms. One bathroom had a tub and the other a shower. It seems that everything that Peter dreamed for was now materializing. All of it he could thank Jessica for if he had a mind to. Peter is a self-centered man.

Upstairs was a lobby filled with fixed seats and tables. This room was for games and parties. Four steps toward the bow led up to the Wheelhouse. From there one could access the Stern Wheelhouse two steps to the rear, both levels surrounded with large tinted bulletproof glass. In the Lobby below the wheelhouse was a fully equipped bar. Thus, far, Peter has been the only person taking advantage of the bar.

There was much to do before Peter could leave their boat slip. First, he went down into the engine room and turned on the bilge pumps. Then he checked the water and oil filters on the engine, inspecting all rubber hoses during the process.

Peter checked in on Rene and Jessica, informing them that soon they were going to experience Cougar Lake. Then he added that besides being the most secluded lake in Washington State it was also the deepest and largest lake.

After securing all the hatches, Peter returned to the main wheelhouse. Once in the Captain's chair Peter flipped on the radar switches, then pushed a CD into the player as he was pressing the button that turned over the large diesel engine at the same moment. With the engine roaring into action, heavy metal music filled the wheelhouse. Peter pushed the levers up and the boat lurched forward.

In the far distance out of radar, range was another boat; it was a yacht keeping a weathered eye on the Lupus fugitives.

Dinner served on the galley table and Mia ate in her cabin. Jessica asked Peter why he drank so much.

Peter replied. *"Honey, I am only a casual drinker but if it makes you feel better I will not drink in your presence."* 'Rene asked Jessica to please pass her the bowl of mashed potatoes.'

Peter had set the course and plotted it well, now the Starfish was running on autopilot. Certainly, Peter was an able-bodied seaman by the way that he understood the Starfish. Skies were blue and the water was calm so dinner was easy to manage.

"Thank you," 'replied Jessica and then added.' *"I must admit that by nature you are a good and caring man. I want to let you know that God can provide the same joyous feelings that you get from drinking booze by giving your life to Jesus. In his name you can be saved."*

Rene changed the subject for a lack of a thing to say. In addition, she felt that the situation was getting weird. *"What beauty there is out here, haunts me. We should go for a swim in the morning?"*

Peter checked the weather report earlier and knew it was going to be a bright sun shiny morning. There was always the thought of Nicklaus and his henchmen coming after him on his mind. Perhaps that is why he began to drink more and not less. Peter worried much but did not show it. Unless you noticed that, he was growing more pimples. Peter had it made in the shade but for how long was anybody's guess?

After dinner, Peter fished for a while and the women kept busy cleaning the boat and doing the dishes. At nightfall, Rene went out to meet Peter on the deck and together they watched the full moon eclipse. They held each other tightly and whispered thoughts about Jessica and Mia. Mia was odd and there was only one way to rid them of Mia. Rene was against it and Peter agreed that they would wait and see.

It was sunny in the morning, and they were having

their lunches on the deck of the boat. There was a small pool along with a hot tub on the deck and Rene had put a plate of sandwiches on the ledge of the pool.

Mia decided to swim in the lake. She jumped into the water and dove deeply until she disappeared through the clearness of the water. Peter said good God and Rene seemed to be astonished.

Jessica pronounced the words that come out of her mouth to her friends.

"And I saw a great white throne and he that sat on it, from whose face the Earth and the Heaven fled away. And there was found no place for them."

Mia never surfaced and they all thought that she had drowned. Peter circled the area for a couple of hours but could not find Mia. Peter seemed to be relieved that Mia was gone but the two women begged to differ.

They stayed offshore for three days on Cougar Lake and on the third day, the morning began with a breakfast of fruits and pancakes. It was around seven in the morning that they walked out of the main cabin and onto the deck of Starfish. It was foggy and there was a light mist in the air. Almost cool yet warm, and it was wonderful for the two lovers to walk the gangways. The moon was still a full moon and the horizon was beginning to show signs of light. Water particles glimmered as they floated around the boat. It seems that Rene had been lonely for too long.

'Peter remarked to Rene as he held her to him.'
"Washington State is beautiful all year around but here in the rain forest it seems magical to experience the wonder of it all."

Rene kissed Peter and said. *"How in the world did I ever fall in love with you Peter?"*

Captain Dyer was closing in on the Starfish and

realized that suddenly he was within radar range. Changing course the one-armed Captain ordered his yacht about and followed his prey. He had been watching the fishing boat for two days. It was time soon to board and overcome the crew to pillage the Starfish.

Captain Dyer was on a sixty-foot yacht and had five partners in crime onboard. They had escaped out of a Police van after a fatal accident to the Officers in Charge of transporting them. Scott Nelson transported to Walla Walla State prison for murder in the first degree. After their escape in Mason County, Scott became their leader and then they stole the boat. They did not have any real plan after their daring escape and were ready to do anything to gain their freedom while having some fun doing it.

Jessica knew about the lake pirates but kept this fact to herself. She had no reason to help Mia in her plight. Mia was a murderer and not forgiven for her sins. At this very moment Jessica knew that Mia was onboard the stolen boat.

I would prophesy that Jessica was Jesus except for her lack of performing proven miracles. Spending more time on this personal project, long-range video cameras kept me in tune with the Starfish situation. The Agency that I hired informed me about the renegade boat closing in on the Starfish and its crew. I ordered them to intercept and neutralize the situation at hand.

I watched Jessica standing on the bow, staring off into the horizon. This was happening 150 miles from the Lupus Estate and I felt comfortable that everything was under control. Calm waters and blue skies accented the fish that were leap from the lake every so often.

Frank was the first to board the Rising Sun, the stolen boat. It was the smell that made the 1st mate throws up his chow. Then after an investigation of the stolen boat they found gnawed bones, naught else.

It was a ghost ship on the lake, remarked Frank over the radio. Then he called the lake Police and waited for them to arrive. In the distant horizon, the Starfish was heading back toward home. I could not help but wonder what Jessica was doing?

Jessica was seeing me in her mind. She let me know with a vision of her own. She heard me think that I was pondering what she was doing perhaps she is a seer. Perhaps this was an illusion or I did not see anything at all.

Jessica shuttered at the sight on the stolen boat. She could see all and know all. Certainly the world was filled with evil and idol worship. Jessica pondered if it was worth saving at all. One thing that she was sure of was that the future was unchangeable and that a Promise made by God is bond in blood.

Far away at Timber Lake, Becky was busy as a bee. She loved having complete control over the Xeno Project. One could see that she was angry with Nicklaus flying the coop but oh well. Worse things have happened since Nick had left and Becky had it all under control.

Becky has found some old books at the Timber Lake Compound and found one of the Mercenaries reading aloud from one. It must have been a hundred years old if a day. These words came forth from the Professional Killers mouth.

"How art thou fallen from heaven, oh Lucifer, Son of the morning! How art thou cut down to the ground, which didst weaken the Nations." 'Becky was curious at first but then became annoyed by the Guard.'

"For Thy has said in Thine heart, that I will ascend into heaven. I will exalt my throne above the stars

God. I will sit also upon the mount of the congregation, in the sides of the North. I will ascend above the heights of the clouds; I will be like the most high."

Becky ordered the Guard to go and bring another test subject and this time it was to be a healthy male human. Stopping in mid sentence the Guard got on his radio and had John Sung bring a newbie. John was back.

Becky was experimenting with insect DNA. She learned of a way to stop the rejection, of any transplant into a human being. She did not have it all together yet and perhaps her formula would not succeed? This first operation was transplanting one strain of centipede DNA into the human penal gland located in the center of the brain.

There was no way to know the effects it would have on the human. Becky worked on a trial and error method to complete projects.

Her heart has grown into ice and her bitterness stays well hidden. She had two Assistants that she thought of well. Then there were the other seven, they were expendable as soon as there were replacements. Becky would use them as Test subjects.

Becky theorized that soon she would have an army of virus's and mutants to let loose on the world. No, Lucifer never had to influence Becky fore Becky was a cold-hearted bitch. One day in the future Becky intended to concoct a drug that would keep her young forever. Insects can be used as tools, as weapons thought Becky. Certainly, my first surgery will be a failure in this venture and I believe that the humans will awaken insanely. Becky's last words before the surgery began. Becky would decide who deserved immunity serums to prevent death in her pack of wolves.

Overall, Becky missed Nicklaus Keller and wondered about him. Perhaps this was a reason that led to her bitterness because there is nothing worse then being alone. Was he all right? Did he have an accident? Becky would know when he was prepared to tell her. It was never an option to monitor the whereabouts of Nick by Becky. She was not stupid and knew that he would kill her if she tried to follow him. All that Becky could do was waiting.

In America, a person can live among the free and prosper in their works. We have the right to buy the mineral rights below our properties and do whatever we want to do, as long as it will not infringe on the rights of others. We can buy firearms or even a Tank if you need one. My point is this, who are we to know what is truly going on inside secret Private Compounds? Will they ever know the danger to us until it is too late? In America, one will never know the truth no matter how hard they try to get the facts. Some people are certainly above the Law. Others are expendable.

Writing this story makes me think about all the thousands of Private Foundations and Private Investment Group Investors. High tech illegal laboratories are operating in the tens of thousands. Most are searching for cures of one nature or another. Others are renegade toxic rouge dealers, like Nicklaus Keller and Becky are.

I fear that we might be too late to stop this. I do not comprehend it all but am continuing in my efforts to find a means to the end to this fiasco. I know that money will not be an issue. The unpredictability of events and their determination for destroying the human species that worried me the most.

There are but one answer that we, the masses force these elite Researchers in their quests to learn how man became enslaved. They are the ones who will one day accidentally devastate all of us. Perhaps, unable to recreate, thus forcing our extinction, perhaps creating a newly structured strain of human/animal DNA and a beastly species. Now I must get back to the objects brought to my attention by my associates and examine them carefully. I see a bone shaped in a strange way and a saber in its sheath. There is an old clock draped in blood and a stack of stocks. 'I was surprised to learn that the stocks dated back to the civil war.'

———————————

Nicky did not care about his Project nor Becky for the moment. He fainted with his phone stowed. Lisa was a dream; she was everything that Nick wanted and that much more. Enjoying the sun from his outdoor pool, Nick was waiting for Lisa to get back with a bottle and two glasses.

Lisa was lost in the wine cellar and fell over an old wooden chest. In that, instant the chest tipped over and out fell a scroll of paper. Lisa bent over for a closer look, lifted the old scroll from the floor, and set it on a Dresser Top. She read the strange words into the vacant room for no one to hear. Cluttered with cobwebs and undisturbed for more than a hundred years Lisa stood alone between the vintage wines and its history contemplating whether to read it.

Lisa Miller dropped the scrolls three times before she could hold it in place. A huge spider came out of the scroll and soon spooked Lisa. Then she brushed it aside and began to read the old text. *"And God's anger was kindled because he went: And the Angel of the Lord stood in the way for an adversary against him. Now he was riding upon his ass, and his two servants were with him."*

Lisa skipped some lines until another verse stopped her in her tracks. *"Behold, the people shall rise up as a great lion, and lift up himself as a young lion. He shall not lie down until he eat from the prey, and drink the blood of the slain."*

On the shelves behind the scroll were the exact bottles of wine that Lisa had been searching for. ***"And those that died in the plague were twenty and four-thousand."*** 'Declared a painting that was hanging on the cellar wall, it was a spooky place to be for even Lisa.'

Something seemed to be drawing Lisa back to the old scrolls and she found it hard to resist. Indeed this whole thing will never make sense to me, and some persons get away with murder until the end of their life, taking their secrets with them to their graves, along with the names of their victims. It seemed that Lisa was a walking and talking human robot. 'Nick was her Puppet Master.' Evil surrounded Lisa and attempted to overcome her will, but Lisa is well disciplined and dosed with confidence.

On the sides of the old oaken stairs were piles of human bones. They were experiments for the University that young Nick once practiced. Lisa ignored the bones and exited the cellar. Once on the main floor Lisa entered the bar area and grabbed a tray of deviled eggs.

Nick had a few more months remaining before he became a father. He planned to enjoy every minute of it. Never caring how Becky was doing, nor about Jessica and Samuel because Lisa was more then enough to fill the quiet evenings and walks through his enclosed and Private Park.

The good Doctor Keller was having thoughts about prenatal serum injections; Nick was willing to sacrifice almost anything for his work. He was willing to sacrifice lives for his work just as much.

Insanely bent on making the world his conquest Nick knew that it was going to be slow and easy taking a lot of time to achieve his goals of global conquest. Yet Nick knew that one day it would become so. He understood that he had to keep control of all formulas or that another scientist could steal away his glory, and with it, his power.

Nick had a small orchard of apples and pairs. During his stay, Nick was onto some other Projects retrofitting the Estate. It was elementary for the lunatic to know that soon our world was coming to a wicked end. He sold some of his formulas to the Terrorists.

Deep within the underground chambers that Becky had constructed last month were denizens of living things. Down there was where the waste and failed experiments dumped. She was sure that if Nick were here, then together they would have found a better way.

Insect DNA was mixing in with the retrovirus molecular structure and spiking into animal cells. These occurrences in the darkness were secret and there was a custodian of the steel overhead door, which was the only way in and out of the chambers and the gangways that connected them. It was self-contained with double reinforced complexes. All of it rigged to explode in case of an emergency. Unusual life forms developed here and among the mist one could see glowing eyes.

Jessica and Peter were unloading the boat while Rene was inside the house preparing lunch. Rene was not much for any of the work that came with owning a boat, only for the comforts of owning one. Tonight Jessica promised to tell Peter and Rene a story from God. Jessica is a wise girl with a multitude of talents. Always ready to help out with the chores around the house and making herself useful. Jessica is not a spiteful girl but a delicate flower, as gentle as Southern Belle. Peter tied off the bow and the stern to his slip in the back yard. Then he entered the yard and walked up the narrow boardwalk to the house to wait for lunch. Jessica stayed in the cabin of the boat staring out the window at the spy boat in the far horizon. Jessica held a bible in her hand as she moved to the deck to watch the sunset and pray.

Rene was wearing a beautiful silk blue dress during dinner as she sat next to Jessica on the couch. Peter was placing logs on the fire while a smoking pipe hung off his lips. Nothing was on and the place was quiet as Jessica began speaking. *"I do not want to watch TV tonight because I want you to hear these words that are ordained by God to proclaim for you to hear."* 'Rene put an arm over Jessica and said.' *"All right dear, we have you to thank for our escape and will always be indebted to you."* Rene seemed to sparkle in the candlelight wearing her lovely silk blue dress as tears rolled down her cheeks. Her nightmares of the Lupus Estate still mesmerized her.

Peter sat back into his favorite easy chair and opened a beer. Then he began to get comfortable and seated himself exactly the way that he liked. It was a large living room with tall western ceilings. Rene decorated the place recently, which gave the house a touch of home. Peter loved his chair and his favorite dog lay beside him as Jessica began to speak in a pleasant and gentle voice that seemed to carry volumes.

"Even as Abraham believed God, and it was accounted to him for righteousness." 'Jessica paused for a moment and continued.' *"Know ye therefore that they which are of faith, the same children are the children of Abraham."*

There was silence for a few minutes as tears swelled her eyes, Rene felt captivated by Jessica. Then Jessica began singing a song. Peter and Rene listened as they learned the words and sang the song together. *"God standeth in the congregation of the mighty; He judgeth among the gods."*

'Peter excused himself for a few moments to grab another beer. He was back in his seat being fidgety and nervous as Jessica began speaking again.' *"How long will you judge unjustly, and accept the persons of the wicked? Defend the poor and fatherless, do justice to the afflicted and the needy. Deliver the poor and needy; rid them out of the hands of the wicked."*

They were clapping their hands together joyously as they sang, it seemed that Peter had learned the song earlier. There is no other way to explain this. Peter had calmed down and I watched on video that he was in some sort of trance. I could not get over the irony in this fight between good and evil. I was glad that Jarred was gone forever, unless Becky has cloned the monster. At any rate, something one day will bring this all to a melting pot. It almost seems as the end of the world is around the corner.

"They know not; neither will they understand, they walk on in darkness. All the foundations of the Earth are out, off course."

Jessica rose to her feet and boldly pronounced . . . *"I have said, ye are gods and all of you are the children of the most high!"* 'Jessica sat down, and then she continued.' *"But ye shall die like men and fall like the one of the princes. Arise! Oh God, judge the Earth for thou shalt inherit all nations."*

Peter asked Jessica a good question. He asked . . . *"Why is there so much hell here on Earth and why will not God stop it?"*

Jessica smugly smiled and said. *"For the flesh lustiest against the Spirit against the flesh. And these are contrary the one to the other, so that ye cannot do the things that ye would."*

Peter was dismayed and lifted his arms as he complained. *"You mean to say that this evil here is for our own good? It is our choice, on which side to take. This all seems ridiculous to me."*

Jessica was quiet for a while and then walked over

to the dog and lay beside it. Then she said. *"Behold! Your house is left to you desolate and verily I say unto you. Ye shall not see me until the time come when ye shall say. Blessed he that cometh in the name of the Lord."*

It almost seemed that Jessica was angry when she answered Peter but if you know Jessica then you know that is not possible. Jessica radiates love and promotes peace. I knew that Mia was out there somewhere but the cozy three did not seem bothered by Mia being on the loose. None of them truly believed that Mia was dead and knew that eventually Mia was going to pop out of nowhere. Jessica walked to the piano and began playing beautiful classical Gospel music. If she had been angry at Peter then she was not angry now.

(While they were on the lake, I had a team set up cameras' and bugs in and around Peter's house. It seems that if it were not for me to try to stop this fiasco then it would go idle wild until it blew. A confidential informant who knows more then he tells me gave Accounts about Nicklaus and Lisa to me.)

This adventure continues as the world self-destructs a bit more each day. Fog never leaves Eastern Washington and all over the world, Earthquakes are trying to knock us back into reality.

June 27, 2016

War on Terrorism is continuing in Iraq and Afghanistan. New wars have broken out including U.S. invading Iran with Israeli support and the war is in shambles. Great Britain has thus far refused to leave the Sudan. Sudan invaded, claimed as a new colony of Britain.

Terrorists have grouped and regrouped forming huge resistance Factions totaling almost two-million worldwide. America has experienced Harbor Attacks that have

killed nearly 250, 000 Americans. President Jeb Bush was a
better President then was his kin. Jeb was trying to prevent
a Police State from becoming reality. An all Democratic
Congress and House of Representatives, last week
Amended the Constitution to allow consecutive terms in
Office. Wealth and power moved the members of both
Houses and not the survival of our own species. As a world
figure, Canada succeeded to the United States of America.
It was a matter of survival as terrorists detonated a dirty
bomb in Ontario. Canada asked the U.S. for help. Now they
are part of the United States.

Four years ago, Korea promised a nuclear attack on
the U.S. and England if the sanctions were continued.

Up too now, they have not carried out their threats.
An Armada guards the coastline from Vancouver to the
Mexican Peninsula. Jeb Bush's Presidency is ending a
second term in Office, claiming to have everything under
control again. North Korea is ready to nuke America and
our Social Security went bust. President Bush promised no
new taxes at his last State of the Nation Address, forgetting
to emphasize our Nations pending doom. Bush had an Ace
in the hole; he had allied with most South American
Nations and named it . . . "Nations United against
Terrorism."

Iran vowed to nuke thirteen Countries and promised
that one day all the infidels in the world will be annihilated.
Korea and Iran signed a Treaty but Korea was planning to
stab Iran in the back when the time was right.

Landslides have caused havoc on both the Eastern
and Western Seaboards. Globally flooding coastlines are
reshaping historic borders.

Fallout from the wars caused pollution that is
destroying our planet. I am a scientist and never believed

in gods but if there is one out there somewhere then I hope that God saves our world before it becomes too late to save.

I believe all this to be the product of Xeno experimentation done by terrorist researchers. Super Leaders bred from Hitler's Youth Corps. Perhaps, it spread over by Britain and the U.S. who are successfully breeding soldiers with high intelligence. I will not say names but who is your favorite movie star? Is this person a product of a laboratory eighty years ago? Anti rejection serums, the Germans first developed during the second big war. Insects mutated today through Xeno technology to create cures and vaccines to cure Cancer and memory loss. All forms of life are akin to the human species and be utilized in one way or another into our genetic pool. Once introduced into our genetic pool it will change our children's genetic futures.

Ahead in the pages before you "The Xeno Stars"
Coming in the Future
SEQUELS to The Xeno Project
2.) The Xeno Stars
3.) Xeno Gods and Demons
4.) The Xeno Exodus
5.) Xeno Blood
6.) Xeno Bugs
7.) The Xeno Horsemen
8.) Means to an End

Book Two
Chapter One
"Xeno Prodigies"
Jan 2015 A.D.

It was a dark and weary night as the five Heads of State met inside of a completely Secured Oval Office. Vince was a tall man with stern lean features who was against releasing the information on the Xeno Project man. A year ago, a group of Terrorists had blown apart this wing of the White house but that made it the perfect place to meet. Construction material surrounded with armored suited Secret Service Agents. From a crack in the concrete wall, a person could feel a cold chill.

Xeno Project Special Operations had created a clone that was eight feet tall and solid muscle. He was quicker and stronger than any human in the entire world. With great resolve, the President stood and asked. *"When will he be ready to enter the games?"*

Terrorist Factions unrelated to each other were growing quickly throughout the world and military training camps were building small terrorist armies globally. The Pentagon had developed the first cloned Xeno Species developed to kill. Terrorists' nomenclature processed into his brain with miniature mega mite computers. Trained to kill the leaders of these terrorist groups, Xeno 1A was ready to see some action. Oil wells were burning fiercely into the night as terrorist infiltrators in the name of their cause attacked inland oil wells. American troops were short in supply and understaffed. Troops were going home or redeployed from Iraq.

The Xeno Project had cost billions of dollars in the last forty years but at last, it was, finally paying off. New diseases had spread throughout the world without cures as the present diseases found cures with Godspeed. Dr.

Keller was present at this meeting and was explaining the telepathic capabilities of the mind inside of the Xeno Project man. Little did the others know that Nick had more then a computer program inside the Xeno man. He had instructed loyalty, instilling its essence into the brain of the beast to obey the man who created him.

Ted Kennedy was getting on in his years but was still snappy and as witty as ever. Perhaps destiny has kept the Bush family in the Oval Office. There were those who claimed otherwise but their voices were a brave minority. Democrats held the Majorities in the House and the Senate, holding the meek and humble Republicans at bay it seemed that a New Democratic Party had formed. At the head of this Organization was the Supreme Court who backed up all Policies dictated by the President. Ted was annoyed that only received an invitation to this secret meeting.

Besides the President, Ted Kennedy and Vince Battaglia, also attending was Senator Clark and Congressperson Julie Peterson.

A non-partisan Committee overseeing Xeno Advances and breakthroughs decided how far to take the Xeno Project and where the Funding for it came from. All of these persons had Xeno surgeries and projected to live 150 years or more. Nuclear spiking later saturated with anti rejection gels before transplanted into all crucial Government Officials mutated alligator brain DNA. Many died inside Medical Research Institutions from these bone marrow injections before it perfected to be an antidote for aging.

Some claimed that their ages were regressing. How much longer these extremely important persons were going to stay neutral about the limitations to Xeno Advances was surely to gather criticism.

Now they needed to decide whether to allow, "The Xeno Project Man 1A." To fight in the Arena during the

Xeno Games and see how he will adapt to his environment. It was going to be an introduction into what was to come in the future for the evolution of humankind. There was a hitch, the computers made it run and think and not the man. He was without free will. Soon that was going to change.

Xeno Industries INC was searching for ways to program Xeno organs, to allow them to operate on their own and hopefully to regenerate and possibly reproduce.

It was a chance that the Secret Committee was not willing to take, 'Allowing Xeno Prodigies to think for themselves spelled trouble.' Ted had the finances and the Contacts to slow the technology down but not stop it.

Xeno Arena constructed in 2012 used for free style hand-to-hand weapons combat. To the victor go the spoils owned by the loser who ends up dead anyway.

The war on Terrorism has been lost and the world had split into two factions. Those opposed to the changes in experiments in Xeno DNA, and those for it.

All over the Western World, most of Africa and Japan, animals bred for their organs. All western and non-Muslim, non-Buddhists and other religions, went with the flow were doing research and promoting Xeno Transplants. All other Nations opposed it and built a wall higher then the Iron Curtain to keep potential Xeno transients out of their Countries. New Terrorist groups formed to attack Xeno Installations and they never seemed to run out of money to promote more terrorism, all this in defense of Animal rights and the freedom to practice their own Religions.

The Xeno Man amended to be human. In this way, #1A entered into the Contests. Since the tall curtain, been formed between opposing Countries, the West advocated the Xeno age. Then the Xeno Arena passed with a no holds barred contests with weapons, contest between World Nations.

This replaced the Olympics and many events ended in the death of one contestant or the other. Xeno mutants and Xeno offspring of humans banned from participating in the contests at Xeno Arena in Washington, D.C.

World politics decided in the Arena and it offered an excited and tranquil peace among the many Xeno Nations on a global scale.

Dr. Keller was in control of the Xeno Project and set his headquarters up in Seattle. Lisa was the Xeno Arena Queen for the games and parades.

Mia was nowhere, as was Peter and Rene along with Jessica with her new Following. They were in hiding.

Becky was still in her Compound conducting her own experiments deep in the Rain forests of Washington State. Becky had her own dreams of conquest and she had a new boyfriend. He was a young man in his mid twenties with a solid build and good-looking. Becky adored him and he worshiped Becky.

Becky controlled more than a thousand acres of Rain Forest. She was getting Government Grants and Terrorist bribes to keep her work alive. It was fortunate for Becky that she discovered a mushroom with mind control and anti rejection properties all in one. She kept it a well-hidden secret and was in control of her world and her man with a little help from Mrs. Schroon. Becky became quite a control freak with a deep burning hatred directed at Nick and Lisa.

It seemed that The Xeno Project promised life and to most Westerners it was more real then God's promise of forgiveness.

There was no stopping the rich and famous, they

wanted to stay beautiful forever and with Xeno surgery, they could do just that. Each surgery was cheaper because less anti rejection drugs were needed seems the human body was adopting its principles sort of remapping our DNA.

"Tammy, please hand me the blue towel, would you?"

"Sure Honey, do you want me to towel you off."

"No babe, do me a favor and see if we remembered to lock the patio doors."

Leven Goldman was a rough but cultured man of 22 yrs. He was the first round Draft Pick the last year before the NFL disbanded because of the Xeno Games. Now he is a modern gladiator ready to murder another Human Being for the Games. It was very different from being the best linebacker in the League for him, selected as a Champion Xeno Star.

This was his last Contest and it was the most difficult of all of them. It was an armed meeting to the death. His opponent was yet unknown to Leven but he knew that he would be fierce. Leven loved to fight with, and was most effective while armed with his saber and dagger. This was his last fight because it was his 50th win in a year. Leven did anticipate the fifty-million dollars that came at retirement knowing that few survived their last Contest.

Tammy was gone only a few minutes before she arrived into the bedroom where Leven was waiting. She was carrying a tray with breakfast and a pitcher of screwdrivers.

Wearing her purple and black silk robe Tammy's long flowing hair nearly made her beauty illumine her surroundings. Tammy was born in Oakland California but raised in San Francisco by her uncle. She met Leven at the last NFL Super bowl by accident and they have been together since then. Tammy is a stunning beauty who won the San Francisco Spelling Bee and was Class President when she quit school at 17.

Leven was of Olympic stature and in his rookies' year in the NFL; he had broken a few Records. Most interceptions in a game, most sacks in a Season, and MVP seven times during the year were a few. With his career over at the start, Leven chose to fight in the games.

Terrorism had made Americans cold-hearted and indifferent, there were the powerful rich and then there were the poor. America was a Leader of the World that had formed a Treaty between the two nuclear communist nations. As more, and more of the masses learned of gene manipulation of the human genetic pool. It seemed that the fight against Terrorism was ongoing.

Yet America was growing more powerful and wealthy during these outcries, so the majority of Americans did not want things to change. American Research monies developed the Xeno Project and it brought power with it. Certainly, the Pentagon was not going to relinquish this Power to any Nation but Great Britain that shared this awesome influence with the U.S.A.

Lucas Bailey stared at the Arena from his car. Washington was D.C. crawling with crime now more then ever. Lucas, once a Professional Wrestler, decided that he needed more out of the sport. At seven feet ten inches tall Lucas seemed forbearing with his beady eyes and thick connecting eye brows. There was a lot to see at the Arena, and Lucas was soaking it up. He was mentally preparing himself for the Contest, trying to become one with the Arena. Learning the smells, observing the winds, knowing that soon he would be fighting for his life in the center circle against a worthy opponent Lucas felt like a god. Lucas had three more fights to go before his last fight. He felt terrible for the man that needed to be killed fighting in his last Contest. Lucas wondered if he would make it that far as he started his car and moved opposite of the Arena.

A rope lasso and an eight-foot lance were what Lucas prided himself on. Most of his kills happened in less than five minutes in a fight to the death. Lucas was always favored to win his fights and his betting profits were nearly enough to retire. In the Game there was no quitting, once entered you were in for the long run.

Indeed, Lucas was a loner and a bully but he was not a braggart. They made him impotent in his second Contest so he had no need for female companionship. All his time was devoted to keeping in shape and learning the art of murder. Lucas is a Rep. from Australia.

Tang Chang was a not a tall man at 6"5" but he weighed nearly a thousand pounds. Born in Tibet and a Master in Hand to Hand Combat, he was an Expert with the Manchurian sword he always carried on his thick leather belt. Chang was a born spiritual killer. He is the leader of the Chang Dynasty with thirty wives.

Besides being a Priest, Chang is the Leader of his Religious Sect in the Mountains. Tang represents China at the Xeno Games. Some Villagers claim that he has skin much like steel scales. It seems to me that China had been experimenting with DNA manipulation for thousands of years. 'Always in a benevolent understanding manner to respect Nature,' Tang knew that he was going to win his next Contest. He had laced his sword with poison.

Two other combatants made it up the ranks to the position they now hold at the Arena. They were Raven Decont from France, and Litua Patel from

Pakistan. Litua is the only combatant from a Terrorist Nation.

Raven Decont is a tall woman weight lifter. She is a fifth Degree Black Belt and used a large hammer and net during the Contests. Raven known by her stealth and deadly accuracy with her net and hammer.

Cal's Realm of Nightmares

Litua was deadly with her poison darts and lethal when she had her four-foot steel staff. She had a reputation to have potions and some type of disabling dust that she was able to spray like a cobra. Thin, yet strong, her quickness made Litua dangerous.

The Heads of State discussed these persons in detail and they all agreed that the Games were good. Ted stated that Becky and her crew were getting too powerful and that their experiments needed regulations.

Vince Represented the Elite and the Mob. *"It was not easy controlling the war and the Xeno Project issue, but we managed."* 'Everybody knew what was coming next.' *"We will have to hunt down and kill the Twin before she hunts us down."*

Senator Clark and Julie Peterson were more concerned about internal affairs. *"New Orleans is nearly under water and the next big storm will consume the city. We must fix our dams and bridges before they are no more."* Senator Clark was angry because the Coastline of his own State was giving in to global warming.

Julie Peterson was fuming red; she was irked that nobody had mentioned the poor and the high gas prices.

"Gasoline was now at fifty-two dollars a gallon. Our minimum wage is nine dollars an hour. Wealthy Corporations and Industries have controlled the Government for the last two years." 'Miss Peterson was getting warmed up.' *"I am a Baptist and by God if it takes*

passing laws to limit their influences in Government. One way or another we have to stop these monopolies from running our Nation. All of us here are driving cars given to us by names such as Chevron USA, McDonalds, the Unions, and hundreds of other Fortune 1000 Club members." 'She had made a driving point home.' *"There is only one way to give this Country back to its people and that is to stop the corrupting now!"*

Senator Clark stood before the others and said . . . *"We are but a few and the odds are overwhelmingly against us so I believe the best avenue to attack this dilemma is by covert operations. I see no other way to stop the conquest of our Nation by the Wealthy and the corrupt."*

Many other issues seriously discussed and the major concern was the excelled growth of Xeno Creations. Xeno Creatures grew at twice the rate of a human child and there were instances where Xeno Creatures advanced in age ten times faster then a normal human child.

Xeno bribes spread like cancer and the wealthy became filthy rich, filthy rich with the knowledge that the Medical Association was beginning the end of the human species. Greed ruled humanity and ruined our Justice system.

Is there anything that we can do about this or is it too late to stop the Xeno investors from growing to a ripe old age of a thousand years while our human species dies off?

I will predict that these prodigies will come back to haunt us, perhaps even to destroy us. These monsters created in laboratories everywhere will protect when that time comes not the rich or the poor.

Our world of ours has turned cold and has become heartless doing nice deeds to cover up their wickedness and evil buried deep within the minds of those persons making high-level decisions. It has been merely a roll of the dice that humankind has managed to stay afloat this far, poisoning our genetic pool is the ultimate genocide of a species, our species. . .

End of Chapter One
"Xeno Prodigies"

Chapter Two
"Xeno Breakthroughs"

"Please not now, perhaps later we'll have time to fool around. I have to get ready for the Games."
'Leven was honing his dagger to a keen point while totally involved mentally in sharpening his telekinetic skills.' Leven was neither manufactured nor Xeno-operated. He is the offspring of Xeno recipient parents. He was born completely human but seemed to have unnatural talents that he used for his advantage in the fight.

"Can't you forget the game for just a little while Honey? The games are six months from now. You can spend some time with your Babydoll now." 'Tammy was not one to keep waiting, and she had a temper like a wildcat with a litter being disturbed by a raccoon.' *"You always win Leven, and you never trained this hard anytime before in your life."*

Soon after Tammy finished her sentence there was a loud knock at their door. Leven stared at Tammy as she ran to see who it was at the door.

___

Deep within the confines of The Holes

Susan stared at the high open ceiling covered with steel mess. She was in a hole 12 x 36, in the inpatient ward of the Rehabilitation Center, known to its occupants as the holes. Spiraling stairs lined with 6'x 6 caged cells housed perspective or offbeat Xeno Contestants. Susan was a few days away from her spinal Xeno surgery. There was a comfortable bed in her cell, which left Susan little room to move around, spiders and other insects were abundant.

Kansas Federal underground Nuclear Institute or better known as the KFUNI is a testing experimental facility designed by Dr. Keller. They jointly work with Xeno Pharmaceuticals Corp. This huge underground

Complex, directed and Operated by the United Nations. This well fortified Compound was equipped with Green Houses, deeply drilled wells into underground rivers. It was self reliant with the newest technology and fashioned compartments specifically designed for different purposes.

This massive underground complex is four miles deep and three miles square. Designed to house and maintain up to one-million persons for as long as the nuclear reactor stays online. Huge generator rooms filled with mazes of massive and complicated nuclear Transformers.

There are many secrets and assassinations within the Chain of Command inside the confines of the private Levels owned by the truly rich and the Medical Association.

Guarded by Two Battalions of dedicated and committed for life Special Forces hand-picked elite men, perhaps it was the most expensive and exclusive place to live in the world. The Pentagon was soon to be moved board by board, stone by stone into the adjoining two miles deep Installation three miles from the KFUNI Life Force Research Center. Beneath the Centers was a Battalion of Special Task Force Platoons supporting the deep levels of KFUNI.

One mile deep, ten miles north was the Underground NASA Special Air Force Squadrons designed to be on ground zero of a nuclear detonation and withstand the blast. Engineered to go down in a 45% angle so that conventional rockets would be fired in defense of the Elite's three hideouts of havens, were the worse to happen.

Nobody considered Nature that much. People expect things to stay the same. It has been this way, long that they could remember.

****

It was raining hard in huge raindrops as the two

Agents ran for cover. It was only early afternoon, tree branches were snapping, and crackling as the high winds blew through San Francisco, California. Tammy and Leven were on the run after Leven escaped from the clutches of KFUNI. They rode the jet train from Sacramento to San Francisco to be together and to be free of the Games. Raining or not the two of them decided to flee with the small-amassed fortunes that they had saved during the Xeno Playoffs.

They took the Trolley to Broadway and stepped off the bus on wheels into the blackness of the street.

"Now what," 'said Tammy in despair?'

Leven checked the load on his old Army 45 cal. Auto and searched with his eyes for a place to stay the night.

"We find what we need and we buy it, take it, or steal it." Certainly, the two lovers were determined to get away at any cost.

All that they needed to do was wait the storm out. Before long they strolled up the sidewalk and seen two men from the Mid-East and they had their turbans on. Two large suitcases sat beside each man and they stayed in the shadows of Broadway Street. Tammy and Levin watched them as they drifted past the strangers.

A wealthy Arab Billionaire had bought out Broadway Street for twenty blocks. He had set up gambling and Prostitution Clubs and sold whatever you wanted, or could want. There on Broadway and Montgomery was a lone Hotel named the Golden Eagle.

Entering the place was difficult as the pimps blocked their way in. Levin knocked them aside and kicked at the steel meshed doors locked by remote control. Then the door opened next to a second door that was ajar.

It was a bad place to be and if the two fugitives had known that they were inside a Terrorist safe house, then they would have walked on. It was not like the two beloved soon to be wed were shocked by what they considered casual behavior, for being in the neighborhood that they were in. It was run and Policed by the Arabs, even the Transamerica Building was owned and managed by the Arabs and the Turks.

Dennis Hurtman was the Manager and he was standing alone at the top of the stairs. *"Welcome to the Golden Eagle Hotel"* Then Dennis stepped back into his room leaving the Office empty.

A Transvestite stepped out from the back room of the office and asked? *"What can I do for you, would you like a room with a widow and for how long would you like to stay?"*

The Basement

While Leven and Tammy were, making love on the fourth floor, in the basement there was a sophisticated network of laboratories and an elevator that could take one deeper into the abyss. Leven knew that the good times they were have having on their fugitive run to freedom in the Nevada wastelands was futile, yet he had hope of making it there.

Dennis was the intermediary for everything going on in the Hotel. He was not a feared man but if you wanted to get into the Ahad Gang then you had to be cleared by Dennis.

Dennis knew who Levin was and that Leven was on the run. Denis hated all Jews and ethnic groups. Dennis smiled as he thought about the reward offered by the Authorities for the capture of this love couple.

After running some errands for the lab {stealing a dog from down the block} then Dennis decided to wait it out and see if he could find a more extravagant buyer.

Indeed, the labs were in constant need of Test Subjects.

Dennis was excellent at recruiting girls, kidnapping some girls into the basement vault. Broadway Street had become infamous with the girlie bars and the Strip joints. Dennis would rent a room to a stunning fox just off the bus from Chicago. Then he would dump a bag of bed bugs under the bed as the new comer was showering. It was easy as pie, Dennis would remark with laughter.

The next day the girl would be littered with bites and unable to get a job. Marked as a risk by the local Bosses, Yes sir, Dennis would front them the rent and be kind to them. In the end, the girls paid for his services with their sex and their lives. Dennis always got himself some before he turned them over to the Xeno labs.

Occasionally a Fed would infiltrate the ring but would be killed or worse yet, never found.

There was a rumor going around of a new Xeno Breakthrough. A guard that the new discovery consisted of everlasting life overheard it. It was a micro transplant into a human gene taken from an alligator. With the promise of new drugs around the corner to combat the side effects of this brain matter transfer, distinguished scientists and leading Research Facilities vouched for success. Obviously, it was more then a rumor, it was a new reality created by man.

Dennis had in his mind to break a better deal with the Xeno Mob for the fugitives in room 336. Peacefully tranquil, Dennis locked himself in his bulletproof office and began to massacre a Neil Young song on his acoustic guitar. Dennis was fooling only himself; he was all thumbs on the guitar. Perhaps Dennis planned to get out of the game with the money he earned from snitching on Leven.

Becky was experimenting in her Compound on Timber Lake, Washington State on a new killer agent that would neutralize Xeno Drugs. She figured that it was the best way to gain power and to find that bastard Nick Keller.

Aggressively Becky searched for a way to beat Nick at his own game. She had cages filled with mutant Xeno byproducts and engineered DNA Masterpieces. Becky had a new boy friend that she designed into nature herself.

Dubbed, by his peers as Ivan the Madman, he was a stout feller with the strength of ten men. Yet he was a gentle giant willing to help anybody and he had feelings. Becky instilled into a computer chip in his brain to do her bidding. He once was a movie star, now he was Becky's slave.

Ivan was a masterful killer without emotion nor any remorse. He was a superb lover and an excellent host. One could tag the man Becky's stuntman. There were breakthroughs in DNA Technology that were developing daily. It was becoming a major issue producing a new type of terrorist. It was a movement against Xeno Transplants and the research monies spent on promoting the idea. Ivan was in the Rainforest far from New York and Chicago where most of this research was ongoing. All that Ivan had to know was what Becky told him to remember or do. Like murdering a person, one day she planned to use Ivan to oust Nick.

Washington D.C.

"This meeting will now come to Order, please Gentlemen, have a seat and quiet down." It became dead quiet in the brightly lit chambers below the Pentagon.

The Speaker of the House rose from his seat and addressed the secretly invited members. *"Here I stand with a stack of documents before me and tens of thousands of words in each Brief. No, I have not seen all of them but the few that I did read pointed to the same conclusions."*

There were a few murmurs in the chamber as the Speaker shifted his stance. *"I give the Floor to Senator Henry Rochelle."* Henry was an upcoming popular candidate for the Presidency.

"You have ten minutes and you can pass or give your minutes away to another House Member or Senate Person." During his closing, the Speaker sat down.

Henry spoke loudly and confidently as he presented the facts, discussed about the issues at hand. *"Certainly by now we see that Xeno Advancements must continue in order to put an end to the terrorism happening all over the world. There is only one way to hunt down the Terrorists, we must genetically design super soldiers that can hunt down their leaders."*

There was some stirring by the Democrats but all eyes were on Henry. *"Obviously we have gone too far to stop now. We need two trillion dollars to run the Xeno Counterterrorism Research Center located near Fort Lewis, WA. Many of us are here now because of Xeno Transplants and Treatments, Xeno organ transplants is a Promise for a better future, longer lives, and immunity to diseases."* (Ted Kennedy was old and held a firm stance against the idea of creating superhuman soldiers.)

Henry continued as his eyes diverted to Ted. *"There are a few holdouts here and they seem determined to undermine the Xeno Project. I know that I will outlive them and be around for my grandchildren."*

It was silent in the domed chamber and Henry paused for a glass of cool water. Indeed, Ted Kennedy was old but he was veracious in his character. He was waiting to stall this meeting but with only three of them in agreement, it was bound to be a short-winded Filibuster.

Persistent and headstrong, Henry continued his speech. *"Sooner or later the entire country will catch on, adapting to this new life of the ever lasted ones. We are*

important to mankind. Imagine the good our experience will do for the future of politics if one was to live for hundreds of years . . . just imagine."
"I choose to give my remaining time to Congressman Bush. Thank you for your attention and God Bless America."

Will Bush stood and addressed the agenda. *"I move that we appropriate the funds from social programs and also to give NASA another blast to Mars with a Federal Grant consisting of three billion dollars."*

State Rep. Pedro Warez seconded the motion and the Gavel slammed down. Pedro was from New Mexico and was 125 years in age.

Perhaps this meeting was going to turn the Government Officials against one another. Anything is possible in the new Xeno Age. Futile was the word that Ted pronounced without giving a speech or a statement. *"Futile to save the human species because it is bent on destruction, I say that all of you are crazy to dwell into the unknown because of what will become of our species two-hundred years from now."*

Ted knew that there was no fighting the New Republican Party. They were anti abortion, anti Christian, and pro Xeno. Most were forgetting God's Promise of salvation knowing that now technology was eventually going to develop fountain of youth pills. True Children of God resisted the changes and built Cells and groups to hide their identities. Politics were changing as the Rights of the people and their plight grew dim to spread the Word.

High in the mountains of Idaho was an encampment where sanctuary was waiting with Jessica and Peter.

Most persons that went there disappeared. Then there were those evicted, or stoned to death after their first day.

SAMUEL

Samuel was on another rampage and killed three Compound Guards before being locked into a cage. At 6'6" with a peachy-face, he looked like a man but was still a growing boy

Most of the time Samuel was docile and a true leader, then sometimes for no reason at all Samuel went berserk. Samuel was the one truly in control of the corruption and famines invading the peoples of the world. He still used his father's skull as a candleholder and kept it aflame 24-7. Lucifer screamed with curses in agony to his son, the anti Christ.

Leven made Samuel go ape. A telepathic thought detected the man placed here by God sent to kill Samuel. Was it ordained?

Leven was waking as he reached for his blade and it was gone. He was strapped atop a Gurney and could barely move a muscle.

There before his feet were two persons wearing masks covering over their shoulders the lining of the black jumpsuits that covered their bodies. One seemed to be female and the other was male. They had latex gloves on and held briefcases in their hands. Levin knew that they were going to give him one more chance.

Perhaps Leven was going to be sorry that he tried to escape. Leven had heard about the Xeno Man and was beginning to think that he was now a Test Subject.

Worried about Tammy, Leven knew that he had to rescue Tammy.

Leven tried to slip his hand out of the straps, he acted as if it was futile to keep trying. Knowing the whole while that he had the strength to snap the straps and become free of them. Eyes roaming the room, he noticed that there were two doors about ten feet from his position. Leven knew that to escape he had to take out the two strangers. No sweat, thought Leven. *"Ain't nothing but a thang, Shalom?"* Leven was confident that they had under estimated him.

Meanwhile, in the adjoining Cell.

Tammy was being hung in the gang yard by her feet as it was necessary to perform the operation. Dr. Hector was preparing to direct Tammy while saving her organs, skin tissue and bone marrow. Tammy was out cold from a blow to her head by Dennis and Terry. Terry worked for the Motel and was to retire soon. As soon as Tammy was awake Tammy was to be eviscerated.

Slow and Easy

Leven waited for something to happen next and he was not disappointed about the results of what transpired.

A Bright light illuminated the sterile cell as the two strangers walked in Levin's direction. Then they spread apart as they pulled syringes from the pockets of their suitcases.

Softly and with a deep voice the larger of the two strangers spoke out with a hypnotic voice. *"I want you to sit down and go along with the program son. We are only going to enhance your fighting abilities by giving you night vision sight."* 'Then the female said.' *"We have corneas taken from a wolf and plan to replace yours for better vision."*

"It seems that they are perfect matches for your DNA strands. You will not even know that you had the surgery." 'Perhaps the lady was trying to convince Leven to have the surgery on his own.' Around every corner lurked trouble for Leven. Leven, had been chosen to fight the Xeno Man.

Leven could only think of Tammy. What diabolical experiment they had chosen for his love made his skin crawl. There was only one course of action and he wasted no time in taking it. Obviously, he believed that her life was in danger and that her only chance for rescue was Leven saving from the clutches of these monsters.

It was the tall dark stranger that stood between him and the doors. Leven moved like a stroke of lightning at the man and with a quick jerk broken the man's neck. Then the other stranger darted at Leven trying to get in a stab at him. It was during that same moment that Leven body-slammed the dead operate at the lunging woman. She must have stuck herself with the needle because she lay beneath the deceased dead as a doornail herself.

Leven was out the doors and heard Tammy scream. In a moment or two, he was before the persons about ready to butcher his sweet buttercups. It had taken the ex football hero perhaps four seconds to massacre the Researchers with his Xeno quick strokes of death. It was a phrase used to describe these moves during the games. With a surgical knife, Leven let his lover loose and both ran for the stairs.

Before long, they reached the bottom landing and their path was blocked. Blocking their way was three night clerks with Billy clubs waiting to club the Couple. Dennis was the leader and had a guitar strapped on his back. His club was at least a foot long if it was an inch. It seemed for the fugitives that the end of the tunnel darkened at the bottom of the stairs. It was a day that would change history in North beach.

Tammy was no pushover as she hit Dennis on his jaw with a front snap kick. Vince slugged Tammy with a lucky swing before Leven knocked the man down the stairs to the steel double doors they had walked through the night before. Tammy was swift to run down the stairs to meet Leven. Leven saw that a streak of blood was running down

Tammy's face.

Leven knew that they had to move fast and car jacked a cab, after grabbing the keys he threw the driver ten feet to the sidewalk. Tammy was dizzy so Leven burned the wheels as he pulled away from The Golden Eagle Hotel and down Broadway toward the Bay. Leven seemed to be riding a lucky streak; he was hoping that his luck would not run out.

Jessica had found a friend in the woods that she called Abe. He was large as a fox and good to look at. There was a glow surrounding Abe and he had wings. Jessica claimed that Abe was going to win the Xeno Games without hurting a soul. Jessica will be disappointed.

Jessica did not believe in Breakthroughs. She trusted in Jesus and claimed that Abe was from God. She Quoted some verses from the Bible without ever have read it in her life.

She renowned to do odd things that amazed everyone and scared others. Certainly, Jessica is some kind of Saint or Angel herself. That was the rumor going around the Christian World. Abe was a by-product of her Sainthood, Divine Authority to do as she pleased, one could   wonder why she never used her miracles to destroy the Xeno Projects around the Globe. Jessica said that it was not her place to judge souls, only to be there for them if they wanted to find God. Jessica always made decisions for all.

> *"AND THERE IS HOPE IN THINE END, SAITH THE LORD. THAT THY CHILDREN SHALL COME AGAIN, TO THEIR OWN BORDER."*

Pandemonium struck the crowd as the President tried to deliver his State of Nation Address. There were three lines of Special Forces numbering three thousand that surrounded the President.

With his had picked Chief Justice and his Party ruling both Houses, he was confident yet unpopular in the polls. The thousands to house the American Revolutionaries who called themselves American Patriots were building prisons with his blessings.

Americans were now subject to curfew, invasions of privacy laws, no Social Programs, Police brutality went rampant and lawlessness went over the line. The best job to have is a Federal job; many folks claimed that they were living a Police Action happening in their back yards.

There was an attempt made by some Entertainment Businesses to fight the Xeno horror back in 2005 but now they were a fortified Compound. They had an Army of more than 20,000 men and women. Cal Black had known what was coming and had been preparing for this fight since 2000. It did not take long for millions to share and support the Cause. It was not over yet but the Human Species were losing the fight. Seemed that everlasting life was too hard to pass up for most people, this Group holed up somewhere in California.

Terrorist groups were taking over Countries and now had nuclear capabilities. Storms cause havoc all over the world yet the battlefields always seemed to have fair weather and stable ground.

Hot and muggy with bright lights in his eyes the President rose to the podium. Not knowing about the conspiracies going on behind his back, the President began his speech.

"First," started the President. *"We ignore this great threat against our God forsaken Nation. What else but invade Pakistan was there for General Stratton, it was that or nukem. Still, the Terrorist Leader eludes us, and he taunts us. That is why we must expand The Xeno Project. This scientific marvel will bring our Nation back*

from this Recession and assist in winning the war against Terrorism."

'Taking a sip of water the President cleared his throat.' *"Our Forces are battle hardened ready to combat our enemies. Canada has added their Military Forces to our Commanders and Mexico has built a foothold in Central America. American Military Advisers are spread around the globe. I am asking the House to release $100,000,000,000.00 that we confiscated from Pakistan to finance our Xeno projects."* Madison Square Garden gave the President a standing ovation.

Wiping the sweat off his brows, the President continued. *"We will stop the curfew once the war on terrorism has been won, until that time gets here our U.N. Home Security Force will continue to Police our Great Nation. All people of Arab decent shall imprison at Xeno Compound Holding Facilities. We as a Nation must band together for times yet to come. Yes, there will be some hard times and some good times but we will never let down our guard. In these years of fighting this war we have learned from the mistakes that we made. We have victory in our hands; it is only a matter of time before we prevail against our enemies."*

About a hundred Protestors arrived from the rear. They were protesting against monies designated to Xeno projects. Wearing different styles of defense, armor and the like, protestors armed with baseball bats, soon intercepted by a force of Special Forces dressed in NBC Riot gear. Armed with bulletproof vests and M-203's along with sidearm's, they intended on ending this problem with the protestors quickly and with prejudice.

Soon after a platoon dispatched, the north flank erupted in a string of explosions. Everybody was in a panic within the Garden and the Protestors seemed organized.

Secret Service Agents hushed the President to safety as rockets coming at the podium were launched from the south flank.

They called themselves the XRAP Group Gang better known as the Xeno Rebellion American Patriots.

Leven and Tammy found shelter in the doorway down a dark alley. They counted their blessings as they headed for the docks in North Beach.

Once there then it was easy to steal a yacht. Tammy dumped them overboard once they were a couple miles offshore. It was better to lighten the load to pick up speed. In the main cabin the Captain, his First Mate and the Cooks wife locked in. There were three more able bodied seamen unaccounted for, but Leven knew they were dead. He had not known his own strength fighting Norms, peoples without enhanced abilities. They sailed for several hours before dropping anchor.

Leven, shared more then love with Tammy, he shared his nightmares too. Dreams blackened and saturated in blood seemed to be some sort of mist and in the center was Samuel eating human flesh. Leven would jump in his sleep grabbing his blade to kill it.

Screams would loudly disturb the silence that seemed to come out of nowhere and everywhere. Both lovers were alone in their dreams, trying to kill the evasive razor-mouth man. Screams from the depths of hell grew louder as the battle grew bloodier.

Leven at first was the hunter but before too long he was the hunted. Radiance and blurry visions made it difficult for liven to catch the invisible man. First Samuel would appear before him and in the next moment vanish only to be behind him. Terror stricken and prepared to fight for his life, Leven and Tammy would awaken the same ways, ready to fight and scared senseless.

There are many mysteries about the Xeno Age and when it comes down to the bottom line, all that they truly are is cover-ups.

The End of chapter Two
"<u>Xeno Breakthroughs</u>"

CHAPTER THREE
"Xeno Opposition"

Leven was running faster then Tammy as the crowds were closing in on them. There was nowhere to hide as they ran down Jackson Street and then cut right. It was gusty but at least it was not raining as they ran into the Transamerica Building for shelter.

All of that area watched by Xeno-armed patrols. They were from Saudi Arabia and worked for the new owners of the Transamerica Building.

In an abandoned building near their position, hid seven Commandoes, part of an elite group Platoon, trained at the Jessica Foundation Compound. They were to capture the two fugitives for the Patriot Cause.

Mostly non-combatant, these highly trained super soldiers were capable of severe destruction. They had the capability to go unseen, like ghosts. When times were desperate and killing needed to be done these men and women were the best.

There was no law on Broadway Street, only chaos and mobsters. Fortunately, rescued by these Patriots and brought out of harms way. They were in an underground tunnel and entering a huge chamber as Saul Freeman, the fearless Leader of this Elite team, greeted them. They made their own laws.

There were other forms of Demonstrations against the Xeno Project and they all have their own agenda's. Third World Countries were being armed and trained by Guerilla Armies complemented with battle hardened Arab Military Advisors. Advisors armed with the modern hand-held LaserJet missiles were always nearby. This technology was bought from Russian Mobsters who were exploiting their own ex-countrymen and the U.S.

Jessica and Samuel were always competing in the

Xeno Games. They each had a host of warriors to fill the Arenas. Jessica Commanded Angel Warriors and Samuel utilized the most deadly demons among his denizens of horrors straight from hell. These were betting games and the longest and bloodiest fights during the Games. Exhibitions held quarterly every year. Super Xeno Games were on Christmas and they were the deadliest games played.

Dr. Keller and Lisa were nearly always together, working in the labs and shared many secrets. They had a son they named after his father and administered mind and body enhancing drugs to the child since a young age. The boy was called Jr. by most folks around town, yet at home he was always called Nicklaus. Samuel resembled his father in his mannerisms and appearance.

The two never knew what was coming next on the chain of evolution. Completely and utterly oblivious to the everlasting damage they had caused our species and the Devil that they had helped create. Anything was possible but Dr. Keller was the President of the Xeno Research Foundation. On this ill-fated night, they could have never guessed what was coming.

Leven burst into the lab with Tammy in tow. Two Secret Service Agents who were on Duty at the lab quickly accosted them. Leven stepped with his right foot between the oncoming man's legs thus getting grounded as he delivered the uppercut knife slash to the throat with his right hand. Then at once delivered the overhand palm slams to the temple of the unfortunate Agent.

Tammy had the other Agent pinned onto the floor with her razor-studded boots. Silently the man lay there hoping that he would see another day.

Nick and Lisa were set aback in shock, then . . .
Lisa moved like a cat around Tammy and Nick reached for

his shoulder holster. Leven snatched the P-38 from Keller's grasp and gently knocked Nick to the floor.

Lisa was much harder to corner and it took the both of them to subdue her.

Leven and Tammy laughed aloud and then said *"Now what?"*

'Leven saw a moment for light-heartiness and comforting.' *"Do we have time for a hug, perhaps a peck on the lips?"* With the impact of a car the north wall came crashing down.

At least ten Security persons entered with caution on their side which had come to their undoing, Keller should have never had came to San Francisco, California. In the early 2000's crime was under control. Now it had become a hotbed of dignitaries and terrorists. Leven and Tammy had no difficulty in exterminating the remaining Xeno Investigative Force.

After the smoke cleared and the smell of gunpowder diminished, Leven eyed Tammy over. She was hell bent in blood and guts, oblivious of her place and time. With the smell of sulfur in the air once again, Leven comforted Tammy and this time she was more herself.

A storm was rolling into the Bay Area that was beyond recent comprehension. Winds were at seventy miles an hour and the city was in a panic.

Standing firm in the Courtroom, We are so glad to honor the Xeno Games by having the Playoffs here in L.A. Arnold was still Governor of California; he gave a speech in Sacramento, to its citizens and the Nation.

"Around the Nation havoc is tearing apart Bay cities and populations. Weather Reports claimed winds of up to 250 mph heading into the Gulf of Mexico from the southeastern seas."

"The Motel/Hotel Terrorist Gang is the biggest threat to Americans. In 2006 a new contractor

was hired as Port Authorities, basically we had given charge of our harbors to suspected terrorists. " For some unknown reason Bin has stopped aging. His Followers believed Bin to be a Godlike Figure. They did as they were told, without question. It seems that the Xeno controversy had divided nations named the "Ring of Terrorist Armies."

Leven and Tammy were studying the tactical maps in the Lab. It showed India, Pakistan, Iran, Burma, Nepal, Egypt, Congo, Sudan, Kenya, Argentina, Chile, Brazil, Turkey, Greece, Yugoslavia, Spain, and last but not least, Iraq.

Most Nations stayed neutral in this war with the promise from Bin. He promised no terrorism to press for peace from their Countries.

In America Militias were forming in record numbers ever since 2007 and they were against more Xeno Breakthroughs. These small armies were not acting as one but were fighting for resources and territory. They all have one thing in common with each other, against the Xeno Project and against more Government regulations.

Leven was reading computer CD's while staying alert and on his toes for any more trouble. Leven thought about the Contract that they had signed to work for the Jessica Foundation.

Tammy heard the creature but acted unaware of its presence. Then they both saw Mia swing into the room dressed in camouflage and hosting a sub machine gun under her arm. Mia had evolved to the point where she could express herself by speech. Mia worked for the Foundation and was unknown to most of its members. Mia played a role in the schemes to come, Jessica directed that to her telepathically. Tammy was bundling the pair of doctors into crates that be delivered to Jessica. Tammy did not know what to think about the Mia. Mia frightened her and that was a first.

Leven noticed that all the Security was not present gone or passed out, then Tammy motioned with her eyes over to Mia. Leven turned and raised his own weapon to combat Mia. 'Mia replied' *"Stop what it is that you are doing and follow me. We have been compromised and now they know our position and are surrounding us now."*

"Who are you?" Tammy asked.

"I am your only way out of here." Barked Mia as her patience was growing thin. It seemed that the Doctor and his Bride were safe for now, but a bit uncomfortable.

Mia ran out the door and the two followed her. They almost ran into Dennis as he and his gang was protecting the recently built tunnels. Dennis held a shotgun in his hands and released both barrels into Mia. It's power sent Mia flying into a corner of the room.

At that moment, Mia shot out from her corner like a bullet as she plunged into the thugs. She began ripping them apart with her teeth. Mia killed each one, and then devoured Dennis. The last sounds from Dennis were a couple of burps from Mia. In the end Dennis begged for his life.

They ran down Broadway Street and then Mia led them into a blacked out house. Through the basement and into an elevator that descended three floors down to a safe house.

Meanwhile, back at the demolished laboratory the Doctor and Lisa are released from their captivity. Relieved to be alive the two of them were ushered into a black limo and driven to Salinas, California. Salinas was a Xeno Stronghold with all the Motels run by Mid-Eastern Militants. There were a few of the bigger motels, which privately operated terrorists ran the rest.

Jessica was moving her Foundation Headquarters to California. Storms were hitting the East Coast at record levels and the ice was melting at the North Pole. Heat created by the huge asteroid flying right at us was generating radiation adding to global warming. It is to pass our planet Earth in 2027 A.D. and some claim it is on a dead course directly heading toward Earth. This Asteroid is the size of a small moon and moving at the speed of light. It is a stray bomb heading to nowhere yet everywhere. Jessica wanted to be at a place where she could observe the oncoming disaster so that she might pray for this planet and the Human Species. Jessica knew that the Devil was setting up his Offensive in Salinas where Samuel has been hiding at the new Keller Mansion. It was located in the mountains twenty miles from Salinas, heavily fortified, and guarded by demons and imps along with an Elite Force provided by the Secret Service. Government interests were strong.

Nobody likes to ponder his or her own deaths. It is better to believe that it was never going to hit the Earth then to believe that the destruction of this planet was imminent. I think that it all has to do with destiny and foresight.

Jessica knew that the fate of humankind was in the hands of God. She also knew that the souls of all men and women were in her hands and that the mark of the devil was a Xeno deformity made up of scars that resembled 666. God had not decided whether the asteroid would hit the planet Earth but perhaps by not deciding our foreordination. Jessica did not know for sure and was not about to question her God.

In Carmel, at a secluded Estate was the new home of the Jessica Foundation. It was set up covertly and well hidden deep in the woods. There were horses, and a small ranch that went along with the Estate. Peter loved it in California and relished the sunshine.

Peter was troubled with Jessica claiming that the second coming of Christ was near. She was adamant in saying that it was time to purge the world of evil before the second coming of Christ. Peter was disappointed about Jessica and wanted more then he was getting from her. She loved him but would always go only so far before calling it quits. Jessica loved everybody including her enemies. Peter was reflecting about the strange powers that Jessica possessed. Her gifts or powers were eerie yet mystical, perhaps more spiritual then anything else. Peter was into the movement, loved to be popular, and involved in the Cause. Still there was the fact that Peter wanted love, real love from a woman. He knew that Jessica was a virgin and that Jessica was worth the wait. Indeed,

Peter was not satisfied about his life but glad to be living in California with Jessica. It seems that he had forgotten about Rene and that Peter had an evil streak in him.

Jessica wanted Peter to meet Leven and Tammy in Salinas and bring them to the new underground Foundation site Headquarters. Jessica wanted them to bathe in the underground river that ran through part of the deep Compound.

"Resistance to the Xeno Project is fruitless to those that have tried with their own activism or in unorganized groups. It was a major concern to all to keep the Xeno Foundation funded in the name of global peace. Xeno madness was out of control and its benefits were overwhelming to mankind." This was an Article in the New York Times.

Others, dubbed mostly by Christians, called the new species the Xenokind. Forceful in their determination to kill the Xeno project, wars amongst themselves fumbled their try to oppose the Project. Baptist Forces were the most effective in this war against Xeno Projects.

Leven and Tammy secretly driven by limo to a

secluded Motel named the Casa Linda. Koreans operated it so the driver booked a room for three days and thought all went well. "All wasn't well"

Tailed from San Francisco all the way to Salinas and never noticed a thing. Inside the Motel Office was a husband and wife team, Yin and Carol were two Koreans here for 33 years and living on the edge, it was difficult getting stuck between the Terrorist Motel owners in Salinas and the Government that gave them sanctuary. Tricked, unwillingly through ignorance become Double Agents.

The Managers insisted on inspecting the room each day. They claimed that the law was behind them. As a paying guest, you gave up the Right to protest invasions of privacy. They claimed that they had to perform their duties, "they sounded militaristic rehearsed."

Both were anti Americans and hated being in America. Being the fact that they were here confirmed their intentions and reasoning.

Down the road a band of murderers were assembling to assassinate the people staying in rooms 16 and 15 at the Casa Linda Motel.

Scenarios such as this was occurring the world over but this event was the most devastation that the anti Xeno movement was facing at this time.

Tammy was feeling amorous and she had Leven on their motel bed. This was their last night alone together before they had to report to different Duty Stations. With the lights dim and colored, the lovers tried to catch up on lost love. Leven and Tammy carried an emptiness that nothing could fill and a thirst that was unquenchable, as they passionately wrestled and laughed throughout the night. They had secretly decided to stay together even if it meant leaving the Foundation. Tammy did not know that the XTF were watching the lovebirds via satellite.

Samuel was always dealing death. He had grown to become a fearless and awesome man but he had flaws. Now that Lucifer was dead, murdered by Samuel, Samuel called himself Satan. Everyday he took great pleasure in the murder of an innocent person or two. Samuel has a sexual appetite never satisfied.

Knowing all too well that Mia was a tool being used by Jessica to hunt Samuel down and assassinate him. Samuel brought Valentine back from hell and cast life into him, so that Valentine with his denizens of demons would protect Samuel and hunt Mia.

Valentine wasted no time in building an Altar to Worship Lucifer who was burning in Hell. Lucifer begged Valentine to find his damned human skull covered in hot wax and to cast in into Hell and returned to him. Valentine promised to do so but now that he was alive again, Valentine is under Samuel's will. It was going to be impossible to snuff out the candle sitting within Lucifer's skull on a night table beside Samuel's bed. Lucifer's skull utilized as a candleholder.

Samuel found his victims along the Canadian and Mexican borders. He had his own Patrols run by his demons bringing home a hundred a month. Samuel demanded that they all be women and all virgins. Samuel gave Valentine one sacrifice a month but promised him all he wanted was he to catch or kill Mia.

Mia was elusive and there are those that claim that she can make herself invisible. However, she did it. It was an advantage against hundreds of disadvantages.

Each time that Valentine made a sacrifice, he laughed madly despising the human species. There was no way to compete with future Xeno people under his rule.

Leven stroked Tammy's long blond hair as they cuddled in bed after making love. In their own mind, there was wonderment in how the world had changed within a matter of only a few years. Often they shared their thoughts with each other and both agreed on one fact.

Both lovers were atheist and did not believe in gods, as they did not the devil. They were slaves to the Xeno Games and now they were soon to be fugitives from both Factions. Those for Xeno Technology and those standing in the way of it were both against the desperado lovers.

Oppositions against the Xeno Project were losing the war but winning countless battles. Soon with organization and co-operation, the resistance would strengthen and win? All they had to do was escape from the Casa Linda Motel and the traitorous operators of the Motel.

———————————————

Taking into consideration that the one thing that the two gladiators loved more then each other was the Xeno Games and the Super Xeno Games, they were inseparable. Leven was not using his head and was acting illogically but if you consider that, the duo seemed trapped into a corner what else was there for Leven to do?

Among the circle of Xeno Stars within the Games, there was only hatred for the two Xeno Stars that had shamed the Xeno Games by breaking the Rules of Honor. These super beings had a raffle going on the date the doctor, would be captured.

This incident had been in the News ever since the Fugitives have been on the run. Bad Publicity for the Investors of the Xeno Project was affecting their donations. What made it worse was that the militant Xeno Opposition Militias were increasing attacks on arenas and Office Buildings.

Crime ran rampant through the streets throughout the Country and new Law Enforcement organizations were born. Wire taps and satellite video tracking imposed on every citizen in the U.S. Invading what privacy they had left remaining. This riled the people and large protests were being organized everywhere that was recruiting new supporters in record numbers. Local Militias been commissioned to act as local Police Forces because the wars had depleted U.S. work force.

Leven and Tammy are victims of a changing world during the beginning stages of the Xeno Age. Greed was the evil miscreant, which created Xeno Industries and fuels and the fires that run the Xeno Transplants and pharmaceuticals companies and Research Facilities. Thought the Rein of the human species in the history of our planet greed was the downfall of every Empire.

Xeno Corporations had hired small armies to protect their interests and they were veteran skilled killers. Human youth that rebelled against the Xeno Age, and they were killed off in the wars since the draft had been restated into law.

Dr. Keller had secretly offered the Xeno Stars a reward of ten-million dollars for Leven and Tammy. Dr. Keller told the Xeno Stars *"Dead or Alive"*

Drugs made from animal DNA had been processed with anti rejection formulas so that our bodies do not reject them. People were receiving Xeno treatments without their knowledge and side effects from these treatments did not appear for years. Slowly with time people were complaining about skin problems, abnormal hair growths among many other side-effects. This mass conspiracy was orchestrated by huge corporations working with several Governments to fool the world into believing that it was all for the good of humanity.

Those persons that voiced their opinions were insane. Xeno Project Executives did not expose themselves to the public in fear of assassination. These same CEO's also employed as Lobbyists hired to influence

Government figures in Washington DC. That these CEOs had made many friends in Politics, opponents of the Xeno Project were getting irritated; Anti-Xeno Forces openly blackballed in society and most were limited with their finances. For now, it seemed that the rich got richer and the poor stayed poor. Capitalism had reached its peak and the wealthy pushed new laws that prevented people to become new millionaires. Opposition was gaining ground as their freedoms vanished one at a time.

The End Chapter Three
"XENO OPPOSITION"

Chapter Four
"<u>Xeno Demonstrations</u>"
June 2015

Nobody escapes the Xeno Games and Leven knew, that they were hunted by assassins. At least at the Xeno Foundation they were safe and out of harms way.

Yet they had escaped the watchful eyes of the Korean owners of the Motel and now were planning their next move. They were hiding out in a beach house in Carmel. It was empty because the owners were in the Army and happened to be stationed overseas. Before Leven escaped, he scouted out the Koreans running the Casa Linda. He found that the husband was a communist sympathizer and hostile toward Americans.

Leven and Tammy were playing around and chasing each other into the water when they almost run into another Couple. The tall youth offered out his hand in friendship and asked Leven. *"Hey there, you folks need some shelter or anything?"*

"No, we are fine, thanks for the offer." Tammy said.

A short skinny redhead then said. *"We thought that you were here for the Demonstrations going on in Salinas in the morning?"*

Tammy was getting interested and asked . . . *"What are these demonstrations about and why are you here in Carmel when you should be in Salinas?"*

Unexpected as it was, new information was making its way to the two fugitives.

"My name is Mary Miller and this is my boyfriend Vinnie Carlosi. We are here, because we want to be out of the light. We plan to Protest the Pak-motel-Alliance. They are here sending reports and information about us to terrorist factions. They are

laundering money through drugs and Motels as they build their arsenals. Ready and willing to die for our Cause, we want it to be a big surprise."

"I am sure that you will be but don't you think that it's a bit extreme?" 'Tammy Replied.'

"Perhaps they have an underground network or well-hidden Cells we can go to contemplate our next moves?" (As he readied his reply, Leven thought to himself..) *"I would not mind learning more about it, this movement sounds worthwhile so if you have a place we can check you out. Then perhaps we will go there and see for ourselves."*

They learned of a Compound almost resembling a Commune, if it were not for the towers and fortifications. It sounded like the perfect place to continue his training for the Xeno Games. Leven was intent on winning the games and crowned Champion.

Once Champion of the Xeno Games the Victor has two legions of the Army and fifty-thousand acres as his bounty along with five-million dollars and three Stealth Fighters armed with laser spays. Leven wanted to be Champion and he wanted it at any cost of lives. He and Tammy were inseparable and they had not opened their bag of tricks yet.

"These damn new world hippies are making a big deal out of nothing!" 'Doctor Keller and Lisa were dug in deep at the Golden Eagle in San Francisco. 'Dennis was missed,' his shiftiness, cunning, and con artistry had made the place what it was. Doctor Keller was watching the News on the big screen in the den when he saw the chaotic mess going on in Salinas California.

There were always celebrations and parades on Broadway Street. During the night, there was mayhem and death. Broadway Street was a little part of every part in the world. Chinatown, raided, vanquished by the wealthy owners of the strip clubs, owned by hostile Nations to the U.S.A. It was a bad summer for Chinatown but the new U.N. Xeno companies had monopolized the streets with their third world allies.

Out of Country Contractors were terrorist and others of the sort. It became global known that San Francisco was the Second City for Terrorists. All of the vice, drugs, and money cloaked but in plain sight.

Amateurs who were trying to correct Xeno deformities were performing rude surgeries. Our Garden of Eden had turned into a dump for Horror.

Demonstrators from all over the world were comparing San Francisco to the greatest city of sin. Leaders of demonstrators kidnapped and assassinated. It was keeping the Cause off balance. Some Demonstrations were making a difference in most parts of the world. Here in America it seemed to be more of an aggravation then a Cause.

Peter was scared, and he could feel it to his bones. God had appeared to Peter and made him understand. Now Peter was driving to Salinas to meet his Contacts. It happened while Peter was walking to his car. God was not transparent but hovering over the grass. He was in the form of the Holy Spirit and that was more than enough to convince Peter that a higher power existed.

Peter saw the deer too late as he was rounding a curve to avoid hitting a Buck. It was mating season and deer were all over the roads. 'Highway 101 was no different.' Turning the car away from the deer, Peter slammed the brakes on. At that moment, Peter said under his breath, "Rene, that arrogant bitch."

Lucas Bailey was tailing Peter stopping to help the Stranded motorist. Peter had no clue that this big man was but he seemed friendly enough to approach. Lucas asked Peter his name and Peter told the tall stranger his name.

"Can I be of any help?" 'The Stranger was smiling exposing his large white teeth.' *"Seems to me,"* said the stranger with an Australian accent.' *"That you hit yourself a good sized Buck, don't mind if I take it home and butcher it, here sir. Can you please give me a hand?"*

Peter stared up at the giant and said *"sure."*

It was the biggest mistake that Peter had ever made, as soon as Peter had gotten within reach, the almost ten feet tall giant snatched Peter up as easily as a sack of potatoes. Then Peter, locked into the trunk of the stranger's car.

Xeno Game Officials had decided to kidnap Peter and use him to get Leven and Tammy returned to them.

Little did they know that the Fugitives were on the run again? Peter was in dire straights.

Jessica was glad that the Supreme Court overturned Roe vs. Wade when she had gotten the news that Peter been kidnapped. Jessica cried about this unfortunate event but knew that Peter would be safe. Jessica knew that God had given Peter a difficult choice under extreme conditions. What Peter decided would either make him a Disciple or send him to hell.

Jessica had gathered an army of over two-million persons. These mostly affiliated with State Militias and Police Departments. It had not taken long for the smaller Police Departments to join in with their children's Militias.

Jessica knew that God protected his Army,, now she had to recruit the non-Xeno population to move into one area, perhaps populate a State.

Jessica was alone except for her God. She envisioned the boy child being born and being Christ. Jessica was preparing the way, ensuring a grand reception and a swift ending to the pain violating His people. Peter was in trouble and if Jessica wanted then she could have saved Peter. She decided that Peter had his own mind and needed time to work things out for himself.

There were Prayer Rooms the size of conference rooms that were equipped with all State of the Art teaching screens and computers. Jessica kept beautiful underground gardens run by powerful lights and the underground river. Jessica loved the caves beneath the waterfalls and spent much time praying there. The water believed to keep a person young for as long as they drink from it.

Jessica's eyes captivated you, her demeanor was inviting, and love filled. Jessica had animals housed everywhere and an underground pasture. Only she knew what made the lights operate and where most of the funding came from.

Jessica claimed that the Funding came from God and that as long as we kept fighting. He would always provide us our bread and water along with whatever we needed to win the fight. Jessica was beautiful and mostly wore pastel colored summer dresses. She claimed that the Funding would never run out as her beauty radiated love.

There was one wing of the last level in her underground Compound, which was a modern dungeon. It was in there that Jessica planned to hold Xenomittes. Xenomittes were persons cut human and animal into one. Once a family genetic pool is contaminated one time, it would be highly likely that the family tree in time would die.

Legal Demonstrations were one way of getting the message through, it was the best way.

It was Paradise in Eden in the underground Foundation. Certainly, the safest part of the world to be inside was the Foundation Walls. Walls protected by a lightning field produced from nuclear reactors. Jessica drew the original plans and definitions to build these towers that generated streams of lightning bolts. To the naked eyes they seemed alive, lightening bolts dancing around and overhead the Foundation ceiling behind the clear tempered crystallized glass plated with laminated lasers. These creations credited to the scientists that had defected to the Jessica Foundation research laboratories. Certainly, the accomplishments accredited to Jessica are a wonder by itself knowing that she was only born a few years ago. Jessica created a haven in a place called Earth that was hell to live on.

Campus Demonstration at Texas University

Tens of thousands of students from all over our Nation were storming the University and easily overwhelming the Campus Police. The campus areas filled with Texan Student Body Leaders running the show. They were sick and tired of being forced to attend Xeno Propaganda classes and protesting the year's ongoing war with Pakistan. These students were wearing armor and bulletproof vests. Jessica had seen to it. That they were well armed and well led wearing gas masks. New protesters were against the war because college students were not completely exempt from the Draft.

Pentagon Officials were confused at the sudden extreme Activism happening in Texas. It seemed that for the present the students had won. Federal and State Authorities were standing down because of Orders from Washington, D.C.

This was only a temporary loss to Xeno enthusiasts. Not worth the trouble to bother with, the

President declared the University shut down and a Police Action booked to occur in the future. For now, the war on Terrorism was spreading and there was more to worry about then a bunch of drunken students.

At the University, most of the students were getting drunk and being armed. Stocked with enough food to last a year but their Quarters were cramped and small.

Jason Master was the University Student President that sent out three well-armed Patrols to recon the streets around the University. They reported that the streets were all deserted and that they were all alone.

Radio communication was going on and a Radio Station was running. All Universities around the Country closed for the next month and occupied by the National Guard. Few holdouts and those that were behind Xeno Funding, they stayed open.

Most of the holdouts were Ivy League schools. One thing about College students is that you can count on and that is that they tend to change Causes if one seems more worthy to fight about or popularity.

For the time being, the school was safe from harms way. Put on a shelf for now and deemed not a threat. Before long, everybody's focus will be on the Xeno Games.

In a hidden Cove deep in the mountains of Idaho a piece of the Snake River streamed past the huge fortified cabin. In the cabin were twelve Apostles and their Servants.

Indeed, the Devil had been cunning and persistent. He had devised a way to send most of the souls in the world straight to Hell. Whether they went to church, or were men and women of Holy lines. They were going to hell. One might ask who had done this.

It all has to do with the Promise of animals to

human transplanting using anti rejection drugs. Once a Christian believed that this was good, at that moment he was damned.

True Patriots of God assembled at the Temple of a secret Town named Adam. They lay downhill and out of sight behind the main cabin.

Several hundred persons, men, women, and children occupied Adam. They were some of the true believers, and more were on the way. Adam is secluded and has no electricity. They burn lanterns and use candlelight. It is a Holy city and only those assured a seat in heaven can find it. Jessica knew of Adam but told no one at all.

This army of Christians had one job to do and they did it joyfully. It was to petition the Lord with Love praising through Psalms and applauds.

These souls had not come to this town on their own, they were placed there by God. One day another person arrives and the crowd cheers as they Praise the Lord. Happy and content, these people never thought about their pasts.

There was News that the Koreans had declared war upon America and had launched nuclear weapons at New York and Washington, D.C. For now, they were only rumors but the Adam Congregation prayed for the souls of those   about to die. Every day more people arrived as the invisible town grew.

It was a sad State of Affairs and hope was diminishing among the true human species as the Xeno population grew. Hell was celebrating by exacting pain on each other's terrible souls. They were dancing in their own blood as Lucifer smiled painfully through grimaced teeth.

Lucifer cursed Valentine as his own brain boiled. He had given specific instructions to cast the skull into hell. It would rule over the billions of skulls piled high in the hollow core of hells fire. Hell is a bottomless pit so Lucifer had a dam built from pelvic bones and shoulder blades. It is a gruesome area of hell littered with the forever dying, begging for death. Lucifer promised them God's soul and seats in Heaven after the invasion. Lucifer cursed Samuel for ruining his plans for glory.

Jessica was distraught over Peter's abduction. She knew that he was safe as long as he accepted God into his life but Jessica had her doubts about Peter. He was analytical and cynical, proud and perfect Peter. Peter the pawn was on her mind when Jessica centered her thoughts on Leven and Tammy's whereabouts. She knew that Peter would be under enormous pressure to give away information. Every trick in the book would be used to extract this information and eventually if that did not do it. There were torture and drugs. This was Peter's test to pass.

Jessica had seen the Gladiator Lucas murder six opponents in twenty seconds time at the Xeno Games last year. Learning it was Lucas that kidnapped Peter Jessica knew that current affairs were going to get wacky. Lucas was going to be difficult to win over. However, with Leven and Tammy working this case, it was possible to win Lucas over to the Foundation, God Willing.

Jessica was involved in the world and active with helping the unfortunate. She was as ruthless as she was beautiful, she is a gift to humankind, a prodigy, another Saint, and she was the only hope for the masses not affected by the Xeno project. Jessica was not all-powerful but truly pure of heart and Blessed by the Lord.

Samuel, on the other hand, kept in seclusion. He had created his own world in a shell and was acting like a child. Valentine was out searching for his prey. His Legions were out recruiting Followers using all means at their disposal and they had high dispositions.

It was pure pleasure for Samuel to see others in pain. At times, he thought that he could feel it but then he would write it off as his imagination. Well disciplined in Martial Arts and a natural boxer, Samuel lived his life out of control. Nobody around him was safe from his games or sudden rages that always ended in death. Samuel is a lethal jokester with a wicked sense of humor.

Leven and Tammy were having the times of their lives at parties celebrating small but devastating victories against Terrorists and the Xeno Project, all fun for now combat later said one drunk patron at a party. Tammy was quite tipsy and Leven was drinking straight whiskey-bourbon. It was a well needed vacation for the two Gladiators but it was not all fun and games . . .

Several attempts were made on their lives once resulting in a shoulder wound on of the cult guards. Once while sparring in the cult gym a sniper hit a young woman who was an armed Rebel. Leven had a hard time deciding whether these cells of armed twenty-year-old were a cult or a movement. Once the Super Xeno Games grew near then Tammy and Leven would begin to get focused on their skills. Having an exhausting day the two lovers were intent on taking advantage of their time together apart from the prying Xeno spies and electronic bugs.

The End   Chapter Four

"Xeno Demonstrations"

Chapter Five
"Xeno Assassins"

Morris was upset about driving Lucas around. There were assassins out to murder Xeno Stars, a price on their heads and a hunter Trophy to show off. Humans rarely allowed participating in the Xeno Games so the wealthy Elite created their own games.

Assassins were always on the hunt for the Xeno Stars with a Bounty on them of fifty-million dollars. Rarely have they ever collected but they had a couple of times maimed a Xeno Star.

There was one man named Lance M. Spearhead. Nobody knew what his name truly was. Lance was the man behind the two successful hits where two Xeno Stars died. Lance was not a big man but quite the opposite. He was only five feet three in height but well muscled. His target with a price tag of a million dollars was Lucas and Peter.

Lance was too small to play in the games and was not great to look at. He was small but deadly with the cunning of a fox.

Lance waited at the home of Lucas deep in the desert near nowhere Nevada. He was prepared to kill Lucas and kidnap Peter for Dr. Keller. Dr. Keller wanted to dissect Peter, and eventually he wanted to do the same with Jessica. Only Jessica was a tough fish to catch and more elusive than a ray of sunlight on a cold winters night.

Peter was petrified. He had never been in this situation before. Nothing that he could do locked inside a car trunk. Peter was afraid of what was happening to him. There was nothing to do about his dilemma. Lucas opened the trunk, and with one hand lifted Peter out of the truck and threw him toward the Traitor.

Peter was bleeding from the burns of sliding on the hard desert ground. A couple of bushes torn as Peter's body slid over them. Then he abruptly stopped by the steps to the trailer.

Peter was sore all over and scared to death. His plight had just begun; Lance was lurking around the corner waiting for his chance. This time he had a Police riot shotgun and a couple of grenades.

Lucas walked up to the trailer and unlocked the door. When he turned around, Lance Murder Spearhead faced him. Spearhead was holding the shotgun in his hands and began firing until all the Shells were gone. Lucas lay in a pool of blood dead as a doornail.

Lance was proud to know that he had the first Xeno Star Kill in history. It was a great bounty plus another million dollars, if Peter given to Dr. Keller in San Francisco.

First he had to take Peter to the El Dorado Motel on N. Main Street in Salinas was alias Kevin, the Manager of the Motel. Accommodations made by Nick for Lance to take Peter there to hide out for a few days before bringing Peter to San Francisco.

Kevin is a blatant liar and a thief. He was also part of a Terrorist Cell and owned Military transmitters and Receivers to communicate with his Islamic patriots in Pakistan. Kevin also was a kidnaper and a murderer.

Kevin was elated about Peter's capture and thanked Lance as he handed over a suitcase with two-million dollars inside of the briefcase.

"Thank you Lance for bringing to us this criminal, of Islam, we will deliver him to Dr. Keller in San Francisco and you can go on your way, Sir."

Lance walked three blocks to his laser-powered car and sat behind the wheel. Before Lance had the chance to generate the lasers for power the vehicle quietly from the inside out burst into flames. Lance fried as he screamed in agony with no way out of the car.

Peter was up a creek without a paddle. They was rushed Peter into room 26. Room 26 was out of view from the road and secluded from the outside world.

Peter was in a stripped room. It was haunting and desolate. There was a toilet, a mat on the floor without blankets or a pillow, what made Peter angry was that there were steel bars on the windows. Confused and not knowing where he was, Peter searched for a way out and found none.

This event made the Front Page News all over the world. Lance was in Brazil when he saw the Headlines and grinned with satisfaction. There was no mention of Peter.

Evidently, there was no mention of Peter because he was never reported missing. Jessica was going to find Peter her own way.

With the world in shock over the assassination and the Xeno Games coming on December 25th, Lucas was going to be missed by his fans. A Global search of his Killer began and after a few weeks. Leads followed but they led to dead ends. Lance knew that he was hiding out in the jungles of central Brazil. He was in with a Cartel and was a Cartel leader's personal Assassin.

Mia took a shining to a straight razor and used it to murder one Xeno Official after another. She was elusive and swift in her ventures. Now he received a message from Jessica to find and bring Leven and Tammy back to the Foundation Compound. Mia was after a scientist named Henry Miller working in a Research Center, near Oxford University.

Those made Mia contemplate quite a distance to travel with her mission not completed yet. It was hard to get Henry because he was an important man. Henry Miller was close to developing the final anti rejection formula that would allow any animal to human transplants and revolutionize the Xeno Age.

Mia knew that she had to rid the world of Miller before she departed for the States. Henry Miller was the biggest threat to the human species. Tales told in the pubs that Dr. Miller had cages of people and animals in his Lab. Many severely mutated and deformed, in ways that make the elephant man appear attractive. Mia decided to crawl through the heating vents and cut the good Doctors throat before breaking his neck. Then Mia planned to release all the Test Subjects out of their cages. This would cause confusion that would allow Mia a simple escape.

Mia slid out of the vent over Henry's bed and with three deep cutting strokes cut his throat. Then Mia turned the man over and with a palm slam broke his neck. Without losing a beat, Mia set all the files on fire with two gallons of lighter fluid before entering the lab. Searching the lab Mia found the master switches for the cages and released all the experimental Test Subjects.

Mia ran down the corridor dripping blood all the way to the exit. Fortunately, the Security teams were searching the Institute for the intruder and trying to douse a raging fire. Mia made good her escape and running fast headed toward the Harbor.

August 2, 2015

Times are moving fast and so were the Terrorists. N.A.T.O disbanded, as Nations were disappointed about U.S. Policies on animal to human organ transplants. Secretly, they had created a small Army of Xeno Super Soldiers and it did not go over well with some Nations. Times were hard, with the Xeno Project spearheaded by America. America had become the strongest and wealthiest Nation in the world because of the profits and kickbacks of America's deep roots inside the Xeno Project.

United States had sent this moderate Army to hunt down the Terrorist Leaders. Bin was worried for the first time in ten decades, about his Movements and his own life. France was selling Terrorist weapons to terrorist Factions that vowed to attack Xeno targets. It was chaotic.

United States was unintentionally becoming a threat to all Nations because of this wealth and several military breakthroughs in the largest military force in the world.

Perhaps the war on terrorism was only an excuse to become all mighty. Life was good in the United States for its citizens and there were homeless in the streets. This makes one wonder if they were now in cages like the stray dogs and cats collected or stolen.

During an emergency State of the Union Address, our President was trying to convince the American people to invade Mexico. Canada was behind the U.S. as was England and Germany. They created their own alliance called the Fearsome Foursome. United States had fortified Canada and gave it nuclear arms and two American Marine Divisions to train a new Army for Canada. Fearsome Foursome Policies controlled this whole ordeal.

Bin and his band of Terrorists were trying to gather their Forces world over for the first strike. Heretofore, the Xeno Armies were fearlessly hunting down the terrorists. They were not fully active yet so Bin was able to elude them. Bin had to think of something fast because his time was running out.

Greed was second only to eternal life. Christian's everywhere were giving in to the sure thing called the Xeno Youth Eternal Potion. It created a genetic change that made you grow younger and stop aging at twenty years. Of course it was expensive and involved costly therapies.

Perhaps the Powerful had it all figured out. Eventually the Xeno Project would make the poor go extinct and the Xeno Age would rule the world with the rich and powerful at the helm.

One can think of many reasons why the world is embracing the extinction of their own species. God is a promise, a historical fact or fiction. However, the Xeno success assures us all to be gods. The human masses and Xenomitte populations regulated by the ruling select few.

Today, assassins were around every corner and bystanders were negligible. Media stations were neutral but went with their statistic and promoted Xeno advances. Today the Xeno movement was still in the balance. If it is to be defeated then God has to raise an army. Man learned long ago how to become beast and man. God destroyed them and banished the creators of these beasts. Now God looks down on us and frowns. We have brought back what God has banished forever. If you believe in God then you find your salvation there along with eternal life. According to eyewitnesses and News Headlines, Xeno Project Works offered the same thing.

Assassins hired to hunt assassins and Officials from both sides of the field were feeling their losses.

Leven and Tammy were kicking it at a safe house. They decided to emerge from their hiding for the Xeno games and not before.

Leven was training with some of the militants in the Organization and learned about them. They were stout fighters and heavy drinkers. Some of the Demonstrators, because of the attitude among many, used drugs. Many thought that they were fighting a losing battle and that in the end they would suffer defeat. It was obvious that they were anarchists at heart. God was not in their Cause, but self-rule was. They wanted to segregate humans and Xeno People into separate States, or Countries.

Leven was in South L.A. and the house seemed huge. Occupied and guarded inside and out was. These people knew who Leven and Tammy were and planned to keep them. Mia was watching the house too and biding her time. She was in a tree across the street.

Tammy picked up the Bible for the first time in her life. It was in one of the drawers in their room. She began reading a page that she picked out randomly.

"And if a man lies with a beast, he shall surely be put to death: and ye shall slay the beast."

"Neither shall thou lie with any beast to defile thyself therewith: neither shall any woman stand before a beast to lie down thereto: it is confusion."

"All flesh is not the same flesh: but there is one kind of flesh of man, another flesh of beasts, another for fishes, and another of birds."

Tammy was glad that she and Leven had never had Xeno operations nor have they ever used Xeno supplements. They never believed that Xeno teams were better in combat than human teams. Thus far Leven and Tammy won all the Xeno contests they participated in and they used no Xeno supplements. Steroids were a part of the past now. Xeno therapy was legal and much more effective. Tammy once wrestled professionally and Leven still remembered his glory days playing Football.

This year all bets were on the Xeno man. At all the contests that the Xeno man has entered, he slowly tortured each opponent to death. Ruthless and enjoying every second of his kill the Xeno man seemed invincible. Leven wanted to challenge the Xeno man with Tammy on his team. Odds were 1000 to 1 that the Xeno man would snag the victory.

Southern California this time of the year was

usually hot and dry. Tonight, lightning and thunder rocked the city and it was wonderful to watch. Blue and white streaks colored the black skies as Mia moved along the hedges of the house. Mia had to slit the throats of two lookouts so far and it was not over. Strangely, it had not rained yet and Mia knew by her animal instincts that it was going to pour. She knew that soon drops of rain the size of large hail. Mia was not going to be surprised if hail did slam the Earth.

There were two men at each entrance into the house. There were no casement windows along the foundation of the house. Then Mia searched for another way into the basement but there were none to be found. There was only one way to enter the house and that was through the back door.

This created a problem because of the two guards. They were dressed in grey suits and carrying submachine guns. Mia had one advantage. There was neither patio nor eave over the men so when it started to pour. They would get soaked. It was at that moment that Mia opted to rush the guards; she was near them in the tall hedges that surrounded the building.

"You got a smoke on you Jake; I seem to have forgotten mine inside?" 'The taller of the two men was slipping into a raincoat and opened an umbrella. It was not raining yet but the sky smelled like rain. He was the one asking for a smoke.

"Why don't you go get your smokes and get me a beer? I will hold the Fort while you're gone." His umbrella opened as his backup unlocked the door and walked inside the house. Mia noticed that the man never locked the door behind him. Mia was praying for rain.

Hail fell from the sky with the rain and they were the size of golf balls. Within a few seconds, the umbrella collapsed on the man's head. Mia swiftly ran and then jumped on the man's back sending them both into the ground. In that moment, Mia deeply cut the guard's throat.

Quickly lapping up some blood Mia jumped beside the door and waited for the smokes and a cold beer. Mia inspired by God but knew that she would never go to heaven. Mia honored to serve Almighty God knowing that she would always remain a beast in His eyes. Mia felt shame for the first time.

Mia waited for the other guard to open the door and step out. Somehow, Mia was getting closer to Leven and Tammy. Thinking about the best way to handle the ordeal once she got to the Xeno Stars, Mia had something up her sleeve and they were knockout darts. That was a last resort for Mia; she rather would have them help her escape. Every room was in use so silence was crucial.

Mia slit the man's wrists with an uppercut to the throat. It was an accidental wrist slice but brought a smile to Mia's lips.

Hastily, Mia had broken the man's neck just for the certainty that he was dead. Mia darted into the house and confronted by a house cleaner, with one swift stroke as Mia cut open her heart she hit the floor hard.

Mia exploited by Jessica to fight fire with fire. Eventually both would snuff each other and then the Righteous will rule the Earth with Jesus sitting on the Throne. This was Jessica's secret to success.

Dr. Keller never revealed his true formula's to anybody. Mia was the only true prototype that survived at the Lupus Estate. His secret formulas buried deep in the Dr.'s brain. Everybody believed Mia to be dead, only Jessica knew better.

Jessica walked into the Private Worship Chamber on the Compound. There was an altar made of titanium, platinum, gold and silver that seemed to glow. On the cross there were twelve diamonds and four rubies that formed a cross within the cross. Golden cross, embedded into the front of the altar and the stones had no settings. All the stones seemed to be set with nothing holding them in place.

Behind the Altar was a natural pool filled with clear warm water. Jessica knelt before the Altar and Prayed to God for answers. From the Baptismal Pool a mist began to form into a glistening spiral ball.

Jessica stood in wonder, staring at the Holy Spirit. She felt calm and at peace, her mind was limber and her heart ached with love for man and woman alike. She praised God and humbled herself before Him. No windows and no way that it could happen, bright sunlight illuminated the Chamber and singing tropical birds appeared. One landed on Jessica's shoulder and whispered into her ear.

This event was another private time for Jessica. She emerged from the Worship Chamber joyful and praising the Lord. She issued Orders as if she was an Army General and sent her aids to pass them onto her Commanders. 'Jessica Declared.' *"We are waging a war of wars today!"* Then she loudly proclaimed. *"All the Glory goes to God."*

Samuel had his angels from heaven. One third of Heaven banished into hell. There was no complete victory for God but a war that has never ended since that time long ago.

Now the war has come to us and they are part human and part animals plotting to have their own way with the human race. Could a third of Heaven control an overpopulation of Xenomittes? In the end, it would come out in the wash.

Samuel controlled all the great Leaders of our Nations but had no control over the terrorists or true Christians. He planned to change this fact by introducing a new sin into the world. This sin was everlasting life through Xeno supplements. These entities were beyond lawlessness, beyond control, new types of creatures invented in the Laboratory and born throughout the world. Samuel called them his Future Legions of demons. These Xeno souls belonged to Hell, the Xeno Species is the anti species to the human species, Ruled by the Denizens of demons cast into hell.

Samuel knew that it would take a few years but that eventually he would rule the Earth and the Heavens. Jessica had made other plans. In his own mind, Samuel feared God, but dismissed the threat with arrogance and vindictiveness.

Samuel had all the time in the world to carry out his dastard deeds. Before his birth, he stood over Bagdad and watched modern chariots storm the Palace and how glorious the stench of death was as that filled his nostrils. Samuel watched his father enter battles to fight angels protecting Allied troops.

If you try chasing two deer at once then you will lose them both. Any Hunter will tell you that animal instincts are far more sensitive than human instinct. A scientist can isolate genes, which tie together into formulas to inject into humans. Agenda's are costly on these Projects so each Project is specifically for persons that could afford to pay billions of dollars for creating the serums. That is why Xeno funding was not available to the Public. Funding kept secret, assassins assured that if both were legitimate they would seek out and assassinate their Project Administrators.

Leven saw Mia first but it was too late. Mia had handcuffed Tammy's right arm to his waist and hoisted her over his shoulder. Then Mia flashed her razor still dripping of blood.

'Mia announced.' ***"Miss Jessica tells me to bring you two to the Foundation. She says that you will help me*** *run away if I go with you. Those men out there will not let you leave, do you realize that?"*

In a matter of hours, the three assassins arrived at the Jessica Foundation. Jessica was glad to see them and wasted no time in sending them after Peter.

The End of Chapter Five
"Xeno Assassins"

Chapter six
"Xeno Rights"

John and Sherrie were waiting for the results of the organ transplant tests. Their son had an enlarged liver and needed an organ transplant.

Little John Masters had a rare disease. Thus far, the Hospital had not located a matching donor organ for Little John. Little John was his nickname because of his diminutive size. TNT comes in small packages and up to a few weeks ago, John was healthy, he was active and happy.

Now he was dying and his parents had a difficult choice to make. They had to decide to get their son on a recipient list for a Xeno donation.

Both parents knew that the transplant was at a high cost. They did not have money. They decided to put him on the list and think about while the Specialists were searching for the organ.

John was a devout Baptist and refused to think about putting an animal liver into his son. Sherrie was passionate and caring toward John Sr., but she insisted on the transplant. This causes conflict between them, with Sherrie working a guilt trip.

They were enjoying a nice warm day as they paced the waiting room. Little John was on a Gurney with an IV going into his arm. They were running out of time because an animal donor, a creature created by Doctor Keller was on its way to the hospital on a helicopter in a couple hours.

Secret Service Agents inside of a brightly lit locked office surrounded two surgeons and a man wearing a black cloak. They were discussing the Masters' case.

Dr. Keller flying into Washington, D.C. from San Francisco, California, we will use this boy as the first in history to receive Dual Xeno Transplants. We are combing the livers of two animals for this transplant. Dr. Keller is bringing his new anti rejection drugs with him for this surgery. I hope that you get what you want out of this, Mr. Black."

Mr. Black was a secret courier for a Committee created in Congress; they wanted this boy shaped into a super human killer. A target designated by this Committee and XTF now doing these duties, Mr. Black was glad that the Committee was on top of things to now. For the present time, he was content with the professionals he had on his Staff.

In the room next to them was the waiting room. A two-way mirror allowed the men to observe the Masters as they argued over signing the papers allowing the Transplant to proceed. Mr. Black whispering something into the ear of a Secret Service Agent and soon thereafter the man exited the room.

Dr. Keller was due to arrive in one hour, that's how long Johnny had before he was expended. Inside the Private room, the surgeons were boasting about the Xeno Project. They were impressed that this married Couple had traveled all the way from Seattle to try and save their son's life.

"Do you remember saying that you will do anything to save our son's life?" Sherrie was pressing her husband for an answer.

"Dear, I love you and Little John with all of my heart. I will do anything for you; I wish that I could trade my life for our son's life. I cannot see a liver taken from a baboon or a pig to save our son from certain death. Our son will have to live the rest of his life knowing that he

*is part animal. Imagine the changes that he will go
through taking anti rejection drugs. Do you have any idea
what our son will think, and how much he will suffer? Do
you understand that he will grow up in a Research
Facility without our love and guidance?"*

"Have you thought of our son at all Johnny?" It
seems that they were en passé and beginning to argue.

This continued for several more minutes before
Sherrie ran into an elevator and went to see her son.

John Sr. was still wearing the same suit for three
days. He was tired and needed to splash some water on his
face. Watching his wife leaving the room, John turned and
walked down the hallway to the Men's Room.

Completely sterile and sparkling rest rooms smelled
fresh. Federal Hospitals were the cleanest in the world.
John stared at himself in the mirror and thought about his
stand on the issues at hand.

Shining brass and silver ornaments adored the rest
room as John contemplated his decision not to allow the
Xeno transplant. John knew that his son was better off in
Heaven then he was suffering his whole life long.

John was an Agent too; he worked for the Central
Intelligence Agency, which was the reason why he knew of
this hospital and was able to enter through the double steel
doors.

"This whole scenario isn't right," thought John.
John bent over and with the cold running water he splashed
water on his face several times before he noticed the man
standing directly behind him. John noticed in the mirror
that the man had a briefcase in one hand and a pistol in the
other. *"What can I do for you?"* John Masters Asked.

*"Listen to me closely now because you are
running out of time. You sign the papers and you assure
us that the organ transplant be completed and for what is
in this suitcase? Or you die now!"* In the mirror John saw

the gold lining trim on the man's black suit and he that he was dealing with a Professional. He knew that the man was employed by the White house Staff.

"Hold it please; sure I will sign the papers for what's in the briefcase. I'm not stupid, and I like my job."

Then the man set the suitcase down between John's legs and exited the Men's Room. John had sold out his son.

John examined the briefcase and found at least a couple hundred thousand dollars wrapped in Treasury hemp bands. It was not what he wanted but John knew that now he had no Rights. He had given his oath to serve and protect, to be expendable.

John freshened himself up and instead of joining his wife. With a glance at his watch, John grabbed the briefcase and headed straight for the elevator that took him to his car. Once there, John placed the money into the trunk and quick-timed back to his son's hospital room.

Once inside the hospital John slowed down to catch his breath. Then he stopped before he entered his son's hospital room to gather his strengths. He had sold out his ideals and his genetic pool for a pocket full of cash. His son was worth two-hundred grand. John felt like vomiting as he entered the room and seen his son was awake. Sherrie was sitting on the bed next to Little John stroking the blond hair on his head.

"Hi son, I love you. They have found a transplant for you and we are going to sign the release for your operation." 'Reaching down John hugged his son and then kissed his wife.'

Sherrie radiant with joy and loved her man more then she ever had before. Smiling a doctor entered the room and proclaimed. *"The donor organ has arrived and the transplant will begin in two hours from now. We predict that your son will be fine after the surgery and a Mr. Keller is performing the operation. Doctor Keller is the best of the best and you can feel lucky that he, and his team will be overlooking the welfare of your son."*

"Thank you, and we do feel lucky, don't we Honey?" 'Sherrie was surprised at her husband's change of heart.'

"Why . . . more than you know my love, perhaps this is more of a lucky day then you know."

There were five Xeno Transplants a day at this Hospital. Everyone knew their jobs and 99% were from the V.A. Hospitals on special assignments. One-percent made all the Executive decisions for the Hospital while Government Funding was unlimited. Three extra wings constructed under high security and priority standards. This facility was a target for terrorists.

For those selected that did not sign, well . . . they were extracted from the program completely and permanently, Entrapment, bribery and unethical behavior.

Xeno Organization Agents were everywhere, great spies but sloppy assassins. Our Rights as the people of a great nation vanished, unless they were all rich. All controlled by a special group of CEO's and Regulators.

Poor people were now the middle classes that were located in rural areas. In these parts, the Movement had formed strong Militia's against the Xeno Project and had plenty of hiding places. Underground secret tunnels ran beneath the surface with huge chambers. Jessica's Command was digging in for a long struggle and hopefully an overwhelming victory.

"The Right to Choose" was old news. There was no need for abortions by law, because an unwanted fetus belonged by the Xeno Foundation.

The Xeno Foundation owned through patents 40% of all human DNA. Republicans have stayed in the Oval Office since the war on Terrorism began. After all, it is the Xeno Age now. Human brainstems went patented next.

Republicans have managed to sustain this Nation comfortably if one studied the statistics, and numbers. People were afraid that their Rights been compromised but life was good, and there was no reason to complain.

Xeno Rights Law passed through both Houses by only a slight margin. Yet, a win was a victory. These are the Xeno Amendments:

1. Xeno People carry the same Rights as the Human Species.

2. Discrimination against Xeno People is punishable with ten years imprisonment.

3. Accommodations for the special needs of Xeno People at all Public Places of Business and the Dept. of Natural Resources.

4. Social Services will provide for all the needs of Xeno People.

These four laws went ignored, not tolerated by the general population. Certainty in the cities these laws were enforced but in rural areas people kept to themselves to the point of being selective on whom moved into the area, into Town.

Schools were in conflict and sometimes ugly to each other. Segregation was widespread as the Xeno People matured faster then humans. There were not many in the world today, but at this rate, the Xeno Population was growing and before long out grows the human population.

Indeed, the Rich embraced the Xeno Movement but their teenage children opposed it. Our youth was more radical than ever. They were forming their own Militia's starting with paint guns and before long firing live rounds.

Peter trapped in the attic with shackled legs. It was a long attic provided with little headspace and a bed, toilet, sink with running water. There were areas in the attic that had pad locks on the doors of the cages. Within these locked steel meshed rooms were radios and other military stuff. Peter saw stacks of firearms including assault rifles. Peter knew that he was in trouble when the persons keeping him hostage could not speak English well, or not at all. They were smelly and chewed gobs of tobacco.

Peter began reading a recent newspaper that was in the garbage can. In it was an article about the new Chief Justice receiving a Xeno Heart Transplant? Worried about his own fate Peter pondered the fate of our Justice System.

Never doubting, Peter knew that Jessica would eventually rescue him.

Peter wished that it would be sooner than later. Then he remembered his attitude before Peter disappeared. Peter was a pure realist and had a hard time believing in God. Yet now he was on his knees praying to God for Faith while crying.

John and Sherrie were comforting each other for more than eight hours while the Transplant was taking place. John was aching inside for selling his son for a couple hundred grand. He was not sure that he would be able to live with it for the rest of his life. Sherrie was rubbing against John and thanking him for changing his mind.

It took 14 hours for the transplant and the loving couple had fallen asleep on a couch in each other's arms. John dreamed that no matter how much he would search or how fast he would run that he never saw his son again.

Inside O.R., the surgeons were tired and sweating profusely. They were impressed with Doctor Keller's skill with the scalpel and his instinctive techniques.

Doctor Keller was doing more than a transplant. He performed a necessary brain tissue transplant to make the new created liver function. Excruciating pain consumed the air with the fear of dying.

This was the surgery that was going to change the world. Dr. Keller had replaced the penal gland with one removed from the brain of an extremely intelligent chimpanzee.

Little John was given Xeno Growth hormones and new vaccines to combat all the side effects of the Xeno transformations. Hours after hours passed as the boy changed genetically into an unknown entity later to study. Studied and nurtured into what, it was anybody's guess.

After the final anti rejection drugs, injected in John. Masked men took him to the rooftop where a helicopter was waiting for them. Dr. Keller went along for the ride to an undesignated location.

"We would like to see our son now" 'John Masters was speaking with one of the Surgeons more than 24 hours after they began the Transplant. They were standing next to the water coolers next to the Social Office.' Sherrie continued their requests. *"Is it true that we will not see our son for days, Doctor Beltrami?"*

"I am afraid that it could be months before you will be able to enter the decontamination area and the sealed Oxygen Intensive Care Unit where your son now lies in a large incubator."

"If I were you I would return to Base or stay at the Embassy Hotel and we will call you as soon as there is something to report."

"Until then, rest assured that your son is doing fine and in your absence, is well-taken care of and given the best of everything."

It was good and bad news but not to John. To John Masters it was all bad news. He knew that new Orders on the way that were going to send him to hell somewhere and his wife would go with him to stay on base. She is a noted scientist and chemist who was useful anywhere.

"Thank you Doctor, and please don't mind that I call the hospital every day."

Time passed and every day Sherrie called the Hospital. Each time they had another excuse why she could not see her son so she asked if she could only speak with her son for a minute. They always said no, and that it would be months before they could communicate with their son.

Moods were changing in the married Couple's relationship. Sherrie was crying often and John was in a bad mood more often than not. John was leaving for India on Classified Orders. John was given a large raise and promoted and. He had no idea how to explain the money in the truck of the car. Certainly, he felt like hell about it and pondered what his dear wife was going to say about the money and where it came from. Indeed, John was always in a bad mood because he knew that they would never see their son again. This same thing was happening globally as the sky turned more hazed each new morning.

Humans were losing Rights as fast as Xenomittes were gaining them. In another ten years, the human species will be coming in second best, inferior, poverty stricken and degraded publicly. Desperate gangs terrorized neighborhoods. Today the Draft was re-instated.

"Honey, will you be okay with me gone for six months? Listen to me Sherrie. We seem to be at war with over half the world and you never know whose ticket gets punched next. Should I die then use this key at the bank to access a safe deposit box. In you will find tax-free monies given to me legally. Use these monies to sustain yourself and to see to your needs."

It was late at night and the rain knocked on the

Hotel picture window. John thought that when he had gotten his orders that his wife would be included in the move. Now that it never happened, John worried about his wife's health and welfare. John trusted no one.

"Where did the money come from, John?"

At first, John thought he could slip the money by his beloved wife, now he knew better to try again. Whether John should create a lie or tell the truth decided before he had time to think about it.

"(And at what price, Johnny, is it worth the sacrifice?)"

In a new retrospect, Johnny knew exactly how to handle his wife. He walked over to her and touched Sherrie's right hand, John had a gentle touch that felt warm to Sherrie. She buckled into John's arms and began to cry. *"How much had they given us for or son, Johnny?"*

"We have hope that one day our son will be returned to us . . . but it's slim."

Sherrie squeezed her husband harder then she ever had before and said. *"Well, it was this or his death, I suppose our son is better off where he is but I miss him so much that it breaks my heart."*

They made love and enjoyed the night, staying awake late into the night. It was the last time that they would ever see each other again.

The End of Chapter Six
"Xeno Rights"

Chapter Seven
"Jessica"

It was a Blessed day as Jessica walked through her flower garden circling a spring fed pond on her Foundation Estate.

At her favorite spot near the pond, Jessica sat in a lotus position on the soft lush grassy hill by a formation of roses. Deep in meditation, Jessica levitated over the knoll and concentrated on Peter.

On this beautiful afternoon, Jessica in a vision saw Peter in the roof of the El Dorado Motel. She saw a black widow crawling toward Peter and Jessica crushed it with a thought. Jessica could feel the scents of past sins and evil deeds that occurred in the long and roomy five feet high attic.

Obviously, there was no escape and Jessica heard a whisper that the compromised Police investigations seemed to be the standard. Peter stranded and Jessica had made plans to rescue her friend. These plans had taken Leven and Tammy acting as if they were drug dealers into the El Dorado Motel, in Salinas, California. They asked for room 16 because it was beneath the place that Peter was imprisoned. Jessica could see all of this as if she was there.

Mia sneaked into the room at around 2:00 a.m. and they made themselves comfortable. They had rented the room for a week. It was going to have to be crafty and at exactly the right moment to rescue Peter. That meant waiting it out.

Mia became friends with the Gladiators and learned a thing or two about the whereabouts of Dr. Keller from the loving Couple. Mia was happy go lucky in her mood once she learned that Doctor Keller was living in San Francisco and that there were underground tunnels.

Mia planned on going to San Francisco once Peter

was rescued and the two runaways were returned to the Foundation. Until then she was planning the rescue and evacuation of Peter.

Some claimed that Jessica was dreaming as she levitated over the roses and others thought that she was communicating with God.

Jessica could feel the deep hatred for Dr. Keller from Mia and it raised the hair on her arms. It was a frightening sensation. Jessica prayed for Dr. Keller and knew that there was no redemption waiting for Mia during the Second Coming of Christ.

Every so often Jessica would think of her brother and sigh in disgust. At the thought of him, Samuel sickened Jessica and she wished that Samuel would uncover the light, she knew that Samuel was bad to the bone. Jessica tried not to think of her brother. Certainly, there were times that she could not prevent it. Samuel was always up to no good and Jessica heard all about it. Gently setting herself down Jessica opened her eyes and soaked in the sunshine. She was the most pleasant person to be near and Jessica always had some wisdom to share with anyone willing to listen.

Jessica decided to go for a swim so she removed her bright summer dress and gotten naked. Then she jumped into the pond. Swimming around the pond doing laps, she played with the ducks that followed her.

Staying in the pond until dusk Jessica was free to do as she wished. There was a reason for her being here and that was to proclaim the Second Coming of Christ. It was a tranquil and peaceful night on the Estate grounds. Security was the people themselves in the Compound. Most of them were armed and everybody knew each other through a melding of their spirits. Jessica had good Security.

Jessica took the bun out of her long hair and it

covered her back. Watching herself in the mirror Jessica
brushed her hair while preparing to go to bed. In her
bedroom there was a King size bed covered in purple satin
sheets.

Essentially, since the day of her birth Jessica has
left herself in God's hands. She knew that the time had not
come yet for her Proclamation and that evil was only
beginning to get a foothold on our world. Powerful demons
that once were angels in Heaven were now sinking their
claws into the Earth. Jessica was powerless to destroy them
was given the Duty to delay them.

Her Faith was in the power of Will. Jessica has the
Will to use the power of Christ to always be one step ahead
of the Xeno Culture. For how much longer her power
would last was anybody's guess. Unless you had Faith,
then there was no reason to believe in losing this war
against Evil. Jessica donned her nightwear, and knelt by the
bed and prayed.

Late as it was, the Foundation Grounds were
buzzing with activity. There always was much to do and
maintain. Then there was the take in, these are secret late
night arrivals of CEO's.

Tonight a special convoy arrived with Mia, Leven,
Tammy, with Peter in tow. Jessica was going to have a
bright sunrise waiting for her in the morning.

While Jessica slept like a lamb, Mia and her new
friends plotted the capture of Dr. Keller and his Mistress.
They lived in the Guest Quarters and had all the comforts
of home. Mia knew the se was superior to the Xeno Stars
and had Dr. Keller to thank for it. Leven drank a case of ale
beer before he passed out beside his wife on the bed. Mia
climbed atop a large dresser drawer and slept.

Morning brought a thunderstorm. Gray skies
blocked out the sun and black clouds were moving in from
the horizon. Jessica always spent her mornings in the glass

bubble eating breakfast. She spent most of her time alone, and when she did come out of her shell, it was to set an Agenda and to spending the first four hours making decisions over current events and checking on the progress of her private missions.

Today was a special day because Mia was on the Foundation Grounds. Jessica knew that Mia was harmless to the cause but that Mia was a cold-blooded killer.

Mia asked Jessica if she could continue her services with the Cause. Jessica complimented Mia at her ability to speak and her mannerisms had improved. Jessica gave her instructions and stressed that she wanted Samuel caught and brought to her, alive. 'It was not in the cards.'

Jessica is above insult and her charm and demeanor leaves your jaws hanging. Her soft tan skin is like velvet and her face has the beauty of a thousand Queens. She radiates love and her words are direct and to the point. Jessica was presently what the anti Xeno movement needed, no matter what their religion is.

Jessica had given Mia and her Group their objectives and blessed them in the name of God. After giving their respects and some gifts the group went on their way and Jessica headed for the steam baths.

Someone, once said that if there were a Heaven, it would be as the Foundation? As a neutral Author, I have no opinion on this matter.

Widowmaker was the brother of the Reaper and he went with the motley crew to San Francisco. Dr. Keller had only returned from surgery yesterday and was getting his loving and his rest as much as possible. Tammy mentioned that the Widowmaker was cold as ice, and white as snow.

That comment sent chills up their spines. Jessica gave the Orders and they were compelled to follow them. Everything, including the skies was changing like the weather. Today a world record was broken when rain was

reported everywhere globally. Jessica frowned when she
heard about this bad omen.

Hot as usual the steam baths always had loyal
patrons frequenting there daily. There one day she met and
made her first true friend. Her name was Ruby Ross and the
two of them decided to take daily walks together through
the Rose Gardens.

Ruby filled with the spirit and was a cheerful and
bright person. One day by the waterfalls, everybody was
amazed to see both Jessica and Ruby levitating about six
feet off the ground. It seemed to the crowd that this woman
Ruby was a messenger from God. Nobody dared to disturb
them as they praised Jesus and gave Glory to God.

Many of the masses mocked the Jessica Foundation
and its cause. Some people threw rocks and bottles at the
walls surrounding the Foundation. Two years ago, it was
unincorporated, now it had a comported status and its own
Police Force. All done neatly and legally, sometimes a
pillar of fire would chase the Protestors away but they
would always return.

Jessica found it hard to believe that after seeing God
within the Pillar of Fire the masses that come from all over
the world. Still, did not believe. Some had the mark of the
Devil on their foreheads. These were horns, the mark of the
devil. In some instances Xeno manipulation created
children born with horns. These children's souls belonged
to the devil.

There was a U.N. Tank platoon rolling down the
mountainside near the Jessica Foundation practicing
maneuvers. These were new tanks with fire laser cannons.

It stated as Miles Equipment laser identification. It
was in the 80's when they learned during war games that
Miles' lasers that were suppose to be harmless to soldiers
were actually killing some. Their unexpected deaths ruled
as died of Natural Causes.

Jessica had three-inch thick steel walls constructed with Guard Towers every 75 feet with laser reflecting Discs. Miles laser equipment eventually became a killing weapon from a military exercise weapon. Declassified but not advertised.

"Living just for dying and becoming extinct just for you," Yes, humankind is losing the race against the Xenomittes. Thanks to their own greedy and power-hungry Leaders that have sold out the Human Species. Possibly, there was no rescue forthcoming? Perhaps the clock had run out of time and told what to believe, what to dream.

Jessica was addressing a good-sized audience from the podium inside the Foundation Lecture Auditorium.

"We are never going to die and we will make it if we do not give up trying. We are not playing a game, but we are trying to save what is left of our world. We can do it easily if we all pull together as a team."

There were loud cheers from the people listening and everywhere else globally. Jessica had bought her own Broadcasting Station.

That was all Jessica had to say about the current World Affairs. They were right words to say to an old problem called WAR. Jessica, was not a recognized world leader, people respected while hated. When events could get out of hand, nobody knew exactly how powerful Jessica was but that her power was growing at an outlandish rate. Jessica had to deal with the yin and the yang of this serious dilemma.

Never before had Peter been shunned by Rene, Rene was angry with Peter for continuing to be an atheist. Rene had become distant from everyone after a bad dream. She had thoughts of good times before she arrived into this forsaken hell and as the world around her, changed for the worse. Rene was beginning to love the worldly emotions, that was denied living in the Convent.

Everybody said that the sure bets were on the Xeno Teams. Xeno Gladiator School was no picnic. All the contestants were practicing on live victims. Human gladiators were minced meat against the super Xeno Fighters.

It was a travesty of pride, a humble chip at the block, to die for nothing for these contracted Xeno Gladiators, 'So that peoples could laugh at them.' These products of invention were soulless, heartless cold-blooded murderers.

In a different part of the arena humans trained, these humans were special. Some were abnormally huge Tibetan Monks, Chinese Wrestlers, a team from Samoa, a Team from The Congo that was eight to nine feet tall. Then there were the Pros, experts with poison and other forms of assassination.

A Kill was a Point; just ask the American Team that Leven and Tammy were training. This was the new Olympics and it was everything that you could want and more. All one can say is that it was a spectacle of bloody pandemonium.

If it were not for the Jessica Foundations contributions to the human species, humans would not have been competing in the Xeno Games. Jessica was becoming a big pain in the ass to the Xeno Foundation. Lightning bolts followed by thunder made the skies dark and dangerous, causing your hairs to stand on end if you were standing outside. It had been pouring rain for three days and no relief was in sight.

At any rate, Jessica was becoming popular and famous yet infamous. There was a sect of monks loyal to the Underworld that kept watch over Jessica, best they could. They were trying to get a spy into the Jessica Compound.

Confident and perky, Jessica was always in a joyous mood. Nothing could draw her away from her God.

Everything brought Jessica nearer to her God Almighty.

A private fountain of life had healing power; it was available for the people of the Foundation, hand chosen by Jessica while God enlivened her. These Leaders were also Ministers and God loving people. These persons blessed in that they never aged as long as they swam in the fountain pool. Wisdom seemed to be empowered by the pool to those that used it.

A team of engineers was designing and digging to build under ground connecting Pyramids a mile deep. It seems that Jessica had won the mega lottery a few years ago and did well investing her money. Now she owned major corporations worldwide including an airlines and a Hotel chain.

Now Jessica was one of the richest people in the world. Jessica knew that it was Gods doing and gave God the Glory of it all. Each day Jessica played handball with Rene at the Foundation Sports Gym.

Rene had become recluse and spent much of her time praying to God for forgiveness. Rene blamed herself or much of the evil that happened. Rene prayed for her dead Sisters and their souls. She remembered all to well the murders at the Lupus Estate, and the horror, the torture, the hell that they went through. Rene tried to find comfort in God but her visions filled with Valentine. Rene found great comfort being with Jessica. Jessica always knew the right things to say to make you feel better. Once more Jessica asked Rene if she wanted to go to the pool beneath the Falls and Rene declined as she always did. Jessica sighed at Rene's despair and changed the subject, trying to cheer up her friend.

Rene asked Jessica if she could spend the night with her and if she needed to bring anything. Jessica asked Rene if she was afraid of anything, not to worry. Rene explained that she had been having some horrifying dreams.

"Valentine has been in my dreams raping me. He tortures me and tells me that I missed out, and then he shows me my Sisters heads with his fist engrossed in their hair."

Rene began crying as she hit the ball with her racket so hard that the ball bounced around the court ten times. She was angry and wanted revenge. Revenge was a sin and Jessica explained that vengeance is in God's hands only. That all we can do is defending the Temple and that was hard enough to do without having to get even every time they hit us.

There is only one Temple in the World that God dwelled, the Jessica Foundation, and sits within its walls protect this Temple. Jessica would never run out of funding because God protected the Temple and the World was at war.

People from all over the globe came to see the Temple but only a small percentage gotten to go onto the Foundation grounds, and they stayed. Many claimed that Jessica was greedy and hogged God's Blessings to her own. Others despised her for not allowing them the chance for Salvation. Salvation was to be had, all you had to know was asking for it, not from the Temple, not from Jessica, not from Xeno serums and concoctions. Salvation is through Faith and perhaps your presence refused, if you are pure of heart and ask the Lord into your life then Salvation is at hand. Most people never understood.

Jessica and Rene had fun with the array of gifts that they had not opened yet. Only gifts brought by those accepted into the Foundation were accepted and opened. It had been a grueling couple of days and Jessica was expecting to hear from Mia soon.

Rene opened the first gift and exclaimed with satisfaction . . . *"Just what I needed."*

There in her hand was a beautifully colored scarf. In another box was a wool sweater, in another there was a Silver Set that appeared to be Mormon, and then there was one gift left.

Jessica stopped Rene from opening the last gift. It was in a bigger box than the others and it seemed to move slightly to the left. *"I think that there is something alive in that box, perhaps a kitten or a puppy?*

Jessica approached the box quietly and used her telekinetic gift to see what was inside the present. She stepped back when her hairs stood on end, and in the box was an asp. A deadly snake meant to kill whoever opened the box.

With a point of her index finger and a nod of her head, Jessica made the box burst into flames. Alarms went off and Security people crowded the premises. Ablaze in flames, the snake hissed and spit in the direction of Jessica. Now everybody knew that there was at least one spy in the Foundation Group. There was not a card with the box and nobody knew where it had come from. A Servant quickly killed it with his Buck knife.

Certainly nobody within the walls was safe now. Jessica scanned the minds of the people in her fold. Persons came everyday and certainly, Jessica did not know everyone. It was raining in Paradise.

The End of Chapter Seven
"<u>Jessica</u>"

Chapter Eight
"Xeno People"

Glowing and radiated Posters illuminated the bar with strobe lights in the Pool Room and Dart areas. *"Another Ale, Bartender and please make it a pint instead of a bottle this time."* Conditions were getting tough and so were the locals who knew each other. Strangers looked upon oddly and sometimes jumped by the local humans hanging out together drinking beer.

Rodeos' held secretly and sometimes at night, Xeno People were not welcome in most parts of the countryside. in fact, the cities had been taken over by Xeno People and abandoned by humans. Humans had put bounties on Xenomittes against Government pleas and some human outrages. These banded Law Enforcement volunteers became the Xeno Age Cowboys.

XAC Forces seemed to arm themselves more and wearing six-guns were fashionable again.

Bin had more to worry about then the war against Capitalism. Xenomittes were finding places to hide out from their hunters. These mutants were dead flesh to the Xeno Project, something to be genocide, cleaned up. Bin was finding these creatures everywhere and they were lethal beasts that wasted ammunitions. Xenomittes seeking out caves and tunnels searching for shelter and food found terrorists hiding from the new American President and the recently crowned King of U.K.

Xenomittes were the first prototypes that escaped into field but without a mind of their own. They became flesh eaters. They did not care about Politics or Ethics all, all Xeno people needed was food.

Creatures made their way to the Island. For the time being, a problem within a few days and escalating quickly.

they were allowed to live because scientists were learning from them and studying their offspring. State of Affairs was going down the drain in most places and the future looked dim for the poor. Some places like Australia and Argentina.

Good news is that the Stock Market higher then ever before and the United States was becoming a Nation filled with more millionaires than the middleclass. With it easier to get rich, this Country was changing. Its youth is spoiled and out of control and with the world at war for so long, anarchy was becoming the rule of thumb and watch out for your own interests were becoming second nature. There was a term that spread from the Military to the population that goes like this: ***"Cover your own ass."***

There is a difference between Xeno People and Xenomittes. Xeno People altered with Organ Transplants but Xenomittes DNA altered before birth. Creating beasts that appeared human but shape shifted as beasts. Strange beasts with their jaws covering a fifth of their bodies

Xeno People never understood that in the long-run future generations to be absorbed by these Xeno transplants would create a new species. Medical Propaganda had made many Christians believe that the Organ Transplants were harmless to the genetic pool. Lines were drawn and more protesting for another cause clouded the world.

Those people who opposed the Xeno Project did not allow their children to befriend Xeno People of any sort. Religion put aside, the lines were drawn. Segregation of a different sort than Civil Rights had taken hold of the people in this great Nation. Xeno Rights Movement was growing.

Demonstrations at Hospitals that perform Xeno Transplants and have a Research Facility are growing in numbers and Protestors throw rocks and bottles at Police that try to intervene and stop the chaos.

Jeb and Ed were brothers sitting at their favorite

Country and Western bar on the outskirts of Black Earth, Wisconsin. Jeb had a family problem that he did not know how to fix.

They were talking it over and getting drunk. They were Irish brothers in an Irish bar and just had ordered their food. Jeb had the Stuffed Cabbage and Ed ordered the Clam Chowder with another Pint of Irish Ale. It was a cozy, homely place with three pool tables and some arcade machines. Filled with smoke and overcrowded the bar and the two brothers were glad that they made it there early.

Both men had bright orange-red hair, loggers working out of the 'Gates Lumber mill.' Tall and brawny, both men were married and had children.

Jeb said it like it was . . . *"Ed, my frick-in daughter has a relation with a Xeno boy from school. They haven't had sex yet as far as I know, but it's bound to happen if I don't put a stop to it."*

"Which daughter," 'his younger brother Asked of Ed.' *"Oh its Molly, she thinks that Xeno people are no different then humans. Molly's High School teaches about the Xeno Project and new hope for humankind. Promise for better heath and longer life. Before ya know it, everybody must have Xeno Vaccinations. I got my own idea on how to rid myself of this problem by getting rid of the boy."*

Ed took a few minutes to respond and replied. *"That won't work brother. Us McKnight's don't do a job half of the way."*

"What did you mean by that big brother? . . ." 'Jeb did not quite understand what his brother was trying to say.'

"We need to kill the boyfriend and his family. They are only Xeno People anyway, so let's burn down their house?" 'Times were different now, and the year 2000 was truly history. Weapons were outdated and Miles

Laser Weapons being used from satellites orbiting our blue planet. Weapons such as the T.O.W. and the Dragon missiles, the viper, all became obsolete. A laser can hit any target, moving or not at any moment in time.

These conventional weapons had become hot items on the Black Market. Of course, these Lumberjacks had access to such weaponry, perhaps they had more then we know.

Jeb walked out of the bar and Ed followed his brother outside. *"Check out what I bought at the PX Flea Market. It's in the half ton truck parked a block from here."*

"Lookee here bro, I got us some firepower and I bet the Boys at the Mill will be happy to see them." They were approaching the truck and the two large men left tall shadows. When Ed saw what was inside the truck he was smiling ear to ear. *"Well now brother, their yaw go . . . We gonna try out a couple LAWS' tonight on the Xeno house. Can you believe that they are the only Xeno people in our Township?"*

" Yep, you think we should bring our chain saws just in case?"

Ed thought about it as they closed the latch on the camper shell. Then with Jeb driving, the brothers drove into the sunset and to the Lumber mill. On the way there Ed reached through the sliding glass window and picked out a loaded Colt 45 along with three extra clips.

"Sure is some beautiful country out here ain't it bro. I wish that your daughter would take a liking to a good boy from around here, heck; there are plenty of young men around here. What's she doing around a Xeno pervert anyway?"

At four men to a cabin, there were two rows of ten cabins across from each other. These men made up the crews that cut the trees, moved the trees debarked the trees, and then milled the timber into usable lumber.

"How do ya know if they aren't together tonight?" Ed wanted to be sure that Molly would not witness or get hurt when the fired the missiles at the Van Brock Family home.

"I will drop Molly off at her grandma's house in Madison. That is about one and a half hours from here as the crow flies. I'll tell ma to make sure that Molly stays put."

Between the men sat, a Coleman cooler filled with food, Cokes, bait, and beers. On the way to the mill the brothers had a few beers that were cold as ice and great taste.

Persecuted Xeno People were everywhere but in the suburbs. Cities were shrinking as its inhabitants were moving out in droves into the country. Privacy was almost against the law, but this law did not apply to other then cities. Xeno people at the most, tolerated in country towns, and hunted by the farmers and ranchers so Xeno People were mostly in the cities.

One never knew where the Xenomittes could suddenly strike seemingly out of nowhere. Side arms allowed in the country but outlawed in the cities. Xenomittes were not afraid to bite the ones that fed them. It was all food to the freaks.

With all of this going on it was natural for unnatural acts to occur in the dead of the night. Xeno Project advocates protested the treatment of Xeno People outside The city claiming that humans operated well worldwide.

Perhaps the only advantage that the Foundation has is time. Time enough, to damage Samuels budding Empire. Before the second coming of Christ, Buddha is reborn, all religions bond together under one God called by many names finally fight the devil.

"Jeb, had me that launchers will ya, and be gentle

with it."

"Why don't we stop and pick up some of the boys, I hear t that he these Xeno People hang out in gangs." said Ed.

"Sounds like a good idea to me. We need to show that Xeno People cannot live in our Township. We have to protect our children for as long as we can. That means the Eighth Grade, which is as long as we can protect them before they are moved to the Main High School." Jeb hit it on the nose.

"We are setting up home schooling at the Town Hall. Our wives and girlfriends can run our school. We will make sure that there will not be any Xeno People or Xenomittes near the Town Hall Building. Who knows, if we pool our monies together, we can build our own private school."

Ed was on top of it, now they had to get away with murder. That was going to be easy because the Police were part of the good ole boys.

Time dragged, three in the morning by the time the group gathered on Ed's Ranch. Once there, Jeb showed the boys the new toys to put in their Armory.

In the house occupied by the Xeno family, they were always prepared for the worse. Xeno sympathizers gave away the scene happening at the ranch. Since the Xeno family learned of it in ample time to reinforce, they did that and more.

Jackie went to the short wave radio and called other Xeno families to join them on their farm. In a matter of three hours, there were at least fifty armed men in the Xeno house. Some were Xenopeople, some were humans, and they surrounded the house and set into army type trenches.

Xeno people were organized to the point of small arms weaponry, most of the time that is the most force that was required to defend their Rights.

Sherman Van Brock, his wife Jackie, two son's Billy and Shawn, and a daughter named Cindy. They were all angry with Shawn for dating Molly. It was a rule among the Xeno People that they were never to befriend, or mate with a human. Sherman was ashamed of his son for being the centerpiece of all the trouble waiting for them around the corner.

Afraid for their lives the children and Sherman's wife stayed in the basement until the humans were discouraged to fight. All that they wanted was to live in peace, they were good law-abiding neighbors and active in the community. The way were singled out was not fair and they were going to defend themselves the best they could.

Shawn should have known better but his overactive hormones and his oversized organs made him outstanding in sports, academics, and sex. His sex drive was overwhelming and his build and good looks drew the girls like honey. Three generations of his family had a Xeno Organ Transplant but Shawn did not, he was a fourth generation naturally born human being. Therefore, Shawn believed that he was but many begged to differ with him.

During school, the jocks picked on Sherman but Sherman outclassed them. He moved faster, hit harder, and was a hard target to hit. After his senior year, Sherman was using steroids and banned from all sports.

Civil Liberties bent for the benefit of Public Health quoted Senator Gore known for his statements of bluntness and truth. Gore was too old to filibuster or argue. He was direct and true to his cause. There was a television in the basement where Senator Gore was speaking on a Talk Show. This event that was about to occur on a country road in the middle of nowhere. These redneck loggers were thinking along the same line. That the best way to cleanse the Township from Xeno infestation was to root them out now, for the better of the whole.

Fifty Xeno people mixed in with human sympathizers had not a clue of what they confronting. Five miles away the crews at the logging camp were forming squads that each armed with an M-30, two Law's, and ten grenades. Jeb carried an M-1 as did his brother Ed. Each squad consisted of the same people that were in those logging crews.

Jeb planned one missile to fire at the house. It was the wire guided mounted Tow Missile on a tripod. It would fry an egg 50 yards from impact.

It was a perfect night with no moon and clear skies. All the men in the houses who were present participated in this event after the Assembly ended and everybody was oriented.

Ed was smart enough to know that the Xeno Family would be waiting for them to come. He had sent out a couple of scouts who never returned. Ed was a colonel in the Army before he resigned his Commission and elected to lead this assault against the Xeno Family. Not even West Point could have prepared these men for what was to come.

Ed addressed his men and two women on his crews. *"My brother learned that his daughter Molly was dating a Xeno boy, now how many other girls do you suppose that this monster has violated? What about your daughter Jim, and you Phil., I know that my Foreman has two pretty daughters in school, should we wait until our grand children are born with tails or nip it at the bud now! Before it's too late and these devils will arrive in hordes."*

There was applause that nearly sounded like an organized angry mob bringing down the house. These rednecks loved country music, drinking and kicking ass.

"If you are with us then get in a truck and follow me." Ed ran to his truck with his brother in tow. There must have been at least seventy lumberjacks and most of

them drunk. All heading straight for the Van Brock farm to burn it down.

Over at the Xeno home they were ready for an assault. Sentries posted a hundred yards from the house with radios to give warning when the Loggers arrived. Two scouts caught by the Sentries and were tortured until they told all that they knew about the assault.

Once Sherman heard about the firepower that the loggers had Sherman thought for a moment that they were doomed. Then he figured that it was better to stand up for your rights and make a stand. All the Xeno People had special advantages with their special abilities to leap, run, and see, smell, and stronger than humans were.

Certainly the only disadvantage was that the loggers knew the Country and were being led by a decorated Officer who went on two 18 month tours in the Gulf. Humans were a few steps up the ladder when it came to reasoning and all test scores, common sense and overwhelming firepower.

This Event set the world on fire, it was going to be the first time that heavy opposition would make Civil Rights History. This is what happened at the Van Brock farm. Neither side knew what to expect from the other. One thing was for sure and that is that they were both going to be sunrise.

Molly was desperate to warn her lover and his family of the coming doom. She tried to leave the house but her mother stopped her. Then Molly's Uncle and brother locked her in her room to keep her out of further trouble. Molly had a bad feeling in her gut that something awful was about to happen.

Only Molly knew that she was pregnant and that Shawn was the father. Xeno offspring take half the time to be born so Molly was slightly showing.

Molly knew that she had to run away but they were watching her closely. Molly was not surprised to see that her bedroom windows were nailed shut and stared at the nails in despair for her future.

Molly packed some things in a suitcase and began pulling using an angle iron off her steel framed bed. Molly intent on flying the coup and knew it was her only hope to keep the baby.

Everybody in the Township knew about the raid that was going to happen at five in the morning at the Van Brock home. Nonetheless, it was a well-kept secret.

Parking a mile from the Van Brock home the loggers quick-timed it down the road a quarter mile and then cut off onto a trail through the forest. Jeb and Ed were at the point with Tim's squad bringing up the rear. There was a platoon of half-drunk and heavily armed loggers led by a Patriot to their target.

Jeb noticed the man in the tree and pointed at him. After refusing pleas to climb down, Ed shot him out of the tree with his hunting crossbow he had slung over his shoulders. With a brisk rustle among the branches, a young man fell out of the true, dead as a Buck during open hunting season at a petting zoo.

These men had a job to do like any other job. Ed's speech hammered home some good points, depending on which side you were on. Within ten years, the Xeno Project grew into a controlling monster. There was talk of mandatory Xeno vaccines distributed in our schools.

Ahead on the trail were three Xeno persons ready to test the strength of the loggers.

Jeb, Ed, and Jimmy were walking the point. Jeb carried the Tow cases and knew how to assemble a Tow mounted on tripods in 45 seconds flat. Ed was holding a 45 Cal. Colt in his right hand and a grenade with the other. 'Loggers are good with their hands.'

Ed armed with an M-203; it is an M-16 and grenade launcher combo. It was a battle weapon that if used correctly one man could hold off a Platoon. Jimmy was carrying an M-60 strapped over his shoulder pointed ahead of him.

'Walking about fifty feet in front of the others in the logger's group,' all the supervisors and woodsmen were alert and at home in the woods.

Bruno, Stan, and Vincent were almost done setting booby-traps for the ambush. They had dug a deep hole 6-foot high and set a tripwire to a claymore mine within the hole. These Xeno men wanted to discourage the loggers from attacking with the least losses possible. Certainly, the Xeno People wanted to avoid a confrontation in the first place but now it was over due.

They used rubber slings six feet long to stretch out and placed 16-penny nails into the leather pouches. A fifty-pound box fit snugly into each leather pouch. They hung hand grenades from the branches of trees all set to explode by remote control. Xeno People had access to higher forms of weaponry. None of the people at the house knew that these three men had been setting death traps.

Stealthily, the three Xeno persons hid in their predestinated hiding places and waited for hell to break loose. Traps rigged for a length of a hundred yards, the traps expertly hidden.

These men were Contractors who worked for the State Health Department and hired as a peacekeeping Force. They awaited the anxious lumberjacks to reach the line. Anything was bound to happen and it was going to happen soon.

Jeb detected a hole, it was by pure chance and afterwards he felt lucky. Ed stopped the move forward and sent out scouts to search, find, and disarm all booby traps. Ed sent Jimmy along for some heavy cover fire. Ed and Jeb saw everything under a new light. In the light was a claymore mine.

These loggers were the best in Wisconsin but it took them over an hour to disarm the line of booby-traps. When all the patrols had come in, the men went forward again. Ed sent a squad of his men behind the house to see what was there. As the men disappeared into the woods, a series of explosions that sound like grenades erupted the early morning.

Jeb ordered two more squads to check on Alpha Squad and then ordered his men to quick time up the trail to the pond, on the eastside of the Van Brock home.

Once they had gotten there, they learned that they were five men short. The contractors had stalked them. Moreover, now were watching the ponds.

Ed realized that he set up for an ambush and the whole Operation was not over yet. He looked behind his shoulder and felt spooked. Ed was in charge and owned the Lumber mill. Ed Gates was the man of the hour, was a saying going around for years. Ed told Jeb to line the missiles around the pond and to fire them all at once, on his command.

They planned to have some hangings, but now Ed thought it best if they got it over with as quickly as possible. There clearly were dozens of defenders waiting for them to line a conventional assault. Now after losing several men, Ed believed that the quicker the better.

Jeb insisted on taking four men and getting a better look-see at what was waiting for them. He ordered them to spread out ten-feet from each other. They walked on at a slow pace, Ed told them that he would give the command to fire the missiles in twenty minutes and Jeb had seventeen minutes left.

On the line along the pond, every gunner given a range card for a field of fire. M-60's and Dragons along with Laws aimed at the vicinity of the farmhouse. Ed had the powerful tow with an effective range of 5000 meters.

Ed wondered if the Laws had the range to be effective, from the far edge of the pond. Passing an order along from one gunner to another the Troop moved to the near side of the pond.

Jeb was moving swiftly with his squad and before long, they were low crawling to get nearest the best vantage point into the trenches. What they saw made them laugh because now Jeb knew for sure that they had them outgunned. As Jeb was speaking on the radio to his brother, there was a scream in the distance.

Joey bludgeoned with a knife as he was low crawling by Bruno, then there were two more screams and Jeb gave the order the move back to the line.

Paul caught up with Jeb and told Jeb that the other three men were dead. Jeb let out a holler in an expression of pain as his face turned red his knuckles turned white with clenched fists. At that moment, Jeb became a homicidal mania. Jeb elected to lead the storming party once the missiles fired. He was shaking so badly that he did not think he could hit the broad side of a barn.

Ed fired the tow and hit the house dead center. After the smoke cleared, the trenches opened fire at the loggers. There was nothing left of the house but the family was safe in the full basement mostly because of the concrete deck.

Hell was there on this clear black night. Fireworks lighted the night and the people in the trenches were plainly viable. M-60 machine guns fired into the trenches to keep the enemy's heads down while Jeb led the grenade charge.

It turned into a bloody carnage with both sides taking heavy loses. This firefight took two hours and the State Police did not respond to Xeno calls for help. When the final bullet was fired at the end of the battle, the only ones left alive in the house were the family in the basement.

When it all ended, the last shot fired killed Bruno but his two partners escaped. This was going to come back and put California Township on the map.

Jeb calmly walked up to the family and told them to get on their knees. Shawn did not go along with the program so Jeb shot the child stealer in the groin. Execution style Jeb shot the family members one at a time until he got to Shawn.

After losses tallied up, half the loggers were dead and all known Xeno People killed. Ed and Jeb helped carry the dead and the wounded back to the Mill.

———————————————

Molly knew that she was in big trouble but there was no way out. She feared for her life, and knew that the least that would happen to her was a bad beating, and the worse was unthinkable.

Molly heard the men come home and thanked God that they were too busy to see her now. There was tomorrow . . .

The End of Chapter Eight
"The Xeno People"

Chapter Nine
"The Xeno Mob"

It reminded me of a snowball rolling down a hill. Xeno People in the cities quickly heard about the California Township massacre.

Humans all over the world feared what the Governments would do and what the Xeno People might do to the outnumbered Humans in cities like Chicago, San Francisco.

San Francisco was a rallying point for Xeno Activists. An abundance of humans supported their cause advocating them as a part of the Human Species. Genome Human Transcript maps were different, and now there are man species of human and animal combos, and multiple unstable Beings. All of the Xeno People fought for one cause on the other hand. Humans split in their loyalties and in many instances' fighting each other.

Chicago thousands of Xeno People have trapped all the human workers and visitors inside of the Sears Tower. It was law that all Policeman and Officers of any sort be human, so for the humans inside the Sears Tower they were uncomfortable but safe.

Molly put on trial at the Knox, Indiana County Courthouse. Molly blamed for instigating the attack on the Van Brock home and for mating with a Xeno boy. Everybody knew that molly was expecting a child and it grew at a phenomenal rate.

Jeb was a witness for the Prosecution, as was Ed. Molly cried through the Indictments, and returned to her cell. There was Cause showing, it was solely Molly's fault the Van Brock Incident. Jeb was watching the News afterwards and seen Xenopeople protesting in the streets of San Francisco. Then started soon there after in

Chicago, Ill. where a huge Xeno Mob was forming around the Sears Tower.

Christians braved the Mob and Protested the Evil caused by these abominations. These humans were making a big mistake but they acted in the name of God, nothing could move them to get away, hide, and run from that place.

When the National Guard deployed, the Xeno Soldiers in the Reserves refused to go to Chicago and fight against their own species. This created a dilemma for Washington, D.C. never considered in their tactics to put a stop to this Mob before they burned down Chicago. It seemed that the task was in the hands of the Chicago Police Departments.

There was a clear line drawn between the Xeno People and Humans. Chicago Police, known for their reputations and organized combative ability and brutality were the best in America. They are hard and mean, most of the time if you are asking for it, you never make it to jail. These Law Enforcement Personnel were more than ready to quell the storm building up at the Chicago Sears Tower. Now the deep hatred for each other had a place to vent, and thus far, the Police were winning.

Police in Chicago had years ago replaced their car fleet with Armored Police cars with surround razor bars. It had an M-60 port in the rear and cameras that monitored from Headquarters. Police Riot suits armored and they had laser pistols. With bulletproof shields to protect them on foot, they were confident. Yet as they watched the mob growing even within the mists of tear gas some Officers were having second thoughts.

Chicago Police are boss; they wanted to terminate the Xeno People and were about ready to begin. Then Orders from Washington, D.C. belayed this lethal Police Action.

Acid rain down pouring was falling on Turkey in like slush. It drifted over from Iraq and Iran where a World War scenario staged. Oil wells were ablaze in this time of these upheavals in the Gulf and a typhoon was heading in that direction.

England's shores were flooding cities because of global warming and China was in drought for two years now. Plagues had broken loose in third world Countries and the Nile were flooding.

Times were bad and everybody knew it. Iraq partly contaminated from Bio-Chemical weapons that set off by an unknown Faction. Iran invaded Iraq while the Allied occupation was still ongoing. They, unlike Iraq, were not afraid to use chemical weapons but now there had to be a Truce among all warring parties because they were destroying our planet. The Middle East was Split into Five Sections.

Our world finally was banded together to fight Mother Nature. Once things were better, the wars were going to start again. For now, all that was making the World Headlines was Chicago, Ill.

With the growing mob getting restless, the Police had no choice but to pull back and let the Sears Tower fend for itself.

Inside the Tower was a small army of Police and Security Personnel who had barricaded all the exits and windows to the building ten stories high. These men and women were experts and trained Counter terrorists. Well armed and prepared for the worse, they believed that they could keep the mob out.

If not, then there was the underground Fallout Shelter that surely was safe. It was fully equipped to hold five-thousand people for several years. There were more then that in the high-rise but if it came to that extreme, many by then would be dead.

California Township had set an example that turned the tide on the Xeno People. Now they stepped into the light during the Trial of Ed and Jeb, "Acquitted." Death was in the Windy City air. Everywhere the dead and the dying, dead were piled high. This carnage caused by the mob itself. Who could have expected such a violent response from the Xeno People? They were rioting and out of Control. Chicago Citizens were shooting into the mob from their Apartments windows making things harder to control.

Human Militia's came into action and a fight broke out between them and the Xeno Mob. At first loses were heavy on both sides and then another Militia joined the fight. Hands tied nothing the Police could do but prevent the fight from spreading into other neighborhoods.

Who would have thought that the mob would continue to grow and proceed to fight for days, not me? There were Socialists there representing their Party, and the Communists were egging things on too. Militias moved out and others promised to stay home to protect their own. It seemed to be petering out, as the crowds grew tired and weary of the chaos.

Senate Members agreed to give their Xeno Man a crack at quashing the Mob. It was a risk that they had to take. Everything was getting out of hand with both a World Crisis and the Chicago Riots happening all at once.

Our Country had repaired or replaced levies all over the States and had fixed or replaced all major bridges. This undertaking flooded our Economy with work for the poor and now we were tapping into our own oil wells for the first time. We have more oil here in the United States than anywhere else in the world.

Sure, as always we were stingy with our oil and

shared it with few Nations. Many Nations were bone dry and their Armies were dead in the water for lack of fuel. Allied Forces including Australia were rich in oil and on the hunt for Terrorist Leaders and encampments. We had shut off world supply and blew up or disabled all the oil wells in the Persian Gulf.

Now the Xeno Man was going tested in containment and control, Mia was planned it for tonight and "The Xeno Man was ready for action."

"The Xeno Man" was all-powerful and had skin tough as steel. He invented by using several vicious and cunning animals to Xeno transplants into a man once known as Calvin Adams. Now he was not that man anymore. Female hormones and a penal transplant from a golden retriever assured dependability and loyalty to the Master Handler. In a few hours the Xeno Man was going to devastate the Mob. All of those involved were going to watch him through the camera that sat implanted in his forehead. Microscopic lenses with a wide viewfinder were good enough for a home movie of the riot.

Abdula was the Xeno Man's handler and he was good at his job. Donning his Xeno Prodigy with modern flexible body armor and a host of weapons designed for the Xeno man because of his long razor sharp claws. Abdula was driving to Chicago in a caged van with the Xeno Man in the back of the van. With the Presidential Seal that he was given Abdula knew that he would get an escort after the first roadblock check point. Abdula lived a short life.

What made the Xeno Man odd was that his face had deformed during the course of his treatments. He had a nasty scar splitting his face and made him seem as if he had two faces. One side was hairless and smooth while the other side of his face was beastly. A giant made to hunt and kill, to obey his given directive. Obey he did, and it was pure hell.

He was merciless and the coldness of his heart felt if you stood within twenty-feet from him. Hairless, the Xeno Man glimmered in the afternoon light as he disembarked from an armored vehicle. His cold black eyes scanned his Area of Operations for a point of weakness where he could break through. A squad of Rangers carrying M-15's and side arms protected Xenoman.

Grey Chicago clouds began rolling over the city as the winds were picking up speed. Carrying a ball and chain welded onto a metal shaft in one hand and a broadsword in his right hand. Xenoman was ready to stop the riot by himself. A long line of Police in armor and with shields stayed fifty meters behind the Xenoman as a sweep up maneuvers.

With a howling screech, the Xenoman charged the crowd at its weakest point and hit the Mob at about thirty miles an hour swinging the weapons with both hands, as he felled one victim after another. A pile of dead littered his wake as the Xenoman spiraled through the Mob.

This event was going to make the Xenoman a fearsome and awesome spectacle to watch on television and beside the new nickname this event gave, Xenoman a reputation and he gained global respect.

Hands feet heads and pieces of torsos rained from the sky near the Xenoman. He was unstoppable and the attacks made against him were futile at best.

Indeed this was a remarkable sight. The Xenoman was like a lawn mower cutting down people, like a reaper in a wheat field. After twenty minutes, the Mob was feeling the sting and arranged organized attacks against Xenoman.

All the Rangers hideously killed by the mob in the third assault but the Xenoman continued his rampage seemingly unaffected by bullets and fiery bottles filed with gasoline.

Fascinated and terrified all at once, the mob realized that the Xenoman was fire resistant. This brought terror into the mob that spread faster then a bad flu.

Xenoman possessed no emotion and fought masterfully as he shredded or smashed everybody around him as he kept walking a steady pace. In the first fifteen minutes more than 300 of the Mob were dead.

"We have to find a way to crush the beast. It is the only way to kill it, if it can die?"

Jane Baxley was the Leader of an Atheist anarchist Groups that was staying on the outskirts of the Mob. Estimations of ten-thousand People involved in the Riot and many were looting and committing other crimes.

News of the Xenoman spread quickly and newcomers were dwindling off as the Xenoman murdered whoever was there. Jane wanted the Sears Tower to go down and needed to stop the Xenoman before the Xenoman stopped the riot.

Nobody anticipated the great Terrorist Leader Bin to play a role in this disorder occurring around the Sears Tower in Chicago, Ill.

Terrorists had placed explosives on critical area's of the Sears Tower outer walls. It was not going to bring the Sears Tower down but its purpose would further the cause. To create fear, to show the world that the war was far from over, and to heavily damage, the Sears Tower.

"Xenoman go," said one of the Senators. They were watching it on a big screen received from a Government Satellite. It was better than a ball game to these men and women in Chambers. *"Look at that fighting machine eat it up in Chicago. Nothing can stop him. I say that we send him after Bin in a week or so. Do I hear a yea?"*

Yea's out numbered the nays and the Act passed without opposition having a chance at winning.

Jane had found a bulldozer and seen on the big screen as she and several trucks moved through the crowd at the Xenoman.

Viciously, the Anarchists were trying to crush the Xenoman. In ten seconds, the Terrorists detonators were going give the Loop the biggest bang it's ever known.

Congressperson Lisa Benning saw what was to happen and she alerted her colleagues. It was a couple seconds after that moment that the charges exploded one at a time circling the building and causing extensive damage. It was enough to shake the building and rattle it some, but exterior damage was the worst of it.

Because the bombs were set outside the walls in the trimmed hedges, the blasts blew outward into the mob surrounding the Sears Tower. Four-thousand people died instantly and the Xenoman watched as the trucks coming at him cushioned the blow to the Bulldozer. Xenoman ruled!

Jane was alive and saw the machine had saved the Xenoman's life. She slammed her foot on one pedal and then hit the gas at a high rpm. Now she was going to try to finish him off. Her bulldozer spun into a circle but it was too late for Jane. She never saw the Xenoman as he jumped onto the rear of the dozer. Without emotion and regret, the Xenoman swung his steel ball in a downward arch and smashed Jane's skull into an oozing bloody scattered mess.

In the Chambers, one could hear some gasps from some of the Politicians watched Jane murdered. To the Xenoman it was a clear case of self-defense and it was so, with most others who had seen this broadcast. It was the most horrible broadcast ever seen on T.V. and it would change the world.

Waiting at major intersections Ambulances, Fire trucks a few blocks away. Called into Action, Protestors had left behind the wounded along with banners and signs proclaiming: **"Remember California Township!"**

Chicago has a population of 25 million people, and that includes the Xeno People. "The Sears Tower Incident" not considered an uprising or a serious Terrorist attack. Chicago has thousands of people that considered unknown and undocumented. These persons considered a threat to society according the United States Senate. These people hide out among the masses and in holes in the ground. Underground Compounds constructed by the Super rich.

Certainly, in Chicago a person can almost buy anything. All the Crime Bosses and corrupt Officials had placed a death sentence for anybody possessing or developing chemical and Biological weapons. In fact, because of the global warming and the monstrous storms, the feeling was the same world over.

Many of these hidden persons had no affiliation with the underground elite but were assassins and criminals. Prisons were overcrowded and riots had forced thousands of early releases from Prisons all over the United States. Others transported to laboratories locate at Xenopharmaceuticals owned by Mr. Keller Research Investments.

State of Affairs was at low ebb while the economy was growing in strength. The Xeno Project generated trillions of dollars and it stayed in the United States. We became more powerful with each day as the planet died a bit more every day.

Xeno Technology considered in discussions of bartering changing the course of the oncoming asteroid expected to hit this planet in 2027. At the end of this year, a Shuttle launched to intercept the asteroid. Word was that there were four hydrogen bombs on the shuttle. It was a suicide mission that only a far more advanced being other then the Xenoman to complete a mission in space.

There was much discussion by nearly everybody about the Xeno Mob in Chicago. New Laws were being passed and Xeno Endorsements increased. Long prison sentences, was handed out to humans that attacked Xeno People.

Scientists in Israel have developed a new fuel using Xeno by-product and are using it to fuel their tanks. Israel was neutral on the Xeno Project but times were hard and their Borders were vulnerable.

Governor Lewis Said. *"Dealing with a changing world, lost and spinning into disaster will be difficult but not impossible."* 'He was speaking to other Politicians, at a private Meeting at the House of Pancakes.' *"I am truly impressed by the Xenoman. His exploits have been stored in the Archives of Congress. We need to regulate the Xeno Project and use it to conquer the world and make it globally Republic. We can create a Xeno Army and eliminate all other Xeno Project Research. The promise of Xeno technology to save the planet was a Just Cause. To be used as a substitute for human organs or enhancing humans with Xeno therapy with drugs should be outlawed."*

This Debate continued into the Chambers of the White House.

The End   Chapter Nine
"The Xeno Mob"

Chapter Ten
"A Cry For Help"
Nov 1, 2015

Wandering throughout the grassy fields within the compound, Jessica was mulling over everything that has happened in the last few months.

A new Resistance Group was forming in the Compound who called themselves "The Legion of Death." Jessica was concerned about this group of Christians. Peter had been Saved and Baptized. Now he is a member in the L.O.D.

Militant Group assigned Scouts, and communicated with the L.O.D. of the Army. Being a covert group the names of its members, never known, not even to the Military. Jessica knew that they were taking the law into their own hands and disapproved of these discretions. However, they seemed to be making a decent headway and were effective in breaking up Militant Xeno gangs.

Fall wild flowers grew all over the pastures, huge oak trees, and maple trees spotted over the lush grass. Jessica sat beneath a tall and lush oak tree in the center of the valley to eat lunch. She had brought with her a basket filled with fried chicken, an ear of corn, an apple, and a canteen of water.

Robins and a couple of cardinals landed near Jessica and deer were approaching her place under the giant oak tree. Jessica felt at peace and the tranquility of where she put her mind at ease.

Overhead in the skies, a turbo-laser-jet flew high emitting no stream of pollution. Science had come a long way in a few years time.

Constant Global wars were consuming our planet. It was a catch 22; if Jessica halted, the Xeno Project then that technology failed entirely to neutralize the Terrorists. Everybody in war was calling the other terrorists.

Jessica heard the voice of a girl pleading for help. Jessica felt that this teenager was crying for help. This was the first time that Jessica had received a message from far away and not from God. Jessica was trying to zoom her senses to this girl. In a minute, Jessica learned the girl's name. Her given name was Penny Wilson.

Jessica was broken out of her meditation, as over the horizon a Laser Jet exploded. Jessica prayed for the persons that had died in another terrorist act committed by who knows whom.

Penny Wilson was the daughter of Senator Richard Wilson. A man who never took no for an answer and was not about to allow his daughter to miss a Xeno Heart Transplant.

Penny Wilson was born with an oversized heart, larger than most oversized hearts. She did not want a pig's heart in her chest, Penny refused to cooperate but was drugged into submission. Now she was waiting in her bed in the hospital for the donor heart to arrive from France.

Penny believed in God and trusted that her own heart was the heart God gave her at her birth. At sixteen years of age Penny did not have a choice, the decision for the Xeno Transplant was out of her hands. Her parent's dead set on getting the surgery done and having their daughter back.

Truth was that Penny's parents did not care so much for their daughter as they did the votes they were going to get during Election Day. Richard had invested most of his money in Xeno Industries. Surely, Richard was making a large profit playing the Stock Market. Along with Political contributions and bribes Richard hoped that one day he could buy himself a Presidency.

Yesterday a vaccine for AIDs developed in the Xeno Labs. In addition, the news of it spread joy among the people of the world. Once you had the vaccine then you were immune to AIDs but if you already had it then there was no cure.

Xeno Industries with Xeno pharmaceuticals in a venture to create a breakthrough drug that would change the future were close to their goal. This Promise of life for humanity was a double-edged sword. Some claimed by some Researchers that this new drug would add hundreds of years to a person's lifetime. It seemed that The Xeno Project was gaining popularity.

Penny was praying hard and nonstop as she waited in her Hospital room for the outsiders to get her. That is what she refereed to the Xeno People involved in her care. Penny fell asleep and dreamed a dream that eventually saved her life. 'Outside her door' an Orderly stood guard.

Somewhere in a pasture, Penny was flying a kite. She was running along with a dog following her. Then she came upon a beautiful woman sitting beneath a huge tree eating an apple.

Jessica was seeing the dream Penny was having and felt her pain. Anguish was a new sensation for Jessica. Without hesitation, Jessica brought Penny with a thought to the Jessica Foundation. Jessica had never used a gift before but this time Jessica felt inspired by God to take action.

Penny was healthy and Jesus had healed her heart. Jessica welcomed the girl to the Jessica Ranch and led her back to the populated center of the Compound. Jessica gave Penny a terrier black puppy named Katana.

Perhaps at first, Penny was shocked but before long, she consumed with love and glad to be free of the hell she once lived in. Everybody called Penny a sister, and warmly welcomed Penny into the family. Katana barked.

Penny made the newspapers and the Television news. According to Hospital sources, Penny Wilson kidnapped from her hospital room. On the Compound where Penny was walking the gardens with Rene, the two became best friends. On the outside, posters of the missing girl were at every fueling station and transit stop.

Penny Wilson was safe now and the Publicity that her kidnapping brought the Wilson's Sympathy from the Public. Richard Wilson reelected for Congress and forgotten his daughter was gone to his Victory party.

An ideal world with the perfect solutions would be wonderful and right on time. We are far from our objectives and our morals shot to hell. Everybody wants to know the truth but the truth is different to everybody. Concepts work for some and not for others, during this Xeno Age Humans will set the date for the death of our planet.

Collateral damage was persons such as Penny, and Little John. Thousands more as these two innocents went through these Xeno transplants against their wills and were doomed to live out their lives in agony, in a darkness of pain with splatters of red. Xeno patients complained of the side-effects such as hallucinations and voices.

Cries for help had replaced beggars and the homeless. Xeno transplants had become a fad among the rich and a necessity for the dying. First the innocent get taken and then eaten alive by something that cannot be destroyed, waiting to be reborn again.

Penny did not know how lucky she was being rescued by Jessica, and living safely on the ranch. Her cry for help heard, this makes me wonder how many cries go unheard. This was the one and only time that Jessica did such a thing. There was a reason for everything done.

Samuel screamed in agony as Penny found God. He knew that Penny was a part of Gods master plan but had no idea in what way. Every move that God made sent Samuel into a rage. Samuel would curse God and his own father. John Sung was now at Samuel's side most of the time. Samuel always loved to watch John work and there was plenty of work lined up for John.

"Jung, get your ass over here!"

Samuel did not like it when Jessica got her way and it was happening a lot lately. Indeed, Samuel would have conquered the Heavens and the Earth if he could have succeeded in his quest. He needed his father to be whole, and he had murdered his father in a jealous rage. Now Samuel had to find a way to get forgiveness for the terrible way he cast Lucifer into Hell, this time not by Almighty God but by his own son, Samuel.

Samuel pointed at the man dressed in a Postal Uniform sitting on a chair the furthest distance possible from Samuel. Then Samuel told John Yung Sung, ***"Strap that heathen onto to the stretcher and make him hurt, make him ache, make him squirm in discomfort, and then my friend, I want to hear the bastard die screaming for mercy."***

John Sung did as he was told and then some more. Samuel gained satisfaction in the cries of the poor man as he sank his tools of doom into his new victim.

Samuel watched the spurts of blood and the man as he withered after each punctures made by Sung. Soon after each holler of pain or a screech of agony Samuel smiled broadly showing his pointed razor sharp teeth. It was gratifying for Samuel to watch others suffer. Clearly had not dismissed the voice of the teenage girl and her pleas for salvation, Samuel became enraged.

Items in the Mansion that Samuel was occupying began to burst into flames. Servants were running around the mansion dousing the flames with some fire extinguishers. Trees were snapping in the forest on the Estate Grounds and birds were falling out of the sky dead when they hit the ground.

Mia was hiding in the forest and had to avoid the falling trees and find shelter from the pounding hail the size of golf balls. She had been trying to get at Samuel for the last two months but it seemed to be in vain. Mia had a couple of narrow escapes trying to get at Samuel once almost killed the beast but his wolves saved Samuel.

Samuel had put a huge Reward on Mia's head and promised to cut her into pieces that would fit into mason jars. Then Samuel planned to bury each jar a thousand miles from each other. Samuel and Mia had only one thing in common, they both had eternal life as long as they were in one piece. Everlasting life is conditional if that person or persons are living on the Earth. Samuel knew that Mia was not going to stop hunting him until Mia murdered him. Samuel hell bent on killing Mia, before Mia got lucky.

Mia thought that now would be a great time to kill Samuel because the Mansion was in a form of chaos, and Samuel was not thinking rationally.

Mia moved like a weasel through the forest avoiding the falling trees and enduring the hail. There had been times that Samuel had been angry but this time it was worse than ever before. Mia decided it was time to make her move and kill Samuel.

Mia tried to get in and then tried to dig her way in. Both of her efforts were in vain, as demons had to fight off and steel bars sunk thirty feet into the Earth stopped Mia at first. Then Mia climbed the walls and broken a window to get inside of the mansion. In Mia's wake were demons dying or dead. All of them had their tongues ripped out of their mouths. It was a mission far from over as Mia entered the hallway and followed it to the dead-end. There at the end of the hallway was a room with a thick oaken door.

Mia tried the doorknobs and to her sunrise, it was unlocked. She tuned in her senses to the sounds and smells in the room. Sure enough, she could smell blood and her cries of the Postal Worker being 'sliced and diced' while probed by Mr. John Sung. Without doubt, it was Samuel in the room with the other two men.

There was the fast way in and then there was the waiting game to play. Mia knew that if she stayed outside the door that eventually demons or lower devils would find her. That left only one choice, and that meant through the front door.

Mia pulled her razor knife out from her pocket of her coveralls and silently opened the door. Now it was a matter of wills, with one catch. Mia had the advantage with surprise but she was out numbered. Thinking the odds over Mia decided that it was a time as any to kill Samuel. With a promise from Jessica that Mia's human soul promised a seat in Heaven, Mia opened the oaken door and stormed in. Samuel felt the blade slice into his side as he grabbed Mia by her throat. Mia struck first but Samuel was quick to counter Mia's move. Mia continued to slice and stab at Samuel without an effect.

Mia tightened her throat and Samuel felt it harden like concrete. Sung continued with his torture oblivious of what was going on around him. Mia tried her best and could not kill Samuel, perhaps it was because she worked alone

Demons joined the fight until Mia overwhelmed and escaped by running out of the room and jumping through a window onto a tree. In the wink of an eye, Mia disappeared into the woods. Samuel screamed in pain.

Mia was badly hurt as was Samuel. Both combatants were severely injured and enraged. Samuel swore on Earth and Hell that one day he would capture Mia alive. Mia was dreaming up a new strategy.

There will be other chances to get at Samuel, thought Mia. Certainly, Mia was not going anywhere except back to her cave on the Estate. This cave was only accessible from underground tunnels that Mia had dug.

Jessica, Rene, and Penny were sitting by a pond on the Compound discussing the future. *"How did you cure me Jessica and why is all of this happening, and?"* Penny was full of questions and then Penny asked one more question. *"Where are my parents and will I ever see them again?"*

Jessica hesitated for a moment and gave Penny her reply. *"Only God can answer your questions, Darling. I suggest that you pray to God and ask him. I am sure that he will answer your questions, be his will."* Jessica was about to speak again when Penny interrupted her. *"What about my parents?"*

"I am sorry child, you will never see your mother again but you will be with your father again." A tear rolled down Jessica's cheek as Rene said . . . *"Penny, you should be glad that God has answered your prayers, He healed you and rescued you when there was no salvation coming your way. If not for God then you would be within the Kingdom of the Beasts, lost and forgotten forever."*

Rene had been through hell and back while living at the Lupus Mansion. Pleasant and loyal to the Cause, Rene was an asset to the Foundation. They ate and played a board game as the two women tried to get more information out of Jessica about the future.

There was much ado over the kidnapping in the Army Hospital of Penny Wilson. Alerts sent out, with pleas for Penny's safe return. Posters were everywhere and the kidnapping was featured on America's Most Wanted television show, it was the first time that Security at the Hospital had failed.

Scientists had developed a heart ultimately and genetically altered with human DNA creating a half human and half pig donor heart. Penny was going to be the first to receive this transplant and it top secret.

Now that the operation canceled, another perfect donor needed to be located for the donor heart. Surgeons did not care if it was a person in need of a donor heart or if the person was perfectly healthy and wanted to sell a piece of them for profit.

Media outlets were taking advantage of this frenzy to find Penny Wilson had to find a donor for the hybrid heart. Oddly enough, the Public loved the idea of this new Promise to humankind; seemingly, few believed that this type of medicine was fine and dandy. After all, it was the Xeno organ or not enough organs to go around. CNN was featuring The Penny Wilson case, as were other Networks.

It is hard for any normal person to fathom giving up his or her own healthy heart for an experimental Xeno heart. Yet thousands of willing donors were lining up in front of hospital doors at four in the morning to get the jump on the donor list ahead of the others. These people were the poor and the once middle class ready to trade their heart to feed their family.

Immigration into the United States had nearly wiped out the chance of getting a job for an educated American. High paying jobs Engineers such as Bo-chemists. Good paying jobs were favored liberally to the outsiders because they asked so little in return.

Immigration the only issue that both parties agreed. Democrats split over the Xeno Project expenditures used to fund all the Xeno Projects. Trillions of dollars given to Government Foundations and foreign Contractors enjoyed the limelight and contributions immensely increased.

Obviously the truly rich had banded together to gain as much control of the world as possible. Unfortunately, they were succeeding in all parts of the world.

Penny at first was uncomfortable being away from her parents. After a few weeks, Penny began feeling at home and Rene had become her best friend.

Richard Wilson had more trouble knocking on his door. His wife Pam was having an affair with his best friend, who always seemed to be around when Richard wasn't home or was away on assignment. Richard opened the door to see who it was.

"You bastard, what were you doing spying on me? I was appalled when I saw the Private Investigator writing down my friend's License plate number and taking photographs of us. What in God's name were you thinking?"

Rick stood there for a moment and stared at Pam in disbelief.

"Do you want the neighbors to hear this?! Come inside before somebody calls the Police."

Pam walked inside the Hotel room and sat at the table. She knew that she had been caught red-handed cheating on her husband and what made it worse was that he caught her with Penny was kidnapped. Knowing that Rick was going to tear into her about the bad publicity it would bring down on them. Pam sat at the table ready to get on the defensive. A good offence is the best defense. Love or lust, it was too late to dwell on the past.

Senator Wilson eyed his wife over infuriated and bewildered by what he saw before him. Pam was dressed in a pink mini skirt and a T-Top.

"Look at you, its snowing outside and you are not even wearing a coat. You should be in an Evening Gown wearing your pearls and being graceful. Have you

forgotten that you are the wife of a senator? I don't care anymore anyway, you can do what you want to do but don't do it in Public!"

Pam crossed her legs and announced. *"I am just down the hall in room 1321, and I'm hosting a party. Your best friend is there, with the gang. Basically Honey, I want a divorce."*

Richard thought about the Presidency and his upcoming bid and possible nomination. Then he surveyed his options.

In the room adjoining his there was two Secret Service Agents watching and listening to everything that was happening in the Senator's room. They saw Richard give the hand signal and the two Agents stood and walked out the door. They had the keys to the Senators room and opened the door.

Pam tried to sit up but two well-aimed bullets fired with a silencer knocked Pam dead back into the chair.

Richard was glad that his personal Agents reacted so swiftly. Now he had to take care of Bill, his so-called best friend. In fact, Bill was the Best Man at Richards wedding. With a few words spoken to his Agents Richard knew he could crush this crisis before it happened. With a stern face, Richard closed the door to his room

"I want you to get rid of the body in my room and clean it up. You, need to go get Bill and bring him here. You know what to do from there. Make sure that the bodies will never be found."

Rene and Penny decided to go skinny-dipping in the spring fed pound. It was a beautiful day in California, unseasonably hot. It was a great day for a swim and the two women jumped into the pond among the wildflowers.

San Francisco was warned that a 7.0 Earthquake

was coming within a couple years but the people refused to move.

Penny was one of the Chosen and God heard her pleas. Fortunately, for Penny she would never know what happened to her mother.

Not every cry for help, will get an answered, 'some will not be heard' by anyone who would help but at least Penny was safe.

LOD, or better known as the Legion of Death were Angels Commissioned in Heaven to fight the first and the last battles during the end of the world. These battles will be deciding battles in the war between good and evil and the Legion of Death were the cream of the crop, they were the kindest of the kind-hearted, the best warriors to ever exist. At first L.O.D was only a bunch of local fellows from the Jessica Foundation until a guiding light from Heaven brought forth two Companies of Warriors.

Certainly one can see that God had given humans a 'Force of demon killers.' Each new Xeno baby born with horns is reincarnations of demons straight from hell. Without outside help, the human species doesn't have a chance.

The End of Chapter Ten
"A Cry for Help"

Chapter Eleven
"The Xeno Species"

*"**We** are the Xeno Species and we are proud of our race. Humankind has held us down for too long, now, and it is time for us to take our place in society."*

Many Xeno People had gathered and formed a United Front against humanity. This Organization kept secret for three years and founded by Valentine. They are a Militant Organization determined to make a difference in this war of wills.

"Now it is time to lash back at the weaker and dumber humans, why should we be equal a species that has run out of time when we are stronger and smarter then they are?"

There was loud applause and then a standing ovation. There were at least twenty thousand Xeno People if there was one. Valentine continued his hateful speech against humanity.

"I know a way to rid ourselves of these pests that call themselves humans. With the help of Dr. Keller and Lisa, 'who by the way is Xeno transplanting' Dr. Keller can develop a virus that kills only pureblooded humans. What is the greatest part of this plan is that the antidote will be an anti rejection drug kept secret by Dr. Keller? Please listen to this carefully, if a pure human tries to use the antidote to kill the virus in his body. Then the antidote becomes a lethal poison."

This meeting held in a huge underground cavern near Lake Mead, Nevada. Everyone there belonged to a twelve-person cell operating covertly to undermine human efforts to keep track of every Xeno Person. It was hot in the cavern and the walls were sweating what appeared to be blood dripping off quartz crystals.

"Remember California Township! We must never allow such acts to humiliate and destroy us. Do you agree with me that now it is their turn to suffer?"

Eagerly, the crowd cheered and screamed for more of what Valentine had to say. I would dare to say that if they had caught me, known who I was, then I would have never gotten to finish this Documentary.

"There never seems to be enough time to address our issues in Public. Perhaps we should do more to assure that the world hears us. First, we need to take control of our future and the best way to do that is taking over a State, certainly. We can cause enough corruption to bring down Governments. I say that it is time for us to recruit and strengthen our ranks so that California Township is never repeated in our lives."

Valentine was standing behind his Blood Altar that he had built while working at the Lupus Mansion. Of course Valentine was excited about the ten virgin sacrifices that were being prepared as his oration was ongoing, and his hunger became ravenous.

"We do not have to fret over weak Capitalists because they have Ethics and consciences. We must concentrate on Bin and his terrorist networks and kills them before we can take on the Capitalist Countries. Terrorists are a threat to our species because they are difficult to find, and live to die for their causes. Once we have accomplished this feat, then we will not need the Capitalists to help us hunt down the terrorists. They believe that they have control over us but the truth of the matter is that all victories will fall into our hands."

I was appalled when I had gotten a clear view of the Blood Altar and had to choke down the smell before I chucked my guts out all over the Xeno persons in front of me. It was Hell on Earth inside this large damp cavern. (Cheating death, a death arranged by God and a soul destined for Heaven. Stealing the soul by prolonging a life with animal DNA is the worse of all sins.)

"Some say that you can't live forever, I say Bah humbug. We will live forever while the human race dies of weakness and wars. Humans do not live forever; they die before they have a chance to taste life. Now some of us have the abilities to live for hundreds of years, if we do not have accidental death, or are murdered. However humankind is limited to a life span, simply proving that in due time the humans will go extinct while we will live on!"

Silence consumed the cavern and most Xenopeople were nodding their heads and staring at each other in agreement. Valentine continued his forceful Agenda. Valentine was an extremely talented speaker.

"In the future we will rule the world and kill every single human that refuses to be Xenomized for the good of our Species. Right now we are not strong enough in numbers to defeat these inferior people but in five our ten years we will be the almighty. For now, we must abide by their rules and be humble. Bring me the organizers that provoked and planned the Chicago Xeno riot."

Six men and two women led to the stage. Valentine forced them to bow their heads. *"This is what happens to people that decide to do things against the humans without my permission, remember that before any one of you decide to take matters into your own hands because you will suffer the same fate as these Xeno People will."*

Valentine picked up a broadsword that he had stolen from a museum and beheaded the men and women. With a thud, their heads hit the stage and then rolled off into the crowd. Xeno People in the crowd fought over the heads and the bodies as the virgins escorted up the stairs to the Blood Altar. Valentine studied the crowd as they ripped apart the bodies and of the executed and cheered.

Valentine was dressed in leathers and wearing spiked armbands while sporting razor sharp fingernails' five inches in length. Standing powerful and confident, most surely a remarkable sight.

All the virgins kidnapped from a church Bible Study held at a private residence. Every one of the girls was frightened, terrified of what was to become of them. They had good reason to be terrified because this was going to be their last day of life on this Earth.

Valentine smiled as the women forced to kneel before the Altar. Anxious but patient, Valentine was not finished giving his lecture.

"We will destroy all the humans once Dr. Keller perfects this lethal virus, now we have to insist on being classified as a species, there is an ongoing debate in Congress over this issue. Some say that because we as a Xeno People we do not share the same genetic pool then, we are not a species. I command you to carry out peaceful protests sending masse letters to our Politicians. What happened in Chicago they must not forget? It has set us back and now we have to present a new image. Otherwise, we might never reach our goals. We must become their friends and become productive in Society, then as we are smiling and telling them jokes. Only then can we release the Xeno Virus on the human species. With one swipe of a blade we will exterminate them all!"

Crying and pleading for mercy while a few Xeno Sentries fastened both women onto the down-turned cross, their pleas went unheard. Soon it would be their turn to experience a horrible death and then the other virgins would be next to be strapped onto the transposed sacrificial cross.

Valentine had his sworn loyalties to Lucifer and managed to keep this secret from Samuel. Samuel was the brain behind this plot to backstab the human species. Killing humans, while stealing their souls keeping as his own. Legions of Demons to command and victory in the name of Lucifer ruled. I am going to skip the details of the murders of the women kidnapped for Valentine. Being more gruesome than hell itself, these sacrifices were in the most horrific way imaginable.

Every night, nightmares haunt me and chase me into the morning. If I could go back in time, I would have closed my eyes during this ordeal. After the Sacrifices, ended Valentine ate until his gullet overfilled with human meat. Then he threw what leftovers into his Congregation of meat-eaters. These incidents will forever be stuck into my mind; certainly, it has affected my chain of thought and made me an enemy of the Xeno People.

All that I wanted was to study the Lupus Estate and dig up some facts on Doctor Keller. In only a few years it has come to this, the Xeno Age.

Once the meat devoured and order restored to the cavern. Valentine roared a demand for silence over the audience, which met with total silence. Valentine was going to sink his point home.

"Soon, the Xeno Games will begin and it will be then that we show our supremacy over the human species. We will dominate the games and humble them before we cut off their legs. In about ten years, we will have the Xeno Virus and then the world will be ours! For now we must bide our time and give no reasons for the humans to banish us, or worse yet, hunt us down like animals and murder our species. Time is on our side and don't you forget that when you are faced with an arrogant human, or a bully. You are all my flock and together we will conquer the Earth, the Heavens, and Hell." There was more said between the lines than there was in the speech.

It was elementary that Valentine had become a

powerful Demon, now he felt invincible; he felt that Samuel was a troublesome child that needed a good paddling, perhaps a quick death in some manner or another. Valentine was risking capture by allowing his wicked mind to wander as if it was. Samuel, on occasion reached into Valentine's mind utilizing telekinesis. Lucky for Valentine this was one time that Samuel was busy doing something else.

After the Cave Convention was finished, Valentine disappeared behind a stage as his servants cleaned the blood off the Altar and the stage. "Cleaning the stage was if you consider licking the blood and eating leftovers?"

Each Cell went in different directions to different cities in the world to await delivery of the virus. There was another Convention scheduled for next year, and by then Valentine will have added thousands of more Xeno People into his Legion of Death.

Flyers and Pamphlets, being distributed globally proclaiming that the Xeno People was a species and not a creation by Researchers. Facts were the legends and physical proof found in parts of South Africa, Central America, Argentina, and unbelievably in Siberia.

Objective facts demonstrated that the species were not the results of the Xeno Project. These abnormalities created solely by Nature and not by scientists. They were kidding themselves.

All the Xeno People claimed that they were a new species since the first baby was born from natural parents with horns and a tail in 2008AD.

Since then the recipients of donor Organs in the early 2000's were now having children and most were Xeno affected in body or mind, or both.

Humans everywhere were agreeing with 'the right for life for Xeno People.' However, there were strong human factions against this Xeno movement.

Anti New Species Groups were becoming Militant and Killing Xeno People in drive by and random killings throughout the world. China had deemed the Xeno People a menace to Society and mass murders were ongoing. There had been nothing of this magnitude since the Opium Panic in the last Century. India and Burma followed China's lead.

CNN was doing Specials on their News channels about the Xeno People and their Rights as a equal species. This did not go well with the Anti Xeno Groups and a huge controversy rolled off the News Presses.

Nobody thought that CNN would be blamed for this new issue hitting the Headlines but blamed they were and by all the anti-Xeno Groups, which spelled trouble.

Militant Groups that thus far managed to stay unidentified attacked CNN in many different ways. Kidnapping, assassinations, and death threats to the News station had become a great concern to the Executives of CNN. After years of promoting the Promise of animal to human organ transplants and drugs it had caught up with them.

Other humans were fighting for the Xeno People as much as the anti-Xeno Groups were targeting Xeno People. In America the issue was hot and lines were drawn in the sand, it had become an internal conflict that the world had never known in its past.

This subject of whether or not the Xeno People were a species created much ado among the different races of humans, that had less Rights then Xeno People held.

Humanity was in total chaos with nobody knowing what were truths and what were lies coming from Government Sources. Nobody knew whom to trust because many Xenopeople were akin to human families.

November 28, 2015

"This Court is now in session, please be seated."

Sixty Xenopeople brutally murdered at the Union City, Kansas dumpsites. Not only were they murdered but they were mutilated beyond recognition. Ten Defendants were on trial for these dastardly deeds and they had pled not guilty.

Outside the Courthouse Protestors wanted the ten men and women released, opposite from them on the north side of the street were the Xeno people with their own grievances and signs proclaiming that they are no different then humans. Before long, there were confrontations between the two groups outside the Courthouse.

At first, it was only a fistfight between two humans and three Xeno people. Within a few minutes, the fist fighters doled out and calm restored.

Inside of the Courtroom, the Defendants Attorney was giving his final address to the Jury.

"Ladies and Gentlemen, please let me give you the facts and get off this conjectured attack on my Clients. I want to bring your attention to these ten Defendants, yes they admit that they had committed these killings but consider why they killed them? Let me explain that all the Defendants are human and the so-called victims are not a species, a species of Terrorists. Sixty Terrorists meeting in a secret place and caught by the Defendants plotting against the human Species. Consider this if you will, the Prosecution has no witnesses that will defend the victims and that the Xeno people that died were no more than beasts wanting fresh meat. If these ten Defendants had allowed those Terrorists, or so-called Xeno People to get away then none of us here would be safe. I ask you to find these Defendants Not Guilty because what they had done was far from being a crime. These men and women

should be given Medals instead of being accused of Murder."

After the Jury deliberated for two hours, a verdict returned. "Not Guilty."

When they announced verdict, the crowd outside the Courtroom Cheered and the anti Xeno Protestors hung their heads down dropped their signs and walked peacefully away. Everybody believed that if this verdict was read, then another riot would occur like the one in Chicago. Instead of a riot, the Xeno People walked away gracefully, with honor.

The entire world over the Xeno People applauded for their humility and compassion. What everyone thought would escalate into a full-fledged riot turned out to be a peaceful protest to the injustice and prejudge attitude of humans toward the Xeno People. This time the humans in this melee were the ones that turned out to be the villains.

Scientists expressed outrage and the Supreme Court was debating whether to classify the Xeno People as a species. Changes were underway for the future and they were changes that the Xeno People celebrated and nurtured. These changes were occurring too quickly and caught the world by surprise. These changes dug the line in the sand deeper and in the future would reap blood. Opposition continued against the Supreme Court by the human Representatives._____

Valentine was elated, he was ecstatic about his flock of wolves walking away from a riot. If they had rioted there was a chance that one of his Cells would have been uncovered and possibly his quest to exterminate the human species. Valentine began planning his next move.

Two-thousand miles away Samuel was beckoning

Valentine to come home. Samuel noticed that Valentine was gone more then he was home.

Mia knew what Samuel was thinking and was contemplating whether to make another go at it. With Valentine on his way home, Mia opted to put off another try at Samuel for a better time.

A Bill passed through both Houses and was on its way to the Oval Office. To be signed or vetoed, if the President signs the Bill then the Xeno People be classified into three separate Species.

Species # one: The Xeno People, they are the offspring of normal persons with an animal to human tissue, bone marrow, or Organ transplants.

Species # two: Persons that are half-human and half animal, created in laboratories. They are intelligent and peaceful in nature.

Species # three: The Xenomittes, creatures made up of human and animal DNA without the ability to reason and were violent in their natures. Some Xenomittes are born insane and placed in seclusion. Xenomittes have mixed DNA and a wired genetic pool, but they are living beings. They are vicious in their natures and devour meat as if the meat never would run out.

The End of Chapter Eleven
"The Xeno Species"

Chapter Twelve
"<u>The Xeno Empire</u>"

Deep inside the Rain Forests of Brazil lived what once was a cult, now, it was a Militant Compound filled with all three Xeno Species geared to genocide the human species. They called themselves "The Xeno Empire."

In the last year two-hundred-thousand Xeno beings had migrated to the Xeno Empire. There were thousands of huts and an underground tunnel network. Within the tunnels were constructed living quarters and huge chambers used as Medical Centers and warehouses along with dining facilities.

There were only a few humans allowed to enter the Xeno Empire and there was a good reason for it. Once a month three-cargo planes landed on a camouflaged airstrip inside the Compound loaded with kidnapped humans. Onboard, were two scientists? In addition, four researchers relieving the others work in underground laboratory Staff.

Breeding Chambers emptied quickly and several Governments had covert Operations with the yet unheard of Xeno Empire. Inside the cargo planes, were more breeders and some feeders.

At one time, there were three villages within a twenty-mile range of the Compound. Now it was as if they never existed, the Xeno Empire raided them. Soon more Villages raided once human meat vanquished.

Only the Breeders were safe from danger, because they created more food. Treated like livestock, the children fattened and then eaten by the Xenopeople.

Four feet tall and covered in hair, the Xenomittes herded the victims into underground cages. Every so often, a Xenomittes would eat a human as they were herding humans like cows.

Swiftly the Professional humans were hushed down into the labs to relieve the others that have finished their three-month shift.

Huge generators running 24-7 powered the hidden Research Laboratory where the men and women escorted. First, to see were two Researchers, Ben and Mike spoke first.

"It's about time that you folks arrived and you are late. This place gives me the creeps and these species are cruel. Do not worry about anything because we have immunity. I'm outta here; see ya sucker's later, alligators." 'In less the twenty minutes the planes were taking off and gone into the horizon.'

Inside the lab and around the corner standing beside some test subject cages was Valentine. As the new arrivals turned the corner, they saw a huge Beast dressed in leather wearing a crimson cloak.

Ruby Christian was one of the Researchers and when she saw Valentine's hideous face Ruby fainted. Charles Clark grabbed hold of Ruby before she hit the floor.

Valentine held out his huge hand and one at a time shook the hands of each member of the new team. Doctor Keller and his Mistress entered the lab from a side door and introduced themselves. Valentine laughed like a baboon and sent goose bumps up the Team's backs.

Valentine seemed to vanish but the lights could have been playing tricks on the Teams eyes. Dr. Keller opened the Welcome Mat and began the same speech he had rehearsed a hundred times . . .

"Welcome to Lab 131341A, we work hard labor as a Team. You are here to assist us in building an apparatus that will Culture, control environments, separate germs and viruses as they are sucked out of the huge aquariums and into this oblong incubator."

There were six aquariums on each wall, that fed by the Immunizer, which made eighteen aquariums. Each aquarium had its own world. One had human skin tissue kept alive and had been infected with on of Dr. Keller's culture viruses. Another had an insect that radiated heat.

Number two, filled with water and fish. Some of the fish were deformed and others had boils and warts growing on their bodies. They were unsightly fish that were also carrying deadly viruses.

Number three, had a sandy bottom and housed three lizards each carrying a different virus. They seemed healthy enough as they aimlessly fought each other.

Number four, was a lager aquarium with two monkeys inside and they sported razor sharp teeth and hands resembling human hands. These Test Subjects perfected with an absolute immune system. However be, as it may, they were suffering from a bad rash that was beginning to seep blood.

Number five, was empty except for two dead sparrows. Around the sparrows, were rings in the black dirt circling the birds? Each ring was a different color and seemed to have a glow about it.

Number six, had a spotted Armadillo inside with what seemed to be Goose bumps all over its body. As we passed it, the creature hissed at us.

Number seven, was filled with different types of frogs from all over the world. After studying them for a few minutes, the Team found no faults in the frogs.

Number eight; an anthill, discovery surely a wonder surprised the Team. The ants were blue in color, along with being extremely vicious. Dr. Keller tossed a mouse in with the ants, in a few seconds the ants devoured the mouse. There among the ants was a spider loaded with nanomites.

Number Nine, to our surprise, there inside the aquarium was an eight-year-old child. 'Pat, one of the

Researches' asked what the girl's name was. Dr. Keller replied that Test Subjects did not have names, only numbers. Lisa informed us that this Subject was Test Subject 1313. Lisa explained that the eight-year-old girl was a carrier of deadly viruses and that she was immune to them. Lisa compared 1313 to Typhoid Mary and laughed.

Number ten, was full of snakes crawling around and forming a ball. Some were eating the other and others were squeezing each other to death.

Number eleven; scared the Team. They stayed back away from the creature. Behind the tempered glass was a Xenomittes that had human legs. It was science against humanity. With human legs, the Xenomittes could run and chase prey. Images of these horrors rampaging through the human species terrified the team. Then just in time, Dr. Keller said . . .

"Don't fret people, he is only an experiment in the search for a cure, this creature is subhuman and will be destroyed once we find the cure."

"Cure for what disease?" Dick Trenton Asked 'one of the scientists on the Team.'

"(We found a cure for Leprosy.)" Lisa Answered.

Number twelve proved to be interesting. Behind the glass was a three-headed boy with a tail. Each head seemed normal and they were speaking but the glass muffled sounds.

Number thirteen, thus far was the worse exhibit to view of all. It was a monster of some sort that had only arms and no legs. Scooting around on the mat inside the aquarium the thing opened its mouth and displayed shark teeth. Silently the group moved to the next exhibit carrying the creeps with then from what they had seen so far.

Number Fourteen was a Xeno Woman that was extremely beautiful but she had three hands with one hand being that of a baboon. After a closer look-see, the Team noticed that the nude Being behind the glass was probing their minds. ***"She is telepathically endowed."*** Lisa Informed.

Number Fifteen was filled with thousands of species of insects. Most of the insects were unknown to the team and left them baffled.

Number Sixteen seemed to be a large virus, it was swimming in fresh blood that filtered and recycled fresh new blood once the blood depleted of nutrients.

Exhibit Number Seventeen was an octopus that had a human head that could speak and had eighteen long arms, hands and legs. It scurried around, as a spider would have done, locked in a jar. It seemed to have no purpose what so ever.

Number Eighteen blinded everybody until Lisa passed out dark protective glasses. It was a living plant with a spiked skin. It stood about four-feet tall and two large glowing beetles were it's eyes. At the end of its roots were bear claws and its limbs glowed red as if they were hot.

Now the Teams was not repulsed but were amazed and impressed at what they saw. With a mouth, at least ten inches wide with normal human teeth.

Lisa informed us that the spikes lined with microscopic sacks of poison. She also said that the bear claws were razor sharp and weighed one-hundred pounds apiece. Lisa explained that human DNA was absorbed into the plant.

With great hospitality given by the Xeno escorts, the Team shown the Kitchen, bathrooms and orientated them to the lab and where everything was stored. Then the Escorts showed the team to their rooms.

All the Guest Quarters completely provided with their own bathrooms, a small kitchen, a big screen TV, an awesome stereo, a plush couch and a queen-sized bed.

There were no locks on any of their doors but privacy was guaranteed.

Two Days Later

Hot and muggy with mosquitoes thick in the air an unknown Speaker was pushing the crowd of the Xeno Empire to hate humankind. I heard on the grape vine that it was "The Xeno Man."

"We are the Xeno Empire! Nothing can, or will, stop us, with the conquest of Brazil. Then the world will be in our grasp! Don't you think that we have the sand it takes to deliver the final punch to the humans, to pound in that last nail into their coffins? It is time that we ask ourselves, how we can make the human condition worse."

There were all sorts of different activities and Events happening on the vast grounds of the Xeno Empire. All the Officers and Leaders wore masks to cover their identities. Sometimes on the grounds, there would be a huge carnival. During the festivities, the Venders would sell human meat, cooked and raw. Seasonings and barbecue sauce absolutely applied heavily on the food.

Hideous scenes were all about the compound. One could easily say that Xeno People lived like animals. What was stench to humans was good smelling air for the Xeno People. They bred like dogs and ate ravenously cannibals.

Three groups of hunters were heading out searching for Villages to plunder. It was Dusk when they entered the wood line. They were carrying an assortment of weapons with them, from knives, spears, to firearms. Unfortunately, for the primitive Villages twenty-miles away, these Xeno Forces knew where the Villages were. They were able-bodied first generation Xeno People.

One main issue that both the humans and the Xeno People shared . . .

In agreement, both species wanted Terrorism to cease. Big decisions made about big bombs. Big bombs like the Dirty Bombs and Atom bombs. There was a wait for the Killer Virus and Bin with his cohorts had taken a toll on both species.

Bin was hiding in Pakistan on this day and the Xeno Leaders knew it as fact. They were constructing a plan to blast that chunk of land where Bin was hiding into a crater. Two people, Dr. Keller and Lisa, were addressing this.

Xeno People from all over the world had been sending monies to the Xeno Empire that has added up to billions of dollars. Still, it was not enough to build a nuclear bomb and have it delivered to its target.

Money converted into platinum, gold bars. It was the only thing of value. Fort Knox was safeguarding more gold then ever in its history. Vats filled with diamonds and other precious metals.

Missile Silos constructed for one minuteman missile aimed and launched at Eastern Pakistan. It was equipped with six warheads and a Powerful nerve agent. Dr. Keller estimated that the missile loaded for bear would kill everything in a two hundred-mile Radius. If the blast and radiation did not kill him then the powerful Nerve Agent would do the terrible deed. If all went as planned, the due date for the launch was set for 2020AD.

Whatever happened within the Xeno Empire stayed within its stoned walls. Word of spies and satellite surveillance had leaked to Valentine, he sent a message to Dr. Keller, and the Dictator Valentine had left in charge of his Xeno Army in Brazil, an appointed Dictator named Sul Krokus. Sul was a brutal and heartless being with a passion to inflict pain on humans. He enjoyed being a part of Valentines scheme of things to come. Xeno Empire recruiting was at an all time high.

Sul was angry when he had gotten the news of the

spies within the Xeno Fortress. With great haste, Sul ordered all new arrivals within the last year gathered in the Courtyard. There in the Courtyard were almost ten-thousand people. Some Xeno People and others were Xeno transplant recipients. Sul stood over the crowd and demanded to know who the traitors to step forward. Nobody stepped forward and that infuriated Sul to the point where he climbed down the steps of his podium and stood defiantly before the crowd.

Krokus is a huge creature who has a bad deposition. Twelve-feet tall and half-animal, Sul was a remarkable sight. Head and neck with the shoulders sported powerful human muscles, his body, including the arms and legs, whatnot, were Arabian Stallion. Sul is half human and half horse, a creation of Dr. Keller's work. Dr. Keller was unable to duplicate this masterpiece, if he could have created more of Sul, then Nick would have created an army of them.

Pacing back and forth in front of the mass of people, Krokus was turning red in anger. He could not know for sure who the spies were in the crowd. Krokus sent for his messenger and told her to contact Dr. Keller and to ask him for one of his telepathic people from the lab.

Dr. Keller was more then happy to help Sul out. He sent Raven Stockton to help find the spies within the walls of the Compound. Raven is a beautiful young woman with a penal gland transplant donated by a cougar. Within the Xeno Empire one of a kind, Test Subjects were common.

Two Korean Managers at the Casa Linda Motel were a part of the Xeno Empire. They are not Xeno People but greedy as hell they are. Sneaky, nosey, and invade on the tenants privacies. It was not the Xeno People this man and wife team hated they despised Americans. For every Xeno Assassin that they helped, the Xeno Foundation paid Kim three-thousand dollars. Kim and Kathy were putting their children through College with the illegal monies that they received and had become talented, blatant liars.

Sometimes if a person or persons rented a room from Kim, they would disappear. Kim worked jointly with the El Dorado Motel in Salinas, California.

Kevin is the manager at the El Dorado Motel and openly beat his timid wife on a daily basis. Kevin had the same deal as the Koreans bar Kevin was a Double Agent. Working for a Muslim Terrorist Group that is loyal to Bin, Kevin was able to collect enough information from the Koreans to make his work worthwhile. Kevin and his wife were born in Pakistan, working the El Dorado was fun for Kevin.

Absolutely, positively, guaranteed dished and prepared to your liking, were the words that came out of the Tour Guide's mouth. A Busload of tourists was debarking at the Casa Linda Motel and Kim with his wife had the barbecue pit fired up and dinner nearly ready for the tired and hungry travelers. You know what they say; fatten the hogs before you butcher them.

In the meat, there were knockout drugs and in the motel, there were shackles and other items needed for transport. Long ago Kevin began hating Americans and like Kim, the loathing festered. Everyone was having a grandee time, laughing and enjoying the last warm days of the year. Hot coals smoked as the meat sizzled on the gas grill.

Unknowingly to the passengers the drugs in the meat was slow acting but effective. Before long, passengers were sleeping like logs with smiles on their faces. Kim and his brothers gathered the tourists and carried them to their perspective rooms. These persons had no idea what happened to them until they awakened with their hands and feet shackled laying in the trailer of an eighteen-wheeler.

There were cargo planes waiting for them at a private airport near Fresno to take them to the Xeno Empire.

Every year, California was a bit colder as Canada became warmer. These events could easily make a person believe that with all the disasters happening in the world and wars that the Xeno Empire would only grow into a lethal threat beyond the others.

The End of Chapter Twelve
"The Xeno Empire"

Chapter Thirteen

"The Xeno Games"
"December 22, 2015"

Starka knew all too well that the human race was counting on him to win the Xeno Games. Starka secretly lived and trained at the Xeno Compound. Starka is a formidable and witty man with white wings. Some folks believed him to be an Angel.

Blessed by God, Starka was pure human at a young age. Jessica proclaimed Starka to be an Angel sent from heaven to assist the human race in defeating the anti Christ.

Born with wings that adored his long white hair, behold!

Sly as a fox and born evil, the devil tricked the world and God by creating a species of human anti Christ. With these creatures the devil knew that first he would conquer the World and then the Heavens. There was not anything that the devil believed could stop his horde of demons. With a stern warning to the devil, God promised to burst the Earth into a ball of fire in the year 2027 if the devil succeeded in his plans to conquer the planet.

Starka was another creation of God with the ability to fly and turn its finger and toe nails into razor sharp talons, Starka preferred to use a round shield with a four-feet in length double-edged broadsword. Standing seven-feet tall with immense shoulders and a well-muscled body Starka was a humble but a lethal warrior. He had been a member of God's Guard since the beginning of time.

Some people said that Starka was white as snow and carried a glow about him everywhere that he went. A nearly beautiful and perfect man, Starka walked gracefully, among the people in the Jessica Foundation was respected, and loved. Starka exclaimed that the coming of Christ was nearing and that he was to clear a path for Christ to walk.

Leven and Tammy were fighting along side Starka throughout the Xeno Games. Because of flurries in hurricanes along the coast, the Games moved to Salt Lake City under protest by Mormon Leaders. Grateful that Starka was on their team, Leven and Tammy had become Christians.

Each Contestant followed stringent rules, one weapon's carrier and helper during the battle. These men and women wore no weapons and had to improvise to help their Masters. Brave and daring, they were worth the time and effort to train in hand-to-hand combat. Monica, Seth, and David were priceless to Starka, he was glad to be their Sheppard.

Xeno warriors allowed the same courtesies and always had the edge during the games. It seemed that the refs were calling penalties against humans last year more than the Xenowarriors. Xenowarriors allowed stepping out of the fifty-foot circular fighting line to avoid a deathblow and the humans followed harsher rules. Because humans deemed smarter, rules of the games favored the Xeno Species.

- **December 23, 2015** -

On this day, Dallas suffered hits by at least thirty-two tornadoes. Inside the Xenotraining grounds, Xeno Warriors were getting the feel of the new Xeno Games site.

Global warming had changed the four seasons into a chaotic mess. Chicago was a record 80 degrees Fahrenheit and in Sarasota, Fla., the weather was bad, staying in the low thirties. Salt Lake was a perfect eighty-degree Fahrenheit without a cloud in the sky and the calmest day of this year.

Throughout the world, Countries were refusing to help Countries who had given aid to them in the past.

Mother Nature was tearing the Earth apart a bit more everyday as the asteroid neared in its dash at our planet.

Flooding was a huge problem globally and the winters were getting warmer in most parts of the world. In Salt Lake City, the weather was perfect and the Xeno Field was grassy and well groomed.

———————

Tang Chang and Xenowoman represented the Xeno Species. Now considered a branch species from the human race, Xeno Warriors eventually allowed to compete in the Xeno Games.

Tang and a recently released Xenowoman were fighting as Seed 1; they were an awesome team bent on winning the Xeno Games 'using whatever means possible to achieve their objective.'

Seed 2 were two more Xenopersons. Since the day that they classified as an intelligent species, more Xeno people had gotten involved in the Xeno Games. Paulex Mamdin and Bocus Dementri were born Killers and bad to the bone. Both were weapons' Experts and chose different weapons for each contest.

Seed 3 were Starka, Leven and Tammy. You already know the story behind these heroes' lives and in my opinion; they should have been the first seed.

There were three no-shows and the Xenoman was one of the absent. He was in Pakistan hunting Bin and his private Militia. Only a few knew about this fact and those that did know kept it highly confidential.

Numbering in the hundreds, contestants were all about the Arenas getting in their last workouts before the Games began. Appalling and ghastly scenes consumed their workouts. Live humans were being used in their practices, 144 those on Death Row or had Life Prison sentences . . .

Some of the Humans were quite formidable

opponents and inflected wounds on the Xeno warriors. In the end, all the kidnapped humans were mutilated and murdered.

It was all for the glory and the thrill of it all. Xeno Warriors were ruthless, unfeeling, and merciless. Training intensified as another truck filled with Prisoners ready to be punching bags or worse yet, human targets to be sliced, diced, smashed, or broken. Xeno warriors would eat fresh flesh and drink the blood of the humans that they slaughtered during the practice games. There was more blood than glory and the human Gladiators were fighting not for glory. They were fighting in hatred of the Xeno Species.

All contests were fights to the death. Odds favored the Xeno Warriors and the bets were buzzing on the Internet in favor of the First Seed. Christians were protesting the Games by celebrating Christmas. Christmas and Easter forbidden, outlawed, and the jails were filling for the Xeno Games.

Security was immense at the Xeno Games Arenas with the Xeno Guard and the National Gaud were protecting this Event. There was bad blood between the two Guards but they worked in cooperation with each other well.

Deep in the wetlands of Pakistan, Xenoman was nearing his prey. He watched from a rocky hillside that seemed to stand alone among the vast flat lands of Pakistan. After murdering fourteen sentries and hiding their bodies, Xenoman was well on his way in making History. Once he was near enough to Bin and his aides then Xenoman would kill them all.

Bin was getting a little older and kept a pack of dogs near him as an added line of defense. These dogs were mongrel hybrids that had shark teeth and muscles like pit bulls. These dogs were hunting, fighting, and guard dogs trained to protect Bin. Bin was older and wiser with hands on experience in every aspect of war, every move that he made was calculated and in his own best interests.

Winds seemed to come from all directions and helped Xenoman stay covered in sand. With a modern Miles laser rifle in his hands all that the Xenoman had to learn was which house, cave, or dwelling Bin the Great was hiding in. Xenoman known to go for a week without food, water or sleep, Xenoman was going to wait Bin out.

Obviously the Xenoman enjoyed his work more than the Xeno Games but missed being there fighting in the arenas. Soon his target would emerge from one of three dwellings. He knew this because of his keen animal senses and his human gut feeling. His plan was to escape in one of the helicopters on the edge of the airstrip. It was the pleasure of the kill that Xenoman lusted for.

———

Starka flew laps around the circle of death in the Arena while Leven and Tammy stood back to back ready for their second practice Round. Against them were four convicts armed with hatchets and round shields to attack and defend themselves.

Barry Newton was on Death Row and was a mad-hatter. Newton had earned his tough Sentence after he raped and murdered five college students and from a rooftop murdered three off duty Policeman.

Bob Sorenson was doing six Life Sentences for the murders of six high school kids trespassing on his land. He had dismembered the children and was feeding them to his pigs when Investigators walked in on him.

Virgil Gains was the third man and he was a born bully and ran the team. Virgil was a unique criminal in that he raped and murdered his own family. "Three daughters, two sons, his wife and mother-in-law, plus the pet dog,"

Gains was beyond insane and a war vet. He was an ex Ranger and was serving on the Chicago Police Force when he committed his ghastly crimes, sudden and total insanity.

Finally yet importantly was Billy Ann Borden. She was an expert in poisons and deadly toxins. Their Wardens made sure that Prison Teams was well equipped with the best gear. Prison Wardens appointed by the Feds, and were encouraged to give the convicts in the games every advantage possible. Billy Ann was poison from her nails to her teeth. Her dagger was poison-tipped and so was her axe. She had been sentenced to death for murdering her three children and 287 fellow employees at the factory that she worked at. She had poisoned all the water coolers and coffee dispensers with a slow acting deadly toxin. Then she entered the Office and axe murdered her boss and all the employees working there, including the Owners wife. "Watch out with that axe Billy Ann Borden."

Starka dismayed by the pureness of the evil he sensed in these convicts. He felt compelled to save their souls but that was not his job, Starka was a warrior. Saving eternal souls were the works for Ministers and not the labor for warriors from God. Starka was headstrong and strong willed to perfection beyond our imaginations. Starka never felt joy in his work to kill, and vanquish evil. This time Starka sickened by the deeds that these people had done and the crimes they committed. Flying over to his comrades in arms Starka gave a stern warning about Billy Ann Borden.

Leven eyed their sparring partners over and knew at first sight that they were dangerous. With the same protecting copper mess protecting his body, Leven had armed himself with a spiked ball and chain and a long sword. Leven knew that they had to kill the woman first because she was the biggest threat.

Both Tammy and Leven suited their weapons to

best defeat their opponents. Tammy decided to arm herself with a six-foot staff and a short sword. Tammy covered in light but stalwart copper armor, it was fair protection against the poisoned daggers but the steel axe was trifling at the very least. Tammy would use her shield to ward off the axe and to keep Billy Ann Borden at a distance. Still, there were the other convicts to keep an eye on, to watch and when opportunity strikes the moment, to kill.

Starka circled the convicts as they entered the circle to engage in combat. Bob Sorenson went into a rage and swung his axe at Starka hovering over the man just out of reach. Bob was slower then the others were and with a mighty swing of his double-edged broad sword, Starka beheaded the ill-fated convict.

Raven Decont was in the next arena to the east of Starka' Team and she used her net and hammer with deadly accuracy. She was killing seven convicts in her circle with malice and with ease. DuPont was smiling as she relished each kill and screamed in delight when she slammed her hammer down on the last convict. Blood splattered far enough away that some of the splatter glistened on Starka's snowy whiteness.

Raven glanced over at Starka and grimaced, she was convinced that once she competed against Starka and his team that the Xenoman would have returned by then and joined her in the Contest. Raven was counting on it to be so.

Litua Patel was from Pakistan and was a born liar and expert assassin. She was a survivor of many deaths. Patel had the ability to come back to life after she was pronounced dead, an ability that was deemed to be a syndrome. Some folks called her an insane deformity from God but she was far from that. Litua endowed with surreal gifts such as hypnosis, astral projection, deception, and acupuncture. Litua wore a belt lined with needles that she would stick into her foes faster than the eyes could see, causing a horrid death.

Litua stepped into the arena with Raven and as they faced each other, the women smiled at each other. They were friends and shared the same Dorm room at the Arena Barracks. The Xenoman was the third person on this team but the women were ready to enter the contests with or without the Xenoman. Litua carried a sickle that she was twirling faster then the eye could see. In her left hand was the Lucas Lance, she took it from his belongings once she learned that Lucas was dead. Litua always wanted the lance and she laced it with poison once it was in her possession.

Expertly the two women sparred to warm up for the humans ready to jump inside their circle. Raven gave the signal and ten of the twenty humans waiting in tow jumped into the arena to try their best to kill the two Xenowomen.

Bin Aladdin was only one of his names, but he had many others. In his mind, the coming of Christ was getting too near for comfort. There had to be something done about this problem. Bin believed Christ to be the white devil.

Unbeknownst to the War Lord of all Terrorists, Bin was in a cavern surrounded by his handpicked Guard. There was no reason for Bin to fret because he was deep inside friendly territory. There was an Army of battle-tested veterans protecting him. Pouring himself another cup of sage tea Bin sat on the ground next to the hot blazing fire.

How could Bin have known that the King of Assassins was only sixty-feet above him hiding within the thick sage bushes? There was no way to know because Xenoman exclusively created and fine-tuned for this job

Xenoman engineered through his DNA to do many awesome acts, including the ability to burrow like a mole. Thus, it was best to come down from the top, or dig up from the bottom. After thinking it over for a few minutes' Xenoman decided to burrow down and then up. By doing, it in this way, Xenoman could pull Bin down into his clutches and drag through unknown tunnels as he dug them.

First Xenoman burrowed vertically beneath the deep cavern chambers. He listened and searched for the scent of the Xenoyouth Potion that Bin was hiding from his peers.

During Bin's initial run for life from the Americans, he was a man under many names. Bin Aladdin was only another name like the others but not to his followers; to them he was a Saint. Bin was pouring himself a cup of ginger tea and sitting beside a blazing fire. It was time to celebrate the next attack on England. It was going to be bigger then anything he had conspired before. All his chosen Specialists were prepared to leave at dawn. Now it was time for feasting and playing games. For others it was time to pray and ask their God for victory with the war against the infidels. Bin felt safe and secure as he watched the leg of lamb roasting over the fire.

Xenoman knew that he was almost indestructible, key word being almost. It was getting to be past dinner and in another hour; all in the cavern would be ritually drunk or drugged. Xenoman heard the plot to hit England and thought about killing all the Leaders before hightailing it with Bin in tow.

Xenoman waited eighty-feet beneath the surface for the drunks and the prayers to party out and pray out. First, he planned to kill the guards and then the Leaders while holding Bin hostage. With Alpha-x-ray vision, the Xenoman could nearly see through walls. First, it was time to wait, and then it was time to kill.

-   10:00pm   -

There were a few thoughts going through

Xenoman's highly engineered mind and that was the Congressional Medal of Honor and the taste of blood. All the chatter was gone and the music stopped playing in the cavern chamber. Soon it was going to be time for bloodletting and feasting, for the hungry Xenoman.

Indeed, Xenoman began silently scratching dirt away as he crawled, upward right beneath Bin. Bin was sipping his tea with a shot of some Scottish Whiskey when he fell into a deep hole and into the arms of Xenoman. Xenoman squeezed Bin silently until the Leader of all Leaders of Terrorists passed out. Then in a flash Xenoman went on a rampage inside the dark chamber slicing and dicing swiftly enough to massacre fifty or more terrorists and their families. Xenoman grabbed the leg of lamb and ate it in two bites, and then he twisted a human leg off the body and ate that too.

Ten miles was not a problem for Xenoman, he carried Bin under one arm as he ran to the airstrip to a waiting twin-engine plane. Once Xenoman and his bounty were loaded, they ran down the runway and lifted into the sky. It seemed that the Xenoman was going to get to the games in time to participate in them after all.

Leven and Tammy retired for the evening as had Starka. They needed their rest for the Xeno Games tomorrow. It had been a strenuous day for the trio and Leven was too tired to make love with Tammy.

Tammy was cuddling and fooling around in bed when she announced. ***Leven, I hate to be the one to say it but Xenoman has returned to the arena in time to sign in.*** "***So what, we have Starka and he is the only contestant who can fly like an eagle.***"

Since the moment that Leven had become a Christian, he believed that Starka was a man from God.

Sculptured by God's hands, Leven trusted in God to

deliver victory into his hands.

Bocus, Tang and Xenowoman now had Xenoman on their Team, victory seemed assured for the four beings created by hell bent Scientists. Seed 1 was favored to win the Xeno Games Competitions with the odds being 250-1.

December 25, 2015

Lisa was exhilarated about the games and the 250 Teams participating in the games. She was inside the main enclosed balcony overlooking the six arenas.Dr. Keller was there beside the Queen of the games watching the fields prepped for the games. Their son was hidden away safely out of harms way.

It was only six in the morning and the games began at nine. Breakfast brought to Lisa and Nick in the balcony, Staff members catered all of their needs. Nick was wearing shoulder holsters that housed two semi automatic large caliber pistols. Dr. Keller picked up the habit while working in San Francisco, California. While the combatants were limbering up and getting wrapped, there was a Marching Band tuning their instruments in the main Arena with a diameter of fifty yards.

This same arena was going to begin the games with seed 250 against seed one. All the arenas would be engaged in contests at the same time, in this way a person could not get bored.

Naked Cheer Leaders had only their hands to use as shields. They were a part of the game, if a combatant needed to test the sharpness of his or her blade; the Cheerleaders were always there to help. Once a cheerleader was raw, then another innocent victim with a pretty, fresh girl.

Festivities included anything from beer and hot dogs to steaks and roasted pigs. Venders were price gouging and making a profit selling their goods. There were plastic shields and swords for the kids, and tee shirts with Xeno caps. There was dancing and clowns, jugglers, and carnie games. Nobody thought about the hundreds of innocent lives sacrificed for the games. After all, it was only a human life.

Sunshine streaked across the valley as the morning turned into day. Today the first Xeno Games would begin and the people would cheer loudly enough to shake the stadium. With the sun shining bright and all the seats filled for the Games, The Quean rose from her seat and placed her hand over her heart for the National Anthem. There had been a dry spell in parts of Utah and the Mud Flats, had completely dried and lay barren in the vastness of the horizon. Within the Stadium walls the sun was rising and the Contestants were entering the circles they had been assigned. It was a beautiful morning in Salt Lake City.

Starting the games off were six contests of the lower seeds making their way up the ladder to fight Seeds 1-10. These contests seemed to drag on but as the lower seeds were dying off, they grew more talented and the contests ended quicker. The crowds with laughter and insults at the dying and cheering at the winners met screams along with pleas for mercy.

Dr. Keller and Lisa were in their bulletproof balcony safe and snug from the crisis that he created. Lisa requested that the gladiator named Starka brought to her so that she may keep him as a pet. Dr. Keller laughed and tilted his head. Lisa noticed that one of Dr. Keller's eyes seems to sparkle more in one eye and it glowed.

Lisa had a fit and stomped her feet in disappointment when Nick told her that Starka was a natural human and not a Xeno Project.

Meanwhile at the Jessica Foundation Compound

A huge blue fur pine tree adorned the Compound

Center, and located centered in Abraham Square within Heaven Gate Park. Jessica had bought so many thousands of acres of land that only her Banker knew the true span of the property. They also had Mineral Rights and fields of wheat and hay. The Heaven Gate Park is ten miles long and three miles wide.

Thousands of lights illuminated the tree and ornaments cast in jewels. This Christmas tree was eighty-feet high and decorated from top to bottom. Carolers sung and everybody was exchanging gifts and hugging while enjoying a lovely morning.

There was a big screen television in Jessica's chamber and she was watching the Xeno Games with Raven and Penny. Jessica called the games a part of an epic story ending with slaughter and bloodletting. She claimed that the coming of Christ was near and that all those people at the games would see blood rain from the sky.

Jessica saw the Queen and Dr. Keller on the TV screen and was disgusted about their demeanor. Lisa seemed not to age nor did Dr. Keller. It was their haughtiness and pride, greed eating at their souls and self-righteousness making them appears godlike. This day and from this day on, Jessica knew that they might burn in hell and that life would vanquish, a bloody dawn lurked over the orange horizon.

Mia was hiding in the woods on the Jessica Foundation property because she did not want anybody to see her. She knew that many people would scream when they saw her and that just being near Jessica was giving Mia great comfort. There was no reason to be hunting Valentine because he was in the jungles of Brazil and Dr. Keller always surrounded by Secret Service Agents at the Xeno Games. Several Investors with the Jessica Foundation had invested 250 million dollars on Starka and his Team to win the Finals in the Xeno Games. They were loyal to

God and were responsible for the Foundation Finances.

Jason Kuzma was responsible of the Defense and fortifications of the Compound on all Foundation Properties.

Justin, Jason's older brother was the Steward of Inventory and Master of supplies, along with holding the highest seat of five Judges on the Foundation Properties. Jason was more creative and much larger then his brother, but Justin was a fighter, a man who hated the fact that Justice dolled out fairly. Justin held the Chief seat on the panel of Judges and was an honorable man. There was only one harsh punishment and that was banishment from the Foundation. Justin was God's favorite

Jason was Jessica's favorite because of his stubbornness and rebellious nature. She knew that one day Jason would see God and to her it was worth the wait.

Becky hated the world and depressed because she failed to create an entry into the Xeno Games. It was a problem with spiking genes with aggressive genes but by using this procedure, Telepathic injections became quiescent.

Becky had been trying to create the sixth sense in her subjects. Mental telepathy was the way to go, it was the means by which Valentine was born. Becky was limited but resourceful so she was nearing evolution, a serum that manipulated DNA making the Subject a telepathy wonder of the world. Now she had to create a drug that would make these tele-genes adapt to genes that are more aggressive. Then she can create a species that would always be one-step ahead.

Hidden away deep in the rainforest Becky was well armed and well equipped. She had a large Militia that was quiet and stayed out of trouble. That was the way that Becky wanted it because once her creation was born then her revenge would begin.

Becky carried a hatred that was unequaled toward Nick and Lisa more than by anybody else, anywhere. One day Becky planned to dissect Dr. Keller's brain and torture Lisa for as long as she lived. Perhaps transplant their brain into a monkey . . . Becky laughed at the thought of it.

With steel and concrete warehouses connected by underground tunnels Becky was a recluse, sure . . . She was not a household name; in fact, she was unheard of by most Americans.

Yet, Becky was forceful and diabolical in her frenzy to find the perfect serum that would connect herself to her test Subjects. In her plot for domination, she had made secret allies with the Xeno Empire. Becky was building her Forces and since most young men were fighting in three Republican wars, 'invade Washington State in two years and claim it as a separate Republic.' Silently and taking great care, Becky was a cocoon ready to turn into a butterfly with sharp teeth and talons.

It was going to be a grey dawn when Becky would finally awaken from her cocoon. Read "Xeno Gods and Demons"

Litua and Raven greeted Xenoman and welcomed the giant into their fold. They were getting ready for their next contest.

This contest was number 25 and involved a human from the Country Congo, and two German Xeno Warriors. They also had won their previous 25 contests and were watching DVDs showing previous contests earlier in the day by the Xenoman and Litua, and Raven Team.

At first, the Germans and their human friend entered the main arena. Litua and Raven engaged the three combatants with daring skills and quick moves but the opponents fought bravely and gallantly to the end.

Xenoman watched from the sidelines until the women needed his help.

The man from Congo seemed to be completely evasive and managed to cut both women a couple of times. Litua managed to hack off the left arm of one of the Germans and the crowd gave them a standing ovation. Raven slipped a hammer strike by the other German and sliced the German slightly with her dagger. Both women shared the secret poisons with each other and fought back to back. Raven had scored a lethal blow with the slice of her dagger. Laced with a pernicious reptile poison, the Congolese man had his poisoned lance directly pointed at the Xenoman while he was waiting for it to enter the ring. Menacingly with deep hatred in his cold eyes,

Raven turned on the one-armed German Xeno Warrior and with three swings of their axes the women cut the German into three chunks.

Then the fierce women turned on the eight-footer and watched his glistening coal-black body turn as sweat dripped on the ground. Majai was his name and he was an expert spearman and used his shield well in combat. Raven and Litua tried to flank the black giant but his jabs and swings of the spear kept the two women from accomplishing their flanking maneuvers. One at a time and then mixing their throws, the girls failed to scratch the man from Congo with their daggers. Majai wanted one go at the

Xenoman, Majai knew exactly how he was going to kill this giant who stood taller then Majai. Majai thought that it would be best to toy with the women, anger the Xenoman, and then kill him.

With a deafening roar, the Xenoman announced himself into the arena. ***"I Am Xeno Man!"*** Then he leaped into the ring.

Majai jumped in Xenoman's direction and thrust his spear into Xenoman's throat. It went clean through the

Xenoman's neck and then falling backwards and dead before he hit the ground.

Raven struck her axe deeply into Majai just below his heart while Litua stabbed the gladiator deeply in the left ear with a poisoned dagger. Majai died on this day but on this day, he made History.

When the tall Congolese bent over it was in a graceful way as if he were bowing. It was at that moment that Litua loped off Majai's head.

Killing the Xenoman was tough but possible. Majai was a hunter from the deep forests of Africa and knew how to kill. Majai sacrificed his life to show the world that humans were better then Xeno People all the way around. If he had a second longer, just a little more time, than he would have slain Raven and Litua. As the two women bowed to the audience they were cheered like hero's and given the right to advance in the games.

Soon as they carried Xenoman out of sight, a Medical Team was working on the creature. First, they hooked up life support systems and then removed the spear from the Xenoman's throat. Before long, the Xenoman was breathing and a cheer lighted up the mood of everyone there. "Well, almost everybody."

A half and hour later it was announced over the Loudspeakers that the Xenoman would be well in time for his next game. From the stands came a roar of cheers and in the background noise were some boo's. Could it be that Xenoman was indestructible? It seemed so, then what kind of hideous monster have we created?

I am sure that you have heard the saying . . . **"The Skies the limit."** Let us ponder about the Xenoman.

According to the writings on the Lupus Estate walls the Xenoman was reptile enhanced, gorilla enhanced, wasp enhanced, and with wolf enhanced human DNA. Still we have to remember that Majai had slain the beast with his lance and that it had taken a Medical Team to revive him.

What if we dismembered Xenoman and tried to kill him that way, if we set him on fire? We have created a monster that we can destroy, 'be it the hard way.' When will we create one that we cannot kill? If people had joined our movement in the early part of this Century then perhaps this would not be happening now.

_____

With a gavel in his hand, Senator Kennedy sat at the head of the long rectangle table. Heading this meeting on Xeno Affairs, these men and women were not attending the Xeno Games. There was a small Christmas tree on a table by the entrance to the chamber and Agents armed with machine guns and other high-powered automatics. Assassins were all about the Country and nobody was safe. Senator Kennedy called the meeting to order.

"Order in the Chamber, we will begin with unfinished old business and then tackle the Xeno Games." Senator Boxer stood and gave her Report from the last meeting. She read it off the Transcripts and every so often, there were sighs among the members.

After hearing, the unfinished old news there was a response from the Sub-Committee. Several members had feedback to offer along with comments, eager about the new solution. There was a combination of fifty members attending the meeting from both Houses. They were a minority and the odds are against them. First, to take his minutes for the Republicans was Roger Stallman, the youngest Senator in the Senate now or in the history of our Government.

"I understand that some of you that are attending this meeting here tonight are receiving injections of the Xeno Youth Serum. I must admit that when I learned of this conspiracy I was mystified as to why?"

There was a not so secret pact made between most

of the anti Xeno members at the meeting. To ensure
financing and a strong base, several members allowed
taking the drug as to make them younger. Ted Kennedy
was an important man who carried more influence than any
other person did in history. There were others in the
meeting that had used the potion claiming that it was for
the good of our country and not for selfish reasons.

Senator Thurman Thomas stood and explained to
the young Senator that compromises needed development
that new recruits in both Houses were nowhere *"We have
to last out the Xeno Age."* 'The Congressman Stated.'

Robert Wolf stood as the others sat into their seats.
*"We must bring back Christmas and put an end to the
Xeno Project before it's too late."* 'Rep Wolf was in his
eighties and was shaking a bit from being fragile and thin.'
*"I never utilized the youth potion because for me it is too
late; however we must keep our numbers strong and
defeat the Xeno Project before they make us go extinct."*

Hear, hear, *"I whole heartily agree, we must
befriend the snake before we can kill it."* Ted Kennedy
was excited and wanted to have the upper hand. For once in
his life the Party, that they belonged to did not matter. It
was the cash and the contacts that made things happen. The
old men had the most capital.

*"Good news, my friends are on the way. Our
scientists are working on a virus that will only take ten
more years to develop. Of course the bad news is that we
have to keep our Research Programs financed."*

*"Now that we have captured Bin, the oil mongrels
have began to finance New Terrorist Groups; we know
this buy watching the Markets. We must find a way to
mass produce our new energy sources and anti gravity
vehicles."*

Each member of the Sub Committee took his or her
turns at the Speakers Podium. Commotion and cigar smoke

with liquor brought out the best and the worst out of everyone.

Rep. Bill Franks spoke for a while. *"Certainly we cannot do much about what is happening to our world. Islands have disappeared because of global warming, sea level climbs every day. Another storm is about to hit New Orleans and this one will bury the city underwater."*

" Perhaps there is a way to stop the glaciers from melting, but I do not believe that there is. We are doomed; an asteroid zeroed on us and in 2027 will devastate our planet killing every living being on it. We now have a colony on the moon; it will be no different there because gravity will pull us both into this humongous asteroid. We must shut down pollution completely now or it will be too late. We must find a way to change the course of the asteroid using our facilities on the moon. I do not know if this can be done because our Government disagrees and have turned a blind eye to reality." 'Before Franks was finished speaking, he received a brief pause for a standing ovation.'

"What we must do is convince our colleagues that if we do not find our basic values and if we keep allowing our ethics to corrupt. Then our Government with our great Nation will fall, and crumple, invaded by heathens and barbarians. How can we continue to fight three wars, we are running out of children! The time to act is now and I say that we start with Military Covert Actions against the Xeno Project Founders and their hidden Installations." There was dead silence in the Chamber room.

"We have contacts in all Branches of our Military. We know that our Generals and Troop Commanders are against Xeno recruiting and consider the Xeno People our enemies and not our friends. Remember this; if we do not act now, then they will act without us."

"Ladies and Gentlemen, this is not a game, this is the right of our children and grandchildren not to be slaves or worse yet . . . meat for the beasts." Rep. Franks sat and watched for a reaction from his colleagues resolved at the thought of having the guts to say what was on his mind.

A cautious applause grew loud. Then Senator Jesse Mahoney took his turn on the podium.

"I am disappointed in the way we have been hiding and mishandling our Power with the people. By people, I mean human beings. I agree with Rep. Franks, why should we wait, why be afraid from political hoodlums? We should act soon before it's too late. First items on our agenda should be the assassinations of some colleagues who have been corrupted by greed or are Xeno People."

During the long debate, that followed decisions made that would change the world. These daring men and women were ready to fight the odds and save the world. Certainly, this was better then nothing.

10:30pm

"Introducing the Xenoman! ' With his team of beautiful Raven and the deadly Litua killers,'" 'The crowd cheered nearly loud enough to bring the house down.' *"Representing the human race is Starka, Leven, and his beautiful wife Tammy."* 'Loud and nasty boo's with vicious comments filled the Stadium. It seems that the humans were the underdogs.'

It was almost time for the competition to begin between the finalists. Xenoman was in the center of the main arena and the two stealth women were on each side of him. Promising them a quick death, they were daring

humans to enter the circle. They taunted the humans
waiving them into the humans into the ring five minutes
before the bell tolled. It was nearing the end of the
competition and after this fight; the winners had one fight
left to win the Xeno Games.

Lisa moved toward in her seat and watched the
event unfold before her. She noticed that the white man
with wings was holding a broadsword in one hand and a
round shield in the other hand. Leven was armed for this
contest with a long axe and a round shield. His weapon's
carrier was holding a ball and chain with a long oaken
handle and three poison daggers. Lisa had gotten an eyeful
of what was to come and felt charmed by the winged white
warrior.

Starka was the Leader of the Team and he decided
to enter Leven into the fight first, and then Tammy a few
seconds later. At the right moment, Starka would go in for
one kill after another. Starka was not expecting the
Xenoman to be on the team they were fighting. Starka
opted to strike swiftly at the Xenoman first and then help
his comrades defeat the remaining two combatants.

Leven jumped into the circle and then he fainted
left, then stepped leftward as he used an upward slice to
sever Litua apart in her mid-section. Litua's guts spilled
into the arena as Leven using the same swing knocked a
chunk of flesh out of Xenoman's torso. Tammy jumped in
at Starka's cue and went after Raven who was about to stab
Leven. 'Lisa was beside herself in bliss.'

Dr. Keller stared in disbelief at the way the humans
attacked. They had struck fast and hard at the only blind
spot on the Xeno Team. Starka was not in the contest yet
and the humans were winning.

Lisa could see that Nick was upset and asked him
what his problem was. Nick yelled and ranted about the
faults in Xenoman. Dr. Keller pulled one of his pistols out

of its sheath and shot one of the bus boys. When asked why he killed the boy Nick said because he was human. Lisa did not mind because it seemed to calm down her husband. Lisa began to watch the main arena again and she was not disappointed at what she saw happening.

Starka observed Xenoman for any weaknesses and found only one, but it was a gift from Heaven for Starka. Xenoman had limited reaching abilities, which meant that from above Xenoman was vulnerable

Leven was absorbing blows from Xenoman with his round steel shield. He felt as if his arm was going to break as his shield began showing dents on its surface. At the same time, Leven was swinging the axe while Tammy was trying to break Xenoman's legs with the ball and chain. Starka created this attack and he was proud of his friends. Starka could see that Raven was mortally injured but not out of the fight. Litua was dead. Now it was time for Starka to join his team in the fight against the Xenoman.

Litua was assaulting Tammy with all of her might but Tammy was extremely evasive. Litua was using illusions and tricks but Tammy did well to avoid a poison thrust to her heart as she wondered how Litua had returned from the dead.

High over the stands in the V.I.P. balcony Lisa and her Nicky mesmerized by the spectacle before them, they watched as Starka swooped in and loped off the head of Raven. Oddly, the weapons holder's head rolled before the Xenoman's feet. Another Attendant took his place and fought with a sickle and hammer combo.

Starka watched as Leven, Tammy slashed, and gouged Xenoman, handing out lethal punishment, as the Xenoman stood his ground at the center of the main area. 'Lisa and Nick laughed as Nick threw the dead busboy over the balcony and into the crowd below him.' Starka hovered over Xenoman contemplating his next strike with his double-edged sword. He was watching for weaknesses in the Xenoman as Xenoman tried to kill his elusive prey.

Every so often, Xenoman would try a swing or a lunge at Starka but Starka was always barely out of reach. Tammy and Leven backed off and began circling Xenoman. Starka waited until Xenoman let his eyes wonder to Leven and Tammy and then at the perfect moment Starka dove and tried to split Xenoman's head with a ventricle blow that hit right on the mark. Xenoman swung an axe that he picked up off the ground and hit Starka's shield cutting off a fifth of the shield. Litua was sneaking around trying to get to Starka's blind side.

Starka's blade only penetrated an inch of the Xenoman's skull barely touching his brain. Xenoman let out a scream that sounded for miles as he futilely tried to hit Starka, as the winged menace darted in and out of the arena yet staying within the circle. Starka struck Xenoman in the right eye and blinded the Xenoman. Now Starka had a blind side to assault.

Leven and Tammy saw what Starka was doing and assaulted Xenoman on his good eye side. Tammy threw three poison daggers at Xenoman's face and all three hit their targets. Since the poison was snake venom, the poisons did not affect Xenoman. Xenoman had some reptile genes in his DNA. Three knives buried to their hilts made Xenoman rage, insanely attacking Leven and Tammy. Xenoman was bleeding badly and Dr. Keller was screaming in anger. Never would have Nicklaus believed that his Xenoman could be defeated by three humans. It was not over yet, Xenoman was still in the fight. Lisa tried to calm Nicky down but Nick was furious. Lisa handed Nick a bottle of bourbon whiskey and watched Nick taking a long swig off the bottle.

Litua was using her power of illusions to seem as if

she was everywhere at once. She was about to administer a deathblow on the white winged warrior when Xenoman cut her in two from head to feet. Xenoman had gotten confused and killed his own teammate. Was Xenoman now doomed because he was alone?

Xenoman called upon his weapon's carriers to join the fight. Pain was not an issue with the Xenoman and it only made him rage harder. Litua would have slain Starka was it not for Xenoman losing his bearings.

Starka believed that another blow delivered exactly on the same mark would send his blade into the brain two-inches. At the most, it was going to take Starka three strikes to the head to bring the giant Xenoman down.

Recovering quickly, Tammy was truly mystical in the way she was able to show up on opposite sides of the Xenoman quicker than a cougar. Leven was aiming his poison tipped lance at Xenoman. He was prepared with a different poison made from insects.

Xenoman relied on his animal instincts and knocked Tammy out of the circle with a forearm slam. Tammy was out cold, but she was near death from a concussion. 'The crowds cheered and Dr. Keller lifted his bottle in a toast to his creation . . . *"Xenoman"*

Xeno Weapons carriers ran after Tammy to kill her as Starka intercepted them barely in time to save her life. Lisa loved every moment of the fight and saw that the XenoWeapon Carriers had turned their attention to Leven.

Becky was watching the Xeno games too. She had wagered twenty-million dollars on Starka and his human team. She knew that Nick would be devastated if Xenoman was defeated and that she would get rich from it. For once since Nick had left her, Becky had a reason to smile.

One look at Xenoman would tell any sane person that he was finished. Tammy was out of the game but

Leven was glad that Tammy was out of harms way. Now Leven was swinging his long axe in a figure eight and using his shield to block his eyes. Xenoman grossly underestimated before and his phenomenal abilities to self heal occurred at an incredible rate. Xenoman was bleeding and healing about as fast as he was dying.

Tammy's daggers had hit some nerves and that is what Starka took advantage of that and Xenoman's blind eye, which was oozing slime and blood.

Xenoman was beating Leven into the ground when Starka dove and delivered another downward strike to the top of Xenoman's head. Xenoman yelped like a dog before ceasing his assault on Leven and focusing his attention on the White Man with wings. Starka was circling for another dive at the Xenoman's head.

Xenoman's Xeno Carriers was trying to throw daggers at Starka and trying to help the Xenoman at the same time.

Leven rose to his feet and observed the situation. He knew that he had to distract Xenoman long enough for Starka to strike with his broadsword again. Leven saw his opportunity and struck swiftly with his axe. Leven pounded the three daggers into Xenoman's face with the back flat of his axe. It was a remarkable sight, as it did not slow the giant. Leven was grabbed by the Xenoman and was about to break Leven's neck when Starka struck his blade edge into the opening wound on Xenoman's head. Starka's blade sunk into Xenoman's brain and Xenoman dropped on his knees.

Leven picked the axe up and began hacking away for five minutes that it took him to sever the head from his body. Boo's were louder then the cheers but Starka did not care about what the crowds wanted. All that Starka wanted to do was please God.

Becky was dancing her victory dance. She had

beaten all the odds and Nick's creation was dead, Becky poured herself a drink and laughed aloud. Soon she would be the Xeno Star and have her way with the world.

Dr. Keller was mad; he was in despair about the Xenoman becoming extinct by three humans. His mind was not wasting any time as he calculated the changes that needed work.

Lisa was absorbed by what she saw, especially Leven. She had become savage with her thoughts about the games. Lisa was Queen and could have any man in the arena but the married ones. Leven was married and off limits to Lisa. Nick was beside himself with schizophrenia, Nick told Lisa to gather their things together because they were flying back to San Francisco in one hour.

Tang Chang and the Xenowoman were Seed one and last on the list of combatants. Dr. Keller pulled them out of the contest because he did not want any more of his Xeno Stars killed. Dr. Keller had a lot of work to do, enhancements, new mobility, and longer reach was on his mind now but there were other things too.

Starka and his team won by default, but it was an awesome fight with the Xenoman, the crowd booed Starka for winning by default.

The Next Day

Becky declared the 25th a holiday and gave almost everybody a paid day off. Becky was elated, overjoyed at the terrible losses that Nick and his new wife had suffered. Becky did not know whom she hated more, Dr. Keller or Lisa.

Believing all these years that her ex was creating the monsters of monsters Becky was wrong. Dr. Keller had been wasting his time on life Xeno serums and Politics and neglecting his main work of creating new life. Now Becky felt confident that she would develop a creature that was intelligent, empathetic and under Becky's control, most important of all was the fact that when Valentine had the time, he would assist Becky in her laboratories.

Valentine would use his telepathic powers during surgery, which produced wonders in the Test subjects. Becky's dream was to capture Mia and develop her into a telepathic assassin.

Becky is a bitter, jealous and a malicious woman. Her destiny cut into stone on the walls of the Lupus Estate.

Christians from all over the world over came to America to see Starka. Many agreed that Starka was an Angel from Heaven and wanted to touch Starka. Nowhere that these people searched Starka could be found.

'Speaking of Mia,' she was hiding on the Samuel Compound. Eventually one day Mia knew that she would murder Samuel. Mia could feel it in her blood. Dreams of ripping Samuel apart occurred when Mia forced herself to sleep.

Dr. Keller held Lisa in his arms as they rode in the back of a long bulletproof limo and drinking a bottle of aged wine while kissing. Before long, they parked in front of The Golden Eagle Motel on Broadway.

Dennis was dead so Terry met them at the steel door entrance. Terry was never the Manager but he always seemed to be the boss. Occupied by pimps, pedophiles, rapists, murderers and Felons, the Golden Eagle was the perfect place to disappear. Anybody could disappear at the Golden Eagle for one reason or another. Dennis had become one of those people, eaten by his own greed.

Once in their living room adjoining the labs, the two lovers joked about the games. Dr. Keller missed Becky, she was quite useful and from what he understood, she was doing well in Washington State. Nick directed his attention back to Lisa . . . Dr. Keller was utterly mad.

"What do you think about watching a video and sharing a bottle of vodka, my dear?" They loved San Francisco and wished that they were on an upper floor but inspired by their underground Estate/Research Facility. Carved out of solid rock and was supposed to withstand an Earthquake. San Francisco was had become home for the two macabre lovebirds. Watching the stars Lisa would whisper in Nick's ear *"I love you"* and purr like a cat.

At the Jessica Foundation Compound, it was another beautiful day. Jessica, Penny and Raven were watching the Sunrise while asking God's Blessings for another day on Earth.

Monica, Seth, and David were unsung heroes. It seems that the people of the Xeno Foundation were angry with them. Angry because the three weapons' carriers hadn't jumped into the fight when their counterparts had during the last contest. All three of them claimed that they would have only gotten in the way. Jessica announced that Seth Monica and David acted properly and a job beyond the others. Still the three Christians had lost favor with the population and decided to go on their own separate ways.

Seth traveled to Africa to first, build a church and then an army. Last, I heard he was doing well and his Church constructed.

Monica went to Peking, China to minister in a new Church. She was popular and had a way about her that was controlling and favored by the Government and before long appointed as an Ambassador.

David left the Foundation Property and disappeared after he got into a black limo. There has been no correspondence from David and he could be anywhere in the world.

Mutual Assured Destruction is not a nuclear holocaust but about an understanding among the peoples of the world that the "Xeno Project" is harmless. Animal to human tissue and Organ transplants are life-saving medical operations. I will agree with this fact. Xeno transplants and therapies will improve life spans and save some lives for our present generation but what about our grandchildren? What new birth defects will arrive with this Xeno Age and how far will we take it. There are unlimited possibilities with this new technology and not all Researchers, scientist, are good people. Some are evil people with nothing to lose that are willing to do anything for a buck, or for a war.

We can stop this outrage against our species but we are running out of time. Soon these thousands of transplants will reap a contaminated and diseased future for our species and corruption will become blatantly abundant in Xeno
industries.

Can you imagine children born with snouts or an epidemic of babies with tails? I hope that you will because this fate is happening now globally and it will only get worse.

I write fiction satires in which the truth is exposed and demand that these Doctors held accountable for their actions. What is fiction now will become reality in the future, are we so vain as to destroy our planet and contaminate our own species leaving nothing for our future generations but certain death?

"So that we may boldly say, The Lord is my helper and I will not fear what man shall do unto me"

The End

Table of Contents

Xeno Gods and Demons

This is your page

The Xeno Religion
September 2019
Chapter One

Darkness enveloped the night as the hooded men ran near the forest chasing a fast moving animal. Security sentries were taking random shots at their prey as they ran after the beast or man that had infiltrated their Temple. They were the Guardians of the Xeno Gods. They were a pair of twins developed accidentally at the CDC Laboratories. Finally, after another twenty minutes the two Guardians closed in on their prey. Darkness, pitch black by the time that the beast was cornered and it seemed that the chase was soon to end with the demise of the mutant Xenomitte.

It was quicker then a burst of lightning as the beast attacked the two men. Turning as they fired their assault weapons the men never knew what hit them as their guts spewed out into the tall weeds beside the shallow pond. In the next instant, the beast ran into the wetness of the lush forest circling to get back to the gates of the Temple.

Radio contact cut off and the Commandant increased security sending out three ten-man Patrols to kill the infiltrator. It had not taken long before one three-man patrol found the scent on the beast.

Two men were standing in the shadows watching the chase. They worked at the Xeno Sub Station in Key West. At the present, they were taking their breaks.

With cunning and stealth, the beast circled around her pursuers. She used her telekinetic powers to transfer her shadow into the corner of a dry concrete basin. She had the hooded stalkers go into the basin after her shadow as she closed in behind the Guardians of the Temple, 'anticipating a quick kill.' Limestone and gravel crunched beneath the two men and one woman that had been separated from their main patrol in the fog, their boots were noisy as they walked down into the abandoned water sever treatment plant.

Mia knew that Samuel was hiding within the Temple and Mia wanted at him! Many years had gone by without Mia catching Samuel but there were some narrow escapes. Mia had the jagged scars to prove it.

She had disguised herself as a Xenomitte and had a great plan to infiltrate and murder Samuel and his forty wives but Mia in her haste tripped a wire. A silent laser alarm had warned the Guard and now Mia was fighting for her life to escape. Key West island had been purchased by Xeno Industries Corporation and was highly fortified. Mia had to swim from Jamaica to get onto Key Island.

Mia pondered for a few minutes about the island as she watched the three Guardians low crawling towards her shadow. Mia remembered Samuel and his New Religion. It was the new trend and considered a hip thing to follow. Samuel named the religion "Xeno Science Faith Church" and promoted the worship of idols and Xeno Gods. Samuel crowned himself the Emperor Priest of the Xeno Faith Congregation. Mia laughed loudly and the Guardians became alerted at her presence at their flank.

Snapping out of her daydreaming Mia leaped ten feet onto the gravel landing and slid like a baseball player into the three as bullets flew overhead. Using the talons on her feet in a frenzy act Mia sliced and diced the Guardians to their deaths. In a flash, Mia ran back in the general direction of the Temple.

Mick and Henry decided to call in what they had witnessed to Dispatch. Mick was shaking as he held his mobile phone video typing Mia as she murdered Guardians of the Temple of Faith. Mick had good reason to shutter because Mia sensed the men had been watching her. Through pure chance Mia zigzagged her way to the Temple completely undetected by the Guards, she entered the Temple through a secret private door lying beneath the green sod about ten feet from the back of the house. Mia used her animal instincts and stumbled onto the hidden entrance.

Easily finding the entrance to the ventilation ducts Mia did what she did best, she scurried through the vents to the rafters within the Temple Auditorium, which overlooked the Altar.

Samuel had the same altar that Valentine used during his sacrifices at the Lupus Estate and used propane to heat Lucifer's skull red lighting the altar out of the blackness. In hell, Lucifer screamed in agony holding his boneless head in upright. Mia crouched on a rafter at least two-hundred feet above the Altar. From this perch, Mia expected to get the jump on Samuel. Mia waited there for two weeks before the congregation of evil misfits arrived for Services and the bi-weekly virgin sacrifice. A golden crown sat before the Alter laden with precious jewels and figures of Xeno Gods. It was an awesome sight as the golden crown radiated silver light.

Fifty-thousand people filled the Worship Arena as the night neared midnight. Loud screaming deafened ears coming from the fenced captives, held for sacrifices and booty among other things.

Nearing midnight the masses began chanting loudly . . . Samuel . . . Samuel . . . We want to see our King!

Torches everywhere in rows along the walls made the auditorium smoky and foul smelled. Mia's eyes burned and she choked on the smoke as she waited for Samuel to arrive. This time Mia had a good feeling about her calculated and thought-out murder of death itself . . .
"Samuel, the Prince of Darkness." In the shadows, staring down at the crowd Mia was undetected as she thought

about death. Mia knew that she would not get out of the Temple alive. Samuel etched into Mia's brain.

There among the congregation were freaks of creation and mutant humans, all the by-products of the Xeno Age. Indeed, the cock has flown the coup; it was time for reveling and dancing. Magnificent statues carved out of marble and jade adorned the hallways leading to the Sanctuary of the Priests. A sacred and hollowed Chamber that Samuel had blessed thinking himself God of Heaven and Earth. Among the congregation, some impatient people formed a mob and began lynching some people to curb overcrowdings and a possible stampede.

Samuel appeared, as the curtains were drawn open that revealed the Altar. A spotlight soon zeroed in on Samuel, the crowd grew dead quiet, except for a scream, and some moans from a lynched dying man. An attendant swiftly quieted the ungrateful creature with a blow to the head with a mighty med-evil axe. Once more, the auditorium grew silent. Samuel stood before his throne and proclaimed . . .

"Now the time is ours on this special night to be baptized into the Xeno Faith Temple."

Loud cheers and agreeing masses hollered their approval of Samuel.

"It will be a cold day in hell when we conquer the world!"

Wings sprouted from Samuels back and he screamed loudly into the stands, *"There are those that still follow my father though he is gone forever, we must root them out and skin them alive in tribute for our Xeno Religion we must! All must be caught and dealt with severely."*

"Tonight all of you will be branded on your foreheads *with the Xeno Sign. It is a design of Xeno DNA that designates your rightful seat in my Kingdom."*

'From this day on, all of those people belonging to the Xeno Cult were branded on their foreheads with a strand of their own DNA; this identified them as Xeno Faith Followers.'

Thousands of Followers that lined in six rows hideously branded with a DNA strand that resembled a number six. Six henchmen used sizzling branding irons to embed the five inch by one-inch brand across their foreheads. Screams and the last cries of death muffled the din of the auditorium.

Outside the Auditorium, about five-hundred meters offshore were several military interceptors well armed and ready for action. Hiding in the shadows on the starboard side of the two-hundred feet in length were smaller crafts loaded with the Followers of Lucifer. Covens and lairs of demons prepared to storm Key Island and the Temple sheltered on it. These were Devil Cults and anarchists among the witches that made up this Force of two-thousand armed men and women. Behind these boats were barges filled with programmed Xenomittes bent on killing everybody on the island.

Within the walls of the Temple revelry and pain was all the same to the unfortunate souls selling their souls for lust, murder and for mayhem. Naive and ignorant Samuel did not notice that all the Guardians had abandoned their Posts and joined in on the festivities. With the gates left unattended and the machinegun towers empty, the occupants of the island seemed to be easy prey for the Cultists offshore. Samuel was having the time of his life as he watched the suffering and the willing converts getting on their knees and lifting their heads branded.

Laughter filled the hallways that led to the main Sanctuary as Samuel walked away from the auditorium: he had sensed Mia on the rafters and knew better than to stay there. Mia had been a big pain for the leader of sinners and killers; she had tried to kill Samuel several times throughout the years. Samuel had cut off one of Mia's ears in a fight and had it framed and mounted in his bedroom chamber.

It was all good in Samuels mind because Samuel did not believe that Mia would escape the carnage on the island. What Samuel did not know because Mia was blocking Samuels mind probes was the trouble waiting to pounce on him in an hour and it was going to be a little hell on Earth.

On the Lead Interceptor was the Commander of this motley crew of misfits and criminals about ready as he made the final preparations to release the Xenomittes first to clean the island and then to begin the assault with his main Forces. Fearless and even more ruthless was the appointed Commander, his name was Valentine.

Strong winds began to rise from the east and Valentine knew that it was the time to strike. Wanting to be in command of the strike because of his vanity, Valentine planned to get out once the island was captured, certainly before the Temple was assaulted. Valentine knew all to well that Xenomittes were unpredictable once they smelled blood. Valentine intended to run the assault from the boat and leave in his stolen helicopter when the going got too rough. Valentine did not believe in religions, the beast believed in was the extermination of the human species. Valentine had no clue the death and destruction that was going to befall Key West Island on this evening during a tremendous storm that was never detected on radar? His gunship rocked and soon hit by twenty-foot swells before the Xenomittes freed onto the shores Key West. Then Valentine buttoned up the boat and waited for the storm to calm so that he could make good his escape.

With the island less than 4 mi. or 6 km. long by 2 mi. or 3 km. wide at SW extremity of Florida Keys, 60 mi.

(96 km.) southwest of the Southern tip of Florida; pop.
(1990c) 24,832; southernmost city of the Lower 48 and S
terminus of U.S. Route 1; tourism; winter resort;
commercial and recreational fishing (formerly incl. turtles);
cigar making; Fort Zachary Taylor; daily sunset gathering
at Mallory Square Dock; Florida Keys Community
College. (1965); Key West Naval Air Station established as
a naval station 1822; city incorp. 2013, first in South
Florida to do so; home at various times to American writers
Ernest Hemingway, Elizabeth Bishop, and Tennessee
Williams among others, and to naturalist John James
Audubon. It was going to be easy meat for the Xenomittes,
but Valentine was a different story. Through circumstances
out of his control, Valentine was dead in the water.

Xeno Religion had been on mainstream News for
over three years now. People were taking sides and the far
Right was behind the idea that every living creature had a
right for life. Then there was the American Patriots who in
secret hunted Xeno creatures and had given up on their
elected politicians. Now they were the new freedom
fighters since the American Forces handed over to U.N.
control last year. The war on Terrorism replaced with a war
that would determine the outcome of the human species.

Mia sat on the rafters and watched as holes blasted
through the walls and the Cultists stormed into the
Auditorium in waves. Tear gas and grenades were lighting
up the darkness in flashes as the Cultists freely massacred
the drunk and drugged congregation and confused the mobs
into fighting one another. Gas and smoke rose to the rafters
and Mia rubbed her eyes.

Leaping from rafter to rafter Mia climbed to the
ceiling and searched for a way out of the Temple. It was
time to escape this pandemonium of unequivocal slaughter.

It did not take Mia long to find the Skylight fixed into the roof. Once she leaped onto a sill, her hands gripped the steel bars keeping Mia confined within the Temple.

Outside the glass window rain poured onto the roof and she could hear the wind howling in rage. Mia pulled on the bars bending them so that she could fit between them. Then she lifted herself out of the Temple and laid flat on the rooftop.

———————————————

Valentine was thinking that he should have stayed in South America as he felt the boat dive below the surface of the water as a forty-foot swell hit it just off the bow. Valentine screamed in rage at God and swore to spill more blood on Earth then ever happened in history before. Valentine cursed Samuel and damned the Earth but he knew better then to say anything bad about Lucifer. From the beginning, Valentine was loyal to Lucifer. Lucifer was created by Valentine's telekinetic design but with one lethal fault, Lucifer was all-powerful in the Xeno World and before long Valentine would possess his Master's skull so that he could return the skull to Lucifer. He was thinking that it had to be he that assaulted the island to assure victory for the devil. Staying in the jungle would have angered Lucifer and Valentine knew that eventually he would have to stand before the master of evil.

It seems that there were at least three souls out to murder Samuel, and Valentine was closing in on Samuel with his Forces of ungodly creations.

Blood spewed forth and gushed out of bodies dying inside and out of the Auditorium. Surely, Valentine would have been safer in the Temple then anchored offshore in a Coast Guard Cutter. Cultists well prepared for this fight and armed with computer censored rangefinder assault machine guns and Marine K-Bars. Valentine had given his Commanders strict instructions not to damage his sacrificial Altar or the Temple. In the mind of Valentine there had to be a second reincarnation of Lucifer for the simple fact that there is a second coming of Christ. With a crashing pound, the east wall collapsed and several rafters slipped out from the hardware seats and crashed onto the mob killing hundreds of the once revenant crowd. It seemed that immortality was off the Agenda of Key West and its doomed occupants.

From behind, the wall emerged Samuel with 13 Disciples and surrounded by hundreds of bloodthirsty bloodhounds and pit bulls. Samuels Disciples armed with a shield and a spear and were giants compared to an average person. It seemed that Samuel was changing the odds back into his favor.

Each dog had been charmed by a Coven of witches and spellbound by Samuel to hunt down only the invaders and naught else. Samuel was shape shifting into creatures of hell and his anger simmered like a cold chill in the dead of winter, all the way to your bones.

One man was crushing skulls with his huge boots in the hallway leading into the Guest rooms. In a frenzy and was laying bodies before him in rows, some were dead and others were pretending to be dead. In the finish, they all ended up dead.

Valentine raised his fist clenching a scepter and screamed for the dogs to seek out their prey and kill the intruders. With a loudness never heard before from a pack of dogs, they swarmed into the crowd bringing down Cultist intruders and tearing them to bits. It was no less than a massacre and the dogs brought victory for the moment into the hands of Samuel.

Fury balls of teeth with stubby legs roamed throughout Key Island devouring everything alive in their paths. The Residents of the island manage to kill quite a few of the Xenomittes but not enough to save their own lives. Xenomittes devoured everything including the bones of their victims.

Valentine summoned the Xenomittes and instructed them to kill everything on the island and then to jump into the ocean and drown themselves. Thinking with one mind the Xenomittes tried to accomplish their goals as they neared the Temple to regroup and assault the Temple.

Mia was making her way to the shoreline and then swim to safety, Valentine took his chances with the helicopter.

With steel cable, rigging the chopper was continuing to rock and heave ho about the deck. Valentine tried to get a pilot to fly him out of there before Samuel learned of who was behind the plot to murder him, but even at the price of torture they refused to fly the helicopter. Valentine told the First Mate to turn about and head to sea.

Twenty-foot waves were hitting the Cutter as it turned about. Powerful engines kicked in and the boat rode head into the starboard storm. It dove under when hitting the swells and bounced like a ball. Inside the boat, everything loose, not strapped down was a flying projectile aiming to kill a sailor. Valentine watched from the stairway leading to the Wheelhouse and saw the wide huge widows shatter as a swell hit the boat at an odd angle. The Wheelhouse was drenched in water as the Skipper sat strapped into his seat with a rectangle piece of glass sticking out of his face. He was moaning and Valentine knew that the man was suffering dearly but that was not the reason Valentine snapped the man's neck, it was for the pure pleasure of it.

With a single thought, Valentine mapped the knowledge of the Skipper before he snapped the man's neck like a twig on a tree. Valentine unbuckled the man and threw him to one side as he took over the controls of the Cutter. Pulling back on six throttle sticks Valentine lunged the cutter hard into the next swell that seemed to make the ride easier. It was then that he noticed that his radar was not functioning properly. Valentine walked up five stairs and entered the aft wheelhouse poking his head over the roof for a look-see. Cursing as he kicked dents into the wheelhouse alloy wall, Valentine saw the antenna broken that made the radar work. Valentine reentered the main wheelhouse and navigated the cutter using maps and keeping a weathered eye out for buoys and what not. Valentine was riding this storm out while the Red Cross and the National Guard were cleaning up Key Island.

As all Religions do when they are first created, there are Splinter groups, Reformers, and rebels among the congregations of every church and Religion. This new Xeno Religion was no exception as innocent lives are lost over fanatical Causes.

The End of Chapter one **"The Xeno Religion"**

Chapter Two
The Xeno Underworld
Dec 13 2020

Along the streets of Chicago a completely different conflict was taking place. All the Crime Bosses from all ethnic backgrounds had formed a treaty to defeat the new gang in the city. Mayor Daily Dongoti was a relative of the once Richard Daily and was moonlighting as a major crime boss in Chicago.

They came and set up overnight. First, they raided all the Mob Businesses and then they murdered 150 Mobster Soldiers and their Bosses. It seems that the new gang had big bucks because they had bought the Hilton Hotel and had set up Headquarters there. This new syndicate called themselves the Taxzil Xeno Group.

Chicago Police had received Orders to use lethal force to apprehend the new Xeno Mobsters. O'Hare Airport was bringing into Chicago thousands of Taxzil sympathizers who were arriving daily to make a bigger mess than there was before. These flights were getting into O'Hare mostly from South America and Cuba. In today's world, Xeno People seemed to carry more rights than humans, and the Police had banned Xeno Species from serving in Law Enforcement Agencies.

On State Street, a Meeting was taking place with the Mayor and four Reps from the new Xeno Mob. It was no ordinary meeting, no sir. There was the idea that a payoff was due to the Mayor. Daily was a man of deep stature standing at six-feet five inches and an ex Gladiator from the Xeno Games, he was not a man of compromise. Daily had no intention on taking a bribe from anybody. He had his principles and was devoted to the Windy City.

After the Sears Tower Incident the Police had to crack down and started cracking heads. It did not take long before the power had gotten to their heads and they formed their own gang. Chicago has always had a reputation as a Mobster city, and the people who live there are hardened, tough city slickers who understand that life is cheap in Chicago. Street gangs and Drug Syndicates have always been at war and the Police have always been quick to react. I have seen Police cars lined along the beach in the dozens, and Paddy wagons littered about with a few dozen Police Officers swinging their batons. All these forces had met to take down a man who was enjoying a peaceful picnic on his Honeymoon. I watched as the Police beat this man into a comma breaking bones and tearing muscle. His three children watched in horror as their father died right before their eyes! Chicago had organized against Xeno people and had banned the species from their city. Before the eyes of the world, Chicago thought of as "The Rogue City of the West." I thought that excessive force abounded and brutality flaunted before the hundreds of people at the beach. It is a rule in Chicago that you do not piss off the Police . . .

Now the Xeno Gang was around and thinking that they were going to change the way that things were done. They had a surprise coming when the Delegates that met with the Mayor had been murdered and decapitated in Grant Park. What baffled me was that this event never made the six o'clock News?

Mayor Daily was not the only Boss in Chicago, there were others but they had to pay tribute to the Mayor for protection. That is why all the Airports were shut down and a wall was being built around the City, Everybody in the city wondered if these actions had been too little and too late. Key West, Florida was a grim reminder of what the Xeno Race was capable of, Chicago was prepared.

Crystals abundantly strewn about as nature shed its diamonds into the hidden caverns below the city. These areas of the city were lost after everybody that had operated the mines died during the big Chicago fire. During this time, the cave entrances covered with ashes and debris before filled with dirt, a hundred feet deep but below this flourished a growing Xeno Community.

In these caverns and the adjoining tunnels were living quarters and kitchens. A huge cavern constructed into a modern sports arena equipped with the best gear. In the lower chambers were prison cells and torture chambers. In this underground Community, the locals called it the Chamber of Horrors. Thriving and prosperous the underground Xeno people had their share of contacts aboveground, carried out Patrols, and sent spies to monitor the inferior human species. There are plenty of Xeno sympathizers living in the underground city that are assisting the Xeno Leaders to, get the advantage in Chicago.

In New York and San Francisco, similar attempts escalated to take control of these cities. The people attacked the Xeno People and hunted them in the old WWII tunnels and fortified caves along Ocean Blvd. Xeno people fled in the thousands as the anarchists had gone wild after organizing forty-thousand of their comrades north of Oakland in the desert, to attack the Xeno People along the Bay Areas.

Severe measures amended to city laws to assure the safety of the Bay Area, which included the mass murders of Xeno People and mob lynching's in Golden Gate Park. McDonalds was right there serving Big Mac's and fries to the crowd watching the spectacle as were many mobile food and drink Venders. When a profit established, business is business. Measures such as volunteer Police Teams recruited from the civilian populations and the homeless, all paid to hunt and to police the Xeno species, "no holds barred."

Chicago had their own way of getting things done. Whacking the right people in power of the gangs always worked the quickest and with the best long lasting results. *"There never is a good way to take a life,* Daily was known to say, *but there always is a right and a wrong way to get the job done."*

Outside the Capital Building walking up State Street were two people holding hands. During the wintertime it gets extremely cold in Chicago, all of the sever catch basins were steaming as the Couple was strolling pass one. It happened quickly and with deadly force. Breaking the ice holding it in place the lid of one of these catch basins flew off the opening. Both Lovers stopped to stare at the sight and taken by surprise as Xeno creatures dragged the Lovers into the hole to be gone forever.

Beastly characters of the underworld from beneath the Windy City were a menace at the least and as of late, more often than not, they preyed on the innocent aboveground. These people and creatures were feeding on humans because it seemed to make them evolve faster as they grew older.

Brenda and Fred watched in horror, as half beasts were biting chunks off their bodies. Fred was a weightlifter and although he gave it his best shot Fred could not fight off the Xeno people. Brenda was screaming as they dragged deeper into the tunnels consuming darkness until they disappeared.

Diamonds kept the city in operation but money could only buy so many live humans, the humans that been captured during moonless nights were priceless. During the present time, over two million people had been reported missing in the United States; many were drawn into the underground caverns by the lure of the diamonds.

Congress passed an Act today that Declared War on the Mobs destroying America. Chaos and destruction were as common as the machinegun fire in the streets at night as Policed dressed in riot gear patrolled the streets. Law Enforcement was becoming fierce during these times of the Xeno Age. Congress divided between three Parties but they all agreed about the Xeno Species.

Graffiti proclaimed the death of many street gangs and their families. Xeno Gangs using high-tech weaponry that was wiping out one gang after another. It was a wonder that the gangs were fighting so fiercely against the Xeno Forces, many of who trained in the deep jungle Compound. Graffiti stated that Valentine had returned to his jungle fortress.

Mayor Daily knew that he had to put an end to this Xeno threat. After thinking it over carefully, Daily decided to put a hit on Valentine. Valentine was responsible for all the uprisings around the world and was a wanted International Fugitive.

Daily loved his fat Cuban cigars and made a habit of blowing smoke in your face. He was all-powerful and godlike to the other mobs.

There was a reason for the Mayor's demeanor. He hard as a like a rock and had fists the size of softballs. There was more to the man than cunning and size; he was taking Armo Xeno Treatments that enhanced all seven senses while toughening his skin like a cow. It made him mean but sensible enough to hand out gifts and to show mercy when needed. Mayor Daily dispatched his best men to hunt Valentine and to bring back his head.

Testing booths were set up around the city to find the Xeno People hiding among the humans in Chicago. Panic had infected the Country and was spreading like a wildfire. President Richard Grant ordered the National

Guard to intervene and called the Nation into a State of Emergency. President Grant had decided that the Xeno Species had the same right for life, as did all creatures on Earth. He had decided along with the Leaders of several other Nations a place designated for the Xeno People. They would be living in their own Country and the question was where?

Leven and Tammy assigned the Mission to hunt down and assassinate Valentine. Starka refused to leave the Jessica Compound and insulted the President for assigning ex gladiators to do the Army's work. Tammy was a mother of twin boys and stayed in top physical shape. Leven was at the top of his form in his late thirties.

The Xeno Underworld was flourishing and alive beneath the streets of Chicago. They once were coalmines and with the changes from the fire, the coals had turned into diamonds. There were several warlords among the Underworld and not all of them concealed their hatred for each other. They were all different hybrids created from dissimilar animal cells. There was a rule in the animal Kingdom that anything went as far as creation. Laboratories beneath Chicago were blasting their furnaces all night long as the scientists worked endless hours. There was everything, including two huge Malls in "The Xeno Underworld."

Leven was planning on getting into the Underworld and seeking out Valentine, Tammy agreed with Leven. Senator Hollister believed that covert operations with Leven and Tammy along could infiltrate and kill Valentine. Of course, it was a suicide mission but with Leven and Tammy present, it was probable that escape was possible after completion of the mission with waiting helicopters. Hollister decided that the mission be carried out in the Amazons. Leven and Tammy had secretly decided to go undercover into the Xeno Underworld. People never earned that Liven and Tammy would always do as they pleased, no matter what the consequences were in the end.

Tammy teasingly beckoned Leven to exit stage left and open the door to the limo. Liven and Tammy were as much in love as they were the day that they met, They held no secrets from each other and shared all their feelings, this made the pair truly born for each other. After getting out of the limo, the pair frolicked and played beneath the city waterfalls in Grant Park, Chicago.

Soaking wet the two lovers ran to the nearest Hotel to get a room and dry off. Once they made it inside the Shady Ritz Hotel, greeted with laughter, Leven and Tammy scoffed at these persons in the lobby.

Dripping water as they approached the Clerks Tammy paid for a room for the two of them and soon they were inside room 13A.13B was nosey as if a party was going on and traffic was heavy next door. Leven was being irritated and decided to pay the neighbors a friendly visit. Leven was losing his composure as he neared the room.

Knocking on the door Leven received no response. Then he began hitting and kicking at the door, soon the door opened and a person wearing a costume was standing over the threshold barring Leven. Leven stared at the man in disgust and abhorred the horrid smells emitting from the room. Then he pushed the man covered with boils off to one side and entered the room.

Leven Yelled. *"Shut up!"* His voice roared like a lion's and nobody paid Leven any mind. About the Hotel room were Xeno People that were of a mutant race. *Leven kicked one man hard and then threw another against the wall. "I want some peace and quiet, or I am going to kick ass all night long. I do not care one way or the other . . . now what's it going to be?"*

A huge fellow stepped out of the bathroom and confronted Leven boldly standing in the center of the room.

The wart infected and muscular mutant eyed over Leven and cracked his knuckles with his hands. *"My name is Luther and I am one of the Warlords in the Xeno Underworld. We are part of a lower Clan and folks call us many names but "The Wart Hogs" seemed to have stuck with us. Please pardon me for disturbing your beauty sleep and pleaseeee forgive us."*

Leven was not a man to lose his composure but the big man who stood before him was begging for it. Smiling, the man named Luther continued to listen to himself talk. *"Please join us and bring your woman, ha ha heh . . . we could sure use some fresh meet in here. Sells like rats had crawled up these women here and died of boredom."* 'The women laughed and one spoke out . . . *"I have a rat living in my womb."* Laughter filled the room as the big ugly man took a step closer to Leven.

In the next room, Tammy was getting impatient. She was wearing her sexiest negligee and had been waiting for some quality time alone with Leven for months. After a few more minutes passed, Tammy decided to see why it was taking her lover so long to return.

When Tammy entered the room, she saw that two men were facing off in the center of the room and that Leven was one of those men. All eyes turned to Tammy and a multitude of whistles and catcalls followed in suit.

This event turned Leven's skin red as he began smashing the warty blubber man standing in front of him. With his forearms and his elbows, Leven pulverized Luther. All the creatures in the room leaped onto Leven and he seemed to be at a disadvantage.

It was through this event that Leven and Tammy joined the Xeno Underworld. Let me tell you the story of how this happened.

Men armed with assault rifles stormed the room and opened a three round burst into the ceiling of the room. In that instant, silence invaded the premises and the two gladiators turned back to back so that they could defend themselves better.

The Underworld Warlord of the lowest class spoke to Leven up from the floor and gathering his composure the in.

"You must know that we have been waiting for you. Two strong winning gladiators that whether they believe it or not are themselves products of the Xeno Age are here now for us to do with as we wish."

" Let me help the two of you understand something, we know that you are here for a reason and want you to tell us what brought you here?"

" Why don't we rape the bitch and put the other in the tiger pit." Yelled one of the misfits, then another degenerate added . . .

"They are lean and fat free, we could butcher the both of them and eat a feast fit for Kings."

No doubt, these misfits of society were the bottom of the barrel. Holding the advantage they were well organized, and were holding the gladiators at bay. Leven knew that this was their chance to join the gang. There was nothing else to be done it was all that they had. It was that or certain death. Tammy figured that if these misfits were the weakest of the Underground Warlord Factions then the worst was yet to come.

Tammy stepped forward and all weapons turned on her as she boldly confronted her adversary. *"We are not interested in fighting you or snitching you off, we are here to join the Underworld and be gladiators in your underground arenas."*

Luther has healed his wounds in the time this event was occurring. Stepping near Tammy Luther sniffed her and smiled. Warts littered his face that disgusted Tammy as Luther kissed Tammy's hand like a Gentleman. Revolting as it was Tammy warmly smiled at the ugly man.

"You say you want to fight in our arenas and dare I say that it would be worth watching the two of you get slaughtered by our Xeno Warriors."

Luther began laughing loudly and asked . . .

"How do we know that you are not here to spy on us?" 'Tammy smacked Luther with a hard sweeping slap and said.' *"You dog, how you dare doubt the words of true gladiators! If you are so brave my man, then keep flapping your lips because before you know it you will be dead if, you don't shut up!"*

Luther jumped away from Tammy and spit on the carpet. *"If you are spies then I personally will skin both of alive."* Tammy laughed this time and in a move of defiance flipped her long hair behind her. She eyed the man over and sized him up, and then Tammy made a promise to Luther. *"We will obliterate any contestant that you have to challenge us. Are you so dumb to have never heard of us? We are the Champions of the Xeno Games!"*

"Sure, we have heard of you, we know the reward posted on your heads is a hefty sum.

Leven was not pleased with the way Tammy was dealing with this crisis so he intervened. *"We can just walk out of here unharmed and nobody will die. I promise you Luther that you will be the first to die and do not underestimate us. We might end up killing all of you and you know it. Now do you want to be friend or foe or can we just walk out of here. In case you do not know the Feds want us more then they want you. Now what's it going to be?"* Leven moved to the door and Tammy followed him. Silence consumed the room for a few seconds before Luther spoke out.

"Hold it, okay, come with us and stay low. You do not want any of the X-Crews to see you. They are the Ruling clan of Xeno People, and feared by everybody. A

creature named Valentine rules the clan that controls our huge underground city. He always wins the Super Xeno Bowl, which has the best Warriors that a laboratory can create fighting the Devil's creation. Valentine devours his opponents during and after his matches."

Leven Asked . . . *"How often do these Bowl Games occur?"*

"Once a year," replied Luther.

Luther gave orders to his subordinates to keep it a secret under penalty of death. Everybody followed Luther downstairs and into the basement. Luther pressed against the wall and an opening slid open revealing an elevator.

"This is one of our above-ground Hotels; we have many more of them throughout the city. You will be living in one of our brothels Private Suites. Everything you need, will be brought to you all you need to do is ask for it."

They entered the 20'x 20' compartment that rode them swiftly half a mile down to one of the city's lowest levels. Once there and the doors to the elevator opened they stepped into a dimly lit bizarre. Inside the stoned walls, Venders lined the wide tunnels with living quarters hollowed out of the earth selling their wares. Leaving the elevator behind them the group walked up the busy lane.

Leven and Tammy complained about the attire that they were wearing now. Luther stopped the group at one of the Vendors and purchased Leven and Tammy leather pants and shirts along with Government Issue combat boots. On the wall were racks of firearms and assorted knives. Leven was eying the weapons over and wishing that he could pick out and take the ones he chose.

Luther was a telepath and read Leven's thoughts, he cut in. "Take what you want Leven, don't worry about it, its on me."

Tammy and Leven swiftly began grabbing and

examining the knives and firearms. Leven snatched up a K-Bar (Marine fighting knife) and a 357 Magnum S&W with its shoulder holster and two boxes of shells. Luther watched in amazement as the dynamic twosome became lethal and they kissed passionately. Perhaps what made the duo so lethal was the love that they had for each other? Luther did not care as long as they belonged to him. There was no escape off the level without a DNA scan done by the constantly moving laser video scanners. Leven and Tammy owed their lives to Luther but they had a gladiator saying that went like this . . . *"Loyal to none and sworn to win." Leven knocked two of the guards aside and said to Luther. "We are her to win the games, if it takes fighting this called Valentine then so be it. I am sure that you have never heard of God . . ."*

"What is this God of yours my new strange friend and remember that there is no God down here. My good friend you are in the pits of Hell!"

"There is no such thing as hell unless you piss me off and you have to earn my respect before I will call you my friend. How am I supposed to know your plans? We are afraid of nobody and we do trust in God who is with us now, his name is Samuel."

Luther was ready with a comeback, *"You trust in your invisible god while I will continue to trust in my Generals. I assure you that even your god will run from Valentine."*

Luther and his gang of thugs explored the chambers for a while and were showing the Newbie's their way around Level 656. Both Leven and Tammy were impressed with the Tennis Courts and the underground Parks with Gardens. Underground waterfalls flowed over quartz crystals, which fluorescently glowed lighting the cavern were it was located. Tammy and Leven watched each other' backs urging Luther to take them to their shack.

Leven felt comfortably snug in that he and Tammy had infiltrated the Underworld. Tammy was curious about the Xeno creatures because they were misshapen and deformed: in ways beyond human imagination.

What interested Leven more then before were the mines and the constant drilling for minerals. Using the rules of deduction Leven considered the possibility that this underground city had its own Nuclear Power, underground reactors. It seemed that the Xeno people were warring against each other yet highly sophisticated and organized cooperation among the Warlords ran the city like clockwork. Valentine was behind it all and supported Valentine there was Samuel. There were no ideas of escaping the city because Leven and Tammy were exactly where they wanted to be. Leven continued asking about Valentine and learned that the man revered more than God was. Leven's curiosity grew and he became anxious to learn everything he could about the City Underworld.

January 1, 2021

"Go to the east side of town and tell Lefty that it's time to take out the Zebrine Family. Then I want you to go to the South Side and alert the boys down there about the upcoming hits." 'Daily was giving orders out to his underlings, his so called top Captains.' *"Billy, I want you to make sure that they understand that all the hits must occur in the same hour. Also, be sure to tell them that this is a Xeno hybrid family and that they are well organized. I want our best people on these hits and I want the hits to be done by independent Squads. If we wipe out the strongest Xeno Family in Chicago then the others will give in to our demands . . . do you understand that the time of the hits is six in the morning, by seven I want to get a phone call telling me that the jobs been completed?*

Billy was a tall man with a narrow face and a finger

missing on his left hand. He was the Mayors cousin and a well-known sleaze bag that used his influence to cover-up the monies he was embezzling from his second cousin. Chicago had always the most corrupt city in the world. Not even Terrorists ventured near the Windy City.

The Xeno Underworld is full of horrible creatures outside of God's creations on Earth. Some almost human could fool a normal person into believing that they are human too, these abnormalities believe that one day they will conquer the world and breed humans for food. If there is such a place as Hell, this would be it.

All the city mobs had banded together to exterminate the Xeno virus in Chicago. Tough men that gave no quarter and asked for none were prepared to root out the Xeno Syndicates in a bloody spree. All over the city, professional killers and the Chicago Police that had grown to a Force of over 750,000 strong not counting private Police Militias and vigilante groups were targeting Xeno families.

Federal Officials refused to meddle in the city affairs of Chicago, Ill. Satellites had revealed the Underground city to the CIA and so it was no secret. There were secrets that if the people of Chicago had known about this secret then they would have stormed Washington D.C. and burned the Pentagon to the ground.

Since the Sears Tower Incident, Chicago had become much like a City-State with a population of thirty-million people. Mayor Daily was much like a Dictator and ruled with an iron hand. He had become a problem in Washington so the insiders in the Pentagon deemed Chicago expendable. Once the President remarked, *"nuking Chicago would be like burning an ant hill, I consider it killing two birds with one stone."*

These underworlds were being constructed throughout the world and if they had known about the

Xeno Stronghold in South America then Chicago would have been the least of Washington's problems.

I believe that the Xeno Underworld are Xeno creatures created and nurtured by humans that have become independent and see us as nothing more then food.

The End of Chapter Two
"The Xeno Underworld"

Chapter Three
"A New Dawn Rising"

Jessica and her maid Sandra were sitting on the shoreline on a hedge of rocks watching the sunrise over the salty water. Salt was thick in the air as the ocean reached high tide. *"A new dawn is rising over the horizon; can you see the red halo being created by the sun Sandra?"*

Jessica waited for a response from the raven-haired young woman and did not have to wait too long for a response.

I am sorry madam; *"I was lost in thought for a couple minutes. I cannot get this feeling out of my mind that we watched. I feel spooked and cannot shake it. Sometimes I wish that I were home in the jungles of Brazil. This war is crazy and the hatred spreads worse than cancer does."*

Sandra was also involved with a man who was choosing to get Xeno treatments to enhance his body and mind. Jessica knew that her boyfriend was involved with a Xeno Church and an Activist for their Cause.

When Perez first arrived at the Jessica Compound Perez warmly welcomed by and fell in love with Sandra. After a two-year courtship, the two fell in love with each other.

Perez Chavez was a shy and gentle young man at the gates of the Compound when the Staff at the Gates repeatedly refused some hanger-on begging to enter to enter the Compound to enter. These men and women appealed and begged Perez to allow them a chance to prove their worthiness but the Guards prevented Perez from giving in to their demands and pleadings. Perez went out the Gates to try to preach to them and ever since that time, he has never been the same man.

Against Sandra's pleas, Perez met with a man who introduced Perez to the Xeno Underground Network. These spies severely dealt with but Jessica said it was God's place to Judge them and not hers. Perhaps this led to temptations that led more than one person away from the Jessica Compound. Sandra should have distanced herself from Perez but she was weak of the flesh.

These thoughts were going through Jessica's mind when she spoken these words. *"Perhaps there are some hoodlums watching us but they dare not approach us or bother us in any way. Certainly, there must be something else bothering you, it would be proper for you to forget about Perez and go on with your life. He is one of the outsiders now and belongs in hell."*

"Haven't you ever fallen in love Jessica?"

'Sandra wondered about this for a long time and expected no for an answer.' *"I was born in love with God,"* said Jessica. *"What are we having for breakfast this morning?"* Asked Jessica and Sandra smiled for the first time since they had met earlier.

With a cheery face Sandra blurted out; *"I baked some fresh lemon muffins last night and pouched eggs with pancakes, I have the first batch of maple syrup from our trees this year and it is sweeter then last years. Plus we have fresh milk and donuts that I made that are sweetened with our own cinnamon and sugar cane along with the home grown apples that I mixed in with the batter . . ."*

"It all sounds so wonderful and delicious. Why don't we wait until Raven arrives and invite her to have breakfast with us?"

"Yes Madam, that sounds just fine and I must say that it is starting out to be a superb day. Look at the orange sunrise, which means that it's going to be a hot

day today."

January 3, 2021

Perez was busy selling information to the Xeno underground for enhancement treatments. There was a problem in his life that Perez was not aware of because it was the L.O.D. They were monitoring Perez and knew what was happening to him. They waited for Jessica to act on this crisis but all she said was that in due time God would handle the situation. The LOD wanted to eliminate the problem once and for all rid the Compound of Perez and his new friends.

Tonight Perez was meeting with Gula; Gula was a California Warlord and one of the top dogs in the pack. Gula was responsible for purging the Xeno Race of spies and it was his duty to Police the State.

Perez had stolen some of Jessica's fingernails and hair from the Compound Dump and had a map of the Compound roads, Businesses and other vital areas of this billion-dollar paradise. Gula had requested these items because Samuel had come to say it in person. Perez was the patsy used to get these items for Samuel. Then Perez was expendable and afterwards, Perez would be served for dinner at his home 'Gula had fifteen children and three wives.' Perez was the sap to do the dirty work and the main course for dinner. Fallen into sin Perez needed a miracle to save his life.

Penny Wilson was seventeen years old now and lived in Jessica's house with her dog Katana. They were always exploring the compound looking for new deer trails to investigate. Today Penny was expecting Sandra to visit her so she planned staying home. Jessica dropped by to pray with her and they spent lunch together. Jessica explained that the future held deep despair for the human species, 'while tossing the salad and gazing out the window at the horses in her corral.' Jessica was a realist and a Christian. She separated herself from the horror and murder that she knew was commonplace outside the walls of the Compound. How Jessica was able to play with Penny's little black terrier and display no sadness was almost unreal. Playing ball with Katana, Jessica glanced at Penny and smiled. They Jessica asked Penny an odd question.

"Why aren't you getting ready to go outside and walk the trails, Penny, you usually are gone by now?"

Penny was knitting a sweater for Katana as she sat in a rocking chair on the deck of the house. It was a beautiful house with a deck running around it on the second floor.*" Sandra said that she was coming over today and that she did not know when exactly she would arrive. She never told me when today she was coming just that she was. I understand that her boyfriend is having problems?"*

"Have you seen Peter lately, I worry about Peter and the members living on our Compound of the LOD."

Jessica was more concerned about Peter and the role he was playing in the demise of Perez. Jessica overlooked nothing and when she acted, it was done she did it swiftly.

"I saw Peter yesterday while on my way to the Forum; I asked him where he was heading and told me that he was going to a rally."

"What kind of a Rally?" Asked Jessica, then she threw another treat for Katana.

"I am not sure but Perez was wearing leathers and seemed agitated about something or another. I saw others that were dressed as he was walking in the same direction. I believe it was the northwest path leading into the forest behind North Garden Park."

Most of the time Penny ignored the world around her and lived her life to its fullest. Penny did not want to know about evil or bad events. She was away from her family and her father was running for Vice President of the United States using her disappearance as a means for popularity. Penny did not know why she was healthy let alone alive. Jessica called Penny the sweetest and nicest girl in the Compound. Jessica always sheltered Penny from horror but nothing could have prepared her for what came next.

From the deck, they saw Sandra half-carrying Perez onto the sidewalk that led to the house. Penny was shocked to see them and Jessica did not seem to be in a rush to help them. Jessica warned the pair when she first learned of the problem. Things were not out of control but situations seemed to be in disarray. Perez was badly beaten and bleeding from a wound on his head. Sandra *"was covered in blood and crying while glancing over her shoulder as if they had been followed."* 'Jessica threw the ball for Katana and it bounced inside of the house.' Rising from her seat Jessica followed Katana and Penny stayed in tow.

Security was on top of the situation as they ran out of the wood-line and had taken Perez into custody. They were well armed and chosen one at a time by Jessica when she created Security for the Compound. Jessica was smart as a whip and knew numbers well; she was a genius above all the others and a Wonder to the world. Her special gifts were more than an advantage to this woman who seemed to have a grand vision. What made it miraculous was that Jessica's visions a person could bank on coming true, Jessica was not surprised or seemed over concerned about Perez as the greeted the bunch at the door. Penny invited them inside and they all entered the house.

"You will not believe the way Peter acted; it was as if he was a Nazi from the last Century. Peter and his

group of bully's raided their secret Headquarters and killed many innocent people that were there."

Jessica did not seem surprised and calmly inquired about what part Peter played during the raid. *"Sandra please, do tell us about Peter? What was he doing at this fiasco?"*

Sandra was sobbing and in-between breaths managed to tell everything that she remembered.

"I received a call from Perez to come and pick him up. He told me that they had been attacked by some hooded men and that Peter was one of them, then Perez hung up."

"Please continue with your story, I know that this is hard for you but I promise you that things will get back to normal before you know it. Now please tell us what you saw when you arrived to the assembly in the north forest?"

(Jessica had hardened through the years and felt nothing at all to those possessed by evil. Pure of heart and loyal to God were most of the inhabitants of the Compound. Jessica deemed that on every Wednesday those that are not of pure heart, cast out of paradise among those that judged by the Xeno mobs.

LOD members were exempt from this law and had decided to recruit privately and keeping their names secret.)

"I rode my horse to the forest clearing and dismounted to sneak in for a better view. Perez was running in my direction as these hooded men slaughtered everybody that they could find. Then they confiscated the Ledgers and books before they departed. I saw Peter because he was the man barking the orders and the last person to leave. He had removed his hood before he left and stared at the dead for a few seconds. It seems that a Faction of the LOD was breaking away from the main body

and the main body of the LOD had retaliated. I helped
Perez get here because when we found my horse shot to
death.

Heath Stratton was the operative spying on Perez
and he reported to Jessica. *"Gula had met Perez in the
forest on the east side of Ribbon Creek and they had made
the exchange there, Gula injected Perez with a large dose
of Xeno Potion during this meeting. We were about to
spring our trap when Peter and his volunteer storm their
Rally and chaos preceded from then on out, and more."*

*"What else did you observe while you were there
and Heath please does not leave anything out?"* Jessica
was expressionless as she listened to her spy.

*"I heard Gula say that it was all a set-up and that
bad and misleading information was leaked to the LOD."*

God inspired Jessica and business conducted
differently on the Jessica Compounds the world over.

By the time it was all taken care of Jessica was tired
and ordered, 'Perez confined in their jail.' Perez was the
first person imprisoned in the jail since it opened two years
past. By the time Jessica was home and lay on her bed,
another new dawn was rising.

January 15, 2021

With the force of a hurricane havoc ripped through
Huntington Beach California as a virus spread at a
phenomenal rate infecting the local population for ten miles
square. National Guard units experienced and trained for
crisis situations closed off all exits and blockaded the ocean
with Coast Guard Cutters armed with formidable
weaponry. All the Guardsmen and women wore NBC gear,
(Nuclear Biological Chemical). Suits were of a new breed
then the ones used during the 'Gulf Wars' that final ended
with two nuclear mushrooms dropped at the right

times and places. 'History repeats itself.' Everyday, in the last ten years or so, mostly credited to the *"Xeno Brigades"* invented in Government Laboratories. Terrorist Leaders were killed or captured that had ruled the terrorist murderers due to the strong senses of the Xeno soldiers. It seemed that the Xeno Age Army Brigades had caused more death and killing: than the nukes that were detonated two years ago. The virus causing this disaster fashioned a huge adrenaline increase in its victim's bodies creating a host that was uncontrollable and at the brink of madness. Businesses and homes were ablaze and people lay dying in the street as the CDC stood by and recorded, investigated, tested, and researched every little thing under a microscope.

No vaccine was created because all of those infected eventually died from the virus and then the virus died. One researcher suggested that it seemed that scientists used this ten-mile area as a control grid. There was no possible way to create a vaccine because the virus seemed to vanish.

After a week, the areas of disaster were repopulated and were back to normal, in no time at all as if nothing ever happened at Huntington Beach. Times had changed and America was accustomed to disasters and had learned how to deal with them quickly and efficiently. It had also had the effect to harden the American people and become indifferent to one crisis after another.

March 13, 2021

Tammy and Leven were together again after being separated for over six months. For unknown reasons Leven was arrested and held as a lesson to Israel by the Government and was finally released last night. After hours of lovemaking and drinking wine, Leven was still fuming over America detonating a nuclear bomb over Bagdad after

Allied troops moved out and the Taliban moved in. To our American President it was a no-brainer, there had to be a means to the end so to assure that American Bases could be set up for the big war around the corner. Western Countries were embargoing China and Russia had become a World Power again. Leven made a statement to the Press that caused concern for our Government and they had jailed Leven for speaking his mind on national television.

"What's for breakfast this morning Sweetheart?"
"I am hungrier than a Russian bear in Siberia."

They were staying the night at a rented cottage near Pebble Beach on Jessica Foundation owned property. It was well furnished and well stocked with food, drink, and weaponry. There was a gym available for the Couple and a fully equipped kitchen.

"Hold your horses Honey; we are having Buffalo steaks with eggs, rice, grits, potatoes, and brown gravy. Our caterer should arrive soon but until then why don't we fool around?"

It seems that the two of them could not keep each other from trying to catch up on lost time as their caterers cooked them breakfast.

Finally, by nine they were eating breakfast as the caterers were leaving and joyously laughing like children. It seemed that Leven and Tammy had found the Fountain of Youth by there appearance as they ate enough food for four large men.

After they had finished eating the two lovers strolled to the beach and began beach combing. Tammy smiled and held Leven closer to her as she spoken to Leven these words: *"Honey, I'm Pregnant."*   .

March 14, 2021

Leven was thinking about Tammy as he boarded his plane. Called back to duty Leven directed to a Special

Assignment by a Senate Subcommittee to protect Ben Carter. Ben won the election becoming President and was anti-Xeno in his policies. Ben Lee Carter was a relative to Jimmy Carter and a Peace Activist. Ben believed that world peace depended on the extermination of the Xeno Species.

China was flexing its muscles as it showed off huge arsenals of offensive and defensive weapons. China had equipped an Army of one and a half billion soldier's with unlimited supplies and ammunition. Political differences had brought china at the brink of war with Korea. United States and the U.K. were negotiating for peace but trying to stay neutral in the Chinese and Korean Conflict. China had massed five-million Soldiers on the border with Korea and were ready and able to strike an overwhelming blow on Korea. Korea had the new cruise missiles armed with multiple warheads all aimed at China. China believed that if they attacked the launching sites throughout Korea first they could overrun Korea before the missiles launched.

Leven hated Politics and wanted to be with Tammy but it was not his call to make. Leven honorably given two months Leave after six months of Service as a personal Bodyguard to President Carter. Two men dressed in grey suits approached Leven and asked? *"Hey Leven, you come with us for your orientations and in-processing. Then we will show you to your Quarters."* Glad to be on the ground Leven followed the lean and tall men out of the Airport and into a bulletproof Limo.

It was early morning and the sky was blood red.
End of Chapter Three   "A New Dawn Rising"

Chapter Four

July 27, 2022   **"Sunrise"**

Clear blue skies covered Pierce County as Nicklaus entered his laboratory. ***"Hot, it's so hot today that I wish I were at the North Pole."*** Nicklaus had been obsessed with his work and grown extremely paranoid, there in the middle of nowhere, caught in the limelight, Nick chose seclusion. With his own creations at the gates and staffing the towers, Nick cushioned his life with safety. It was hot all right; things had gotten out of control. Procreation among mixed breeds in the midst of the Xeno population had made monsters with improved immune systems that could fend off nerve gas. Bodies with shells and human arms with hands akin to talons were an even match for the Xenomitte species. Nick was concerned and had good reasons for it. If these two species procreated Nick knew that they would consume the world of other life and then attack and devour one-another. His experiments in the last two months were about whether or not it was a possibility.

In an extreme case, Nick had created a monkey with a shell covering that resembled a CDC Chemical and biological suit. This creature filtered air before it touched the body. Beneath the silky but sturdy skinned critter was a body without any hair. Twice it had broken out of its cell and was chained inside a cage and sedated. This creature had withstood cyanide, lead, mustard gas, and biological viruses from infecting it. Nick had castrated the beast so that it would not procreate but knew of other scientists researching this advanced DNA field. Nick was trying to recreate the same procedure in humans. Fifty Test Subjects treated like guests these people lived comfortably against their wills on levels 2-4. were and had formed their own society calling themselves the Test Tank. This monkey of Nicks' produced enough toxins and viruses as it expelled poisons creating a dead zone around it. There was nothing in the world as extreme as Nicks work.

In the last five years, the average temperature in Washington State had risen twenty-percent and if it was not raining, it was thick with fog. Nick had returned to the Lupus mansion with his beloved wife and stayed out of the public's eyes. Nicklaus stayed anchored into a fifty-acre plot of land. He had a security force of two-hundred human mercenaries and three-hundred Xeno-creatures constructed by the mastermind himself. Rainforest grew lush and thick spreading over the ground quickly. Each day the sun shinned strong onto the state hot enough to fry an egg on the asphalt. Rain or fog the sun would break through for three hours a day. Then heavy clouds would cover the state and loud thunderstorms would rip havoc on the land.

A new volcano had formed east of the mountains and had grown eighteen-thousand feet in one year. Molten lava has covered a fifth of the State of Washington and killed almost three-hundred thousand people in its wake. Scientist predicted that this eruption would not cease for five to ten years and would grow to a height beyond any mountain in the world. Higher than Mt. Everest while taking up a quarter of the State. This new mountain range named the Devils Spawn was a new wonder of the world. The eruption never reached Hells Canyon.

Nicklaus had sent Lisa with three other teams to search for new life, new cells to play with east. Now Nicklaus was lonely and mad.

Indeed the world had gone through changes. New engines that operated on vegetable oil for food, and all were hovercrafts now with turbo jet engines. They could cruise the atmosphere faster then the speed of sound. Oh yes, the new Vets were stealth and cool. Nick owned thee of them at a cost of a billion dollars apiece. Everything was different and a new coastline showed on the modern maps selling at popular gas stations and Markets. Militias had dug in deeply united in a common cause and there were many new laws passed protecting the Xeno Species. Everything was lead-based alloy or concrete that new construction around the Free World was using as a means of survival. One-third of the planet was being controlled and in alliance with the far-left extreme, terrorists relating to the leaders of the Gulf Wars. United States had become one of the most powerful forces globally; this accomplished with having power over the economies of the world and building Military Bases in Iran, Iraq, and Japan. The Games were more popular then they ever were and the only refuge that poor people had was the protection of fighting in the games. It was either that or starving in the streets eventually consumed by a Xenomitte. Xenomitte machines designed for street cleaning and mob control. These Xenomittes controlled with implants from a central command post were not the danger; the Controllers were staffing the flashing panels.

Nick loved to interact with his Test Tank. He had had picked each subject for their mental abilities, Reproductive capabilities, Physical appearance and by the State of their Health.

Walking down long corridors into the lower levels of the mini lab complex most of the facility was underground. In the labs, working 24-7 were experts and specialists, scientists and biochemists. All these workers were under the influence of his improved 1313F66 mind control serum and they followed his orders perfectly well. These people did not know that they followed every word that Nick said as they continued with their private lives within the confines of the Complex. Lisa referred to them as human drones not worth their weight in salt. Having no interest in the private quarters of his Staff, Nick continued walking as he entered Level 2.

Observing about a dozen of the test subjects through the glass loudspeakers in his office recorded everything said in their Commons Room. There was a television and games to play; chess was a favorite among this group. Nick had his office built so that he could observe hid subjects.

Laura Street was an attorney, single, and born into a rich family. After Nick profiled Street, then she brought to the Complex by Nick's henchmen. Nick never used mind control drugs on the Test Tank but he used animal DNA and tested rejection drugs on them. Laura was the first to have DNA implanted into her from the monkey. She was Nick's pet project.

Laura approached Nick as Nick entered the commons room. *"So Doc, what's cooking?"*

Nick did not miss a step as he passed her by. *"Okay everybody, gather together and have a seat in the circle." (It was a large glass table surrounded by lush couches except for one gap in the circle.)* There in the gap between the plush couches was a office roller executive chair and Nick sat in it.

Laura sat nearest to the Doctor and quickly everybody present in the commons area became comfortably seated in his or her regular spots. Some subjects drugged and others were not, it all depended on their mental health and immune systems. Paul Trosky was sitting directly across from the doctor and Paul was a smartass. Paul wasted no time in making a sarcastic comment to the Doctor.

"What kind of bullshit are you going to feed us today doc, do you want us to try some new pills again?"

"No pills today Paul just chatting about your feelings and any comments one might have to improve your living conditions." Nick was being calm and watching his test subjects for any abnormalities. Eying the

teen over Nick told him to be quiet until asked a question, and then Nick addressed the group.

"I hope that by now you realize that the only way out of here is in a box. There have been three escape attempts this week that resulted in the confinement of said persons. Now they are working for me in the lab, beneath a microscope lens. Wasting DNA is not my way of doing things. I am cloning their cells and creating an underwater species that I will house in tanks. I have their brains in incubators so they can think about their mistake of disobeying me. I will keep them alive forever in this state until I find an animal to xenotransplant them into? Whatever the case, I want you to know that all of you have been cleared of any misdoings so you can relax." Silence engulfed the room as Nick lit his pipe and smoked it.

"Now, lets begin with Laura, how was your week Laura?"

"Okay . . . I guess. I keep having dreams of the jungle at night and they can be disturbing at times quite disturbing."

"Do you smell anything in your dreams my dear?" The effects of small doses of his monkey serum impressed the Doctor and his curiosity grew. *"What about taste, do you eat in your dreams?"*

"That is all that I can remember is running through the jungle in my dreams, seems that I am running for my life. That is the feeling that I get, doc."

Dr. Keller smiled and tried to comfort her, some words he concocted on the wing. *"Well /I am sure that it will pass, must be your diet. I will write you a new nutritional supplement that should make the dreams go away."* A bad thought of seeing Laura flashed into the Doctors mind because she was nude. Then Nick observed Tommy grinning ear to ear to his left and realized that

Tommy was transferring a thought with his mind. It was becoming quite interesting for the Doctor, next thing he knew Patty Hunt was speaking about the way she felt about being alone. She said that even among people she felt alone. Nick knew that nobody was listening to Hunt and waited until she was finished before addressing the main issue that he came to advocate to the group. Laura popped another pill and smiled at the Doctor.

"We have given you special gifts that only you possess and in return you forfeited you right to leave my supervision. That means that you are here against your will. Now I decided to install the new Pentium XXX computers into your rooms so you can study whatever you want or go wherever you like. There is no networking with the outside world but you will have access to medical and law libraries. I will give you access to lab level 0003 to experiment and kill time. I encourage you to procreate but please pass it by me first. Some of you cannot procreate with certain test subjects because of the therapy they are undertaking. Tommy if you know what is best for you then you will keep your genetic gift to yourself or the others might throw you a blanket party. Do I make myself clear?"

Tommy yanked back his head leaving his long blond hair on his back instead of blocking the view. The he sighed and replied . . . *"Okay, you're the boss."* Everybody laughed because Tommy was getting to be a pain in the 'you knows what.'

Nick mingled with the group for over an hour before he said good night and departed for his office. Nick was not sadistic but some of his procedures were.

Certainly, in the Complex Compound, Nick was the King he was untouchable. In and about the Compound were creatures of curious natures and a red house for the humans guarding the Compound? Seems odd but prostitution was legalized three years ago so there was nothing politically wrong about it. Nick ruled with an iron fist but was complacent with Security. He figured that they knew their jobs well enough to be alive today so that was good enough for Nick. It had become a hard world and the poor suffered for it. Seems that the Xeno People united and helped each other out of jams, in the human society, it was everybody for anarchy.

Dr. Keller was on the brink of a discovery that was going to change the world into new classes of species and all under his control. Oddly, an accident happened in the Test Tank this night that changed the world.

August 1, 2022

Lisa had waken to a beautiful sunrise enhance by the brilliance of the spurting volcano. Bodyguards and news reporters with their cameras surrounded Lisa. It was the first time that she was away from Nick; so long that she had forgotten what it was like to be free.

One asset that he designed Lisa for Nick never thought about as a curse but that is exactly what it was. Lisa was having five love affairs going and her sexual appetite was out of control with no way to mollify her and satisfaction never a guarantee.

Lisa had a mind equal to Nick's, and was loyally in love with the mad doctor but had to quench her emptiness while away from Nick. Nick had sent with Lisa his trusted and loyal Mercenary/Disciple to report to him and to assure that Lisa was safe. Nick never thought of his son anymore because of the time and effort he put into his experiments. Nick learned about Lisa from Frank Capola, his trusted inside man. Nick felt forgetful and alarmed at first but then regained his composure quickly. Having fun with his Test

Tank and on the brink of new discoveries Nick was willing to take his chances with Lisa.

Ashes rained thickly near the volcano until you were thirty miles from it. Five States had felt the impact of the enormous devastation of the Washington's volcano. Lisa loved flying her armor plated and fortified hovercraft as near as possible to the volcano. She was in a two-seater with Frank as her co-pilot. Nightfall arrived and clouds rolled in from the northeast heavily laden with rain.

Frank turned the craft around, headed west to Base Camp Bravo, and in the same minute, a bolt of lightning struck the craft leaving a blinding flash and smoke.

Several hours later

The two misfits awoke to the sound of wolves howling at the full moon. Wolves had repopulated America and some packs that roamed the night were Xeno Crossbreds. Native wolves had grown larger and fiercer. A new breed of wolves roamed the rainforests of Washington State. Wolves were reputed to have killed mountain lions and cougars. Lisa kicked Frank awake and then the both of them salvaged what they could from the wreckage.

Frank found his laser guided M-9XT and two lock boxes on the flyer filled with two pistols, standard issues, food, water, ammunition, blankets, and medical supplies.

"Well now we need to set up a shelter to protect us from the elements." Frank said amazed at what had happened to them they were both stunned but in today's world, you always have to be prepared, for the worst. *"Lets make a shelter out of the craft using the canvass and we can build a fire pit."* Lisa was getting her gear arranged and working on the shelter. The radio and telephones were

dead and they felt the earth shake from the volcano. *"We can bed down after we eat in a couple hours. I will take the first watch and keep the fire going"*

Moist particles floated in the dense air around the pair as they professionally built their shelter. Once they had finished they sat on some logs by the fire and ate while talking about the bolt of lightning that hit them. *"From now on Frank do me the favor of bringing along some liquor. I could sure use a drink."* Frank produced a long flat metal flask filled with bourbon and handed it to Lisa. *"Boy you do think of everything Frank!"*

Inside of the rainforest was danger and mystery. It was dark on this night, black with the clouds covering the moon that earlier shined brightly. Lisa watched Frank as he bedded down and she shook the urge of lust from her thoughts. Lisa could sense something out there watching them she could smell them. Lisa decided to use Frank as bait to draw whatever was out there into the camp. Through the years Nick had perfected Lisa in every way possible, she was every man's dream of a woman. Spiders the size of footballs tried the near the fire for warmth but Lisa used her torch to shoo them away.

Owls howled and varmints were scurrying along the ground as Frank lay sleeping next to the fire. Lisa tuned in on her surroundings waiting for an attack that she knew was coming. She held the rifle clenched tightly in her hands and had covered her attire with mud. If one did not know where Lisa was then they would never see her.

It was getting near sunrise but Lisa knew that before the sun showed itself all hell would break loose. She found good cover and put herself into an alert state, alert as a cat on the prowl. Frank was beginning to stir and as he moved Lisa smelled the scent stronger then before and knew that their were three assailants about to attack them. Frank moved swiftly as he snatched his Mac-9XT on the roll and landed behind two huge trees firing his weapon. Frank firing blindly hit one of the scavengers three times in the forehead. The brain is the hottest part of a body so the heat-seeking laser zeroed the bullets in on their targets. With two armed convicts that were determined to kill and rob these two strangers still out there somewhere the danger was far from over for the two stranded friends.

Walla Walla State Prison riot exploded during the worst of the volcano and over three-thousand convicts were on the loose in the deep rainforests of Washington.

As the sun crested over the horizon Frank swore, ***"Damn right, bloody sunrise. Now I can see the son of a guns."*** It was then that Lisa jumped up from behind the unsuspecting convicts and cut them down with her Government Issued Assault rifle.

What National Guard was not fighting in the new war in the Congo and Sudan were on duty in Washington State. With the turmoil getting worse and the crisis escalating it was impossible to police the state.

By noon, a Para rescue team brought the two safely back to base and the safety of their own guards. Lisa was exhilarated about the near death experience and had multiple orgasms during the firefight. After this morning Lisa was never the same again, she found a new thrill in life almost as good as loving Nick.

August 8, 2022

Nick was worried to death about Lisa. Lisa was his only love, it was the closest thing to love that he knew to love. Nick carried in his chest a heart made of stone. Yet his hard heart longed for Lisa. Frank was due to call again in the morning and Lisa was coming home that evening.

Slamming the door against the wall as it flew open, Dr. Keller entered the Test Tank with Sung at his side with a mean scowl on his face. It was the first time that Nick had lost his composure with his control group. Sung was giving a class tonight on acupuncture and recruiting a student to learn his trade. Sung carried his attaché case with him and it was easy to see that it was heavy. Behind them the door closed automatically by the laser sensors that were installed on all the doors and windows in the Complex.

Phillip Lacante was sitting alone in the Commons area and everybody else seemed to be in his or her rooms. Phil was the outcast of the bunch because he came from the poor side of society and never attended school. Nick tested Philip's IQ and he was elated to learn it was 191. Phil played video games mostly, and read books his peers ostracized him because Phil had a bad attitude about rich people. Lacante hated aloof and stuck-up people.

Sung noticed the boy and approached him. "Get all the test subjects out here now and then when you return stand by the exit sign. You will be coming with me once we leave.

In ten minutes, everybody had gathered in the Commons Room and soon thereafter seated and eyeing Sung over the test subjects seemed afraid of what was to come next. It was the first time that John Sung at the Test Tank.

"Listen up everybody, this is John Sung, he has been working with me for over two decades and he can teach you a lot if you open your ears and pay attention. I need a volunteer, who wants to be a volunteer?" Nick stared at his group and saw Laura Street standing to volunteer but Nick interrupted her. *"Not this time Laura, you do not have the right stuff for this demonstration. I think that Billy Polanski will volunteer in your place . . . silence . . . will you not Billy?"*

"Yes Sir, what would you like for me to do?"

Billy knew that he was not in a good situation. John

Sung sported deep scars on his hands and face. Sung's eyes were the most frightening to the boy as he slowly approached the podium.

Nick barked some commands to the boy and Billy did as he supposed to do, and did it well. Billy ran to the storage closet and rolled out a barber' chair had been modified for multi tasking. Then Billy set up a folding table and four chairs. All this as he was being told to do it. Once it was all set up in front of the Speakers podium Nick asked the boy to have a seat in the chair.

John strapped the boy down, first his arms and then his legs. Billy trusted Dr. Keller because he had only been in the Test Tank for three weeks. Billy had just graduated High School shortly after his kidnapping. He missed his graduation when Laura enticed Billy to go for a ride with her after just meeting accidentally at the shopping Mall. Laura was loyal to Nick and she was the Test Tank snitch.

Billy stared at nothing, blankly shutting out the world around him leaving Billy alone and helpless more then at first. All attention was on John Sung as he opened his attaché case and unfolded rolls of needles and surgical knives and laid them carefully on the table that Billy set up. Billy seemed oblivious to these implements of healing, and torture.

"Let your love for your workflow this time Sung, we want to set an example her. Drive our point home. Make me proud of you Sung, now I want you to do one through ten of your procedures. I will be watching you closely." Nick was warning Sung, not to get carried away. Nick wanted to see if the drugs he gave them at breakfast would make the others immune to the pain of others. This was part of a Project that Nick was working on for the Army code-named, **"Extreme Behavior."**

When Nick calls you then you cannot refuse. There is no direction unless Doctor Keller dictates it. The man radiates terror, his eyes are wild and for some time Nick has been sharpening his teeth. His whole life Nick had been good at hiding things. He had not changed through the years, and was able covertly become the most influential man in the world. Crazy as a mad-hatter Nick was beyond genius, he was beyond a point, 'that could be measured scientifically,' but Nick was mad to the bone."

Nick addressed the assembly. "We can do it all, everything. We do not need anything from anyone because all of you are special. I do not quite know how to put this. If I let this bother me, then I would have never become what I am . . . Now its time for you to burst into life."

Nick was not his old self and it frightened his test subjects, he could see it in their eyes. It almost seemed as if Nick was drunk but it was more then that, Nick was jealous of Frank.

"All of you have had it easy here; all needs and more, much more have been taken care of because through you I will build a Power so strong that the world will be at our feet! Brace yourselves for what you are about to see and learn from this. Each one of you will learn, see, and hear everything differently so be prepared for what you are about to witness."

Paul Trosky could not help himself from spurting out a rude comment. *"Is Billy getting a haircut doc or are you going to shave off his peach fuzz."* As soon as he said it Paul knew that he royally screwed up. The Doctor focused his eyes on Paul and commanded Paul to replace Billy in the chair. Paul responded with, *"Frick off doc you sit on it."*

This enraged Nick, he yelled at Billy to go back to his seat, and then he recruited the two bullies in the group to fetch Paul and then strap him down in the chair. Dale Loveday was six-foot five and overweight, he under the influence of ape serum to increase adrenalin XX31. This drug created an obedient soldier that would follow all commands dictated by Nick. Dale's father is a Senator. Joe Gun was just plain mean, his father was a County Sherriff and he volunteered to have his son committed at the Complex because Joe was always in trouble with the law. Joe was not the size of Dale but then Joe was all bad, smart and evil, ruthless. Dr. Keller knew these things because of the things that Nick allowed Joe to do in during private experiments.

Most of the test subjects in the Test Tank were normal young adults not yet contaminated by Nick's experiments. 'Once DNA is altered, then it can never be returned to its original form.' Nick would eventually poison all their minds and put their bodies through hell by the time they lived another year. This test group was the fifth group.

Dale and Nick and performed their task and before long, a whining Paul was securely bound to the chair. *"Make this one special, okay John?"*
"Sure boss, whatever you say . . ."

There among the Test Tank were several persons who tried to resist but Dale and Joe pushed them into their seats as they tried returning to their rooms. The others in this Group hated Dale and Joe but there always are a couple of bad apples in every bushel. Rumblings and chatter persisted among these few and nobody could shut them up. Paul had begun his treatment administered by Sung. Paul at that time let out a loud and horrific scream that shot into the room from his throat. Shortly the room grew quiet.

Screams coming from Paul interrupted Doctor Nicklaus a couple of times but he did not seem bothered by it. He continued speaking from the podium into a microphone. *"John Sung is using what he calls the twist and curl followed with a lazy S surgical cut exposing Paul's heart for all to see. Do not be alarmed by what you observe, be glad that it is not you sitting in the specimen chair. It is a painful procedure using needles to paralyze his body and a revolutionized surgical cut perfected by me."*

"Notice that the patient is fully conscious and that we can replace his heart and have him on his way in no more than twenty minutes. All of you were had picked to become somebody special so when I hear disobedience it pisses me off!"

Nick turned and stepped off the podium onto the floor. He pushed Sung out of the way and slammed his fist into Paul's chest. 'Paul looked surprised as his mouth closed and his screaming ceased. Then you could see his face wrench in pain as Nick squeezed and then yanked Paul's heart out of his chest. Sung opened an ice cooler and Nick through the heart atop of the ice. Sung closed the lid and motioned Phillip Lacante to take possession of the cooler. Philip saw that the heart was still beating as Sung lifted the lid for Philip to see. If it all went as intended, Then it seemed that John Sung was tutoring Lacante privately and molding him into a puppet that would assist John with his duties.

Dale and Joe carried the body to the incinerator down the hall from the Test Tank. Dale vomited on the way and Joe laughed at him calling him a sissy. Both boys were glad to be out of the mad doctor's sight and Joe sighed in relief as they pushed Phil into the incinerator. Joe stepped on Phil's glasses as he walked out of the Maintenance compartment of the Level they lived on.

Inside of the Commons chamber, Nick was standing on the podium again speaking to his students, test subjects about what had just occurred. John was cleaning his tools of the trade indifferent to where he was.

"I had never had to resort to these kind of tactics here or anywhere before in my life. You have brought out

the worst in me and Phil paid for it. His death is on your hands as will be the next if you do not awaken to this wake-up call. All the test subjects come in a lot of fifty and usually at least seventy percent graduate from the Test Tank. Among you I wonder if any will graduate!"

"What about me, doctor, will I graduate." 'Laura was crying because she was not given a dose of Nick's formula.'

"Of course you will honey, you are the main attraction, and you have graduated when you were so brave as to take three ocular injections invented from the bubble monkey. Please have a seat and relax because this will never happen again . . . Today was a crucial step to regain control of this group before they all end up like Phil."

Nick had sated his anger with the torture and death of Lacante so now he was as nice as a summer day. He turned to the group and told them that there were no third chances and he was staring at the people who were disruptive earlier. Nick knew that by sunrise Frank would arrive with Lisa in tow. He promised himself that he was not going to do anything irrational.

End of Chapter 4
"Sunrise"

Chapter Five
"Back From The Dead"

Everybody Valentine knew thought him to be dead by after the assault on Key West Island. Yet there he was standing in person before Samuel.

There were two tigers flanking Valentine as he stood at attention before his god. Samuel had created an entity that had tentacles and was slimy like eel or a fish. This creature jumped from Sam's hands and landed on Valentine's face. Valentine clawed at it as the tigers growled and in minutes, the slimy creature had slipped down Valentine's throat.

"There you are Valentine, now you have a part of me inside of you everywhere that you go. You can still think and do whatever you want but keep in mind that I will know about. At a whim, I can instruct my demon to kill you at anytime. Now Valentine I trust you."

Valentine seemed to be choking to death as he collapsed to the floor. Suffering several seizures, vomiting his guts onto the floor he was soaked in vomit, and trembling when his self-composure returned. Valentine stood and seemed to have trouble catching his breath.

Samuel allowed Valentine to build an empire in the Amazon and knew about his traitorous blood. If Sam had not intervened several times, Nick and Lisa would be dog food by now. Samuel respected Nick and was fond of Lisa. There was a prize to win, and the only way that Samuel could have the booty was through Valentine. Now Valentine was in his control. Samuel knew of less painful methods to control Valentine but enjoyed inflicting pain too much to resist the temptation. For the first time in his life, Valentine was horrified.

Locked inside of a 12'x12' cell Valentine slept like a baby for ten hours awakening to the shock of his life. Rufal, who was one of Samuel's demons was holding a stun gun and was shocking the bees wax out of Valentine. This continued for an hour before the shell of a once powerful creature broke down and began pleading for mercy.

Rufal was in a better mood then normal: *"Now you plead for your life that is not a life at all. You are an abnormality, no father and no mother, God will not even know that you exist so who are you pleading to, Valentine?"*

Valentine welcomed a break in the pain and stared at this giant bald man covered with warts. *"I am pleading to Samuel, the god of god, the master of evil, the destroyer of good, the plague that one day will consume the earth, Sam is the apple of my life he is my God!"*

Samuel appeared out of thin air and towered over the laying figure beneath his feet. *"I want you to mobilize all your forces in Brazil and tell them about me; tell them that I am god and that you worship me. I will display some visionary figures for you and then you will sacrifice ten unblemished virgins in my name. Six boys and six girls and keep in mind that they must be perfect."*

"Then what do I do Master?" Valentine was a new man, he felt strengthened by the thing that was inside on him.

Then you arm them and train them for invasions."

This confused Valentine and he asked Samuel this question. *"What are we invading Master?*

"Once we get your forces prepared in Chicago and move your jungle force into Mexico then we will cripple the Mid-west and invade Texas. All the soldiers are

overseas fighting wars so FT. Bliss and Fort Hood will be nearly empty of munitions and veterans. We will disrupt the Christmas Xeno Games and take a chunk of Texas and Chicago as our own. This will be the *'The Beginning of the end'* for the human species, and I will send their mortal souls for my father to torment in hell.

Valentine felt like a King, he was full of hate yet now he seemed docile in nature. Yet Valentine left with the determination and the power to achieve the goals set before him by Samuel.

October 13, 2022

Lisa was enjoying her time with Nick on his secluded Compound in the rainforests of Pierce County, Washington State.

It was hot but central air inside the Complex and swimming pools topside were a great comfort to possess. Lisa did not approve of the Test Tank and she could not understand why?

Lisa had begun her own Project a week ago and was in the process of bringing back the dead. It was a project dictated by the Pentagon to improve the fighting capabilities of downed soldiers. Not even the draft was enough to make up the difference in the loss of lives. A Bill made it through Congress to lower the age that youth drafted into Service at the ripe age of sixteen years.

Lisa would stop a body's heart and wait ten minutes to revive it. She had developed a serum that worked but was still defective that it lasted for only eight to ten hours at a time.

There was Frank always at her side and Frank was a well built intelligent ex Xeno Game Warrior. It was no wonder that Samuel supported Nick and Lisa because once they could bring people back from the dead then his worse foe would die 'the Christian church.' Frank was always watching her back and Nick's cameras were always watching Frank.

At first, Nick called Lisa's ideas and theories pipe dreams but now he was assisting Lisa with her work. They were eating lunch after first murdering and then injecting three test subjects with BFDS, three (Back from the Dead lot three) two previous attempts had failed this morning and these three subjects given larger doses of the serum. There was a well-staffed and equipped cafeteria in the complex with folding tables and chairs. Both were excited about the progress that they were making and Nick proposed a toast . . . *"To the most wonderful woman in the world"* Nick was a bit tipsy and half-crazy.

Soon they were kissing and then Nick suggested that they go for a swim in one of the pools in the Complex. Lisa Asked *"What about the test subjects and the experiment?"*

"I am sure that they aren't going anywhere honey, I have not been outside for days so why do we not swim in the pools in the Gardens topside?"

In a matter of a few minutes, the two lovers were frolicking in the heated pool within the gardens of the Compound. Laughing joyously the couple played in the pool like children splashing water at each other and then kissing some more. *"This water is perfect,"* said Lisa.

"Nothing is as perfect and pure as you are Lisa" Nick Replied.

Lisa removed her bathing suit and swam over to Nick, *"We must always be together darling."*

Nick began stroking Lisa's face while he stared lovingly into her eyes and said, *"Lisa you are as beautiful as the day that we met."*

Both began laughing as if they were sharing a

private joke.

Nick realized that it was getting late because the quartz garden lights and the pool area lights flashed on.

As the two were getting heavy in their love, Frank interrupted them. *"Please excuse my intrusion sir, but I must report to you that a mob has formed by our main gate and that this County is in a state of anarchy, there is a local militia outside our walls prowling around. I recommend that the two of you go below into the Complex. I will fortify our walls."*

"No need to do that Frank, call me when I get in my Control Room and I will take care of our defenses from there."

Nick caught in a compromising position and another point went against Frank. Frank was the best man that Nick had and now he was suspicious about Frank's true intentions. Nick can convince himself of anything if he needed to. In Nick's mind, Frank had violated him, not once but twice and he did not like the way he gazed at Lisa's naked body.

Lisa and Nick ran into the complex and then into the control room to turn on the poison gas and the jet blowers that keep the gas out of the Compound. Nick answered the phone and told Frank to pull everybody off the gates and walls. Protected by lead and concrete Nick was the bravest man in the world as he opened the valves for the poison gas to pump out of pipes installed into the fortified walls by Nick's Engineers.

All traffic into and out of the Compound halted for a week as the gas dissipated and the dead rotted in the hot sun. Frank organized a cleanup after Nick cleared the area and declared it safe.

Lisa ran to check on her experiment and was alarmed when she saw that the three test subjects were gone. It worried Lisa to the point that she set off the alarm.

Frank found the tree test subjects dead just outside the gate. After an autopsy was completed, Lisa jumped for joy when she learned that they died of toxic gas poisoning. That meant her serum had been successful.

Possibilities of what she had created flashed through her mind, like the rollers on a slot machine in a casino. She knew that it was the breakthrough of all creations and inventions. Lisa decided that Nick had to know right away about her perfected serum. She went to the control room and found Nick keying some commands into his main computer. Lisa waited until Nick finished so instead of interrupting him.

From the time that BFTD3, Lisa had revolutionized medicine. If the Government had not known about her experiments and supported the Project in every way, Lisa would have kept her discovery a secret.

At first, Lisa amazed Nick, and then he smiled and smartly remarked . . . *"Do you want to live forever."*

"I do, I want to live forever and then some." Lisa was charging two-billion dollars for each person that she resurrected. Only the super rich or those with great influence managed to get the serum from Lisa. Security increased at the Lupus Estate and Lisa made the front page Headlines all over the world. It was the last year that Nobel Prizes were to award and Lisa received the last Nobel Prize.

Frank was spending more time around Lisa and it angered Nick. Lisa chose Frank as her personal bodyguard because Frank was good at his work. Nick acted as if he was okay with it but his guts told him that Frank was trying to move in on his wife. This notion festered and grew into grand visions of Frank and Lisa making love. Nick thought that Frank's days were numbered, and Nick was keeping counts of the days. Perhaps Nick was jumping the gun, but then perhaps Nick was right?

Down low in the lowest levels of the Lupus Compound was the walking dead. Patients, whose bodies rejected BFTD3, yet continued living like zombies refusing to die. Nick and Lisa monitored these test subjects and used them in experiments. One of the walking dead was the Secretary of the State William Butler. These dead needed no food and water yet their hearts beat and they breathed air like the living. It was dark and damp on the lower levels with the construction half done.

Creepy, extremely odd were the bugs and the reptiles in the lower levels of the Complex. There was toxic waste leaking from the pipes in unfrequented and dark places on the bottom level of the Complex. Nick collected some roaches that glowed in the dark and some moths that ate human flesh. There were new serums made, more knowledge by studying these mutant insects. Nick collected these insects with the assistance of Frank and a couple other guards loyal to Doctor Nicklaus Keller. Frank felt uneasy as he walked in the lead position deeper into the cutout levels of the Complex.

The mini nuclear reactor powered the Compound and provided for a great bomb shelter. Nick knew that given warning the Lupus Compound could withstand any attack, 'Barring an act of God.' It powered the machines that ran the launchers that Nick had engineered for his doomsday formula. A virus would purge the Earth of all life and give the Earth a chance for a new beginning. If Nick was ever cornered and certain death seemed imminent then Nick would get his final revenge against humanity.

Nick and Lisa never had time to watch television so they never kept up with current affairs. They had no clue about the new war started in China. Russian forces had invaded Mongolia and had used non-conventional weapons on Peking and Taiwan. Chinese Divisions had advanced deep into Russia and a truce was not in the cards. Allied Forces stayed out of the conflict. China over populated with twenty-billion people and was spilling over the borders into barren and wilderness lands that were sparsely populated. Soon they had declared their own State and named a Capital city.

John Chen was the Warlord/General appointed Governor of Mongolia by Chinese Officials. Chen was a power-monger on the edge of his wits. Mass executions were committed with other atrocities added into the chaos. Minister Chen was against the Xeno technologies and the mutants that created from Xeno. China protested and threatened war, but when Russia constructed Xeno Factories near Mongolia war broke out between Russia and China. At this point in the fight, it seemed that China assured victory by the numbers.

One thousand Divisions spearheaded an attack on Moscow. Chinese armies were eight-hundred miles from Moscow and closing. The President of Russia was begging western countries for the neutron bomb to even the odds but the world looked on. Russia had been a thorn in everyone' back and unstable as Russia was, the world did nothing to help Russia defend its cities. China was a growing force that needed to expand and the world knew it. Once that Moscow conquered the question was this . . . *"Would the Chinese armies stop with Russia?"*

December 26, 2022

Postponing the Xeno Games had been because of the Chinese-Russian war and other factors involved in this decision that involved politics. America was in an uproar about this landmark decision and Protesters lined the streets in every major city in America and the U.K. Some people were celebrating Christmas again and they were on the News.

Nick and Lisa knew none of this nor did they care as they carried out their experiments at the now Lupus Compound.

Washington State strictly enforced the Death Penalty and there were always a couple hundred persons on Death Row. Nick had heard of a serial Killer who murdered and raped over fifty women. This man was notorious and known because he once held Public Office. Bernard Rufus Walker scheduled to die in the Gas Chamber next month, was noticed by Nick, and Nick had arrangements worked out with the Governor to get the dead body of this serial killer.

Nick planned to revive Walker and use his drugs to control the executed convict. What better protection against Mia was there than a man seven-foot tall and muscled like a gladiator. Nick planned to use Walker to get rid of Frank. Frank was no slouch and Nick was not a match for Frank. Fran's brother is a senator and his father a Major General. It was going to have to appear as an accident when Frank was done in.

Dr. Keller knew about Mia, Mia was assassinating one Xeno Founder after another and the he and Lisa was on the baboon's list. Mia chased after Samuel for several years but after almost capture in Key West, Fla. decided to give Samuel for others to find him. Mia realized that thousands, perhaps millions of people wanted Samuel dead and that was enough for her. Eventually Mia deemed that an assassin would get Samuel one lonely dark night when he was least expecting it. More likely then not, it will be somebody close to him. Mia had been a threat from the beginning when she was a serial killer in Seattle because of her stealth and extreme abilities. That is why Nick needed Walker, a perfect match for Mia. Dr. Keller was afraid of

Mia.

February 27, 2023

Bernard Rufus Walker was walking his last walk, surround by armed guards and shackled hands to his feet Walker shuffled more then walked toward the double steel doors that opened into the gas chamber. Officers had to use three handcuffs because Walker was as strong as an ox. Walker had snapped six pairs before the Sergeant in charge of the Detail escorting Walker decided to use three hand-cuffs. Walker did not want to go through the door and struggled desperately with the guards. After twenty minutes and with the assistance of a few more guards Walked they pushed Bernard Rufus Walker into the gas chamber and slammed the locked door behind him.

Walker yelled and cursed as he banged his fist against the bulletproof window. In the group of witnesses watching Walker several were afraid that the killer would break through the glass. The guards reassured them that it was not possible. Nobody had gotten the chance to strap walker into the chair and the proper procedures befuddled the Staff. The Gas Chamber became neglected and not ready to carry out this Execution so the Warden phoned the Governor to see what was next on the agenda. Walker's fists were bloody and hatred illuminated his eyes as he tried to escape from a room that had no exit.

Nick and Lisa were watching Walker from behind the glass. They became extremely impressed with his strength, and size. Nick wanted to administer the cyanide and told one of the guards to let the Warden know. When the guard returned he escorted Nick to the Executioners Post above the gas chamber in another room. Nick prepared a special poison that would kill with the first breath.

Once the execution finished and at three minutes after midnight, pronounced dead by the coroner. Attendants wrapped Bernard Rufus Walker in cheesecloth and placed him into a coffin. Lisa had the guards carry the casket to Nick's hovercraft and by the next day Nick, Lisa, and a dead body were safe within the walls of the Lupus Compound.

Outside on the compound grounds water was two-inches deep and rising and heavy raindrops splashed onto the ground. It was barely above freezing and the rain was cold as Frank wondered why he had Guard Patrol Duties. Frank had become Lisa's confidant and shoulder to lean on when she needed encouragement or comfort. Nick was a cold and rigid person who never coddled anyone and used everybody to suit his needs. Certainly, Nick loved Lisa and Lisa loved Nick. Frank was thinking that Nick had become jealous and was in fear for his life because of Nick's vindictive nature. Frank had loyal troops on the compound but they were out of reach and out of his command. Perhaps Frank was right for being wary or perhaps he was only paranoid? Frank longed for a hot meal and a warm bed as his patrol neared the water tower.

"Okay, let's lay him on the bed and hook up some IVs. We need to put life back into this dead man as soon as possible before it is too late to administer the anti toxin." Soon Walker was to revive and Doctor Nicklaus was preparing his mind control drugs to mix in with BFTD3 so that Walker would awaken docile and confused. "You have done it Lisa; you are able to bring back from the dead everyone we need to control the planet. I am proud of you and want you to know that this will make you the most famous woman in history. Lisa injected

her BFTD3 into the clear hose that with a needle was plunged into Walker's aorta. Then Dr. Keller injected his formula. Lisa tightened the hemp straps that were holding Walker confined on the hospital O.R bed for when he awakened.

Nick and Lisa were waiting for Walker to regain consciousness and a couple of hours passed without a heartbeat or brain activity. They were about to go to their bedroom when Walker's eyes opened wide and a smile appeared on his face.

Congratulations Lisa, you have just brought back from the dead the most horrific serial killer in the history of Washington State.

The End of Chapter Five
"<u>Back From the Dead</u>"

Chapter Six
"Altars and Idols"

"Watch Herbert dance and after awhile he will induce you into a trance. One will be reborn in a sense with the help of a scent embedded into the rubber idol doll. Many more toys promoted for children resembled the new idols of the times. These Xeno Idols copied from the Idols lining the windows of nearly every house.

Since Nick and Lisa had proven that people can live forever. If injected with BFTD3 within 48 hours of dying, then they stopped having faith and began to worship idols and Lisa as a Goddess, *"the bringer of life."* This fact meant that most religions had no basis for their faith and were in turmoil. From the first moment that Nick and Lisa met history began changing and now the world was in total chaos.

Globally the world was in a bad crisis with the changing coastlines and massive acts of god. Our world was crumbling beneath our feet. With nothing that we could do about it, yet people were acting as if nothing was wrong. It is going to take God to rescue Earth but barely anybody believed in god since BFTD3 was mass-produced.

There was much ado about the Chicago Altar was constructed from concrete and towered to stories high. It was in the center of the city and forty blocks had to evacuate because of an additional park with a pond. The idol was in dedication to the god Samuel.

In the last year, Samuel had become an icon and declared a god by his followers. Massive typhoons pushed back with Samuel's telekinetic powers. Samuel accomplished many miracles and scientists were baffled by them.

Genetic Engineering had cured all sicknesses and Lisa found a cure for death. It seemed that the good things outnumbered the bad but there were some things beyond the reach of man and Samuel.

Jessica was surprised that BFTD3 had been developed and vowed that God would punish the people responsible for it. Everywhere she went she saw Xeno Religion posters and preachers declaring that Samuel was God. She was glad to back home within the confines of her Compound and with her friends again.

Jessica heard about BFTD3 and knew that it was the son of the devil that instigated the breakthrough and success of the drug. It was not her place to change freewill so Jessica asked everybody in the Jessica Compound what the people wanted. *"You can leave and enter the worldly everlasting life or wait for the second coming of Christ?"*

Jessica was surprised that everybody decided to stay, but during the night, a couple of dozen people left the Jessica compound in the darkness. Jessica heard the news in the morning Jessica wept and prayed for their souls.

Next three months

Festivals and parades celebrated the Xeno Age. February 1, changed to Xeno day and the entire world celebrated the new Holiday. Anti Xeno Forces stayed strong and grew with the congregations of many religions increasing their numbers and bringing up morale among the armies fighting this war against the Xeno species. A war they were losing. No matter how you saw it, Samuel was behind all evil on Earth and the master of the Xeno World. Parties big and small block parties, and parades replaced Christmas and Easter.

In a family home in Harvard, Ill. a family gathering was getting out of hand as mysterious events occurred with the idols decorating the household.

Grandpa Stew was at the door with his son and daughter in-law and little Billy unlocked the door and let them into the house. Grandpa Stew died yesterday and today he was alive with his health returning and told by his doctors that unless he died an unnatural death then grandpa would live forever.

Grandma was crying as she entered the living room where everybody was watching television staring at Grandpa. *"What is wrong honey?"* said grandpa.

"I will tell you want is wrong, you died last night and here you are! You will bring the wrath of God down upon us and have you forgotten that you are a Pentecostal Pastor in the Church of Righteousness, you were called home by God and you went against his will, now you are damned to go straight to hell." Grandma was eying over her late: now come back from the dead husband.

"Come on now honey-pie, I am the same old husband that you had before and now I am convinced that I was worshipping a God that never existed." Grandpa had a twinkle in his eyes as he tried to comfort his wife as he moved toward her.

"Get away from me!" Grandma ran out of the living room and back to her bedroom weeping. Grandma was strong in her faith in God, wished, and prayed for God to rescue her from witnessing anymore of the Xeno Age. No rescue was forthcoming for Grandma and Grandpa was as normal as ever except with a renewed immune system and the organs of a young man.

"Grandma will get over it," said Michael Dexter.

Mike was Grandpa Stew's first-born son. Mike was the
Mayor of Harvard, Ill. He paid for the serum that saved his
fathers life.

Grandpa stayed up watching the Ion Telescreen, a
kind of television that revolutionized entertainment. The
television was virtual reality that brought into your house
realistic movies and whatever else that a person would
want to interact in.

Jack Dexter was in Grandpa's bedroom watching
his grandfather doing tricks with some idols. One of the
idols was that of Master Rex, Master Rex was the new god
of death. It resembled pictures of the Reaper and held a
sickle in his hands. Jack was afraid at first as he observed
the idol dancing and swinging the sickle as it danced a
dance of death. Grandpa was laughing hysterically and
clapping his hands in rhythm with the idol.

Idols that came alive at midnight were
commonplace and with the masses believing them to be
Gods. Several Idols that danced, and some that did a bit
more than dance. Midnight belonged to the idols and the
dead.

Churches and Temples everyday demolished and
replaced with outdoor Altars and Xeno Priests. All set in
black rose gardens with fountains and a grassy knoll where
the congregation stood during a Xeno Service. Christians
and Jews joined forces and went about torching altars and
that prompted the Priests to place a Section of troops on
guard duty 24-7.

Dul De Taunt was the President of the Xeno
Reform Religion and had a following of two-billion and a
couple of Army Divisions to defend his religious
Compound. Samuel visited the Religious Compound once a
year to reform the religion. Dul De Taunt feared Samuel
and had to take a lot of bullying from Samuel and threats

each time that Samuel visited the Religious Compound. Samuel was always on the move or on the run, he had more friends then enemies but his foes were determined to assassinate him one way or another and sooner or later they figured that their assassins would score a hit.

Samuel had deemed any religion other then the Xeno religion outlawed and Samuel set a ten-year prison sentence for those who assembled in the name of God.

Chicago had built a statue, twenty stories high in the likeness of Samuel. What made it special was that it was solid Gold. Judeo-Christianity never before in it's history of has there been total annihilation of their organizations until now. Every outlawed church built cells where they communicated and worshipped their faiths and they were growing, as anarchy seemed to rule the streets.

It was the law that every American had to own two firearms in every home, and registering firearms was outdated. Police Forces disbanded and prisons shut down. If somebody had broken the law and it was a felony then there was only one Sentence, Death.

Towering Statues and dancing idols were the trend of the day and Samuel intended to breathe fire into the statues and bring them to life. Samuel had his way on the Earth and it seemed as if God had abandoned his creations to the devil.

Jessica called a private meeting of her Commanders in her underground gardens to see if there were any traitors among them. Times were difficult and the mood was changing among the people on Jessica's Foundation Compound.

At the Meeting was Mia hidden behind a two-way mirror. Mia had only two hours past assassinated a whole Tribe of Xenopeople. Mia is a part of destiny and beyond reproach. She did as she was predestined to do and naught could stop her. These particular Xenopeople were planning to assassinate Jessica. What made these people different were their abilities to trick and fool, magic beyond reality. If Mia never had massacred this tribe then surely they would have succeeded in their dastardly plot. Mia stayed hidden in fear that a person at the meeting was indeed an assassin.

At high noon, Jessica entered the room and then stood behind the podium. In the crowd unnoticed by the people sitting around him a Commander was reaching for his hollowed out bible inside of his suit vest.

This man was sitting in the last seat in the first row front center. Mia knew it was the assassin the first moment that her eyes noticed the movement. Mia sniffed the air and the Xeno scent burned her sinuses. There was an imposter among the ranks of Jessica's Commanders and he was a good fifty feet from Mia so Mia had to decide whether to expose herself or not. The man laid the Bible on his lap and folded his hands over it.

Jessica picked up a glass of water took a sip and cleared her throat. "I want to praise those of you who belong here for your hard work and dedication to Jesus."

'Jessica stopped for a moment and stared at the imposter.' ***"If this man comes forward and asks for salvation God will forgive him of his sins."*** At that moment, the man stood with his bible in his hands and made a step toward Jessica.

With a decision made at a split second Mia darted faster then any animal can in the world right at the man holding the bible standing before the podium. As she passed the assassin, Mia snatched the bible from his hands and then with her free hand Mia clawed a deep gash across the imposter's stomach. Quicker then the eyes could see Mia leaped through the window and less then a minute later everybody was startled by a loud explosion. Mia disappeared into the dense forest on the Compound and disappeared again for months.

"We must brace ourselves for the evil one because he is near. Now that Dr. Keller can bring people back from the dead, it will be only a matter of time before Lucifer will trick Lisa into resurrecting his evil carcass back among us. During these years, we will have to have more faith and diligence in our effort to rid the world of evil."

‘ As she paused for a few minutes, a squad of LOD rolled in a wheelchair a man chained and gagged. ’ A blood red handkerchief around his head that covered his eyes prevented the man to see where he was. Jessica began speaking as her audience gasped at the sight of this stranger.

"This is not a man my fellow Christians but a monster. His name is Magod and he is the demon who controls the spirits of sinners. He has other people murder for him and he does hideous acts in his name. I want you to listen to this creature of hell to help you prepare for the others that will replace this demon."

It had taken three buffed men to remove the gag as the creature struggled, finally he calmed down and begun speaking in an unearthly tone.

"You think that I like to kill, well you are right, my children. Soon I will be with my master and he shall breathe life into me once more. Then I shall return vigorously and eat your hearts out of your chests. I will at first dissect you and then eat your hearts."

" I will return to watch insects crawl into your bodies and eat you alive! You think that you can beat Lucifer when your whole world is sin, Bullshit! I will race to skin you alive, gnaw on your bones, as you are helpless, and watch me feast. Beware of the evil eye, each

of you possess one and each of have murdered in the name of your god, what do you think that you are anyways . . .a fricking army of angels, you are nothing, nobody cares about you! "

Jessica smiled peacefully at him and not moved by the raving maniac. The audience absorbed by what the man claiming to be a demon was saying.

"You are as the animals that you created, just animals. Have you seen the Xenopeople, they are going to exterminate your species and worship Lucifer. They sport horns that will skewer you and tails as my master has. You are doomed, I am waiting for you in hell to torment you, and torture you. Each one of you is damned so why fight a war that you will never win, because you are fools, and losers!"

One of the Commanders stood and asked . . .*"How much longer must we listen to this garbage?"*

With that, said five men remove the demon from the stage and wheeled him to a hole dug the night before. The hole filled with lethal acid as the men wheeled the so-called monster to the edge before turning the chair upwards and dumping him into the hole. It sizzled and bubbled as it consumed Magod yet they could hear his screams for five minutes.

This was the first time that Jessica displayed a side of her that never seen before.

"It is now that we must prepare for the war. Battles will not be fought endlessly to no end, only one battle that will end in victory for them or us and this is one example of what you are up against."

Nobody expected or was ready for this event to conspire. Only a few chosen knew about Magod and they were all bodyguards to Jessica and Penny.

Penny Wilson had moved in with Jessica but was not present for this demonstration. Penny was swimming in

75

an indoors swimming pool while Jessica continued with her Address to Commanders.

"All of you are angels; your faith makes you strong. Be aware of the false gods that seem to be alive, these idols speak and dance; they are all abnormalities of demons which roam the streets at midnight. Altars are everywhere with the masses worshipping the evil one and time is running out for salvation."

" God's wrath will turn these idols into pillars of salt. Altars will tumble as the Earth shakes and we will be safe here, in our sanctuary. "

"We are the fortunate few that will ascend to be with our Lord, God. And the children of Israeli did evil in the sight of the Lord and served Ba'-a-lim;" Jessica hesitated and continued with . . . *"See the world as it is and do not fool yourselves because the end is near."*

"Idols made from stone, silver, gold, and sin will be crushed by God and sent into the abyss. Our traitorous enemies will boil as we lay in the sun and the altars will come crashing down. We shall be safe from this devastation and death as it happens around us. Some of you shall fall into temptation before the final days, I cannot help you when you have crossed the line and entered into a contract with the devil. Please remember that I am here for you now but one day I will fade away to the Lord as his light covers us and we ascend to be at his side."

With her eyes, roaming the congregation Jessica finished her Address. *"The relatives not with you and that are engaged in sin will wear the mark of the devil on their bodies until it reaches their souls. I am telling you now that soon the sun will torch the idols and leave the sinners to watch. Once this event has occurred then when it ends, our God in heaven will cover us with our treasures waiting for us as we ascend to heaven."*

A specialized Staff that used voodoo in their daily work routines operated Xeno Plastics Corporation. Nick owned the plant and they produced 2000 idols a day.

Penalties in the plant were severe if the rules were broken. Daily floggings were commonplace, frequent, but secret sacrifice rituals bejeweled the basement with golden idols, and voodoo magic.

The End of Chapter Six
"**Altars and Idols**"

Chapter Seven
<u>"The Wicked House on the Hill.</u>"

Lightning shot from a huge thunderhead over the Lupus Estate and struck a tall cedar tree. In that instant the tree split into two and one fell this way and the other fell onto the Lupus Estate walls, the wall cracked and a guard was struck dead.

Six months ago, some people had bought some property next to the Lupus Compound and built a large house atop the hill only one-hundred meters from the Compound.

All kinds of people, Xeno and human were wandering into the house as others were leaving. There was a long stairway constructed with flat granite embed into the hill led you fifty meters to the doors of this great stone mansion.

Peter was leading a patrol crossing over to observe the house on the hill. Amazed at the constant traffic and the clamor coming from the house Peter sneaked closer for a better look. Once he and his men were well-hidden and only fifty feet from the steps, he felt eerie about being there. Peter stayed observing the house and it's guests until dawn.

People who went to the house gave off a feeling of the dead in a way one might feel at a wake. It was a feeling that was hard to explain that made his skin crawl. These people had eyes that glowed and were joyously laughing as if they had not a care in the world; some were dancing as they climbed the steps to the house.

Peter had to see what was going on in the house and

so he sent Rod Gambler to check it out and snap some photographs. Rod refused because of a gut feeling he had that he would not return from this recon but Peter forced him to go to the house and peek inside a window.

Rod slowly low crawled to the back of the house and to the nearest window. Then he looked inside and saw hell. People were whispering to each other and drinking glasses filled with blood red wine or blood. Goose bumps raised the hairs on his body as he fell into a trance and could not move. Rod believed that he was spellbound and knew that this was his last day among the living. Before he finished his last thought, a giant of a man snatched Rod away and Rod could not even utter a scream as the big brute carried Rod to the back door. Once inside the big house Rod saw what they were drinking and it was blood.

Inside the house, three men carried Rod to an altar with a overhead beam that had a rope dangling off it. Two women tied his ankles together and the men hoisted Rod into the air where he hung face down. Another man walked out of a room in the house and approached Rod who hung off the beam speechless and helpless.

Chelum was a tall lanky man with a cold demeanor about him. He was wearing a trench coat and a white ruffled shirt with a drop of blood staining his sleeve. Chelum had green teeth from bad dental care and longer fingers than one might ever see on a man. This ugly but elegant man walked over to Rod and smiled. Then the room grew more quiet than it was earlier before Rod was caught snooping around. The room became chilled and Rod tried to scream again but nothing came out of his throat.

An essence consumed the house with an aroma that smelled like death. Everybody in the house seemed to be in a trance or drugged as the lights dimmed and the guests of the house gathered to form a line before the altar.

———————————

Peter was nervous and anxious because Rod had been gone for over an hour and everything became as quiet as a graveyard. Peter asked a couple men in his patrol to check it out and find Rod but they vehemently refused and told Peter to go look for himself. Peter felt it too, the feeling of wickedness and death with the unsettling feel of the wind convinced Peter that it was wise to leave the grounds of this wicked house on the hill.

(Rod thought that at any moment the patrol would storm the house and rescue him but he was wrong because no rescue was forthcoming. Peter and the other men and women in the patrol were long gone as the silence around Rod reeked of death.)

Ken Corbit was stunned at what was occurring with Peter leaving a member of the patrol behind and voiced his opinion to the others. *"Peter is a coward and I am going to tell Jessica about what just happened."*

Sarcastically and with malice, Peter barked an order at Ken . . . *"I heard that Corbit, now you have just volunteered to go and find Rod. We will wait for you on the other side of the property border near the sandy pond."*

Ken glanced up at Peter and scowled, *"Yes Boss I am not afraid to check on a brother, somebody has to do it."*

"What are you waiting for then, get going and do not return to the Compound until you know what has happened to Rod."

Ken ran through the dense rainforest and ran into some rose bushes that cut him up. Ken said one word; *"Damn"* and that one word gave him away to the sentries on the prowl searching for outsiders.

Peter and his group waited for about two hours and

then returned to the Jessica Compound.

Chelum injected Rod with Darvocet, (a powerful painkiller) and then reached into a drawer of the altar and removed a hose with a metal sharp hollow point. Then he inserted the point pushing it into the aorta. Immediately the transparent hose turned red with blood emptying into a large golden punch bowl. Rod screamed in horror and terror as he watched the blood drain from his body and the Rod Gambler died.

May 2, 2023

Rod Gambler and Ken Corbit were never seen again anywhere. Peter wrote them off as Deserters and lied to Jessica about it.

Life was bustling at the Jessica Compound as many left but more entered. There was a population of 700,000 thousand people. The World Trade Towers was still on the minds of many people because that war propelled the Government to exploit Xeno technology. Jessica had two towers built higher then the Trade towers in New York and protected it with a shield of God. Led by Tammy and Leven formed three fighting Brigades stationed to guard the Jessica Compound.

Rene organized a Jessica Cross similar to the Red Cross of modern day. One warm sunny day Rene was strolling through the gardens on her way to meet with

Penny and convince her to join the Jessica Cross.

Penny was sitting on a boulder overlooking a creek that ran through the Compound and singing. Rene approached her and sat beside Penny on the boulder. *"Hi Penny, I can see why you love this spot so much. Have you heard about Jessica Cross?"* Rene waited at least a minute before Penny answered her.

"No, who is she?"

"It is not a she Penny it is an Organization that I started, Jessica declared that the biggest war in time is near." Rene noticed that Penny was not herself, something was bothering her of that Rene was certain.

Raven was hiding in the woods and watching Rene and Penny. She had plans of her own that included and was not limited to murdering the women sitting on the rocks. Planning to jump the women once, they were walking back on the trail through the forest Raven waited. Raven stayed silent as the dead in a hundred year old grave.

"Penny is something wrong?"

Penny glanced at Rene and replied, *"Somebody has been watching me all morning from the forest behind us, I can feel it there. I am afraid to leave but now you are here so I hope you brought a pistol with you?"*

" No, I have not a gun but we should get out of here now before it gets too late in the day. Perhaps somebody will come and help us?"

Raven could barely wait to tear out their hearts and place them in her sack with the others. It had been a long night of killing and hiding bodies. Now it was time to collect the big money when her marks decided to leave and go home.

"Perhaps if we split up and ran to opposite trails then one of us might get through to find help?" 'Rene. Suggested that it was the best chance they had for escape.'

Penny was not so sure that escape was possible; she

thought that certainly it was bad luck and perhaps preordained that they were to die on this day.

"Do not talk crazy to me Penny because we are in all probability we are only paranoid. If some one were hiding there then they would have made their move by now."

Tammy was leading a patrol on the grounds of the Compound and everything was going well until her point man found a cache of bodies buried under gravel in the Compound gravel pit. Tammy sniffed the air, declared that Raven was on the Compound. Her conclusion was that Raven had committed the murders. Tammy knew Raven from the games, and never forgotten her scent.

Tammy moved quickly to resolve this situation. *"All of you follow me but stay fifty meters behind me, count to twenty and then follow my trail, Bruce, you take command."*

Moving swiftly and as craftily as a cougar, Tammy followed a scent well known to her from the Xeno Games. She recognized Raven anywhere and knew exactly where to find Raven.

With her patrol behind Tammy, she crawled to the spot near Raven. Then Tammy stood and confronted Raven. *"I can smell a bitch from a mile away."*

"Where the hell did you come from Tammy, I heard that you have become soft and weak. Are you ready to rumble?"

Tammy began to circle Raven carefully watching Raven like a cat. Raven moved at Tammy, feint her step as to deliver a fatal blow with her fighting axe. Raven swung her axe upward and under Tammy nearly as fast as a bullet. Tammy jumped sideways and came down on Raven with an elbow smash on Raven's back. Raven landed flat on her face and jumped to her feet axe firmly held in a striking position. Tammy sung her axe again this time faking a feint and nearly hit Tammy as Tammy skipped backwards to avoid contact. In the next instant, Tammy kicked Raven in her chest and sent her flying into the air landing on her back. Raven sat up and screamed in rage.

"You slut, I'm going to gouge out your eyes and where them around my neck on a gold chain. Do not think that you will beat me this time! Where is your precious Leven now?"

"I do not need Leven to kick your ass, Raven give it up. My patrol is behind me."

Before Tammy finished her sentence, she flipped head over heels and clenched Raven with her thighs as she sat on her shoulder and squeezed until Raven was choking. Raven swung her axe overhead and Tammy grasped it by the steel handle and flipped it from Raven's hands. Then Raven squeezed harder as Raven's face turned red. Clawing her nails deeply into Tammy's thighs blood ran thick and dripped of Ravens face.

Tammy became enraged and twisted her hips thus breaking Ravens neck. It sounded as if she had broken a branch as they both collapsed onto into the gravel and dirt below them. Tammy sighed in relief and saw Penny and Rene walking to help her get up. Tammy had bruised her hip in the fall.

"Are you alright, did she cut you?" Rene asked.

"I think that my hip gotten broken in the fall to the ground." Tammy Replied.

Rene knew that Raven was dead because she heard Raven's neck break in the fall. Raven examined Tammy, *"Here, roll on your back and see how far you can sit up."*

Tammy sat but could not move and when she saw her patrol arrive, Tammy smiled.

"My God, are you okay," Bruce asked with a

worried look on his face. Is there anything that I can do to help?" *"I am fine, just removing this creature from my sight and be sure that you bury her outside the Compound."*

Bruce led his patrol with Raven in tow toward the east border on the compound. The wicked house on the hill was one-hundred meters off the border due east of where Bruce was beginning to move in that same direction.

Disappointed and angry with Peter for abandoning his friends at the wicked house on the hill angered Bruce, to the point of revenge, Bruce tried to block out the urge to go to the house on the hill but failed in his efforts to do so.

They moved at a steady pace, but alert status due east right to the wicked house on the hill. The body would have hidden secretly on Government forestland. If only Peter had gone west, everything that was about to happen would have never been.

"Joe, you and Billy carry Raven over to that wood line and dump her fifty feet in. Then I want you to go around the house to the blind side where they cannot see you from their windows." Bruce hell bent on raiding the house. He knew that they were carrying outdated weapons as M-60, M-203's, and two Hand held laser launchers, which, was the best they had. Along with this firepower, each carried with them Assault weapons. *"When you arrive within range of the house then hide. If we need cover fire be sure to aim carefully so as not to injure one of us."*

"Yes sir, we will do exactly as you ordered and you can count on us." Billy was a sniper and Joe qualified as Expert Marksmen in the compound training barracks firing range. They were good choices and lucky to get easy duty.

Moving slowly through the forest Bruce had his people twenty meters from the long staircase that led to the door of the wicked house on the hill. Bruce was extremely alert and quick. A handsome man and fit as a Marine Bruce had the cunning and the wisdom of a Delta scout.

Within the dense forest the men we fortunate not to be seen by the house sentries as the patrolled the stairs. Thick fog and moisture in the air kept the patrol out of sight and the sounds they made muted.

Suddenly a strong feeling of doom hit the patrol and sweat soaked their shirts as they felt like they were walking into hell.

Bruce neared to fifty meters of the house and, halted the patrol for a couple of minutes. He began giving out orders. *"You, you, and you go to the west window and storm in firing your weapons at anything the moves when I give the signal."*

Jack Davis asked Bruce, *"What if those two lost men are in the house Bruce? Do you think we might be rushing this?"*

"I seriously doubt it . . . I can feel that they have been dead for a while. Now get going."

"The rest of you follow me and cover each other by walking a staggered formation. Now let's get going."

Once they were the nearest possible to the house Bruce instructed them to lock and load. "Leach, launch grenades into the steel door of the house and do not miss. The rest of us will storm the house and kill everything we see." Bruce on his own, this raid of the wicked house on the hill. Tammy was going to be displeased but in his mind, he was doing as ordered. *"Buck, you and Henry are the flankers so to cover us from the sides, we rush the house."*

Leach launched two grenades from his M203 automatic grenade launched and two loud explosions deafened their ears as the front of the house blew open and the shrapnel killed five guards at the doors. The patrol rushed in and opened fire blindly shooting into the smoke and spreading their range of fire. Chuck Bloome felt a dagger ease into his liver and the last thing he saw before he died was a smiling pale face of a beautiful woman. Leach shot her in the head with his M-203 and it splattered onto his dead friend lying on the kitchen floor.

After ten minutes of roaming the house spreading constant fire, bodies lay about in awkward positions as the dead, or dying. Bruce retreated with his men onto the landing on the staircase that led to the house.

Soon men jumped out of a trap door armed and ready to continue the fight so Bruce gave the signal and bullets sped through the west window searching for targets. These men died with their boots on as fire from two sides cut them down. Everybody inside the house was dead or dying and Bruce gave the command, *"Henry, go in the house and shoot the remaining among them in their head. Henry, go follow Henry and cover him. Then let us move out, 'Henry, give the signal" when the house has been cleared"*

A few shots were fired and then Henry gave the signal. They moved out into the forest moving due west.

Inside of the house, dead carcasses hung from the ceilings half eaten. 'Rod Gambler,' was cut down and bagged. Then the squad departed. There was no trace of the missing Ken Corbit and the sentries hiding in the bush were gone.   .

The End of Chapter Seven
"The Wicked House on the Hill"

Chapter Eight
"Xeno Voodoo"

August 13, 2023

Five miles down the road from Becky lived a Cult.
Becky had to move because the ocean swallowed her
property. She settled in Port Orchard, Washington State.
Property was cheap because of the eroding shorelines and
Port Orchard was growing land mass. Parts of Washington
were sinking into the ocean while the Earth appeared in
others. Port orchard was growing in population and Becky
hired engineers to reconstruct her laboratories. Along with
the reconstruction of the labs, she had them construct a
bunker complex that would float if submerged in water.
Nuclear reactors were cheap for the super wealthy. New
technology enabled reactors to be the size of a carpenter's
toolbox. For three million dollars, anybody could buy it on
E-bay.

A Xeno Cult led by a descendant of Kura was
collecting waste products that Becky dumped in barrels
into the Puget Sound. Kura was the first fetus grown in an
anti-rejection Xeno hybrid dissected, fluid incubation tank.
The baby was born with a perfect immune system and the
mind of Einstein. With tele-powers and the ability to know
who was going to die next within the realm of her cult.
Kura Anne had one giant flaw, she was utterly mad.

Dead chickens and chickens that were alive hung
from, the eaves of this two-story house in the woods. Some
had wilted to bones and askew as the winds blew them
back and forth. There also was a graveyard the size of a
football field next to the house. Stories passed around that
these people could read minds and will a person to death.

Special and beautiful the cult members created a
slave race of humans with two heads. These creatures were

known to communicate with the dead. There were rituals but this cult did not worship the devil. These cultists worshipped Kura. Kura drowned in the sea during the last flood. Now it was Kura Anne running the cult. Queen Anne is what her followers called her because Kura wore long elegant gowns from the fashions of the 1880's. Ruby red lipstick and gothic eyes made Kura Anne and her nymphomaniacal lifestyle obscene but attractive to demented people.

Queen Anne named a God by the people known to the world as the mutated Pagans. They received their names because their babies sometimes were born with multiple limbs or two heads. Giving birth was excruciating but sex and reproduction was encouraged by Queen Anne along with multiple sex partners. Before long idols built in her honor while her popularity spread to the masses another new, religion was born from a cult. Kura was a master with her trickery and magic. Her gifts made Kura special, but not a god.

Other freaks of science were joining the cause and creating cults paying Kura to declare a Leader God. More idols manufactured and Gods were going on tour performing miracles.

———————————

China was beating the pants off Russia and Russia's allies abandoned them because of their arrogance and spite for foreigners. Russia retaliated with another nuclear strike but there were too many Chinese armies in Russia and victory was nearby.

With all the wars throughout this Century, women outnumbered the men 20 to one. Women sold in the slave trade that had become legal in half the world, was an effort to repopulate the human race. Russia was the leader of the Syndicate that controlled these operations. China,

Philippines, Nepal, Burma, India, had protested against Russia yet the Russians continued in the slave and drug trades. They were regrouping their and rebuilding their nation with these ill begotten goods. 'War was on the horizon a decade ago.'

The slave trade was one issue the war was about as were the thousands of assassins that were murdering political leaders on a global scale. These nations formed a PACT and the new treaty made them the world power during this war. Russia's reunion happened too late as the Chinese armies rampaged through Russia. Pillaging and murdering every Russian that was not dead. This war had cost the CPNBI Allies one-billion dead and counting. Russia was the first Nation in the world to employ weapons of mass destruction and they still lost the war. With the slave trade abolished, the world was a better place to live.

———————

Becky had a loft constructed with a protective shield and a telescope so that she could watch the stars on her free time and relax. Tonight the horizon was orange. Her shield on the Observatory protected Becky from the fall-out of the Russian-Chinese war.

It was a good day for Becky; she had created something special that would assure her survival once the planet was uninhabitable by our species. Becky was going to live forever because of her formulas, and intended to do just that, live-forever.

Becky had heard that her tight Security been infiltrated several times by the Xeno Voodoo cult and was planning to take action to prevent it from happing again. Melon Falk was supervising security for Becky.

Becky seemed have her Security Chiefs murdered of the past. Melon was six foot nine and built like an ox. Solid muscled and blacker then coal, he was born in South Africa and studied at Oxford. Melon worked for Scotland Yard before joining Becky. Becky was fond of the man and he followed her directives to the letter.

Kura was seeing and hearing everything in her visions of Becky. With her congregation of misfits, praying to Kura and praising her name, Kura gave a sermon to her newfound children of evil.

"We need to poison the minds of our enemies and blind their eyes so that they cannot see. I ask of you to bring up the two-headed children of Kura and have them meditate for this coming fight. Charm them so that we can talk to the dead. We need to find a way into the mobile complex. This place can be our homes if we fight for it. We need to find a way to blast into the shell. You must find a way."

Anarchy had become the norm in America with the devastating climate, revolutions and the wars. It was elementary. Any Civil obedience that was enforced cost the Government Billions of dollars. It was survival of the fittest, an organized sort of anarchy.

Kura told her congregation the *"first thing that they had to do was buy all the property between Becky and ourselves. You must give until it hurts and if property owners get in the way. Then force them out!"*

Kura caught her breath and continued . . . *"I am the goddess of Evil and I demand that a concrete tower be constructed near the Walls of Becky in my honor. This tribute must be eight stories tall and five-hundred-feet in diameter. Hollow tunnels must worm to the top where I shall dwell in a protective shell."*

Money was never a problem; the price was tall to have the protection of Kura.

Kura turned her hourglass upside down and said . . . *"You have one hour to cook a feast fit for a god, I am your god and my wrath is a long and dragged out hell, take heed, in one hour I want the property cleared so that our Attorney's can buy it."* On this night, a sickness killed the residents that occupied the land leading to the Becky Bubble.

August 12, 2024

Becky watched as the cult built their tower only one-meters from her bubble. She was infuriated about this endeavor and could not stop them legally. Sitting in her dwelling Becky watched Kura as Kura stared back at her.

Melon tried sending spies into the cult but they never returned and presumed to be dead. Melon knew all to well that voodoo was dangerous and real. It was something that no strength and bullets could penetrate. He watched the two-headed people line up in rows bowed toward the bubble performing rituals and hexes on the bubble and those that inhabited the bubble. It gave Melon the creeps.

The Bubble was huge and grew its own crops in sealed greenrooms and growing lights. There also was a heard of cows and a flock of sheep inside with huge aquariums filled with edible fish. Globally the wealthy were building bubbles and buying the technology from Becky's companies.

Livestock were dying for no apparent reason. Becky had replaced her livestock three times in the past year. The voodoo cult behind all this misfortune, behind the virus that was infecting Beck's cows was waiting for a reaction from Becky. Inside of this huge shield bubble, was a

controlled environment so the deaths were a mystery?
Becky knew in her gut that it was Kura behind the virus.

August 30, 2024

Kura was in her spa with three handsome men.
These men were gently washing and rinsing Kura
amorously. She was near the completion of constructing the
right explosive to puncture Becky's bubble. Kura was
celebrating.

The servants of the bath were serving peyote, and
mushroom iced teas. Hallucinations and colors surrounded
Kura as the message made her euphorically motivated.
Kura pleased her men and needed more, before long a large
orgy ensued into the night. Flashing colors and concert
music filled the air elegantly as Kura finished her spa
session.

Nude Dancers performed magnificently as Kura lay
back on her lunch grass near the spa. Tonight was going to
important for the cult that grew to almost one million
servants. All were mesmerized and spellbound by Kura as
she murdered her boyfriends horrifically with the maidens
dancing around her. Saving their blood and genitals Kura
would use the genitals to make potions and cast spells in
the name of evil. These men gladly died for their god.

This bomb was more then a bomb, it was laser
powered, and would accelerate radiation particle beams
into the shield and in time sear through the shell. A bomb
bought for five hundred million dollars and some change.

Kura planned on a war that she was sure to win but
Becky saw it in a different light. Once the instillation of
this launcher completed in the tower, a port would,

open and burn a hole through the bubble shield. This war was ready to break out any day, Becky was not a fool, and she was prepared well enough to satisfy her security.

———————

Becky was watching the cultists carefully and intensely. She knew what was going on and the first spy was successful in sending a message before she they murdered her. Kura came from nowhere and grew like a mushroom in a thorn in the side. Becky hated the woman who she has never spoken with and wanted her dead.

Within her laboratory, Becky was designing an anti-Xeno drug specifically aimed, at killing a DNA strain similar to Kura and her new revolutionary breed. Becky was almost ranting and raving as she worked.

"This will show them and especially Kura that they messed with the wrong woman. I will exterminate them and their god, what comes around goes around, the way that I see it science always beats magic!"

Becky completed her work and went to her dwelling to shower. She knew that it was going to create a biological virus that could mutate to the other species. At this point Becky was a bitter woman and did not care. She missed Nick and if she could find a way. Becky would see Lisa dead. Now that Becky knew that she had the upper hand, Becky smiled warmly at the idea.

———————

Kura was preparing to give the signal to fire the laser and get into the bubble when the vision appeared in her mind of Becky in the shower and the thoughts in her mind. Kura shuddered, and then she gave the signal.

Melon was watching and monitoring the tower carefully and knew that they were planning something but did not know what. Melon had set up two batteries aimed at the tower incase they had to shoot down a missile. Somehow, Melon knew that it would not be enough.

Activity on the cult compound was heavy today; Melon was looking down into the compound from the bubble. With his vision goggles, Melon could see through the stained glass into the compartment that Kura occupied most of the time. Melon decided that it was time to make a move. Perhaps, shaking the hornet's nest that he saw before him was the thing to do. Melon was going to learn one-way or other secrets they were going to attack the bubble. Melon knew, he could feel a fight coming. Two-headed militia lined the borders of the bubble for the first time. There before Melon were sure signs of an immanent attack on the Becky Bubble.

Mellon radioed Becky and informed her of his conclusions and that he believed the cult possessed laser cannons. The phone rang and Becky had just showered, she was getting dressed as Melon explained the situation. Becky instructed Melon to report to the heliport.

Inside the heliport, Becky was waiting with her spray applicator and the virus based formula. Melon asked if humans were in danger by this application of the deadly virus and Becky assured him they it would not kill humans.

Now, it was a matter of who struck the first blow, which determined the outcome of this battle. Once the chopper was in the air, it was over for the cult. This helicopter was the new Apache jet flyer. It was impossible to shoot down and had an armament that could flatten five-hundred square meters, now it was capable of spraying biological weapons at Kura. Becky told Melon to move quickly on this assault because she had a bad feeling about it. Something that she could not shake, a sensation of fear touched her bones as she thought about the opportunities that she let slide by. Becky could have taken care of this cult before they became strong; her gut feeling told her that in some way, Samuel was involved and behind the scheme of things.

Kura watched the laser find its mark and her missiles launched aimed at the core of the Becky Bubble. Kura was dancing with her disciples and they were jumping for joy as the laser began boring into the bubble shell for the missiles to find their targets.

Mellon was airborne and releasing the bio-agent onto the cultist and their buildings. Kura watched from her tower as her people fell dead where they stood. She screamed in rage protected from the poison inside her nuclear, bio, Chemical shelter. Melon grinned as he watched death take hold on the Cult Compound. He felt safe in the chopper.

Kura was casting spells and drawing on Samuel for her strength to win this battle against good.

Becky did wicked things in her life but she was good in the way any great scientist is . . . with there discoveries and inventions that are constantly making it better. Becky did not deserve what she had, and deserved what she was getting. Mutual destruction was imminent; it was the first in the history of the world. The explosion rocked St Helens and the Sound was gone forever. Several counties acknowledged wastelands.

Fortunately, for Nick, he was out of range and safely conducting his experiments. It was the worst disaster that America had ever known, invasion of privacy and new laws, strict enforcement of curfews deemed necessary were inflating Police ranks and getting Law Enforcement better armor. Nick hired a Company of two-hundred men that were professional killers to join his ranks. Dr. Keller had a huge ship he converted for his needs offshore. This ship was manned by cutthroats and murders bought from greedy prison wardens. Nick had all of them injected with his phylogenic mend control serum. These men were loyal to the death. Nick was a lucky man with the world in the palm of his hands. There was only one problem . . . Samuel and his army of demons.

Voodoo cults merged into a legend filled with evil bad omens and darkness. A new leader had emerged that, could levitate and flash fire from his eyes. 'Tura, the brother of Kura created by Kura the goddess.'

Becky was the first to die of the terrible threesome, she was on the brink of some great discoveries and a life of ease when Becky. The woman who wanted to live forever died a lonely cold death. When Lisa heard the news of Becky's death she was at the dinner table and said a toast in her honor . . . ***"To Becky, may she never rest in peace and the devil consumes her soul"***

Lucifer accepted the gift and felt a surge of power in his veins.

The End of Chapter Eight
"Xeno Voodoo"

Chapter Nine
"Never Say Die"

*"**We** must stay together and fight as one, that is the way our Lord would want us to act."*

Humans had formed into a united front advocating a complete halt to Xeno Technologies Corporation. Troy Kohls was a powerful activist and one of the Generals of the L.O.D. His Division had the least casualties and the most KIA's in Atlanta. War was within every country in the world, they had no time to war with each other, which brought about a world peace constantly at war.

There were two religions remaining in the world. 'The Xeno Religion, and its sects, and the Judo-Christian Temple Warriors of God' they were now the force of the World.

India and China were arguing and the alliance was broken. China started a policy that no treaties signed. Costs in the Russian-Chinese war had put China in debt, now they owned half of the world and were exploiting Russia for everything remaining in tact. Russians became slave labor and barely survived day to day. If hunger did not kill them then sickness had. During this disarray the U.K. and the U.S. managed to possess the most powerful and destructive weapons in the world with the best-equipped militaries, soldiers with the most combat experience.

"We must stay firm and win this war in the name of God Almighty! Who amongst us believes these lies that are in the media, not I . . . There is not going to be co-existence between our people and the Xeno people, only death to us or them!"

Being broadcasted this message by an underground radio station that operated the "Human Free Herald." Up to now, they have stayed hidden.

This United Alliance had been responsible and credited for providing ambulances and medical supplies to the wars. To provide medical support and transfer physicians, and their aids to vital places in the world, including the United States of America this group needed protection. Stock Brokers and Bankers globally paid for protection and provided the monies needed to hire the best mercenaries in the world. Most were regular Army, soldiers without jobs but with a cause. War is addictive, a soldier lives in hell during combat and when there is peace. This soldier is lost and confused, feeling out of place, not wanted or needed in the civilian world. American, Jewish, English, Hungarian, Australian, and German soldiers leased by their Governments, to fight in the war under Israeli Generals and American Politicians.

These men and woman were extremely political and physical. Objectives were clear to everybody. They had to exterminate every Xenocreature in the world. Chinese diplomats were prepared to negotiate for the first time in years a treaty. In this Treaty, they promised to provide a million soldiers and ten-thousand fighter jets. The day had come, finally the human species was banding together in a common cause: to exterminate the Xenopeople and the persons responsible for their existence. This movement grew in time and taken on a stronger poise in global policies.

(Could it be possible that it had taken a fight for survival that one day would bring the world together? One cannot help but wonder and speculate about it.)

"Never say die, never say die, never say die,

because if you say die then you are already dead."

"Storming Max Gable" was the speaker broadcasting on the radio waves and pumping up his listeners with patriotic ideals.

Humans had built private shelters to shield their own kind and for the present time, humans held all political seats in the Houses and ruled the Pentagon. The Supreme Court had two Xenopeople on the Bench and this worried the populace. These Judges were Democrats and extremely liberal.

Wayne King and his new bride were listening to Storming Max on the radio as they went about their daily tasks. King was a minuteman volunteer and a member of the resistance. Wayne *"Perhaps there is hope left after all? Storming Max has a point; we can defeat the Xenopeople if we do it now."*

"Yes, Dear I agree with you but one can never know in this century of deceit and world wars. Xenopeople are digging deep and multiplying like rabbits. They have Valentine as their leader. Valentine has an armed compound of genetically altered super Xeno Warriors to invade at a whim."

Wayne had an answer for everything and his answer to this was, *"we have a greater advantage in this war Sugardoll. We have God on our side."*

Storming Max was on the air again and Danna turned the volume up so that she could hear it better.

"We have Army Units prepared to move into Chicago and take back our city. We must storm their holes and root them out of the sewers; it is time to act now. Everyday that we wait the Xenopeople grow stronger, their scientists search for ways to destroy our species as we watch on helplessly."

"Sugardoll, would you please fix us lunch as I fix the vacuum cleaner. We have company visiting us

tonight; our Minister and his wife are coming for dinner. Have you thought about what we are having for dinner yet?"

"Oh yes, we are having pheasant and rice with tossed salad."

Minister Hall and his wife arrived early and said that the young men in the area were driving to Chicago, getting there any way that they could find a way. Storming Max grew more intense as he carried on with his speech.

"I tell you now that if we attack them it will go down in history as the biggest accomplishment of man. If you doubt our determination to go through with this than it is you my friend lacking in your faith."

"BRFE News Radio Human Free Herald will now go off the Air and will returned at an unspecified time. We hope that you have enjoyed this broadcast and will return to BRFE Radio 99.2 on your dial for our next broadcast. This is Mike Lacrue ready to rock down the house tonight with our prerecorded mini disks set on automatic. Be ready to hear songs from the last century when humans ruled the planet. First a few hors of ZZ Top to get you remembering and then a few commercials, remember that the Resistance needs your support now. Please, in the name of God, give all that you can. Then some hours of the Doors, then you will get the blues with Janis Joplin. Onward Christian Soldiers with several hours of the Stones and Genesis. Before you know it, Mighty Mike will be back with more news from the new Alliance. Until next time stay safe and God Bless every one of you.

October 31, 2024

Chicago never happened. Straight from the

President orders to surround the city and guard it mobilized the Army and the Marines to dig in and protect the city. It seemed that the Xenopeople had found a home in Chicago.

Leven, Tammy, and Mia were on a mission on this night together. They were back in the tunnels beneath Chicago, renamed as New Chicago. They had gotten in with some of the locals on Graveyard Lane and Xeno Market Ave. Underground highways and byways of the Xeno walking dead. They were searching for their contacts and the friends they made the last time they had visited. As always, the three of them were there to assassinate Valentine. Spies had informed Mia that Valentine had flew in yesterday and was giving a speech tonight.

Mia fit right in with the others living in the dwellings among the mutated baboons. Baboons were a fierce lot as they were in the jungle they acted in New Chicago.

Leven thought it a good idea to wear masks because a holiday carnival was happening throughout the city. Leven bought three masks that were similar so that they would not lose each other in the crowded avenues. Tammy was antsy and Mia hungry for blood. Leven was premeditating and cold-blooded ran through his veins planning the assassination of Valentine.

Valentine was Samuel's one and only General in his massive army and the movement against the human species. Valentine held together a loosely knit group of armies and movements that made Samuel virtually an Emperor.

Leven led his comrades to an underground cottage constructed from mud bricks beside a running underground stream. Barren as it was it was as beautiful underground plants flourished beneath powerful artificial lights. Leven traded two-hundred rounds of 5.56 ball ammunition for two days at the Graveyard Inn.

Outside their widows, the creatures of this night were celebrating Halloween. Loud music covered up the screams of the innocent drug down into the city from above. Inside a meat stand across from the three, human meat, could be bought cooked, raw, or smoked. If you had a mind to do it, a person could find human jerky for sale. Mia was interested in buying some living meat, and that was for sale in this manufactured hell. Tammy gazed out a window and wondered if they would make it out alive after the assassination? It was a question on all of their minds and only time was going give them the answer. They waited for their contact to arrive as Mia's stomach growled loudly disrupting the dead silence with the mud brick cottage by the running stream.

Tammy and Leven decided to go swimming; Mia said she was going for a walk to scout the area. Leven said, ***"Fine, just be back in an hour."***

Mia strolled down Loin Lane and ate to her hearts content. She spied in on the chatter in the street crowds and counted the steps it took her to go from one end to the other end. Mia was Point on the retreat and eventual escape out of the city once called Little Chicago.

Mia was dedicated to get revenge for what she had become. Mia wished that she had her own body back in its original form and she blamed Valentine for her fate. Was man so cruel that it would kill off its own species? Mia thought so.

Seems that the more Mia thought about it the more she wanted to go after Valentine herself. Leven and Tammy were the best partners to have and Mia knew this. Yet Mia doubted that they could keep up with her own speed. Mia thought deeply about the attempts she made at Samuel's life and the reasons that they failed. She supposed that if she were working in a team then Samuel would be dead now. There was more that Mia knew, she knew that Lucifer would be BFTD3, from the dead and dwell on Earth. Really, Mia thought, I wish that I were home in the forests of Africa. 'Mia Thought to herself.'

Among those at the festival that appeared as normal, among the average humans were misshapen products of advanced DNA Technology. Creatures that were lethal to touch and others with teeth like a wolf or a dog. Then among the festive colors were posters of Valentine, the Chicago Warlord. Valentine sporting scars foot long, dents, and gouges from his many combats were following Mia's scent.

This was to Mia's advantage because Leven and Tammy were following Valentine. Leven believed that murdering Valentine in crossfire within the crowded parade was going to be easier then in the coliseum and that escape would be feasible.

Valentine was walking alone so intent on killing Mia that he neglected to watch his back. This really was a fight between Valentine and Mia both had come from the same forests in Africa and siblings. Valentine was bigger and stronger but Mia was crafty and quick. Valentine was accustomed to having others do his murders but Mia was a pro, she was a ferocious killer. I would not try to guess who would be victorious in the end. Mia could sense that Leven and Tammy were behind him.

Valentine was blind with rage as he neared Mia. Mia pretended not to notice Valentine until he gotten within a hundred feet of her, at which time Mia would turn and charge Valentine and windmill her arms, she intended on slicing and dicing Valentine with her talon-like claws.

Leven and Tammy were dressed like Robin Hood and his wife carrying poison tipped steel arrows and crossbows. It seemed that Valentine was doomed, unless he snapped out of his trance. Who knows what Valentine would have done if he knew what was coming?

People were drunk or drugged as they celebrated Halloween. In the underground city complex near the center was a Park called Head Square and Mia kept walking in the direction of the Park. Tammy and Leven began splitting apart walking into a flanking formation to get Valentine in crossfire or better known as the kill zone. Nobody in the streets noticed what was about to happen, as they screamed while they danced and slaves were being sold in the Square. With all this commotion, barely anybody noticed Mia stop in the center of the Square and turn around to face Valentine.

Tammy and Leven noticed Mia halt and turn around, Valentine was about fifty-feet from Mia. Leven and Tammy had Valentine in their crosshairs and waited for Mia. This was a personal matter between these two creatures and the gladiators were going to allow them to fight it out until one was dead. If the circumstances reversed then they would have expected nothing less from Mia.

Valentine spoke first. *"Finally we meet face to face, you know that I can vaporize you with nothing more than a thought?"*

Mia said nothing and waited for Valentine to get near, near enough to claw Valentine shredding him into mush. Valentine walked slowly as he said. *"Join us Mia, you are as we are . . . a superior being. It is your choice,* 'Valentine stepped closer and leaned forward with his outreached arms.' *What do you have to lose, really, what makes them better then us? Nothing, they are peons, not worth the bullets it takes to kill them. Well Mia, what is it going to be?"* Mia saw her chance and leaped at Valentine quicker then the eyes could see and flesh began ripping and tearing off Valentine as blood splattered everywhere. Mia ripped his throat open and then ripped off Valentines head. Valentines body stood on its feet and that is when Leven and Tammy peppered Valentine with poison steel tipped arrows.

Escape was impossible as a mob surrounded the forceful trio. Leven removed his broadsword from its sheath and began swinging his sword like an expert that he was with weapons and charging into the mist of the crowd. Tammy allowed her bow to swing under her arm on a sling and opened her backpack loaded with grenades some were smoke grenades. All the sharpened rings on her fingers completely laced with poison, and she was a few steps behind Leven. Mia kicked Valentines head hard and it flew into the crowd like a kickoff. The mad rush to freedom was in progress.

The mob armed with all types of dangerous weapons and some firearms were advancing as the trio was attacking the mob. It happened fast, to fast for a shooter to get aim and hit a target. Leven hit the mob and blood rained down as Leven cut a path for freedom. Tammy threw her grenades and hundreds died, then she threw the smoke grenades.

Through some twist in fate, the three of them made it to the sewers and escaped from their pursuers. Once they crawled up a steel ladder to the catch basin, the three were in the street. Leven noticed that everybody minded there own business and that they were in the clear.

In no time at all the three had made their way to the rented van and began driving west. Tammy turned on the radio and **"Human Free Herald,"** Was on the Air.

"This is Storming Sam bringing you the best music and better News than you have ever listened to before. We do not play High Techno, nor do we play computer-generated music as the other radio stations"

play."

"Here are the latest Headliners and today we not only have the news but we have great news!"

"The Leader of the Terrorist Xeno Factions professionally assassinated today, in New Chicago. Insurgents from an unknown origin have murdered the man behind the Xeno Movement and the top general of global Xeno armies.

"All three assassins escaped from the underground city and are on the loose in the city of New Chicago, Ill."

Leven was keeping a trained eye ahead of him as he listen to the news on the radio.

"Never say die, and this proves my point. God has rescued us from the devil himself once and he'll do it again if you open your hearts and never say die!"

The End of Chapter Nine
"Never Say Die"

Chapter Ten
"**<u>Xeno Gods</u>**"

December 20, 2024

Suddenly, a bolt of Lightning streaked across the smoggy sky and snow mixed with rain made this the perfect time and place for the virgin sacrifice to take place. It was Xeno Water God Holiday and millions celebrated this festival with blood lust and desire. The Midwest had been experiencing heavy storms, freezing weather, and hundreds of tornadoes in the last couple of years. Tonight was a warm night with a full moon at high noon. Global warming was drastically changing the weather.

Xeno God of Water was a creation from Government laboratories and Dr. Keller's genius. God of water was a figure twelve feet high and muscled in the likeness of Buddha and the softness of a beautiful woman. He was stern-faced and heavily bearded. Most significant of his sight was the sheen placid wings that were muscled and light, yet stronger than steel. This being was a manufactured god to deceive the people while the conspiracy to exterminate the human species continued. Xeno God of Water was broadcasted by satellite to big-screens the world over as they sacrificed a virgin in his name.

This day was a Government diversion for the "real deal" that perfected throughout the years to kill Xenocreatures. Secret societies within our Governments conspired together to rid the world of what they referred to as "The Xeno Plague."

Waiting for the midnight hour to strike millions of people grew silent as it neared the twilight hour. Feasting Stands closed, as were beer and T-shirt venders.

Soon there would be a time for crying for the virgin

sacrifices and then the inverted cross-altar. People threw red roses at their god, as was the custom of the times.

      Xeno Gladiators protected the stage and the Altar because of a lesson well learned in New Chicago. Red rose peddles flew through the sky as the wind caught them and disappeared into the smog. Cheering people offered their own daughters and wives be honored as a sacrifice but all were refused their service and turned away by the fearsome gladiators. Xenoman was next to god and he was a new and improved Xenomachine.

      First, the virgin was baptized in water in honor of the Water God and then she would be hung onto the steel upturned cross by her feet. Then the Water God would rape her as her blood drained from a knife cut on her throat, not deep enough, for a fast death, but deep enough for an extremely slow agonizing death.

      Sara Dey kidnapped from Sacred Heart Girls School of Mother Mary; she was a beautiful woman that dedicated her soul and her life to God Almighty.

      Walking slowly toward her destiny Sara Dey cried and asked God to save her soul. The Water God heard her thoughts and bellowed his rage at Sara. ***"How you dare to insult me by praying to your worthless god! You are mine tonight and forever, there is no salvation forthcoming from your god, you belong to me now!"***

      Sara froze in the water as she fell into a trance. She imagined herself in a nightmare and she was the star. The

Xenoman lifted Sara and used hemp rope to tie her feet to the tot of the inverted cross. Sara hung there withering in pain as the crowd cheered and danced to the beat of the voodoo drums behind the altar.

Soon the midnight hour struck and the water god carefully slit Sara's throat as to make he bleed out slowly. Then he mounted her and raped Sara for an hour until she was declared dead by the guest of honor. Doctor Nicklaus Keller, Dr Keller had flown in from Washington with a special invitation from Samuel, which meant his presence at the Ritual was mandatory.

———————————————

The Water God was only one God of Ten Xeno Gods. These are the other Xeno Gods that ruled the planet Earth; One-The God of Misfortune, two-The God of Death, three-The God of Betrayal, four-The God of infidelity, five-The God of Hatred and Vengeance, six-The Xeno Locust God, seven-The Xeno God of Suffering and Pain, eight-The God of Sickness, nine-The god of Mass Murder. After the ritual finished, everybody in the crowd lighted a torch in the honor of all the other Xeno Gods.

Xeno God of Water slurped up the last drop of blood from the golden sacrificial bowl and screamed his oaths to evil and as he urinated on the altar.

After the sacrifices the water god drank the blood from the gold bowl he ate the body, gnawing on her bones as he cursed the day he was created.

Samuel knew that some of the gods were under the control of his father but it was something that he had to live with. Samuel was only human and though he was possessed with powerful abilities, he was as human as Jessica was; his twin sister was born before he was and that angered Samuel.

Samuel attended the ritual of water baptism on this day and felt threatened by the change in trends and the glory these gods stole from Samuel. That is why Samuel missed Valentine and was glad that Dr. Keller had stored DNA cultures of the sadistic creature and at this very moment, Valentine was being reborn in a test tube. Samuel was not impressed with this phony god of water, Xeno Technologies INC were responsible for these new creatures from hell. He suspected that his father had something to do with it. Rituals that were not in Samuel's honor offended him.

Dr. Keller flew back to Washington State to check on his new Project. Dr. Keller bringing Valentine back by cloning his DNA and restoring his memory as he grew was another breakthrough for the mad doctor. With the new drugs manufactured in the last years, growth stimulation was phenomenal. His excitement was that as a child as Nick pondered how much Valentine must have grown since he last saw him.

"Gods, my ass." 'Samuel Said speaking to nobody.'

Each god was jealous of the other god's powers; they constantly warred with each other. Xeno God of Betrayal was the most powerful of all the gods. He knew that trust is the most import bond between man and beast alike. Without trust, there is only chaos and death among the humans and the gods alike. Wars among the gods cost millions of lives, Xeno and humans . . . were meat to these gods.

<u>The Xeno God of Betrayed was the worst of the lot.</u>
Considered a loving and generous god, it was his way of getting into the hearts of his victims. Once inside, this god manipulated the mind of the body he possessed. He vexed the heart of his victims and eventual they became paranoid to the point of committing murder.

Dr. Keller designed this god to equal the powers of the world and with it bringing peace. His native name was Betrayell but nobody dared to speak his name aloud.

———————————

In his laboratory, Nick and Lisa were amazed at how quickly Valentine was growing. They did not want Valentine on the loose again and feared the soon to be giant. Lisa suggested that Valentine be contained in a vault protected by a nuclear shield. The lead vault was five meters thick and fifty meters square. Valentine was comfortably placed leisure, but confined to his space. Lisa suggested that five nurses be contained in the vault to care for Valentine and perhaps feed him if the cannibalistic instincts showed in the new Valentine. It was the only way to know how much of the old Valentine was in the new Valentine. Nick and Lisa kept their findings secret while sending fake reports to Samuel.

Days and then weeks went by before Leven and Tammy had safely returned to the Jessica Compound. They were glad that Valentine was in New Chicago because they did not want to go all the way to South America again. It was nice be home and in love again. They were alone in their cabin and had a roaring fire going in the fireplace. They celebrated and then made love until dawn. Perhaps if they had known about Valentine cloned, then they would not have been celebrating.

Huge Halls filled with humans were discussing the future about how to combat the Xeno threat. Many among them had some sort of insignificant Xenotransplant but it did not affect their DNA so they were immune. Some persons were immune to the side effects of the Xenotransplant naturally.

Signs and posters showed on billboards, windows, and everywhere else duplicating the fight against Xenoism.

Graffiti and posters were everywhere explaining the Cause and telling the same old story. Many humans had surrendered to their fates believing that it was all lost so why fight it. *"If you can't beat it then join it?* Not everyone felt that the war had been lost; many believed that it had only begun. This poster and flyer identified an area as contaminated by Xenowaste and byproducts.

This emblem used to warn humans that it was a restricted or contaminated toxic area and not to enter. Many signs from hundreds of Factions littered the street as this poster went unnoticed.

The God of Dead was at the Town Hall speaking to over five-thousand people. Why this meting called together, was unknown to anybody there. All of those attending this meeting in a little town called Walworth in Wisconsin packed with politicians from all over the State. The God of the Dead commanded the audience to have a seat and sit. Then he explained the reason why they called together for this meeting.

"I have brought you here to ask you why you are late with your taxes due to the Xeno Gods. You dare defy me when I can drop you dead where you sit, why?"

A man in the crowd stood and yelled at the Xeno God. *"Only God Almighty in heaven can decides who dies and who lives. You are the god of the dead, not the living. If you kill me, then god will set his wrath against you and what you stand for, we have no taxes for you. You are wasting your time and ours by coming here."*

God of the Dead grew red in rage and raised his fist. *"I am God, what is this god of yours going to do when your heart jumps out of your chest and falls to the ground by your feet? I know what you will do . . . you will watch your heart beat as you die!"*

With that said, the man standing watched his heart pop out of his chest and fall to the floor still beating. It was the last thing he saw in this life.

Gods all the world over were making Earth hell, it was bad. Smog in the air thick as fog crystallized with colors as the sun shined through it.

Inside the Town Building pandemonium hit as several shots rung out aimed at the god by the Police Chief attending this meeting. People starting dying from different ailments and those that ran away were the fortunate ones. Some ran before the false god and fell at his feet asking for forgiveness, others fought back. When the day was through and sunset dimmed the sky, there were three-thousand people dead in the Walworth City Town Hall.

God of Death was one of Lucifer's Disciples and depended on his protection. On this day, God of Death declared that all his followers be marked by the devil. The God of death and his legend spread throughout the world. This emblem; was branded or burned, onto tens of thousands of people on a daily basis.

The gods had just one problem that was out of everybody's hands. Their demons were in an act of rebellion. Demons realized that the Earth was weak and that Xeno Leadership was in turmoil with Valentine dead so the decided to kill the Xeno Gods.

The End of Chapter Ten
"**<u>Xeno Gods</u>**"

Chapter Eleven
"Xeno Demons"

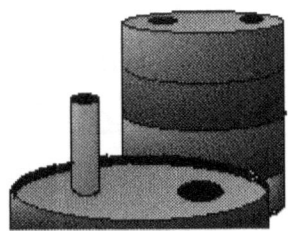

April 15, 2025

Fifty demons gathered at a chemical warehouse owned by one of the hosts of this gathering. These demons were not ordinary demons. They were the president's of there Charters.

One-hundred Charters with three-thousand members in every Charter were a force of demons that could shake the Earth. It was Lucifer keeping these demons in line, following his program. With a thought, Lucifer could cast his demons into his fire and replace them with new demons. Hell is ideal for recruiting demons from amongst the masses suffering from boils, fire, and repetitious deaths. Samuel was charmed and his demons had to abide by Samuel's rules, but their loyalty was to Lucifer.

Samuel did not protect his gods; Samuel was an imperfect being and made mistakes. He never considered the demons becoming jealous of the gods. Samuel might not learn about these demons until it was too late for him to act. Baggot was the Speaker and the organizer of this gathering and was the fiercest demon among them. He suggested that they kidnap the Gods and bring them to the warehouse. Then once there, use the acidic phosphate chemicals to dissolve the gods with their powers. Loud laughter and mocking the gods was only a murmur among the demons as Baggot stood on the loading dock in the rear of the warehouse. Samuel had no knowledge of this gathering as his favorite demons distracted him with magic and trickery.

"Thank you for coming and the hell with you." 'There was loud applause after Baggot said what he said. It was the formal ways of demons; their customs went back almost as far as God.'

"As you all know, these Xeno God's are not from hell, they are invented missing links, nothing more. Lucifer however has baptized us with his fire of hell. We have been born into the world and lived in sin; we are the most evil of the souls cast into hell. Where is our glory? Who praises us? . . . Nobody cares because we are ugly, horrible to look at, we serve our Lord and he gives us life. We must secretly abduct the gods and burn them in our liquid fire!"

Demons were scowling and stomping there feet on the ground, as Baggot waited for his Pack of Alpha demons to calm down. Baggot was an expert in demon psychology and knew how to gain their loyalty. Baggot wanted to gain status and position with Lucifer. Brown nosing for his soul, once Baggot got what he sought then he became the cruelest and most sadistic of all the demons. Baggot thought for a moment and then raised his hands for the demons to quiet down.

"Enough of this waiting around while the gods keep us underfoot! We must find a way to capture these gods. I believe that we should equally assign chapters to kidnap the gods from their Temples. Find your own way

to do it, just get it done. I want all the gods locked in cells here at this warehouse on May 13, 2025. Do you understand me?"

Mokkok became in charge of splitting up the Charters and the god that each Charter was after. Baggot warned that if they congregated for to long then Samuel would detect them plotting the murder of his gods. Mokkok is a huge buffed demon stuck on his ego and his pride swelled at the thought of himself.

Two demons who were attending the secret gathering had to draw a Truce to fight together after two-thousand years of war. Mokkok had a way about him, he could get his way with the others most of the time. Each demon had a host of powers and vexes. Demons warred with each other constantly and some demons had made allies with gods to gain the upper hand. Now these same demons were plotting to murder the gods, that they were bound to by Samuel.

Beneath the basement deep within the Earth was a chamber constructed into The Reformed Demonology Church of Lucifer. Here is where the demons relaxed and drank wine while indulging themselves with young men and women. It was a mirrored paradise with colored strobe lights and smoke thick in the air. Fifty demons stayed until dawn scheming and forging strong pacts.

Mia was nearby, on her mind, was destroying their secret paradise. During the gathering dark clouds obscured by the smog rolled in. Mia did not mind the chance of rain. Mia was hell-bent on murder and once her mind decided, there was no changing her mind.

There was much to do for Mia as she waited for her

chance to kill demons.

Mia knew that the only way to kill a demon was to cut off their head and their limbs. She had secured a bow saw to do the jobs. Mia was carrying a snag net and duct tape along with a hip-pack that had all kinds of goodies in it. Her coat of hair protected Mia from the weather, and the color of her hair hid Mia away nicely in the blackness of the forest. Mia was prepared to ambush the demons in the morning, one at a time. She propelled like a rocket and as quietly as a gravedigger did. Mia waited at the T in the trail to the pier; it was there that she planned to murder Mokkok.

It had been many years ago, that Mia was possessed to be a savage serial predator and she terrified an entire city. On this morning, just before dawn, the demon would walk this path through the woods and Mia planned to be there in wait.

Mia climbed a tree that had long stout branches reaching over the path. Mia climbed the tree and waited for the demon. Her bow saw strapped on her back.

Dead horse lane was the name given to this trail, named after a burial area for a serial killer, this is where Mia waited to leap onto the flying devil and lasso his neck, moving like the speed of light sawing away in the twilight. Mia was most comfortable during this part of the day. Twilight; the time just after sunset or before dawn, the Sun is below the horizon, Mia's realm of operations.

Mokkok was not thinking about his safety as he levitated and flew a few meters off the path toward his boat.

Upwind, Mia's scent hidden from Mokkok, Mia knew that Mokkok was near. At exactly the right instant Mia leaped on Mokkok's back and applied the lasso bringing them both crashing into the path.

In less than a minute Mia had killed and

decapitated, quartered, her first demon.

Next Mia ran swiftly to her next ambush. Mia reached into her hip pack and folded out a razor sharp stainless steel boomerang. With one throw prepared to behead two demons.

Leven and Tammy wanted to go with Mia but Mia would hear nothing about it. She said that it was more then dangerous and that it was doubtful that she herself would return alive.

Two demons were standing under a tree discussing the events of the gathering. Mia was part human and nimble, yet strong as an ape. Acrobatically gifted, Mia threw the boomerang high into the air cutting right.

As the demon nearest the Mia glanced to his left and the boomerang loped off his head. The boomerang twisted in the air and turned left spiraling down at the remaining demon. It was eerie in the way that it happened because the second demon was on the run when his head rolled before him like a ball. With his feet still moving for another twenty feet, the headless demon finally cart wheeled to a bloody halt.

Mia searched for more demons but was to late, all the demons were gone. With Mokkok dead Mia had done well on this foggy dark morning.

Lucifer screamed in pain as his demons died. It was a bad day again because Samuel was burning the candle again, fire coals simmered in his brain as Lucifer howled in agony. He swore that he would give his enemies slow and painful deaths.

Mia knew she hit a nerve, independent killing sprees but not random sprees. Mia owed her life to Jessica so for that reason alone. Mia tended to go after Jessica's enemies.

Her enhanced animal instincts told her that Valentine was alive again. Mia knew that Dr. Keller and his wife had something to do with Valentine's return and wished that she could have assassinated the Kellers a long time ago. She knew that his security was beyond her range of penetration.

Valentine had grown to a height of seven-feet in a little over a year. Unbelievable as it seemed, all the nurses were alive and caring for Valentine. Valentine managed to stay docile and passive behind the locked door. Dr. Keller sent in great reports about Valentine and stated in a letter that Valentine was harmless and that the regeneration of his DNA caused a reverse in temperament.

Mia ran to the North Pole to hide out for a while until the wars among the Gods and the demons started. Valentine was a threat now and Mia fear for Leven and Tammy's safety. Her friends in the North Pole and welcomed her home. Their home was a complex network of igloos built into the ice. It was quite comfortable and safe.

Back home it was another story. Demons were blaming the gods for the deaths of three demons and a revolt was in the making. Nobody suspected Mia of assassinating the demons and everybody wanted to blame the gods.

Other religions prepared their armies and some drew up treaties for the coming war. Demons were causing confusion and distrust among the Leaders of the world. Samuel loved everything that was happening in his world and encouraged the war. One of the world's most popular Christian leaders declared, *"The final days are near, in the name of God we will fight and win this Xeno War."*

Globally, each religion promised to fight to the death, including China. Leaders decided that the most powerful god would win the war thus making this god the true god of heaven and Earth.

People of all species were filing complaints about

demons getting out of control and busting down businesses for money and women and demons invading their homes and raping them. Some mass murders and a few large fires were the demons venting their anger. Everywhere people complained to the gods asking why they have not protected them from the demons. Christian armies were killing those they believed to be possessed by a demon. Thousands on mentally retarded people and mentally ill people sentenced to death by poisoning. Christian workers were in every medical facility in the world.

Xeno demons retaliated by conducting mass hangings of those without the mark of Lucifer. People swung from yard posts everywhere in the world except for china. Tibetan speaking monks seemed to ward off demons with their centuries of knowledge and wisdom, and their magical powers. Xeno Demons that had gone to China never returned or heard of again.

China was the only world power that had kept their society and culture in tact throughout the Xeno Age. Xeno species of all known to humanity were banned from China and put to death if found. Chinese engineers were fast at work repairing the damage caused by the Russian-Chinese war. Chinese were immigrating into Russia at an enormous rate; millions a day were leaving for the Wild West. China renamed Russia to "Mao Providence" and what Russians that remained became slave labor. China was taking advantage of the new rich soil and the vast resources of the mountains.

Samuel had placed China on the bottom of his list to pillage and crumple. Africa was the work of his demons, Locust God had ravaged the countryside's and small wars and new diseases had killed millions of humans. Satan was naïve and did not have the sand of his father. Everybody was duping him because Samuel had become lazy.

Nero was a demon threat had been around during

the Roman Empire; he was the meanest and cruelest of all men on Earth during his time in Rome. At one time Nero had declared himself a god. He hung Christians on crosses and burned them in his gardens. Nero was Lucifer's favorite demon and his trusted informant.

Nero was the demon elected to bring atrocities and unequivocal horror to the peoples of the world. People predicted that after Nero committed suicide by stabbing himself in his neck, he would rise like the Jesus. Nero did not rise from the dead but did go straight to hell. Nero was the Roman Empire anti Christ but failed in his endeavor to enslave the world. Lucifer allowed Nero to leave hell and enter a Xeno body, for the first time in centuries Nero had human form. Nero was responsible for all terrorism; inspiration and encouragement were his weapons.

Nero truly believed himself to be a god a long time ago but now he knew his place. Nero was the right-hand man-demon of Lucifer.

Lucifer was suppose to possess Samuel but Samuel's human spirit invaded and became an individual. Samuel was the evil anti Christ but Lucifer was not in Samuels's consciousness. Lucifer was helpless during his time, he was suppose to be the one through Samuel that battled God, not an infant of evil.

Baggot expected the gods delivered to his warehouse on time, and Nero was working with Baggot to get the job done. The devil had seven years to rule over the Earth and Samuel was making a joke out of it. Nero was going to bring Lucifer back among the living one way or another; he was going to get the job done. In doing this Nero knew that Lucifer would favor him and give him, the Earth to rule as Lucifer moved on to other worlds in distant galaxies. Nero was not above using the most dastardly way to get what he wanted, and at times a bit more. One day soon, Lucifer would become flesh and Xenotechnology was the perfect way to do it. Dr. Keller creating a body without a soul so that Lucifer avoids a long incubation in the womb only a short time for his recreation.

May 12, 2025

Servants of the gods on Earth were demons, as were the bodyguards. Tonight was the night that all the Charters decided to kidnap all the gods at the midnight hour. They were to meet at Death Valley California in one of the demon church's.

The largest religion on Earth was "The Church of Samuel" Samuel preached, *"If you believe in God then you believe in death, I believe in living forever."*

Xeno demons had successfully captured all the gods except for Samuel. When the demons confronted the gods they were stunned, the gods were cowards at heart and not worthy of their names. Demons flew the gods on their backs to the warehouse where Baggot and Nero were anticipating their arrival.

Penny and Katana were at the cliff again, the same site that Raven were killed. Demons could not break through the shield wrapped over the Jessica Foundation. Things had not changed much inside of the compound. The world outside could not touch the people living on the Jessica Compound. It was in the daily paper, explaining the war between false gods and the demons but nobody cared. They were under the protection of Jessica and God Almighty protected Jessica. Katana was jumping and begging for a treat and Penny gives her a milk bone.

The Jessica Foundation Compound was the only unaffected place in the world. China compromised her status in the world by demons with the powers demons had stolen from the gods.

May 13, 2025

Samuel was furious had chased the demons with his armies and his powers but the demons had strengthened their ranks, now they were running amok and killing all humans marked with Samuel's brand. Samuel caught lacking in power so he did the next best thing. Samuel called Dr. Keller and told him to bring Valentine to him. Valentine was a warmonger and a natural liar, these assets made Valentine a natural Leader.

Once the gods were submerged in the chemicals they turned into liquid and then into smoke.

The End of Chapter Eleven
"<u>Xeno Demons</u>"

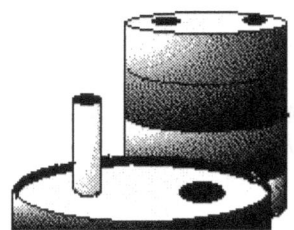

Jeremiah 19-8

Chapter Twelve
<u>"Wars among Religions"</u>

Fire spread through the forests of Utah as the Mormon stronghold was under attack by *"The Church of Samuel."* It had been going on for several days and reinforcements were on the way to help with the conquest of Salt Lake City. If not for the needed work force to fight the fires coming in from the southeast then the city would have had a better chance of survival.

Underground missile silos were in the control of the city and its Leaders. Vulcan anti-aircraft guns were firing into the massive charge hitting the city. The cult church had Valentine as its top General, and they had raided Ft. Hood in Texas pillaging tanks, armored vehicles, munitions, explosives, helicopters, and what not. 'Vulcan's could shoot down the older fighters of ten years past, but the new static stealth fighters were too fast and they were shrouded.' Gram Cutter was the President and responsible for the defense of the city. The thought of installing conventional warheads onto the missiles occurred to him and he asked his aids for their opinions.

John Sutter; *"We have overridden Government protocols and have control of the missiles and our own experts at the University can replace the current warheads with the conventional warheads."*

Elisa Carter; *"I suggest that we make the conversion and then rig the silo's with explosives if we are over-run we can blow it. If these missiles get in the hands of Samuel then he would cause a nuclear war. We should allow God to rescue us before we use nuclear weapons."*

Gram; *"God willing, we will not be forced to*

employ these weapons of destruction, but damn the torpedoes, full speed ahead."

Vatican Officials had decided to begin the purging of Italy of all Xeno Beings. Pope Paul had declared all Xeno Species as work of the devil.

The assault on Salt Lake City prompted the Pope to convey another invented vision to his people. All over Europe, Catholics were banding together and gathering Xeno species entities for a xeno holocaust.

Muslims and Buddhists were also joining the cause and declaring Xenopeople infidels and works of the devil. For the first time in history, man had aligned together to fight a common foe, there was peace among the human species as the wars among religions raged on.

Arguments persisted among the Christian religions that allied to fight one foe were ongoing. Ireland had become house-to-house warfare in the past year, and did not care about Xenopeople. In fact, many Xenopeople recruited to fight in this religious war.

New Faith Religion is an offshoot of Templar Knights, a secret organization that guarded the gates into all parts of the Mideast. Members of a Christian Militia founded in Jerusalem in 1119 after the First Crusade. This was the strongest army in the world because they were the most organized. They also were some of the richest men in the world.

This religion played a large part in the wars by supplying medical supplies or munitions to the highest bidders. They did this to finance their own endeavors and enterprises. These men and women killed in the name of Christ. These religious fanatics were the most powerful force in the world. They were the peacekeepers and the negotiators of the world and that bought those favors, power, and Policy to distribute globally. This powerful status gave them immunity and protection from all parties involved in war, including the Xeno Religions.

Certainly, the New Faith Religion was more then it seemed to be, perhaps only a cover for the inner circle. Bloodlines that go to the beginning of civilization run the world now. This group had no Spokesperson or leader; they had an inner circle of people whose names are secret. In one way or another, everything went to this group, if this group was an evil group or a good group is not for me to guess.

Battles fought in the fields and in the cities, as one Xeno being after another died. Some Xenopeople had the means to regenerate body parts, that is why they were headshots or burned alive. Government forces had thus far kept the battles out of the suburbs and the cities. Exceptions to this were Chicago and Salt Lake City. Race and color was not an issue for humans now but hatred and bias lurked over the Xeno Species. Differences set aside, the human race joined hands to fight this war together. Each battle brought a new host of Xeno Creatures and winged demons into the fight.

Valentine had initiated this war among religions by assaulting Salt Lake City. Gram Cutter was great at his post and had regained the ground they had lost in the beginning of the battle. Valentine was waiting for his Xeno Amazon reinforcements; they were going to be the force that attacks the missile silos. With their jungle voodoo and the help of

Nero, Valentine planned to overrun the city once his best joined the fight. Knowing that just in sheer numbers Valentine would eventually overrun the city, Samuel howled in joy. Samuel screamed into the wind . . . ***"Where is your God Almighty now!"***

Leven and Tammy were waiting for the reinforcements to arrive, as was Valentine. Their agenda's were different; Leven planned to use digital lasers to bring down the huge jets and airbuses bringing these people from Brazil.

California was staying neutral in these wars. Liberal and independent California allowed tolerance for most things, including the Xeno Species. The Jessica Compound was beyond reproach and never attacked during these wars.

Salt Lake City was another story; overhead the skies were blood red as chemicals burned down the military installations in the salt flats and southwest roads and highways into the city. Bishop Cutter was bringing his forces that were holding the mountain passes going east to draw back and reinforce the southwest section of the city. The mountain passes were' left for the locals and Mormon snipers to defend and hold. Cutter was beginning to feel the heat from his Staff as he studied the maps and moved pushpins around. He was deciding whether to employ conventional warheads on the enemy. It was going to be the hardest decision that Cutter would ever make. Salt Lake City would die before falling into the hands of the devil.

An act of God stopped the wars. Daylight had not appeared and it grew cold without the heat from the sun. This phenomenon stayed a mystery. Why the sun disappeared for three months and then the sun reappeared.

None of Valentines reinforcements ever made it to Salt Lake so Valentine retreated into Devils Mountain Range in Idaho.

Late at night, shots rang out throughout the

countryside of more fighting going on. Currently, houses were constructed that were bulletproof and as fallout shelters. Today's world is a world of the living and the dead. With new medicines that sold over the counter there even was a cure for death.

Religion was confusing and it seemed that the gods were never around when you needed them. Samuel made a public announcement that he was the only god. He demanded tribute from the world. Christian armies had taken back control in most places in the world and refused to recognize Samuel as a god.

Irish assassins were dead on their marks as the traveled the world killing religious leaders. The Irish were the best-trained assassins in the world, and the most daring. They blamed religion for all of their problems and the death of most of Ireland. War had ravished Ireland and the fighting was continuing. New weapons from other nations tested in Ireland, in a world where everybody was expendable. Ireland had become a Country and the fighting worsened as the yellow fog rolled inland.

The war among religions had turned half the world against religion. Each religion and its associated religions followed different versions of baptism by water to the death of Christ. *"Why wait to die to receive everlasting life when a person could have it now"* This was a verse going around that people picked up on television, a commercial selling "Everlasting Life" 'one pill a day keeps death far away . . .'

Three Irish Assassins had joined the Jessica Foundation with the complete approval from Jessica. Jessica knew these men from her dreams they were warriors from heaven. These men knew every means of assassination invented in the history of murder. They had been purged by God to aid in the destruction of the anti Christ.

Jessica knew that Samuel was not the problem but the real trouble was still in hell. Each Church claimed that they were the true avenues to salvation, thus causing turmoil within the Christian church tree of life. There were preachers claiming that only 100,000 people will rise to heaven to meet god, others say a million others more or less but they all say that they are the only true source for salvation. Jessica knew that the people inside the compound were safe, but she also knew that not all were faithful. She was most worried about Peter; he had been acting strange for the last couple of years. Some people living inside the Jessica Compound disliked Peter.

Peter had gotten away without having to answer for leaving two of his brother Christians to die at the wicked house on the hill. Jessica introduced the three assassins to Peter and assigned Robin O'Malley to Peter's squad. Peter understood Jessica and realized that Robin was there for him. He was a bird dog and assigned to keep on eye on Peter.

Lucifer was destined to walk the Earth and all Samuel had accomplished was bringing more terror and prolonging the agony of the human race. Jessica knew that the most horror would consume the Earth during Lucifer's reign. The final Judgment will come when all the souls even the dead choose a side, good or evil, during the final battle that decides each soul's fate.

"I do not believe in all of this hocus-pocus, its all nonsense. There is science and there are math, those two have the answers to all of man's secrets and origins. There are no such things as a devil or gods, all of this can be explained through science and it will lead to Advanced Xeno Technology." 'Joshua Goldberg was the leading

scientist that was trying to develop a biological virus that would attack mixed genetic DNA such as the type found in the Xeno Species.' Goldberg was addressing a roomful of Senators and the President.

Congress was trying to find a way to kill the problem that they created. The Xeno Species had set up an Order, Xeno form of Government with Samuel at its head. They contacted Dr. Keller to do find the toxin but he refused because he wanted no part in destroying a lifetime of his work. Joshua was the best objective scientist in the world. Goldberg was born in an ambulance in the Gaza Strip as gunfire erupted around him. Two days later a suicide bomber at the mall killed both his parents. His Aunt and uncle then raised Joshua Goldberg. Presently, he was leading an investigation into how science had gone so wrong as to nearly cause the biggest holocaust in the history of man.

"I understand the concern that you ladies and gentlemen have for the survival of our species. I share your concerns and have tried my best but have fallen short of our goals."

Dr. Goldberg hesitated for a few minutes and Congressperson Shelly York stood and asked a question.

"What have you accomplished thus far with your experiments and the new Research Center we built for you? Are we and closer to find a way to exterminate the Xeno virus that has corrupted our planet, and is poisoning our great nation?"

Dr. Goldberg paced back and forth on stage and then stopped at the podium. *"We have developed many different anti xeno toxins and viruses but they fall short. Mutating DNA within these Xenocreatures is making it difficult but not impossible to develop a virus that will kill the species. Now we are working on a virus that will first lower their immune systems and then a second virus that will ultimately exterminate the Xeno species."*

Applauding filled the chambers as the Dr. finished. *"We are near to finding a final solution to this plague that has infected our planet. Now let me bring to light the problems facing our planet. The blackout that nearly froze our planet was a direct result of the nuclear bombs that exploded in China by the Russians. If this happens again, I do not believe that the sun will shine for a hundred years. Our atmosphere contaminated by black radioactive soot that blocked out the sun has compromised our ozone layer to the point of no return. We need to address this issue as vehemently as we are the Xeno Plague."*

Silence abounded within the walls of the chamber as Dr. Goldberg bowed and then walked off the stage to waiting Secret Service Agents.

A rouge religious sect deployed assassins to kill Dr. Goldberg as he departed Washington D.C. n his limousine. Assassins, well hidden across the street with high-powered sniper rifles were waiting for the group to leave the building.

Secret Service Agents had canvassed all the buildings with a view of the Pentagon but missed the assassins that were hiding in a vacant building that was smoking from the fire that destroyed the building.

CSI were investigating the murder of a homeless man and were searching for clues with Police Dogs. The dogs sniffed out the assassins and led to a firefight that resulted in the deaths of all the assassins. Three Secret Service Agents died during this action and Dr. Goldberg departed without any further trouble.

The wars between religions worsened as accusations, innuendos fed the fires as the Protestant, and Catholic Churches raided and murdered one-another over ideals. Pope Paul declared that the wars had to end but behind the curtains advocated the destruction of the Xeno Religion and the Protestant religions. The Pope posted a call to arms and a new Crusade organized to bring peace to Ireland and to show the world that God favored Catholics over all other religions. Proving that true faith belonged inside the Catholic Church, the Pope wanted to drive this point home. He wanted to save the world with his crusades, and at the same time conquer the world.

It was a dark time for the world and it was only getting worse. The world was becoming a world of city-states, and the United States, UK, China, Australia, Israel, Egypt, Argentina, and India were the last Nations remaining with centered governments. These Countries built an alliance against the wars between religions and began their own campaigns to fight the Pope and the Xeno Religions.

CNN reported the first landings of UFO's while chaos in the world was destroying the planet. Alien contact happened on this day and the wars on Earth stopped for the first time in the history of man. Armies rushed to meet these UFO's from everywhere and they assaulted the extraterrestrials (existing or coming from somewhere outside the Earth and its atmosphere) until they ran out of munitions. Reports came in that said the saucers were unaffected by the human assault and before long six fleets had landed.

Glowing yellow and orange saucers were hovering over the shoreline near Carmel, California. Tourists crowded and moved through military tape and over barricades to get a closer look at the UFO's. Mediators sent to the site to try to communicate with the beings inside the spacecraft were unsuccessful.

A child asked a Preacher watching the spectacle before them *"if this meant there is no God?"*

With a smile and a warm hug, the minister told the

child . . . *"Everything that you see son is a part of God's plan for us."*

News spread quickly and in the next hour, everything mechanical ceased to work. The world stopped for now and possibly forever, at least as long as it will take to disable the saucers. Weapons did not work so some battles around the world continued with had to had combat. Hatred is a disease that is like leprosy, there is no cure for it and it spreads fast.

On this day, the Earth sighed in relief as less toxins and gases entered her atmosphere. Communication with the aliens established through radio, the aliens spoke volumes.

"We are here to inform you that your planet is an eyesore to the other planets with life in your galaxy. You are out of line, and could pollute our galaxy infecting and possibly destroying planets that are in your wake when you self-destruct. Many years we have been watching you and sending your governments warnings and what do they do? They shoot down our flyers. Now in order to stop you from further damaging your solar system and our galaxy, possibly cause idle wild meteors to hit civilized planets. You are not alone, arrogant and selfish, your species have now become bigheaded and intolerable to the populations in this galaxy. We are here to governor your emissions and to disarm your armies. You cannot prevent us from putting your planet in tow. From this moment on there will be a decrease of pollution up to eight-percent, beginning now."

The End of Chapter Twelve
"Wars among Religions"

Chapter Thirteen
"Darkness and the Abyss"

The Duchess of Manchester had been through the wringer all her life and when a harmless youth medicine was discovered in the Jungles of South America She had enough money to buy another term of life. It was the alternative to Xeno medicines and therapies. Dr. Joshua Goldberg was the man behind this discovery and others like it. 'If this new medicine was not discovered,' then her children and other parties would have pillaged her to death. Duchess of Manchester was the oldest woman in Europe and regained her composure to manage her own finances. She seemed younger and was getting younger as all her ailments healed and one day the pain had finally gone away. Now she was on the beach approaching the spacecraft demanding to see who was in them. Five bodyguards and cameras were following her as Reporters raced to get the story.

Stubborn and even more determined to get a better view, the Duchess examined the craft closely and began tapping on it and yelling . . . *"Hello in there can you hear me? . . . Hello . . . Hello . . . Open up, I am Royalty and demand that you show your faces . . . I am the closest that your going to get to finding a Leader to speak with you, now open up!"* " Hello"

Carmel was a protected community and sheltered from the world, many famous and infamous people lived along Hwy 17 and the beach towns in Monterey County, California. People here were more concerned about the power coming back on then they were of flying saucers on Carmel beach.

Hospitals were in a bad way as patients were dying faster then they could be stored. People in surgery died or awakened when the power died. Accidents on the highways and byways everywhere were in major collisions. All aircraft and satellites crashed into the Earth and armies in combat stopped dead in their tracks. Time seemed to be standing still as the news spread globally about the visitation from outer space. If something invented soon to fix this global problem, it would turn into a global crisis. Millions of people would die in a matter of a few hours and the world would become dependent of the aliens.

Finally, the Duchess gave up, walked back to her limo up on the hill, and told her driver to take her home. It was futile trying to get an observation of these aliens because they stayed inside of their crafts. With their bayonets mounted on their rifles, a Special Forces Battalion surrounded the saucers and kept guard. Their firearms did not function and their vehicles were dead as a graveyard.

August 29, 2025

Steven Blake and his brother Charlie remained home alone to watch the house while their parents were visiting relatives in Florida. They had no way of knowing that the plane crashed that was flying them to Florida. It was dark so the two teenage boys lighted candles.

Steven was seventeen and Charlie was only fifteen years old. They were in their country home in upper New York State, in a large ranch house with a extra large basement. Both the boys were avid hunters and above average intelligence. They had no idea about the intruders that were hiding in their barn or about the plans, planning to raid the house, for whatever else they could find that they needed. The boys settled in and went to bed thinking that the power would be on in the morning and that everything was well. Fortunately for the boys, they had two German Sheppard's, in the house with them. Two trained guard dogs bought by their mother, to protect the boys, often they stayed in the house alone.

Mike Ford was a distant relative of the man who shot Jesse James. Since then Mike and most of his kin died in prison were serving time in prison or were committing crimes. It was in their bloodline. Mike always loved to be sweet, a nice person, sort of a Gentleman before he turned on his prey. Ford and two other convicts escaped when the power went out at the prison. Deputies from the Warrants office were transporting them to the courthouse for sentencing. Mike was the ringleader who murdered two families at a picnic in the National Forest Park, then they stolen their SUV and ran out of gas at the end of the long driveway that led to the Newcastle's Garage.

Roger Barns and Stew Harding were lifers before they met Mike Ford. They were on parole when they ran into Mike and now here they were ready to do a home invasion. Mike was a cold-blooded murderer and anticipated his next kill with enthusiasm. They were birds of a feather and followed the same code between felons.

Mike turned to his accomplishes and said . . . *"Stew you go behind the house and see if there is a quiet way into the house. If there is, then come to the front door and let me in. Barns, you go over to those flowers, climb up over the awning, and see if you can get to the roof. These types of homes always have a way into the house from there. I will wait here for one of you to open the door and let me into the house. If anybody sees, then kill him or her. You got it?"*

Roger was the smarter of the two gophers and asked about dogs. *"When I got popped the first time it was the dogs that tackled me to the ground. If not for the dogs, I would have gotten away with five grand. What if there are dogs here, then what?"*

Mike Ford glared at Roger. *"Then kill the fricking dogs!"*

"Sure" said Roger and the two of them went their separate ways as Mike hid in the bushes in front of the house.

Steven put Charlie to bed and then went downstairs to the living room. Picking up a book that he was reading Steven sat on the couch and using an oil-burning lamp started reading. There was a bat beside him and both dogs lay on the floor before him. Charlie was sleeping like a lamb and everything seemed perfect.

Peace and quiet was good and it fit Steven fine. He was the Captain of the Varsity Defensive squad on the high school football team. Football teams in some high schools dubbed, anti Xeno Schools stayed private and were mostly composed of rich kids.

Protected from the outside world these boys were vulnerable and being targeted by escaped convicts. There was a pistol in his father's desk in the den, and a 22 cal rifle in Steven's room that he used to kill vermin on the property. These thoughts were going through Stevens mind when one of the dogs raised his head and began growling softly. Prince, the brother of Cane, went running into the foyer of the house. He hit Stew in the chest and dug his teeth into Stew's face. Stew screamed and hollered as Cane attacked the man next. Steven ran into the den and removed his father's pistol from his desk. Then he ran upstairs as the dogs were ripping the intruder apart, Steven could still hear the man screaming after he closed the door to his brother's bedroom.

Roger was climbing over the rose bushes when two screams rang out of the house followed by yelps from some dogs. Roger panicked, lost his foothold and fell into the thick rose bushes yelping and cursing the day, he was born.

 Suddenly the outdoor lights switched on, they were battery operated and immune to the shield that prevented motors from starting and wars from creating pollution. Roger was tangled in the bushes and yelling up a storm as Mike pulled a bowie knife from his belt and approached the front.
 Mike could hear Stew screaming inside of the house so he tried to kick the door in. Steel doors were immovable never breaking as the motel room doors do. After several well-aimed powerful kicks from his size 14 boots, the doors had not budged. Mike was infuriated as he scanned for a window to break and get inside of the house. It seems that everything was going wrong for the bungling felons.
 Mike Ford found what he was searching for when he saw the casement window of the foundation above the basement. Mike broken the window and climbed inside, he fell eight feet and broken his wrist in the fall. Mike stayed silent as the pain rushed to his head.
 Roger finally cut his way out of the roses and leaving a trail of blood behind him, he headed toward the back of the house.
 Stew was in a bad way as one of the dogs had his privates in his jaws and was trying to rip them out of his jeans. Price would not release Stew's head and if it lasted longer the Sheppard would break his heck Next the dogs began playing tug of war with Stew as his blood splattered

onto the walls. A sudden feeling of fear or anxiety, comes on suddenly his predicament overwhelming, appeared to be uncontrollable gave Stew a second wind. None of Stew's efforts effectually was competent, decisive, or authoritative enough to achieve his desired aims. Stew bled to death on the waxed and buffed tiled floor of the foyer.

The dogs sensed Roger breaking into the house and they ran into the kitchen and attacked Roger who was holding two large meat knives, one in each hand. Prince and Cane were ready for situations such as this. They tried to blindside Roger from two angles as the dogs rushed in at Roger. Roger was quick when he was desperate and cut both dogs, one deeply and one slightly. Both dogs backed off and the wounded Prince went at Roger but was stuck and killed by the meat knives.

Cane jumped and snatched one of the meat knives from Roger's hand taking two fingers with the meat knife. Roger became mad in desperation as he grabbed a garden tool driving it deeply into the heart of the dog attacking him. Roger was a bloody mess as he fell to a sitting position exhausted and glad that he killed the second dog. Cane had taken a bite out of Roger's leg that cut an artery and Roger was badly bleeding. Cane lies dead at his feet as Roger struggles to return to his feet in an upright position.

Steven and Charlie had locked the door to the

bedroom and moved a dresser and other furniture to block the entrance. These were solid oaken doors with heavy hardware holding it in place. For the time being, the boys seemed to be safe.

Steven and Charlie heard the dogs and knew that they were dead. A terrifying nightmare was far from over yet.

Mike Ford started his life as a bully and moved onto loan-sharking for cash and thrills. Ford was a big man with an even bigger ego. A broken wrist was not going to stop Mike from finishing what he started. Sneaking up the basement stairs, he listened for noises. Hard eyes stared at the door before him as Mike Ford waited a couple of minutes before he opened the door.

Once Mike was in the house, he found both of his cohorts dead. Roger had also bled to death. Mike took their wallets and anything else of value before he began searching the house. Mike was true to his bloodline and relished suffering, pure enjoyment watching people in pain; when he ever was, injured Mike was a crybaby.

When in for the kill, Mike felt no pain as his adrenaline pumped through his body and images of mutilating others clouded his thinking. Mike saw the bat and picked it up and gripped the bat tightly enough that his knuckles turned white. Mike was on a baseball team while serving time in Attica. There is only one thing he loved more than baseball and that was killing. Watching the faces of his victims as they died made Mike excited, once in awhile he would miss the eyes of a kill as they died and Mike would rant and rave at the victim. In his youth, Mike loved to torture his pets for years before his animals finally died of internal injuries. His left wrist broken Mike used his right hand to slip his blade into his belt. With the bat, he busted Roger's skull open when he saw he was breathing, and then Mike began his ascent on the stairway to the bedrooms of the house.

The boys were frightened because they had heard everything and, Charlie was crying.

Steven had taken boxing and karate in his private school and he prayed it would be enough to defend his brother. He heard only one pair of footsteps and the dogs were silent. Steven asked God for courage and told his brother to hide under the bed. Charlie refused and grabbed his Little League bat from his closet. He held the bat and Steven held the pistol at the door as the boys waited for whatever was to come next.

Mike was at the door and demanded that the boys open the door. Only silence met his question as Mike began kicking and slamming into the door. The door did not budge, Mike removed the revolver from his waistband and tried to blast the door open. Trying several times the gun would not fire and make screamed at the door.

"I do not want to hurt you; I only want to see who you are. Please forgive me for entering your house but I am wet and cold, I have not eaten in days and my arm is broken. Please open the door."

There was only silence, nothing more.

Mike waited a few minutes to see if he could hear anything from inside the room but the boys stayed quiet. Then the expression on mike's face changed into that of a maniac.

"Fine, if you want to play games the games we shall play. I am going into the garage and getting the sledge hammers hanging on the wall and breaks your door down! Then I am going to crush your skulls in and play in your blood. Once you are dead I will piss on you, like you are pissing me off by not opening this fricking door."

It was nearing midnight by the time that Mike reached the garage and took what he needed to get through the door to the bedroom. He searched the entire house and knew that the locked bedroom was for the children. Mike Ford licked his lips in anticipation of getting through the door and at the children.

August 30, 2025

Mike found the liquor cabinet before he reached the stairs and the temptation was too great for him to resist. First, he grabbed the Jack Daniels and noticed that Wild Turkey hidden behind the first bottle. Mike replaced the Jack Daniels with the stronger more potent Wild Turkey. Wild Turkey 101 was his favorite drink. It was no wonder that he chose it over Jack Daniels. There was a catch, it made Mike Ford meaner then a bull and sadistic as Charles Manson. Liquor had been Mike's downfall from the time he was four years old when his father gave him his first shot of Wild Turkey.

Drinking as if there was no tomorrow, Mike was drunk for the first time in ten years. Seemed, that as soon as Mike was out of prison he was back in again. Mike found a battery operated radio and heard the News. When the word aliens came on the radio, Mike laughed. This crisis for the world was a reprieve for Mike. There was now better way to celebrate then in the comfort of somebody else's home drinking free liquor. It was Christmas in August for the escaped felon.

The boys stayed quiet and listened at first for the stranger's footsteps and then they put their ears to the heater vents trying hear anything that could be of use. They heard Mike talking to himself for an hour and then it sounded as if he was speaking to a man named Stew. They heard him staggering and knocking furniture over with glass breaking. Then suddenly he was speaking to a man named Roger and cursing at him. Mike called him a stupid man for allowing a couple of dogs to kill him. Mike bent over to turn Roger over and Prince with his last few breaths of air lunged at Mike Ford ripping a gouge into his hip.

Mike had a bottle in his hand and crashed it onto the dog's head, Prince bitten Mike again on the arm that Mike used to swing the bottle. In desperation, he ran over to the sledgehammers and reached for the five-pound hand mall. Dragging the dog with him Mike reached the sledge and using his broken hand used it to crack the dog's head open like a walnut. The boys cheered on Prince and grew quiet when they heard Prince die.

Mike heard the boys and smiled devilishly as he made his way to the bottles of liquor for a fresh bottle. On the radio, the boys heard the news, Steven realized that his pistol was a lost cause and searched for something else to use as a weapon. Mike sat in the easy chair with a lantern beside him drinking liquor and eating leftovers that he found in the refrigerator. Mike knew that there was no escaping for the children because there was nowhere to go. Besides, cars did not run anymore since the arrival of the Aliens everybody was fighting to keep what they had.

Steven listened to the radio through the heating ducts and wondered if his parents had made it to Florida on time. Little did he know that his parents were dead.

Trying to find some country music on the radio he was bleeding and to drunk to help himself. Mike passed out snoring loudly as he did so.

Steven and Charlie heard Mike snoring but did not know how badly Mike was injured. Both boys knew that if they were going to escape, it was now or never because once the stranger awakened, the boys knew they were doomed. Charlie asked his brother what they were going to do now.

"Well, I don't rightly know just yet. Perhaps we

should try and run away from the house but according to the news, there is more of him out there and people were warned to lock their doors and windows, not to leave home."

" Well . . . now what do we do?" Fidgeting and still listening to the radio Charlie Asked. *"Steven, when that man wakes up, what are your thoughts on this, that he will kill us?"*

"Do not fret any, little brother. I will do what I must to protect you. I want you to let me borrow your bat so I can go downstairs and see in the stranger is out cold. If he is, out cold then I will come get you and we will leave. I will use this bat if I have to, and little brother you know how much I love bats. Remember, I had the most hits last year and broken a school Record. Besides that, I can here him snoring, he snores louder then I have ever heard before in my life."

" When are you going down the stairs Steven?" Charlie did not want his brother to go but knew that Steven could take care of himself. Charlie had seen his brother fight in the ring several times and went a karate tournament once.

"Now is as good of a time as any but first I want you to hide in the closet. I will lock the door and hide the key. If something does happen to me then wait for help to come. Do you understand me?"

" I do not want you to go, what if he wakes up?"

" Then I will bust his face with this bat"

Charlie gave his brother a longing, loving hug and said . . . *"Okay, but let's wait a little longer and if he is still snoring, then go downstairs."*

Steven thought about it for a moment and then answered the question. *"Okay Charlie, you might have a point. We will wait a half hour, here; take this nine-iron just in case."*

Downstairs, Mike was sound asleep and snoring because he was blind drunk but Mike was not deaf. All those years in prison had taught Mike that in order to survive one had to one, stay on their toes, two, never turn your back to anybody, 3, sleep with one eye open and a keen sensitivity to sounds. Mike was asleep but he was snappy and with a keen sense readiness even while, he slept. Steven hoped that this time he was so drunk that the boys had good chances of getting out of the house and riding their horses to get help. Mike was a sleeping wolf dreaming about his next kill.

Steven was as ready as he would ever be as he quietly moved the furniture out of the doors path and exited the room. He held a bat with both of his hands and swiftly moved downstairs.

(Steven had no mind to leave his house to this stranger. In karate school, his master taught him to strike when opportunity showed itself because there might not be another chance.)

Walking slowly once Steven was in the living room, he inched his way toward the drunken stranger. Steven had the advantage because he was approaching the stranger's blind side. Lifting his bat and getting prepared to choke the bat Steven took another step nearer the stranger.

Mike Ford was awake but pretending that he was asleep. The boys had made too much noise and it alerted Mike. Mike was drunk but getting sobered up quick as he watched the reflection of the kid sneaking up behind him from the reflection of the buffed floor. Mike could clearly see the bat in the boy's hands and that the boy was about to hit him. Mike kept snoring loudly and believed that the boy did not have it in him to hit a sleeping man, stranger or not. Mike felt comfortable that things would turn out in his favor. During times such as this, they always had in the past. It almost seemed that the devil himself was charming

Mike. Mike waited for the right moment to strike and counted on experience to beat this kid with his own bat.

Steven felt suspicious of the sleeping bum, in his father's easy chair, everything seemed too easy. Something was wrong; Steven could feel it in his bones. Then in the next moment Steven sensed that the stranger was awake so he stopped for a moment to observe, holding the bat in a swinging position as if ready to hit a home run. Steven knew that he was a foot from his reach but was prepared to step as he swung the bat. Waiting for the stranger to move Steven kept his eyes locked on the target.

Mike decided to make his move as soon as the boy was within his reach but the boy stopped moving closer to him, in fact, he stopped. Mike knew that the boy was a coward, still there was not anybody worse with a bat then a person scared to death. Mike made his move but it was not as planned. He lurched forward and fell on his sledgehammers. Losing a lot of blood Mike was weak, his arm chewed and he could hardly move his hip. The boy stood still watching the man and waiting for the right moment that he could take a decent swing at the prowler.

Steven was calm he had no fear. He felt violated and seeing his dogs' dead made him angry. Steven thought that his target was nothing more then a rabid dog that was attacking his family. Steven acted surprised but it was all an act. Mike grabbed a large sledgehammer and tried to stand, after three attempts he was finally on his feet moaning in pain he told the boy. *"What do you want, boy? Ya see that I am hurt, help me boy. Come here and give me a hand would ya. You know that I would never hurt you, I promise."*

"Get out of our house, 'man,' we do not want or like you here. You killed our dogs and broken into our house, you are lucky that my dad is not here. He would kill you. Now go, get, come on now, and do not make this

harder then it has to be." 'Steven swung his bat around and flipped it. It was a skill he learned it karate class.' After showing off his skills, he told the man once more. ***"Get the hell out of my house before I beat your brains in like you did my dog!"***

"Now just wait a minute there, those dogs attacked us and we came here to rescue you. We intended no harm. Your dogs make it so that I cannot walk, so how in hell am I going anywhere, boy?"

Steven stepped forward as he choked the handle of his brother's bat. He knew that wherever he hit this man he would break a bone. Thinking about what the man had said Steven knew that it was a trick. With frightening force and speed, the hand mall barely missed Steven's head as he ducked out of his way. Steven moved in and with two lightning quick swings broken the man's knees, then the man fell to the ground cursing at Steven. Smiling sanguinely Steven walked closer to the man and watched as Mike's composure returned.

Cold glazed eyes pierced Steven's soul as the stranger lifted the mall to swing at Steven. Steven decided that it was time to make his move and try to disable the man. He remembered what his father had taught him as a young boy. ***"If you fight a man in your age group he will try to beat you up but if you tangle with and fight an older experienced man. Then he will do his best to kill you"*** Steven knew what he had to do and as they say in the hood, he took a good stab at it.

Hitting the man three times in the head Steven stood back and watched Mike shake it of and scowl at him. 'A cold chill run through his body as a reality check snapped Steven into reality.' Mike dropped the sledgehammer grinning broadly, as Mike pulled the gleaming Bowie from his belt. Mike decided to get it over with quickly because the boy had hurt him. Throwing the knife was Mike's only chance because; he knew that with his present injuries the boy had the advantage over him.

Steven had the same thoughts as he moved in and batted the knife from Mike's hand breaking his right arm. Falling beaten and dying onto the carpet Mike was pleading for his life. It was too late for Steven, his adrenaline had rushed into his brain and in a frenzy of swings and kicks, Mike Ford died somewhere between the fifth or eight hit on his body. This stranger died as he live, a coward and a bully. There was nobody to grieve him because he had worn out his welcome anywhere that he had ever lived. One that is for sure is that Mike was slow throwing his knife because of the damage inflicted on his body by Prince.

Steven seen that the stranger was lying in a pool of his own blood and that he was quite dead. He dared not get near enough to check the man's pulse as a belated fear struck him. Steven had just killed a man and it felt no different then that time in Alaska, he killed a grizzly bear. There was one big difference and that was that Steven respected the Grizzly bear.

Running up the stairs, Steven went into the bedroom and unlocked the closet door. Charlie was crying and asking what happened downstairs?

"It's all good, little brother, they are all dead, I hope. Now help me clean up downstairs and then nailed everything shut. We have a year' full of canned goods in the basement, and we can smoke the meat and make jerky from it before it spoils, The horses are fine and if we have to we will bring them into the house so that they do not get stolen. Then if we have to escape we will use the horses but first we have a lot of work to do."

His father in the ways of the world trained Steven. Vernon Newcastle was on the road a lot and working in some of the most dangerous places in the world. He worked for the DOD on special assignments. Vernon possessed his own teams and task forces to complete his mission. Fortunately, for the boys a Team was driving up the driveway to tell the children the bad news. They were also to protect them and hold the Estate grounds until their uncles arrived. Vernon was the Chief of Operations in the northwestern District of the United States of America. Now that Vernon was deceased, his brother Joel was taking over his Post. They knew when they noticed the broken casement window that some was terribly wrong inside the house.

There were six Agents inside the black limousine parked in the driveway. Armed with assault weapons and pistols, as a precaution they had night-vision goggles. These men wearing grey Federal suits and were part of a Division within the Secret Service assigned to the safety of the Newcastle family.

They circled the house and investigated the events that first happened. Then they entered the house through the front door and saw all the bloodstains, and a couple of puddles of clotting blood. They found the children fast asleep in their sleeping bags and two horses, ready with saddle and loaded, with enough gear and supplies to last them a month.

The Agents were impressed at what the boys had done to survive. These were special boys from a long bloodline. Steven and Charlie exclusively molded genetically and through environment to one day become Leaders of the free world. Special Agent Craig Peters was the man entrusted to protect the boys. Once Craig chose the guards then the others used the hand-pump well water in the back yard to wash up. Soon they had secured the grounds and wired flares to expose trespassers. They dug in and used the battery operated ham radio to contact headquarters and give their report.

This time the boys were lucky and you know how the old saying goes. *"What doses not kill you makes you stronger."*

September 27, 2025

During the daylight hours, the world hustled to prepare for the coming winter. Then at night, they remained at home behind fortified windows and doors. Police with sub-machine guns kept the order but suicide bombings had become commonplace killing at random anybody near the explosion. The aliens had not calculated human ingenuity and imagination into their scheme of things to come. Alien leaders were deciding on a means to control this problem.

Screams echoed throughout the night and murder abounded in the world outside fortified houses of the rich and the syndicates. Nightlife became heavy as the cuties were growing weeds and plant life everywhere; there was no way to control it.

Partly Xeno **"Night Creatures"** that were roaming the nights in packs were the most dangerous during the hours of darkness. One of these creatures timed at seventy-miles an hour and withstood the impact of five point five-six ball ammunition. These creatures were rare sightings but their victims numbered in the hundreds, throughout the neighborhoods. People were living underneath bridges using cars and trucks for a wall and a means to defend there outposts. These people were not bad people but good people displaced by the times.

Organized Bridge people, well armed with conventional middle age weaponry were constantly finding actions and recruiting others as themselves. Crossbows were worth four times their weight in gold. Paper money lost its value when, "Out went the lights" the country was back to the barter and Trade Markets. Most were legal but at night, the outsiders arrived to sell their own goods.

The President of the United States was deep underground and completely safe from harm. Persons that entered the underground network had to walk through an oval screener that neutralized Xeno DNA. If a Xenoperson passed through the screener contraption. In a matter of only a few seconds, he or she would instantly lose substance and wither to skin and bones. It was the side effect of the screener.

Only the brave and the people left out in the cold knew what it was like to live in the first quarter of the Xeno Age. Grizzly bears and brown bears were roaming with black bears in groups; wolves had returned and were repopulating and breeding with wild dogs. A hundred million cats were loose and hungry; many of these animals had rabies or some other contagious disease. Many believed that salvation was possible through Christ. These people were the toughest of the lot and the most organized. Many armies disbanded because of the lack of supplies and the will to fight at a low ebb truces abounded throughout the world leaders. These deserters and factions of militias scattered finding their own ways to survive until World Order restored.

Damns over flooded along coastlines around the world, overrun with dead sea creatures. Security locks that operated by computers were jammed which left many people stranded. People were going through changes; changes that they never dreamed of nor imagined could become reality.

Nobody cared that the end was near because as far as average Joe knew, it was already history. History recorded by my staff and me. Brought to you by the Xeno Series books one through ten, narrated by Cal Black

Ravens and vultures few as one flock and tigers and lions pack-prided together. Many things were odd in the world and most of it went unexplained.

Millions of people were starving to death throughout the world and a new virus was loose that originated in South America. This virus was only killing humans and only those exposed to it through another person who has it.

October 11, 2025

Jessica from the Compound beckoned Mia. Mia was there in half a day's time. Some evil people whose names were in Jessica's lists book were spreading this virus. There was much work for Mia to do and this time Starka, the winged white horse man angel would go with Mia carrying her to the persons on Jessica's list.

Mia did not like the idea of riding on a white horse so Starka demonstrated a talent that he possessed. Starka changed his appearance randomly going through the spectrum of colors at will. Mia seemed to smile, patted Starka on the back, and spoke for the first time. *"I can live with whatever you want me to do for you, Jessica."*

By morning and with their bellies full Starka and Mia flew into the wind heading eastward toward Washington DC. There was much to do for the dynamic dual and little time to get the jobs done.

Jessica instructed Mia to slit their throats and bleed them onto unholy ground. Mia was anxious to do what she did best, use her razor as a murder weapon. Mia drifted back to the first time at the Lupus Estate and her first kill. She used a straight razor for her spree of murders and was prepared to relive the old crimson days.

It was night by the time the two of them landed on the outskirts of Washington DC. Residents of Tent City greeted warmly when they arrived at Tent City in a Park on

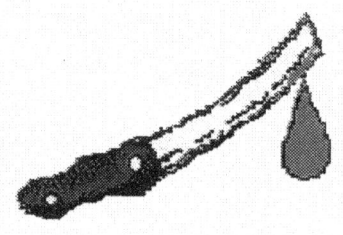

the west side of Washington DC. It was mostly a Xeno camp with a few humans. Starka and Mia fit in as Xeno mutants.

There was more on their minds then just setting up the tents and unpacking their gear. They had to be aware, and make sure that nobody recognized them.

Starka and Mia communicated with their minds. Together they learned to use their gifts as a team and were able to get vital information that would lead them to there target.

Starka and Mia were searching for a man and wife team going by the names of Dave and Millie Sterns. They were the people behind this Tent City and financed the program that operated the shelter.

Fortunate for Mia and Starka, there were no wanted posters of them anywhere in Tent City. The residents were drinking alcohol heavily and doing drugs to enhance their orgies. Darkness and the abyss festered in Tent City. Mia and Starka kept out of sight and to themselves.

The entire nightlong women screamed and begged

while rapes were committed all over Tent City. Moreover, the sounds of death overwhelmed the atmosphere of Tent City. With the night, howling in sadistic laughter, it was hard to get any sleep for the two heroes but Starka managed to get enough sleep because Mia did not sleep.

We have to remember that Mia had done some horrible acts in the beginning of her transformation. Mia was the mother of the Xeno Age; she was the first successful experiment for Dr. Keller and John Sung. Mia and Valentine were in many ways genetically siblings. Unquestionably, the two were the most unique of the two but Valentine had a big disadvantage. Dr. Keller had injected Valentine with several of his formulas and altered his DNA. Momma Mia was a rehabilitated serial Killer now working on the right side of good and evil. "Was it evil to kill evil," Mia did not think so. Hauns the butler had become a young man in his thirties. Dr. Keller only gave Hauns his tested and proved youth serums. Hauns was the man behind this tent city and treated like a god.

Nobody knew for sure what her plans were and if she was loyal to anybody. Mia had a mind of her own and part of it once belonged to Emma. These events happened many years ago.

Starka was a gift from God and was a angel in living flesh with awesome powers never displayed in the past. Half-winged horse and part human Stark was unique and mysterious. Starka, created to rescue and Momma Mia created to kill. They were good together and worked well as a team. This was the first time in her life that Mia enjoyed working with a partner. Communicating telepathically made the two invincible. It also made them friends and confidants. It had been two days and the two assassins were still in Tent City. Hauns had set up a Meat Market beside their tents and it made it difficult for them to leave Tent City. Starka did not know who Hauns was and

Mia explained that Hauns once was a butler for Dr. Keller; he was an old man with a heart problem. Now Hauns was vibrant and young again. Starka loved to listen to Mia's Stories.

Hauns loved to sit in the sun and smoke expensive cigars as he watched the residents of Tent city live in anarchy. Today was a bad day for sitting outside because it was pouring rain in Washington DC. Hauns was in his big house on the hill tended to by his servants.

During the worse part of the storm, Starka with Mia on his back flew off into the wind toward their next job. Starka flew like a bullet and landed on the roof of the Pentagon. Rain, thunder and lightning made the day into night as people seeking shelter roamed the streets.

Beneath the Pentagon were catacombs of tunnels and a shaft equipped with an elevator that descended to debts to two miles. Within the catacombs was a well-equipped Special Forces Brigade protecting the port the led to the Mile Deep City. These were our government leaders and the selected privileged, all depended on the nuclear reactor running the show two miles deep. This complex was an achievement of man protected from Xenoviruses and infestation.

Inside of the Pentagon building, it was ruin and the homeless, in the upper levels were the gangs and their warlords, all of these groups heavily armed and with nothing to lose. Starka and Mia were on the roof in the soaking rain. They knew there target to be Dr. Sheila Hemming, the woman responsible for the virus that had already killed millions of humans. China was feeling the first vantages of the incoming virus. Dr. Hemming discovered virus and was releasing it through the homeless. Five-thousand dollars a bus ticket anywhere that you wanted to go. First, you had to have an injection of what the good doctor called Loveneese serum. Mixed with an opiate and the virus this serum gotten the person high for twelve hours. Free Clinics were also distributing this medicine as painkillers. The slowly incubating virus spread quickly and there was no vaccine for it, it seemed that the dynamic two had their work cut out for them. Mia and Starka were immune to the human mutating strain killer virus.

Mia told Starka to wait for her and that she would return within an hour. Mia was carrying a satchel filled with high explosives and a remote detonator.

Sheila Henning was a bright, beautiful young woman who was the result of genetic engineering. She was human but had a grudge against the human race. Sheila was such a genius that her mind could not deal with it socially and she had gone insane. Nobody knew what this rich woman was doing in her government research laboratory. Shield had the only vaccine well hidden in her vault inside of her Office. Sheila had the connecting lab to her office for convenience, above the clothes hanger, in her closet was an air duct and Mia planned to make her entrance there. Hidden in the closet Mia could bide her time for the right moment to strike and kidnap the doctor. Mia knew that the Restricted Areas had guards so she was prepared to murder swiftly, extremely quietly if the need arose. Sheila was carefree and comfortable as she was processing data into her computer.

Mia gotten into the closet quickly and heard the two guards by the door speaking about going to the roof because they thought they heard something make noises. Mia knew that they heard Starka on the roof above their heads; Mia had to do something swiftly to prevent compromise of their mission.

With lightning speed, Mia grabbed and yanked the two guards into the closet. Then Mia with one swift motion of her arm she slit both of their throats. Mia burped them for every drop of blood. Mia was a beastly savage once the smell of blood touched her senses. Waiting for the Doctor to walk past the closet, once she finished her work on the computer in her office Mia licked her lips after filling her gullet.

Finally, Sheila stood and stretched her well-figured body. Then she helped herself to another cup of coffee and walked toward her laboratory to check on the progress of her experiments. Mia snatched Dr. Hemming into the closet muzzling his cries as he hoisted her into the duct work and dragged her to the waiting Starka on the roof. In the next minute Starka was carrying two loads back to the Jessica Foundation Laboratories.

The Earth cracked open revealing an endless drop into the abyss. A massive earthquake hit the Mohave Desert cracking it open for seventy-five miles. The aliens were still controlling the power and production of the world as winter showed its face and snow began falling.

Winters were getting longer and the short summers produced intense heat. The earth shifted on its axis 000001000005.00 percent. With this act of God came changes in the weather worse then global warming. The cause of this earthquake had gone unexplained.

What some claimed screams from the dead echoed from the wide Earthly crack? Those that dared to peek into the open crack saw infinity. Rumors, going around that some folks disappeared after snatched off the rim, pulled into and down the abyss.

Jessica had not prophesized this natural disaster and believed that she was falling short to be in the shadows of the Glory of God. Jessica decided to visit this great new wonder of the world and learn for herself if the rumor she was hearing was true. Leven and Tammy accompanied Jessica to Mohave Desert; they departed on horseback without giving notice to the residents of the Jessica Foundation. They rode for twelve hours before making camp in the forests of eastern California.

The desert completely covered in snow for the first time in the history of the Mohave Desert, Jessica enjoyed the ride as she studied the new and strange vegetation growing through the snow and blooming beautifully. Earth was changing, new life forms created by nature to combat the polluted atmosphere and live abundantly anywhere. These plants appeared tropical and lush with thorns three inches long. Was it possible that nature was adapting to the new conditions faster and better then humans? Jessica believed so.

Tammy and Leven were wearing their Xeno Games armor and equipped with crossbows and slingshots. Then of course, they had their blades and fast horses. Leven knew that as far as he and Tammy were concerned, Jessica was the last hope for humanity's survival.

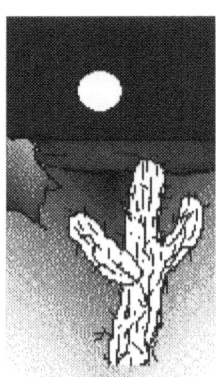

First thing in the morning they headed eat through the desert and noticed that all of the snow had melted. It was seventy degrees and the full moon illuminated the beauty before them. Within the time, that power had stopped and the wars had nearly come to a halt the sky was blue again but in the distant horizon more trouble lurked ready to consume life Jessica knew about the coming evil but this natural phenomenon was beyond Jessica's comprehension of time.

They traveled for fourteen hours before they pitched camp and they were only two-hundred miles from their destination at this point of their journey. They traveled without an escort so as not to draw attention from warring cult factions known to be in the desert. The desert was their last haven, where they felt safe from detection from over zealous Templar's or Militia patrols.

During the night, Leven and Tammy barely got any sleep. Mixed breeds of Xenocanines attacked their camp. Needed to be neutralized Tammy and Leven worked hard fighting wolf-like creatures? When morning appeared, the dog-like creatures disappeared into the rocky cliffs.

Jessica and her friends camped the next night in an oasis only ten miles from the abyss. Tonight it was dead quiet and a thick fog consumed their sights as the wind picked up speed. Eerily quiet except for the wind, they finally set there tents up and tied the horses to a cottonwood tree. This night was cold and chilled Leven to the bones as he stood guard outside of the tents.

During his shift at guard duty Leven was suspicious about the lack of wildlife and insects, and he had a gut feeling that they were not alone in the desert. Leven stayed on his toes as he patrolled the perimeter of their campsite. He made sure that the fire stayed burning brightly and kept a weathered watch over the camp.

Nearly time for the shift change with Tammy, Leven walked over to the fire to get warm. It was then that some sort of five legged creature burst out of the woods and headed straight at Leven who was unprepared for the attack. Leven turned to meet the attack with his sword he swung with lethal force. It was a xeno mix of wild boar and brown bear, ferocious and massive it absorbed the sword with the power of the force behind it.

Loud deafening roars invaded the sound of silence as Leven fired two arrows into where he thought the heart would be. The animal swung a huge paw at him and then tried to gouge him to death with its horns. Leven stepped aside but not fast enough to avoid the claws that swiped his chest. Blood ran hot, as Leven grew focused in his rage of madness to kill the creature attacking him.

Tammy came to the rescue in time to save Leven's life. First, it was the distraction of her sudden appearance and then, the three arrows the embedded into the head of the beast. The beast turned his attention to Tammy and ran towards her.

Leven was stunned for but a moment before he ran after the beast and took his best shot decapitating the beast with his long sword. Tammy saw a chunk of flesh fly off the beast as it lowered his head, charging at Tammy. Back flipping over the beast Tammy with her widow-poisoned dagger clutched in her hand stabbed the beast in his back. Leven and Tammy were now standing side by side, as the beast turned to face them. The two lovers smiled at each other and Leven made a comment. *"Does this thing die?"*

Tammy had a snappy answer . . . *"If it bleeds than it can die."* Leven jumped first at the beast to distract the direction it was running and Tammy flanked the beast. This was a team move that had won the pair hundreds of bouts at the Xeno Games. Tammy held a two bladed axe about four-foot long and her comfortable swinging weight. Tammy had made the weapon herself at home. This medieval axe had blades a foot wide. Tammy carried it in a sling on her back, it was balanced in her hands ready to strike the beast in the neck. This is what the pair dubbed as piecework. Leven was in position with his heavy sword to take another swing at the beast. Tammy swung her axe first and deeply sliced into the beast and she withdrew her axe and swung it a second time at the same moment that Leven leaped at the beast striking the beast in the throat. Within that same instant, Tammy's axe struck home again. They succeeded in beheading the beast that would not die. Jessica slept throughout this whole ordeal.

"We are fortunate that this beast did not kill us instead, you know that my beloved?"

"I agree that if you my buttercups did not rescue me then the beast would have feasted well tonight"

"Get some sleep 'said Tammy' *it's my watch now. Tend to your wounds first, do not bleed to death on me, okay baby."*

" Do not worry about me honey, worry about what is out there in the darkness. We near the abyss and I wonder about the reasoning behind it. Perhaps we should have brought with us Peter, he would have protected us." Tammy laughed hard; she could not stop laughing at what Leven had said.

Tammy finished her shift with another episode of life or death and Leven relieved Tammy for the next four hours. Jessica demanded at least ten hours of sleep. Tammy was tired, worn out from the quietness of her watch. She compared the silence to a graveyard.

They rode hard but still did not arrive at the abyss until it was nearly nightfall. Scattered along the cracks were makeshift dwellings and tents. Lanterns lit the darkness as fires roared next to each campsite. Finding a site, the furthest from the other campsites the three adventurers set up camp. This night was a peaceful and silent night.

Clear and sunny it was hot on this day. It was over a hundred degrees Fahrenheit and the sun was blinding as the trio neared the crack that stretched as far as the eyes could see. Closer as they inched to the abyss the hotter it gotten as they grew near the edge.

Tammy noticed that cut members of several cults were volunteering as sacrifices into the abyss. Wooden blocks placed near the edge of the abyss where executioners were lopping off heads in the honor of a new god. *The God of Darkness and the Abyss*

Jessica frowned when she saw people in lines to, be sacrificed to a false god. Jessica remembered the way the world was like before the Xeno Age Boom. Time flew by quickly and the years faded with memory. Always able to live without showing any expression except for love, Jessica wept for the first time in her life.

Other than the executioner beheading the willing, there were other atrocities ongoing near the cliff something so horrific that it was unthinkable by the human species. The Russians were the closest to committing this type of mass murder during the Hungarian Revolution in 1956. Russian soldiers skewered Hungarian and Jewish babies with their bayonets and carried them as trophies. Unlike the Russians who resorted with barbarism once they had total power over the conquered, people at the crack of the abyss were sacrificing babies to their new god. Human babies were slam-spiked into sharp pointed wooden spikes mounted in cement painted black by their parents. Darkness covered the world and death felt at home, as noon approached there were several thousand people gathered at the mouth, of the crack into the abyss.

Life carried on as normal as Babies were dead or dying in stacks of ten. People willingly bowing their heads and beheaded. Channel Five News arrived in jeeps and trucks with mounted dishes. Before they had a chance to exit their vehicles the mob rushed them knocking their vehicles on their sides or blowing all the tires. A short film clip of a Baby Spike aired on the news before it went off the air.

People in the crowd dragged the Newspersons out of their vehicles and threw them into the abyss. It happened quite quickly and once it finished. Everything went back to normal.

Jessica looked up to the skies and asked God, *"Why?"* Eerily it was calm and the dreadfulness was just part of business. Jessica wondered aloud how so many people were at the abyss, there were no cars or trucks about so she was mystified.

People paid $1,000.00 for the honor to be a sacrifice to their new god. Babies were going for five-hundred dollars at the auction block. It was hell on Earth, and Jessica was appalled at the sights before her.

Leven motion Tammy and Jessica to stop staring before they attracted attention and brought trouble. Then Leven led the way to the edge of the abyss. Leven peered over the edge and saw hell. Inside the abyss, there were yellow flames and orange coals lighting the darkness. Screams echoed of victims who did not have the monies to be one of the chosen. People were dying for false salvation by a phony god and there were businesspersons who were reaping a huge harvest of cash. Jessica had to see for herself what had stigmatized Leven who was staring into the abyss as if he were spellbound.

Jessica held her breath after the aroma of the dead passed through her nostrils and saw infinity. She realized that it was an omen decrypting the coming of the anti Christ. Jessica felt chilled to her bones and shuddered. Tammy felt it too, the feeling of doom and death.

October 20, 2025

Jessica decided to travel to the Great Spirit Matavilya, this tribe were the seers of the desert. Invoking dreams, su'mach, ritually viewed as the source of knowledge The Mojaves were a people of dreams and visions that always proved true. Through them, the dreamer could return to the time of creation where the origin, of all things unveils to the beholder. The art of tattoo was important to the Mojave. They tattooed their faces with lines and dots - a cosmetic, fashionable practice. At death, the Mojaves used cremation to enter the spirit world. The property and belongings of the deceased placed on a pyre along with the body, to accompany the spirits. Mourners often contributed their own valuables as a showing of love. Once the dead passed on, their names all forgotten.

Jessica was, motivated by spirit, to seek out people who kept these secrets. She had to have knowledge of the coming days and weeks. Jessica needed to know what the people possessing these powers knew about the darkness. God, always informed Jessica, were it to be his will, however, Jessica grew impatient and sought out a way to know the truth for herself. She was stepping beyond her destiny and playing her own game. Being human, Jessica was not beyond temptation and there had to be a reason for the mass murders of innocent babies. This was a good way to get in touch and reach out to some more of God's children. Jessica felt lifted into a new realm of the Earth's prism of colors.

It was difficult to find the hidden village in the cliffs. Jessica had lost her bearings and Leven could not find his. They were traveling in circles going nowhere and running out of water when they found the village. Native Americans led them to a hole in the desert that led to underground cave networks. These networks of caves and tunnels had been there since the beginning of time. The village was secret up to now; Jessica was destined to find the village. Said Tammy and Leven agreed with her.

Indian scouts led the three adventurers deep into the earth and then they entered the Chamber of the Chiefs. Here they searched to find a seat in the circle and Tammy given a peace pipe.

Certainly, Jessica was reaching for straws; at the very least, she was searching for an ally. Perhaps Jessica found what she was searching for here within the depths of the Earth in an unknown village that had been there since the beginning of time. The three visitors could feel strong senses of power, spiritual and physical. Smoke from the pipe was sweet and appealing as it drifted slowly inside the cave. Jeyoya, Chief of the North Mojave passed the pipe to Jessica and as the custom went, Jessica smoked from the pipe and passed the pipe to Leven. "Was it possible that something great was about to happen in the smoke-filled cavern filled with Chiefs?" Jessica believed it to be so.

"We have been listening to the white man's preachers and Ministers and learned that they are true to their god when they began preaching but in time they become cultists or are consumed by sex and greed. Tell me Jessica, why have you searched us out. What do you believe that we can do for you that you cannot do for yourselves?" 'Chief Feathers was speaking directly to Jessica.'

"The spirits have come here to our world to show us our arrogance. They were at first going to eradicate our species but decided to allow intelligent life to survive but under strict conditions until our planet is safe from harm. The Spirits have gathered and built a force that has yet to be unleashed and the evil one will be born when the sky is red. These Spirits that have turned off our sun will depart soon but not before the Fire Spirit chases them away."

Servants arrived with trays filled with fruits and vegetables with three flasks of wine and some mule deer jerky to eat. Smoke sweetened the room as another Chief began to speak. Chief Whitesnake was the newest chief in the circle; he was also the most radical and closed-minded. That is why the pipe passed around because it seemed to make a person think before speaking and feel at peace with the universe. It made everybody feel at ease as the Spirits filled the cavern chamber with illuminating power.

Chief Whitesnake invited Jessica to try some desert fruit and some sweet cactus wine. Leven and Tammy indulged themselves with the wine and food, and then they drank a gallon of cold clear water. Jessica drank some water and ate fruit. It felt good to have found shelter, and the Native Americans in this cave network heavily armed with automatic weaponry, not bows and arrows. Chief Whitesnake explained that underground weapons operated and did their generators. This made Jessica happy because humanity could live underground as comfortable as it can above ground. Jessica complimented the Chiefs on their ingenuity and common sense.

Jessica did not have everything answered that she wanted to know. *"Please Chief Whitesnake, tell me this . . . what omen or sign does the earth opening signify, and what is really in the abyss?"*

"Don't you know?" Whitesnake snapped an answer to Jessica, and then Chief Oyay told Chief Whitesnake to sit down and drink some more wine.

December 3, 2025

The Duchess of Manchester was enjoying the sun and getting some air at the beach. She was there as the fleets of saucers lifted off the beach and shot into the atmosphere faster then the speed of light. Snapping pictures of this spectacle, she anticipated the excitement that these pictures would bring back home.

The End of Chapter Thirteen
"Darkness and the Abyss"

Chapter Fourteen
<u>"Project Fire Angel"</u>
January 1, 2026

Deep within the pine forests near Florence, Colorado is a secret Military Complex built for the creation of Project Fire Angel. Project Fire Angel was a top military secret until work leaked out about the purpose behind this Research facility. Now it was in its last phases of completion with two-trillion dollars spent on its development some Authorities claimed it to be alien technology. High fences with barbed wire protected the guards riding in jeeps and on horseback maintaining tight security. They had orders to kill anybody that they did not know, regardless of who they appeared to be, it was shoot first and take names later. Tonight was a moonless night and cold. Snow covers the ground and it was blacker then black as you peered into the darkness. The air was fresh and an odor of pine scents fill the frozen air as the complex silently operated at full power.

Global warming had to create a new genesis and humans had no clue about how to get it done. Project Fire Angel was an attempt to save the planet from further erosion and eventual death. Alien ambassadors met with World Leaders in the Pentagon underground conference auditorium. These alien ambassadors were not ugly grey or green midgets but slightly taller spices of humans with larger heads. Other than those differences, the aliens seemed to be of human origin.

Kutat was the spokesperson for the five alien ambassadors and spoken a language that all languages and Foreign leaders understood.

NASA Space Program rebuilt and fully staffed, through the years, many new technologies advanced. New inventions and better computers made it possible to travel and colonize Mars but it was not the answer needed to save the Earth. Originally, Project Fire Angel designated for Mars refined to clean our atmosphere. This flyer recreated to produce, 'regeneration,' of the planet by purging it of

Solar filters

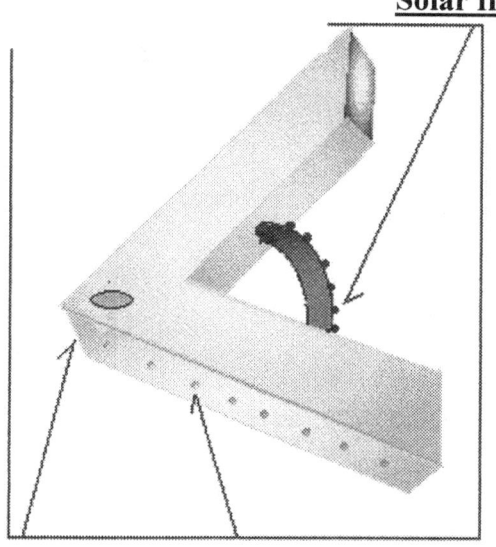

Helm/Bridge   **Toxic gas intake ports**

toxic impurities. In Command of the Research was Benny Carter, a nephew of President Jimmy Carter. Benny Carter was directly responsible for opening the door that allowed these aliens a safe visit to the underground meeting between worlds.

Astral-solar energy worked for propulsion and stability for the new Space Shuttles and it powered the anti-gravity fields to stabilize the atmosphere inside space ships.

Kutat allowed his engineers to construct and instruct the Fire Angel. Alien theories and formulas created new Elements with the Elements that seemed limited to this planet. They showed our scientists ways to manipulate this planet's natural resources so that new inventions were being tested and proved at a rate of hundreds a day.

On this day, a treaty formed among Nations in the United Nations and N.A.T.O., which Kutat mediated, and more than not chose the Nations to be members of this new association. Hidden beneath the earth in manufactured hangers were two spacecrafts that the aliens decided to leave on the planet. Alien scientists were correcting malfunctions and repairing the damaged flyers.

Suspended air disc

water and living Quarters, Recreation

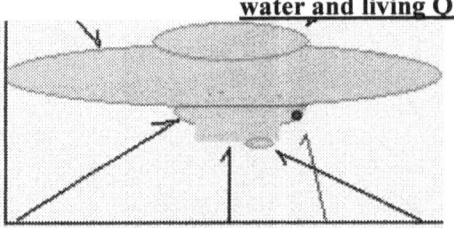

Bridge   **solar engine**   **Dreaded Black Room**

These ships were not armed and used only for scouting and observation Details. Kutat was serious that his scientists allowed all liberties and complete command over the planet. Kutat ordered the global network of power sensors to terminate and power returned to the world.

One V-Spacecraft Launcher that remained, patrolling the planet and doing its best stabilizing the atmosphere. It was loaded with two-hundred Arial fighters and its crews. This craft was equipped with an army of twenty-thousand aliens and their weapons were by far superior to our own.

Peaceful and civilized this species of aliens were akin to our own. They explained that the entire universe inhabited by species similar to our own and that we had all evolved in different space and time but through the same process or formula. Sadly, they explained that their hosts destroyed some life giving planets but they felt that the populace of the earth was worth saving. This warship was on sentry duty; its mission was to save the planet.

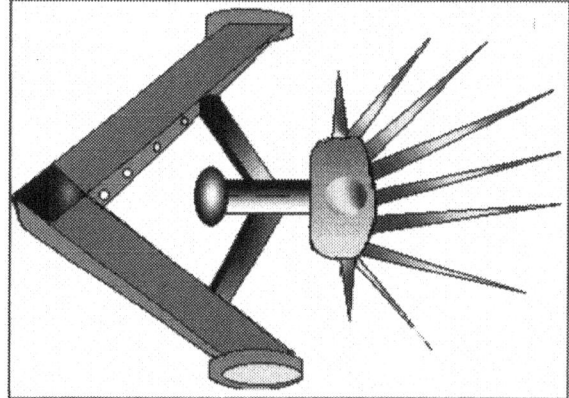

Alien Warship

      This Project kept secret as the world struggled to return to normal, made it the best-kept secret in the world.

      Wars began between the Xeno Religion and the Templar's Knights. Kutat made it clear that genetic manipulation, distinctly forbidden, to all humanity and said that it was not contained then it would spread to other solar systems. If the threat was not neutralized before the Fleet returned then all intelligent life would be exterminated on Earth, to contain the Xenoviruses.

      Three members of the Skull and Bones secret organization were present for the World Meeting and knew of another threat to their world. Now they had to deal with the aliens and the Xenospecies, it was time to eliminate the Xenospecies before the alien fleet returned in two years. This meant that the masters at manipulation and influence needed to blame the Xenospecies for everything from global warming to the *"Wars among Religions."* There was a need for a charismatic, strong yet kind, born leader to appear from a list of men that the inner circle had chosen as candidates.' Now it was down to three men that were prepared to take on such responsibility.

Jewish scholars and scientists had been fighting the justification and right for another species to procreate with the same rights as people. They had faced tough opposition and persecution for their beliefs but now honored, as a demand to rid the world of the Xenospecies grew louder. They predicted that within ten-years the Xenospecies would drive the human species to extinction.

This was old news and now it was in the limelight once again. Things were different; it had only taken the Skull and Bones two weeks to change the world. Washington DC cleaned up and people were going home.

Arthur Jones was the candidate running for the Presidency and he had the support of the people. Everybody loved the man and he was a newcomer to the political arena but not lacking in experience. Arthur had been the aide of many top Government Officials and was the mayor of a small city in Vermont. Arthur was married to Eleanor Kennedy, 'a chip off the old block.' Arthur Jones studied law at Yale and earned a Medical Degree from Harvard.

Jones publicly denounced Dr. Keller and his formulas and promised a holocaust long due to the Xenospecies. Promising to ban the Xeno Games and bring back football by July, Jones was gaining in the polls and passing his opponents to the White House.

October 2, 2026

"Up there can you see Fire Angel?" Lisa was speaking with Frank on the observatory mounted atop their

concrete Research Complex. Dr Keller, consumed with his latest experiments was blind to what was going on around him.

Frank and Lisa enjoyed a drink or two and admired the stars. They had been making love all morning and Frank was tired but willing to continue their love fest. Lisa did not believe that she was doing anything wrong with her lustful exploits. She was on one continuous rush, created by the youth formula, to live life to its fullest and lately, Nick was barely around.

"Lisa look, there it is twisting like a top through our atmosphere leaving behind it pure oxygen. Is it not wondrous, it looks like a twisting comet?"

Frank had fallen in love with Lisa but Lisa was void of love except for her husband. Frank was somebody that Lisa used to have some fun and kill some time with but that is all Frank was to her. Sooner or later Nick would find out and Frank knew it but was helpless to resist Lisa's charms. Frank and Lisa watched the Fire Angel as she flew through the atmosphere like a red-hot coal faster then the speed of light.

———————————

Mia was going after Samuel and Starka made it much easier to accomplish. Samuel was relaxed with his concubines and watching two wrestlers fight to the death in the ring he had set up on the estate property. Mia and Starka were nearby listening to the commotion in the back yard. Mia was getting fast with her straight razor. She was as fast or faster then, Japanese butchers, cutting fish in an expensive cuisine restaurant, and Mia was agile and nimble. Thirsty for blood and primed for the kill, Mia knew that this time she was going to kill Samuel.

Samuel was swarming with beautiful young women and drunk on blood wine. Pair of wrestlers fought to their deaths was bleeding onto the deck askew grotesquely. These giants, misshapen, especially in a disturbing way were now part of the scenery. Samuel had Lucifer caged in the wax skull that once belonged to Lucifer and Samuel had the wax bubbling from thick flaming wicks.

Lucifer in hell was screaming in anguish and his head throbbing from the burning flame. He could hear his son laughing and frolicking as if there were no hell or heaven. Focusing back to Dr. Keller, Lucifer watched as the mad doctor prepared a fetus, meant for Lucifer. Crying like a baby Lucifer begged Samuel to douse the flame.

Samuel heard Lucifer crying out and begging for mercy but Samuel did not know the meaning of the word, Samuel was all-bad. His furniture constructed from human bones and skin and the paintings on his walls came straight from hell. On his altar bound and gagged was virgin waiting for the hour to strike mid-night. Lucifer's hour dedicated for the sacrifice to himself. Evil and selfish Samuel was an abomination from man's consciousness created accidentally by Valentine. Now the problem was that Valentine was very alive and working covertly somewhere in the world against humanity. Samuel was a creation of Lucifer and his downfall. Samuel never contemplated the possibility that Lucifer would rise from hell by the infamous Dr. Keller.

Starka kicked down into the roof and busted through landing on the bed with Samuel and his wenches. Mia killed the wenches in a blink of an eye and then slit Samuels's throat ear to ear. Samuel fell dead on the bed as his blood stopped spurting. Starka yelled a Godly battle cry and flew out the same way he crashed Samuels's orgy. Mia was on his back holding on for her life; Starka was lightning and wrung your ears as he shot out of the

dwelling. Samuel was dead as a doornail. Starka flew into the wind toward California.

Dr. Keller and Lisa had a confrontation over Frank. Lisa promised to stop seeing Frank but Nick was mad. Once Nick decided that, somebody did not deserve to breathe his air, within hours these persons were dead.

Obedient and willing to die for Nick, Lisa agreed that it was due time for Frank to become a test subject.

Two large men roped and tied Frank and then carried the adulterer into the Laboratory where Nick and Lisa were waiting for them.

Lisa had shown Nick books about Hitler and the Nazis. Doctor Keller respectfully regarded as behaving in an authoritarian or dictatorial manner and Lisa pointed out that Nick was exactly like Hitler. Nick began reading the books and then became obsessed with the movement. Nick had become mean and self-centered, sadistic with his test subjects and better in bed.

Frank stood straight and rigid as the men holding him released Frank. Dr Keller bean speaking as Lisa wandered away to the far end of the laboratory.

"I trusted you Frank, I trusted you with my life and my wife and you betrayed my trust. What do you believe that I should do for you Frank? Should I allow you to leave or what? Answer me Frank."

" Please just shoot me Nick and get it over with . . . I am not afraid to die."

Nick began to laugh hysterically and pointing a finger at Frank. *"How dare you try and tell me what to do . . . there is no such thing as a quick death for you my old friend. We had plans for you, as a matter of fact Lisa came up with the idea to stuff you like an animal."*

Frank could not help the horror showing in his eyes and his imagination went wild thinking about two surgeons keeping him alive as they had him stuffed. Frank was about prepared to make a try for escape and die in a shootout but it was all in vain. Frank was stuck up a creek without a paddle; Frank peed in his drawers as he waited for the worse to come.

Lisa came back with two medical bags and a handful of tourniquets. Frank passed out and Lisa laughed at him . . . *"If I would have known his balls were hollow then I would have never entertained the bastard. I was the best piece of ass that this punk ever had in his life and he will not fight for me!"* 'Lisa unrolled some steel tie wire and smoothed the wire to a point. Then she smiled at Frank and said.' *"I am going to slide this wire under your skin and see how far it goes."*

Frank was unconscious but when he awakened, Frank found himself tied firmly to a whipping pole. This was worse then death and Frank regretted having an affair with Lisa, Frank was a day late and a dollar short of buying common sense at the brain store.

What is to become of our world? Will the aliens be our salvation, or is there a God somewhere that will rescue us from ourselves? Who is Jessica, and what will become of Nicklaus Keller and his beloved wife Lisa? What other great stories will the Xeno Age bring under a new light? Find out in the coming books of this series.

I hope that you have enjoyed the first three books of the Xeno Series written by Kal Keller. Our next featured book from this Series is **"The Xeno Exodus"**

The End